PRAISE FOR *THE RULE OF ONE*

"Ava and Mira's world is an all-too-believable mix of advanced technology and environmental collapse . . . In their debut, Saunders and Saunders, themselves twins, lend an authentic voice to the girls' first-person narration . . . Readers are in for a fast-paced ride, poised for a sequel, as the twins embrace their father's call, in the words of Walt Whitman, to 'resist much, obey little.'"

—*Kirkus Reviews*

"Dystopia fans will enjoy this adventure set in an all-too-plausible future America."

—*School Library Journal*

"Utilizing a sf-fantasy setting and a survival-oriented plot, the Saunders sisters are careful to promote growth and differentiation between the twins . . . There are parallels to current news stories, such as immigration, environmental resources, and an autocratic political system. Try this with fans of James Dashner's Maze Runner series, Margaret Peterson Haddix's *Double Identity*, or such clone books as Rachel Vincent's *Brave New Girl*."

—*Booklist*

"Twin storytellers Ashley and Leslie Saunders are modern-day soothsayers who beautifully spin a suspenseful tale of the not so distant future. Pay attention—this could be what *1984* was to 1949."

—Richard Linklater, Academy Award–nominated screenwriter and director

"Ashley and Leslie Saunders have created a masterpiece in this dark futuristic tale of twin sisters who must share one identity in a society where control is the order of the day. Intense and descriptive, the twists and turns this story takes, as well as the obvious love the sisters share for one another, make for an unforgettable journey."

—Kathy Parks, author of *The Lifeboat Clique* and *Notes from My Captivity*

THE RULE OF ALL

ALSO BY
ASHLEY SAUNDERS &
LESLIE SAUNDERS

The Rule of One

The Rule of Many

The Rule of All

THE RULE OF ALL

ASHLEY SAUNDERS + LESLIE SAUNDERS

SKYSCAPE

⽥ SKYSCAPE

Text copyright © 2020 by Ashley Saunders and Leslie Saunders
All rights reserved.

Published by Skyscape, New York

www.apub.com

Amazon, the Amazon logo, and Skyscape are trademarks of Amazon.com, Inc., or its affiliates.

ISBN-13: 9781542008297 (hardcover)
ISBN-10: 1542008298 (hardcover)

ISBN-13: 9781542008303 (paperback)
ISBN-10: 1542008301 (paperback)

Cover design by David Curtis

Author photo by Shayan Asgharnia

Printed in the United States of America

First Edition

To our editor, Jason Kirk,
our gratitude will never cease.

PART I
THE WAIT

MIRA

I shouldn't be outside. Any number of dangers could be lurking in the Dallas streets, hiding in every corner like the State Guard's cameras once did. Loyalists could be watching me, following me right now. Waiting to take me. To take back their capital.

This city isn't theirs, I remind myself. It's Common ground. It was and is my home.

But for how much longer?

A surge of paranoia stings my insides, jolting my mind into high alert. I rip off my reflective sunglasses, which keep sliding down the bridge of my sweaty nose, consumed with the overwhelming need to see the frenzied streets with my own raw eyes.

It seems like Common Guards populate every inch of pavement downtown. Streets so hot from the sun, if I peeled off my UV-protective gloves and touched the concrete with my bare hands, it would scald my skin like a branding iron.

So hot you could fry an egg, my father, Darren, joked when Ava and I were small. Then, schools and businesses would close if temperatures topped 120 degrees. Today, the walkways are teeming.

Rebellions don't just shut down because of a heat wave. Dallas can't afford to "close." Not if we want to win.

Common Guards stand in the odd patches of shade, outnumbering citizens three to one. The sight of bright-yellow paint slashed across their bulletproof vests should comfort my unease, as the color marks them as soldiers on our side. The problem is, anyone can wear a disguise. And these days, it feels impossible to identify whose side anyone *really* plays for.

An impatient pack of bicyclists ring their bells angrily at the horde of pedestrians, who pay no heed to the flashing red of the crosswalk. I move with the unlawful foot traffic, weaving through the free-for-all, stealing glances at the exposed forearms of the commuters around me.

What once signified an ally of the Common is now mainstream. Friend or foe, everyone here in the metropolis bares identical cuts on their inner right wrists. Half-healed incisions that signal what once seemed impossible: microchips are no more.

My greatest desire, the hope I've carried with me my entire illegitimate life, has been realized. I got what I wanted. What my grandmother Rayla was calling for. The people have cut out the chips that were embedded in their skin the very minute they were born.

Most did it to be free. To join up in arms with the Common and fight for our future. For others, mistrust guided the blades that extricated their microchips. They know *our* side controls the NSA tracking system now. Or so Owen and Blaise assure me, Rayla's onetime hacker accomplices who now head our Cybersecurity Team.

But no one ever truly knows who's watching.

Below a twelve-story ad telling people to "Save power to gain power," I spy a camera dangling from frayed wires. The Common blinded all the surveillance that served as Governor Roth's eyes. He's no longer watching us; he's gone.

But paranoia dies hard in this city.

I make a sharp turn with the hurried crowd, all huddled beneath parasols or hats. Pulling my scarf low over my eyes, I squint at a woman moving toward me on the walkway, noting her deft fingers as they reach into her satchel. *Does she have a gun?* Citizens can carry weapons now. Anyone can get their inexperienced hands on a military-issued taser gun or a pistol. Even a next-generation assault rifle.

I plunge my hand to my gun belt and unlock the safety catch of my pistol. Loyalists, lackeys who still choose to follow the governors, might still move among us. Lying in wait for the perfect moment to strike.

It's been twenty-one days since the Common rose up and the Texas government fell. Since the Battle for Dallas, the night of truth and reckoning. And in that time I haven't fired a single shot.

How much longer can that last?

As the woman in the hooded dress nudges past without so much as a glance my way, I crane my neck and search the sky. Or as much as I can see of it through the crush of skyrises, their hundred-story tops so tall, it feels as though we walk beneath a steel trap.

I half expect to see a hypersonic missile dropping down on us, sent by the displaced Texas State Guard. Or the growing flame of a warhead, delivered by any number of global enemies aiming to take advantage of our vulnerable state. Our weakened government. Our far from *United* States.

The list of our enemies is long. Ava's taken to writing each of them down on the back of her trusted map, forming a game plan, calculating who will come for us first.

I glance down at my wristwatch: 5:15 p.m. The hottest time of day. Right now, enemy number one is the Texas sun. Although I'm outside, it feels as if there is no air. My lungs breathe fire, and with every passing second, the idea of melting into a puddle of sweat seems less like an exaggeration and more like an inevitability. *I have to get inside.*

Five blocks later, I finally arrive at the building I ventured the sweltering downtown streets for. I slip into the alleyway, avoiding eye contact with the two hooded figures scavenging the overflow of rotting garbage from the dumpsters.

Food has been especially hard to come by these days. Almost as hard as hope.

The stench of waste nearly knocks me over before I reach the back doors. I quickly rummage through my pockets for my set of newly minted keys, noting the out-of-commission microchip scanner peppered with bullet holes.

Suddenly, I hear footsteps approaching, fast.

"Should you be out here alone?" a man's muffled voice shouts from behind me.

I steal my fingers around the bows of several keys, ready to use them as shanks. I whip around and then drop my guard, recognizing the glacial-blue eyes of Ciro Cross. The Common's benefactor scurries toward me, his six-foot-three frame covered in sweat-soaked khaki, a white visor cap with wrinkled face and neck capes masking his famous face.

"Where's Ava?" he asks, turning his head in search of my sister.

"Where's Barend?" I retort. I nod to the empty space beneath his wide double-canopy umbrella. The steely soldier is usually fixed to Ciro's side.

Neither of us should be out here alone. Ciro is worth millions, and I'm worth . . . well, whatever a second-born twin who revived a rebellion is valued at today. The bounty keeps rising, every state's governor willing to suck their budget dry for the prize of capturing the Traitorous Twins.

As a rule, I can be found at my sister's side. She is my eternal guardian and I am hers. But lately there's been an unspoken understanding between us that we both need time apart. We crave it. And with every passing day, where it feels like all we're doing here is waiting—stuck, useless, on the defensive as always—I seem to seek the distance more and more.

We're searching for our own ways to heal.

I squint toward the end of the alleyway and try to spot the tips of the live oaks that peek between the uniform gray buildings, just three blocks away. Trees that make up the city's cemetery.

My family lies buried beneath that soil.

The queasiness comes on sudden. My heart sinks into my stomach. I blink, and the bullet hole in my grandmother's forehead sears across my eyelids. My knees nearly buckle, but I catch myself.

Never appear fragile.

Not if you want to win.

"Well, thank goodness—or shall I use the new catchphrase—thank *Goodwin* you are here," Ciro says, closing his umbrella and leaning on it like a walking stick. "I seem to have mislaid my keys."

He rips off his cap and flashes me one of his old winsome smiles, but it's strained and awkward. Smiles are another rare commodity these days.

"Ironic, considering your tattoo," I say, knowing my words will sting. I'm in no mood for company.

Head bowed, Ciro fiddles with the cuff of his right glove, revealing the black and yellow ink of a diamond-topped skeleton key.

"It was quite vainglorious of me to believe I had all the answers," Ciro mutters, his cherubic cheeks flushing with embarrassment. I can't help but stare at the unsightly scar that bisects his scalp. A poorly healed gash he earned from a baton strike to the head the day our team was captured and very nearly killed by a Texas State Guard firing squad. He's traded his once buoyant curls for a military buzz cut, as if he wants people to see his wounds, to know what he's been through to get here.

Or maybe he just wants to remind himself.

Ciro's a far cry from the high-ranking boaster I met in Canada—the twenty-year-old boy who once vied to become the Common's leader.

"I've learned no one has the answers to anything," I say, picking the correct key on my second attempt. I twist the lock and push through the glass door, Ciro following close after me. "Life is just a game of guesswork. We're all pretending we know what we're doing. That we're in control. But no one knows a goddamn thing."

Ciro frowns down at me as he locks the door behind us. "I presume there's been no word of him, then?" he whispers, voice tight with concern.

There's no need for hushed conversation. Though my eyes have not yet adjusted to the dimness of the hospital warehouse, I know we're the only two in here. The storage room is always empty, vacant of people and any scraps of medical supplies that once filled the teeming aisles.

It's why I took the back entrance. To avoid running into anyone.

"I'm here," Ciro says, pointing out the obvious. "I know you have Ava . . . but I am here if you need me. Would you like to talk about him?"

I let my silence speak for me. Three at a time, I move up the stairs behind the shelves that previously housed surgical instruments, hoping Ciro and his questions won't trail after me. Unsurprisingly, I hear the soft clicks of his umbrella turned walking stick only a few steps behind.

Everyone's too scared to leave me alone.

As for the "him" Ciro keeps referring to, it's a coin toss.

I snap my eyes out the floor-length windows that greet us at the landing and stare at the thirty-story wanted image glaring back at me from a building's facade. Mere weeks ago, it was my own face that adorned these streets, flashing on every high-rise across the country. *Wanted.* A single bold word signifying that I was criminal. Dangerous. That I didn't belong.

Now the face glowering above the incriminating word belongs to the man who sought to condemn me. The reason the states are at war. The reason the Common came out of hiding.

Former Texas governor, Howard S. Roth.

He's been missing for three weeks since he deserted and fled his capital, stealing his illegal second grandchild away from us. From me.

Theo.

The boy who was my mission. The estranged Roth living a peaceful life in Canada before I ripped him from his ignorance and dragged him into my mess.

Sweat pools in my eyes and pours down my nose. I feel my panic surge, exhausting and all-consuming. Spinning away from the governor's looming scowl, I stumble for the hallway. I free myself of my sun-protective layers, peeling back my gloves and scarf, fighting for a gulp of air.

My thoughts are at once sluggish and dizzying. I feel as though I move beneath a weight meant for a body much stronger than mine. But I fear closing my eyes, for even as I blink, the faces of those taken from me flash behind my lids.

My grandmother, father, mother.

Theo.

He's always there, waiting for me when my consciousness drifts off into darkness. His face is faded like the others. As pale as his brother, Halton, was when death took its rigid hold.

Is Theo lost to us—to me—forever?

I try to shake his screams from my mind, but they only increase, sounding like loud alarms, as if he's warning me of some impending peril.

Get a grip, I chide myself, remembering I'm not alone. *You're no use to anyone like this.* The ruinous effects of heatstroke and insomnia are taking their toll. I can't let people see.

Ciro appears at my side and slides open a window, to little effect. He hands me his umbrella to lean on, which I begrudgingly accept.

"I realize I'm a northerner not yet adapted to the Southwest climate," Ciro pants, looking as if he's just stepped from a shower, fully clothed. "But shouldn't the air-conditioning down here be world-class? How can any Texan expect to outlast the summers?"

We stand motionless, listening to the rattling hum of the AC working overtime. Lifting my hand, I discover the vents above blow nothing but lukewarm air. It's too hot outside. The units can't keep up.

They can and they will, I chastise myself again. Dallas can take the heat.

I shove the umbrella back into Ciro's gloved hands and straighten my shoulders into the posture of someone who is spirited and fortified. Maybe if I keep pretending, I can reclaim the girl that I once was. No, the woman I fought so hard to become.

A woman who knows—*knows*—she deserves to be here. Not merely existing, but *living,* loudly and unapologetically.

I make a sharp left turn, avoiding the network of hallways that lead to the main entrance, to the doors that open to hundreds of exam and delivery rooms still bustling and open to the public.

The Family Planning Center can't just close because of a rebellion. New life enters the world every second of every day. With so much loss, this thought should bring me comfort, but instead it quickens my pace. *What kind of a future will they be born into?*

A doctor in clean white scrubs strides toward me from the far end of the corridor. I nearly stumble, and it takes every shred of my self-control to refrain from cowering.

Men like him took people like me away.

"Afternoon, sir," Ciro acknowledges the obstetrician as he passes. Recognition flickers across the doctor's eyes as his head whips back at me in a double take.

Tell me I shouldn't be here. My old fury ignites like dry kindling and I hold my glare, goading him to say something. I refuse to hide in here. This former epicenter of the Rule of One has been revamped and revolutionized. It's now a place to find who you are.

"Afternoon," he says faintly, hastening his pace.

I wonder if he knew my father. If he was—or still is—a Roth zealot. How many Multiples did he deliver? How many times did he tell a mother to choose?

Another turn and I reach the wing I came here for. My heart lifts when I spot the new frosted glass sign etched above the open doors. An exuberant tree, twin trunks interlocking, it's lush white and yellow branches reaching skyward.

My aunt Haven established this center. After a lifetime imprisoned in labor camps across the state, never knowing who she was—that she had family, loved ones, a *history*—she made this place her fight.

WIth the Common's backing, Haven seeks to rejoin what was separated. Here, inside the very walls that tore parents from their second-born children, my mother's twin seeks to make broken families whole.

It's here that I, too, seek to feel whole. It's the only place I can hope to find respite. To know every sacrifice has been worth it. Or will be.

"Last week I witnessed a seven-year-old boy meet his sister for the first time," Ciro says as we enter the extensive lobby. He has to shout above what sounds like the high whirs of a windstorm. "Half sister, of course, but it's all the same. Blood is blood."

Turns out there were thousands more out there like Theo. Children of perfectly—or disastrously—timed affairs.

Straightaway, I move to one of the four industrial-sized fans—the source of the rumble—their circular, bladeless design making them look disturbingly like faceless heads. Besides us, they're the only other occupants in the room.

Today, the orderly lines of chairs are empty. They were empty yesterday. Empty the day before.

"More will come," I say, turning from the hot air that blows back the loose flyaways of my messy bun. I've let my hair grow out since I stopped running. Dyed-blonde tips, with my natural red roots. I'm still trying to figure out who I want to be. "More will come looking for their sons and daughters."

11

Freed people from prison farms all over Texas, thousands of second-born orphans, live at the Center, waiting for someone to claim them. Haven and the Common Elders look after the youths in the meantime, but a hospital isn't a home.

"And sisters and brothers," Ciro adds as he collapses into a chair. Though he still shouts over the fan, I catch the soft wistfulness in his voice.

All at once it hits me why Ciro visits the Center. Why he even requested a key. He must search for solace here, the same as me.

Ciro misses his family. He wants to be around other siblings, those who understand the bond.

"Still no word from your sisters?" I ask, dropping into the chair beside him, looping my arm around his. "Or your parents?"

Ciro barely manages to shake his head. His hands, usually as animated as his words, sit limp in his lap. He sighs. "The worst part is the not knowing."

The way the Canadian president likes it.

After our takeover of Dallas, Ciro's face made global news, revealing his pivotal role within the Common. Since then, his parents and three sisters are unaccounted for. As illegal migrants in Canada, anything could have happened to them. But my shrewd guess is that President Moore took them. Had the wealthy family arrested and imprisoned. Just to prove he could. *They're probably in the same cell he threw* me *in.*

My stomach clenches, remembering the biting pain of the feeding tube.

"We will find your family," I tell him, squeezing his hand with as much conviction as I can muster. *Just like we'll find Theo.* "Never cross a Cross, right?"

Ciro smiles, a real one this time. It makes him look young and hopeful. "You're right, Ms. Goodwin. And good *will* win."

A loud crash from the other room sends us both to our feet. I reach for my knife that isn't there. *You gave it away,* I remind myself. To Theo.

Maybe he's using the blade this very moment to finish off the governor. To make his escape back to us.

"It sounded like shattering glass," Ciro whispers as we advance down the short hall, our hands hovering above the guns at our hips, ready.

When I spot the broken window of Haven's office, I start sprinting.

The moment this building was claimed by the Common, I scraped away the vinyl letters beside the door—"Director of Family Planning"—with my own sharp nails. Now, in its place, someone has slapped up a metal plaque with five letters still dripping with red paint.

GLUTS

My hand dives for my gun, my feet poised to run after whoever did this, but Haven's voice stops me short.

"Mira." The novelty of hearing my name spoken aloud, in Dallas, is still fresh and jarring. This is the city in which I spent eighteen years "playing" Ava. I was only ever Mira belowground, in our family's basement.

"Haven," I say, advancing toward my mother's twin. She flinches, like she's still adjusting to owning her real name. She only just learned it the night she reunited with Rayla. The night my grandmother died.

"Did you see who did this?" I ask heatedly, fuming at the violation of the office, *of us*. I snap my head back and forth, for the first time cursing the lack of surveillance. *Having no cameras is a double-edged sword.*

Haven points to the ground on the other side of the smashed window. Ciro and I follow her into the room and see a girl splayed across the bamboo flooring. Her raven hair covers half her face, but I recognize her at once: Mckinley Ruiz, my former classmate, Halton Roth's onetime girlfriend. Even passed out, she somehow maintains her snooty expression. The last time I saw her she was laughing as I was sentenced to die on the Capitol steps.

"She didn't see me coming," Haven says calmly, like this show of violence doesn't faze her. She holsters her pistol, tossing her silver-streaked red mane behind her shoulders as she kneels. "Knocked her on the back of the head. Twenty minutes before she wakes."

I toss Haven a pair of zip-ties. "Where are the Common Guards?" I ask, exasperated. Mckinley should never have made it this far.

"No Guards," Haven answers, shaking her head like she's seen enough Guards to fill two lifetimes.

Ciro disappears, then returns with the plaque, the sound of glass punctuating his every step. He holds out the thin sheet of metal at arm's length, as if the five-letter word could reach out and strangle him.

Ciro's a fourth-born. Three times more undesirable than even a twin, some would argue.

Before I can take the plaque from him, he throws it down and stomps his heel again and again, denting the metal, smearing the letters until the slur is no longer legible.

Chest heaving, he looks to me, then Haven. He sways, like he's exerted the last of his energy. My aunt grips his shoulder, her quiet sturdiness his new leaning stick.

"*Glut* is only a word," Haven tells us, her bright emerald eyes shining into mine. "It only has meaning if we let it."

I nod, trying to allow her words to resonate, but an echoing storm of boots yanks my focus away.

More vandals? Attackers?

We stand behind our weapons, squaring up for a fight, but it's Ava and Barend who come rushing in. They wear matching scowls, their urgency and outrage radiating like a force field. I step back, my mind reaching for the worst.

"The Texas Guard is here," I say, much calmer than I feel. I listen for the sirens, harnessing all my fear into my grip on my gun.

Ava shakes her head and flings back her oversized hood, not a lick of perspiration spoiling her shimmering red locks. *She must have used*

Owen's air-conditioned car to find me, I think fleetingly. I was sopped in sweat thirty seconds into my slog across downtown.

Is that where she goes when she leaves me? To Owen Hart?

"It's Alexander," Ava says, spitting the name. She wastes no time with inquiries about the smashed glass or the unconscious girl on the floor. "He's leading an unauthorized search mission without us."

"If we don't leave now," Barend announces, "we won't make it to Guardian Tower in time." Clad in a Common Guard's uniform, he barrels for Ciro, hooking him protectively with his arm. "Let's go."

The very idea that Roth and Theo could be tracked down and unearthed without us—without *me*—there to witness it feels unbearable.

Between my tireless nightmares I've dreamt of nothing but the shock on Roth's face as he realizes he's been caught and the game is finally over. Won.

And Theo. I dream of Theo's amber eyes, wide-awake and alive, staring into mine, knowing I found him. And knowing—*knowing*—that we can make a place for us to belong.

"If we want to make it," Ava cries, holding out her hand for me, "we have to run."

Don't we always?

The first thing I notice when we push through the back doors is Owen's car. If ever I'd call an inanimate object gorgeous, it would be this blinding-red luxury model. I expect to see Owen standing watch over his transport, but instead spot only a Common Guard, face wrapped beneath the woven cotton cloth of a military-style shemagh. Ava sprints to her, instructing the Guard to help Haven with an arrest at the Center.

It's still strange seeing a soldier carry out our orders. But Ava wears the role of a leader like a second skin. She commands so effortlessly, so sure and decisive, skills I've yet to master.

The car doors open like the wings of an eagle, and we all pile in, Ava behind the wheel. I snap my head to Barend, our veteran driver, in surprise. *My sister doesn't know how to drive.*

He raises his shoulders in a dismissive shrug, but I note the set of his jaw, so tight he could crack teeth. "Apparently, Owen's very particular about who drives his car."

"He only trusts me," Ava says, hitting the accelerator before the doors even seal shut. She drives as wild as our grandmother, stopping for nothing. And no one.

We burst out of the alleyway with a neck-jerking left turn toward the heart of downtown. Ava pounds on the horn, warning the sluggish, sun-drunk pedestrians. No one tells her to slow down or be careful. *Careful* doesn't get you anywhere in a rebellion.

We even speed past a Guard SUV, and instead of racing to pull us over, the two soldiers hold down their wrists in the Common salute. They can't see our faces through the one-way windows, but they must recognize the car and assume we're on a mission.

"So Owen tipped you off?" I ask Ava, popping my knuckles, anxious to catch sight of the glistering glass ball of Guardian Tower. Owen keeps close company with Alexander, a fact I don't much care for. But it also means he can keep a close eye on him.

"Alexander received intelligence this morning," Ava answers, eyes never leaving the road. "The drone left for the Island of Houston half an hour ago."

Houston? Despite myself, hope surges through me like a taser shock.

This could be it. The uninhabited city, the drowned metropolis, is the perfect place for Roth to hide. After a dozen failed search missions—from Albany to Detroit, Austin to Phoenix—this could be the one.

"That pompous ass really thought he could keep this from us?" Barend sounds off from the back seat. The normally inscrutable soldier lays his anger bare. He eyes my headrest in front of him, looking like he wants to punch out his frustration, but Ciro keeps Barend's hand firmly gripped in his. "Who does he think he is?"

"A Roth," Ava jabs, smacking the horn harder than necessary. The relentless beeping overpowers my racing thoughts, until my mind grabs hold of just one. The four words Alexander screamed at me the night Theo was taken.

It's all your fault.

I'm the one who led Theo to Dallas. The one who made him shout his truth for the world to hear, and now he's gone. Stolen.

Lost.

It's my fault we lost our father too. Ava and I swore to each other we'd get him back, that we'd rescue and save him. In the end we couldn't even find his body to bury.

Sweat stings my eyes, but I gaze out unblinkingly until Guardian Tower fills my view, soaring high above the city and smoldering in the heat.

This is where our father died. Where Governor Roth murdered him in secret like a malicious coward. Level 102. Cell 148. Thousands of miles and a border away, I watched the hours-old surveillance footage that captured the moment Roth shot him, my greatest protector, first in the kneecap, then between the eyes. Ending the life that gave me life.

I've never before dared enter the prison and former Texas State Guard headquarters, yet now I have no choice. My body jerks forward as Ava jumps a curb and slams to a halt directly in front of the Tower's entranceway.

The car doors pop open and I fling aside my seat belt as six Common Guards rush to stop us. Ava and I keep moving toward the glass entrance, Barend and Ciro close at our sides. We remove our scarves and hoods, revealing our faces, and all the soldiers back off but one. Kano, my old mission mate.

"Finally!" Kano says, pulling down his olive-colored shemagh. "I thought I'd have to break up the party without you!" He throws me a stirring smile, casting the damp, loose strands of his topknot away from his deep-set eyes. Even impending war in high summer can't dim his mischievous gleam. He lives for trouble.

"The latest?" I ask as we sprint inside the high-ceilinged foyer, bee-lining for the elevator bank.

"The drone just reached the coast," Kano answers. "A little island retreat for the runaway governor? Seems promising to me . . ."

Microchip scanners jut out from the walls beside each elevator door, like thin steel arms ready to reach out and stop me. *They're out of commission,* I remind myself. Once symbols of control, the devices are just relics now. Metal bones of a dead regime.

"Dallas should not be a museum for the past," Ava says, echoing my thoughts. She stabs the scanner with the butt of her gun before entering the circular elevator, as wide as our old basement. "The general should have ordered them ripped down the very first night."

"He did, but Alexander suggested it was a waste of his unit's time," Barend says, the sharp disapproval in his voice as cutting as the blade on his duty belt.

His unit? Alexander deserted the military when he fled to Canada with his illegal family some eighteen years ago. Shouldn't he be court-martialed, rather than officially reinstated as a high-ranking officer?

"Control room," Ava yells as the last of us crosses the threshold. The elongated doors pound closed, inches from my nose, each displaying the Texas Guard seal. I wait for the elevator to shout back "access denied," fully believing Alexander capable of deleting our voices from the admittance list, but the numbers on the dull black wall start rising. Twenty, seventy, one hundred. I feel no sensation of skyrocketing upward, past the countless floors of prison cells, the thousands of solitary concrete rooms overflowing with so many of our enemies.

Yet the two most important remain empty. One for Governor Roth, the other for Director Wix. I personally captured and saw to the swift arrest of the last head of the Family Planning Division, but someone let—*helped*—the Director escape. Before I can dwell too much on this oversight, the doors slide open to a flurry of pandemonium.

It sounds as if we stand in the center of a hurricane. At first, I think it's more industrial fans, but then I realize the uproar is audio from the search drone.

The UAV is flying into a superstorm.

The dome-shaped control room, with its arched, low-emissivity glass walls, offers a famed, breath-stopping 360-degree view of the capital, but I only take notice of the bright screen that hangs high above the bedraggled head of Alexander Roth. Live video shows blurry overhead footage of a stilt house, battered and caked green with mold and decay. Violent waves hammer against its four twenty-foot concrete supports as the ocean surges higher and higher, making the house look like a lone breakwater trying to save a city that's already drowned.

Would Roth really shelter here?

"Sir, do I have your order to move in?" I hear an anxious Guard shout over the crushing winds.

Right as Ava and I charge into the room, Alexander whips around, his crisp navy-blue uniform striking against his wall of twenty camouflaged soldiers, all dressed for combat.

Does he think he's sending them to the Gulf Coast? Right into an approaching hurricane?

"You've always lacked vision, but I see you're completely blind!" Ava yells, throwing her hands up toward the screens. "This is a trap!"

"No, Ava, this is it!" Owen fires off somewhere near the control panel. "The bastard's finally in our crosshairs!"

Alexander's beady eyes catch mine, and I can feel the hate that radiates off him as the distance between us closes. It's a burning rancor that seeks to cut me down and make me disappear, like I *let* his son disappear.

"Remove them from this room, *now!*" Alexander snaps.

Two soldiers break from the line and barrel toward us. Their bulletproof vests bear the rebellion's yellow slash, from hip to heart, but the batons in their hands speak a different story. Are these Guards loyal to the Common, or do they serve only Alexander?

Or is one of them the governor's gunman that I've been waiting for these last three weeks?

The pistol in Ava's hand tells me she's asking herself the same questions.

"Looks like we're going to have ourselves a little rumble," Kano yells, not even trying to conceal his delight.

"Alexander, call off your henchmen!" Owen shouts, standing on the balls of his feet like he's in the grip of an inward duel: move to our aid—to Ava's—or remain at the control panel. "Texas made or not, this drone has a lifespan of about twenty seconds in these winds before it's ocean litter!"

Four more strides would have told me just how far the Guards were planning to go to remove us from this room, but a stentorian shout erupts from the elevator door. "Stand down, soldiers!"

Emery.

The two soldiers go rigid, their bodies jerking to attention. I sprint past them for the screen—*I have to be the first to see; Theo, are you really in there?* Throwing a cursory glance behind me, I spot Emery standing beside the general, chest heaving, jaw and fists clenched. Clearly, she wasn't told of this mission either.

"Move in!" Alexander shouts, undercutting Emery's order for all soldiers to stand down.

In a surprising move, Owen disobeys Emery and slaps a button on the panel. The shaky drone footage suddenly displays on every screen throughout the room, encircling us. I swallow my panic at what I might see—*or not see*—inside the dilapidated house. I grip Ava's shoulder and watch the search drone dive, as agile and quick as a bird of prey.

"Just in time; knew you'd make it," Owen greets us as we reach him. His smile beams like a five-hundred-watt bulb. "Heat sensors show ten bodies in there."

But a shadow crosses my sister's face. She glares at Alexander, who paces the shellacked concrete floor, his trembling hands pulling at his tangled hair.

"This doesn't feel right," Ava presses.

The UAV swoops to the far side of the ruined structure, where an entire wall is missing, most likely ripped off in a previous storm. The rainfall batters against the drone's lens in sheets, making it near impossible to discern any detail beyond the ten distorted shapes of bright yellow.

"Clarity Mode, dammit!" Alexander commands, and the blurred images instantly snap into focus. He stifles a cry.

It's like jolting awake from a hazy bad dream, only to see the nightmare clear in front of me.

Ten bodies, aligned in a straight row along the edge of the exposed room, sit cuffed to metal poles, the savage waves of the Gulf thrashing against their knees. *How long before the water is above their necks?* All wear identical yellow prison uniforms, a single word in black on their chests: "COMMONERS."

"What is this?" Alexander cries out, hurling the Guard who pilots the drone from his seat.

"This is a setup," Ava says, a hollow despair softening her usual edge. "The governor was never there."

"Theo!" I shout over the shrieking gale. "Do you see Theo in there?"

Alexander's long, pale fingers frantically stab at the control panel, driving the drone forward, but the man-made machine is no match for nature. The raging winds and rain keep whipping the UAV left and right. *And I can't see their faces!*

"Enable face recognition!" Alexander screams, his voice cracking in desperation.

21

"UNABLE TO IDENTIFY" scrolls across the screens.

Stupidly, I stand very still, squinting my eyes, like this will do any good to stabilize the jerky spasmodic footage and focus the line of captives. The longer I look, the more my stomach lurches, bile burning the back of my throat.

Please don't let me see him.

Yet still I search for the beacon of Theo's golden-brown hair. The identifiable curve of his athletic shoulders. His characteristic fighting spirit, pulling against his zip-ties.

But all I can make out are flashes of the white gags tied around the sopping wet faces of the Common members, a lone purple star stamped over their lips.

"All Commoners will be exterminated," Emery reads slowly aloud, somehow deciphering the jumbled text scrawled on the back wall. "The future belongs to Loyalists. Long live the governors."

Just then the drone loses the battle with the storm and starts spinning downward, plunging into the roiling sea. The screens cut to black. The room falls into a dead stillness, the audio from the drone lost.

"Son of a Glut!" Owen screams, shattering the quiet. He winces at his use of the offensive curse. "Sorry. Son of a *goddamn governor!*"

Alexander grips his metal chair and slams it onto the floor. It doesn't break, so he picks it up again, but Emery stops him with a lift of her hand.

I sprint for Alexander, seizing him by his rumpled lapels, forcing him to look at me. "You can send your soldiers," I plead. "There's still time! You can save them. *Him.*"

Theo.

Were you in that house?

The bags under Alexander's bleary eyes are as black as his stare. "It's all your fault," he utters, slapping down my hands. His words sting more than his touch.

Ramming past me, Alexander drags himself from the room, his flock of Guards remaining where they stand at attention.

Ava grabs Emery by the shoulders, her face hard and inscrutable, the Goodwin way. "Please," she whispers.

But we both already know the answer.

"We can't risk more lives," Emery says flatly. "The Common members will drown long before our Guard could reach them. I'm sorry."

"So we just let them die?" I exclaim, unable to accept this truth. I blink and see Theo's lifeless body buried beneath the sea.

No, I tell myself. *He wasn't there.*

"The Loyalists led us to that scene with the aim to make us feel helpless," Emery tells the room. "It was a mistake. The more they take from us, the stronger we will become."

I want to believe that.

I need to. Because looking around the control room now, I can't stop my mind from thinking about how many more of us will be taken before this all ends.

Emery dismisses the soldiers, straightening her blazer as she leaves with the general, whose normal bulldozer frame has shed at least fifteen pounds since his time with the Common. The last wisps of hair on his bald head have disappeared, sacrificed to the cause. *Life as a dissenter has been hard on him.*

Before the door closes, I catch Emery withdrawing a fidget cube from a hidden pocket, her deft fingers working the buttons and wheels so expertly, it's clear she knows the stress reliever well. Her responsibilities after the coup must be weighing on her more than she lets on.

"Alexander just cost us our last search drone!" Barend shouts, throwing a hammer-like punch into his left palm, and then emitting a sharp hiss at the pain. Ciro removes his synthetic leather gloves and takes hold of his bare hand to soothe him.

"I really thought we'd get the bastard," Owen murmurs, the last of his vibrant radiance snuffed out. "The intel was surefire. I really thought this was it."

All at once the heat proves too much and standing feels too big a task. I plop my backside on the hard floor and stare up at my sister, too scared to close my eyes.

I don't want to see the vacant, swollen faces of ten Common members who have less than an hour left to live.

"We're going to get Roth," Ava states with enough strength to sustain us both.

"And Theo," Kano says, taking a seat beside me. "He might have been a spoiled northerner, but he showed us he's one resilient rebel. He's still out there, and we'll find him."

I want to believe that too.

THEO

There's this spot off the coast of Vancouver where I'd go to get lost. It was one of those hidden beaches that's a forty-minute slog through trees to reach. The place somehow managed to avoid ever becoming a geotag, which meant I usually had the knockout sunsets and pebbled shores to myself. Pretty ideal. Just like my childhood.

My parents first took me there so I could learn how to fish. A rich person's hobby I never got the hang of. In British Columbia, civilians need all these special sport-fishing licenses that cost a family fortune to procure, and of course, my dad had them.

My dad had everything. Or so I thought then.

The fish don't feel pain, mijo, he told me when I caught my first Pacific jack mackerel, as big as my forearm. I cringed when I saw that the white-bellied fish had swallowed the hook whole. My naive nine-year-old eyes were centered on the steady line of blood dripping from its open mouth. But it wasn't audibly moaning or screaming, so I was dumb enough to believe him.

Looking back now, I understand how the fish could have been such a fool. It trusted the shiny bait, because why not? How could it have known the lure was just a lie? A sham?

I, too, swallowed all kinds of lies whole. My entire identity, for example. My whole family's identity, actually.

And my dad was wrong. The hooks *do* hurt. A lot. I feel every jagged cut, the deep and the shallow, created by the incalculable lies he fed me for eighteen years.

Life has been painful since the wool was ripped from my eyes.

"¡Mierda!" I scream when I hear bus-sized tires speeding across the rocky, rust-colored sand. *Shit!*

The Beast is here. I made it ten minutes longer than my last attempted jailbreak, but a tracker drone wasn't even used this time. *And yet they still found me.*

I refill my lungs and scream again, if for no other reason than to let the world know how pissed off I am. I've long since cast off any hope someone useful will hear me, no less help me. There's no one else out here in whatever bone-dry hellscape I'm trapped in.

Concentrate.

Three minutes is all I've got before the Beast catches up to me.

No, that's being optimistic.

Less than a minute.

My legs are beat. My path is a Hail Mary sprint straight through thorny vegetation. I'm so cut up and sore, it's a miracle I'm able to move at all. I'm dehydrated to the point I've seen multiple heat-induced mirages on the horizon, and the real kicker is I have no idea *where* the hell I am.

Somewhere in no-one's-land, Texas. A whole other world. I'm easy pickings.

But the desire to survive is a hard instinct to kill.

I take stock of my surroundings. Where can I hide? Large mountain ranges, spiked like a dragon's back, tease of shelter in the distance.

Too far.

Eight-foot-tall shrubs that smell like rain are scattered across the valley.

Too sparse.

Those are my options, and they for sure won't do me any good. I know because I've already tried them both on my previous failed escape runs.

That's it. My less than a minute of freedom is up.

Like a black angel of death, the Beast hurtles in front of me, skidding to a stop at an angle to block my path fifty feet ahead. The sun's reflection bounces off the sizzling metal of the giant military vehicle like a laser beam, impairing my vision, and I'm forced to draw back.

On cue, the front door bursts open, and a Guard dressed in all black charges me like a grizzly at a dead sprint.

I try something different this time.

Instead of running the opposite direction, I stand my ground. It's the gutsiest move I've attempted yet, but I wait until the last possible moment, right up until the Guard can almost grab me, before I spin on my heel, causing the Guard to blow clear past me.

My success is short-lived. The Guard rebounds fast. Blindsided by sheer muscle, I pitch forward to land hard in the dirt, ripping open my palms and the knees of my pants. I manage a few defensive kicks that land nothing but air before I'm manhandled to my feet and dragged toward the armored vehicle that looks like a limo on steroids.

The back door of the Beast opens, and the Guard unhands me. I can feel the AC from where I stand, but I won't be tempted. I dig in my heels. Or what's left of them, anyway. The soles of my runners have all but melted off, and the bottoms of my feet are cut and seared so bad it feels like I'm balancing on the tips of newly sharpened knives. Every step I take is self-inflicted torture.

But I could have done it. I would have. Made my way back, I mean. To Mira.

"Get in," the Guard orders.

"No thanks," I tell him.

His hands, puffed up like fattened sausages from the heat, make their ham-handed way to his utility belt. Dark shades conceal his eyes from me, but he's for sure glaring down at the symbol I crudely carved into my right wrist. Hate burns from him, almost crueler than the sun's blaze.

His name escapes me, but the Guard who looks like an extra-large reptile with his scaly, sunbaked skin can't seem to remember mine either. He keeps calling me Roth.

My last name's Wright, I told him time and time again, back when my resolve and pride were still intact. But now it feels like almost everything about me has been shattered.

A Guard's baton can do that.

The soldier jams his metal club into my ribs, making sure to block the vehicle's window with his mammoth frame, so no one sees. His pudgy thumb presses down on the handle, and the electric shock of a taser jolts me backward. I bite my lip hard, tasting blood, and absorb the pain in seasoned silence. After three weeks with this guy as my personal guard and travel companion, I've learned to take a hit.

I drop flat on my back, my head narrowly missing a rock the size of the Beast's tire, and squint up at the blinding sky.

Even if I wanted to, I no longer have the strength to get up. This really is it. There's no fight left in me.

Why won't my captor just leave me here?

The Guard grabs a handful of my overgrown hair and hauls me up from the dirt.

"You might be a Roth by blood," he spits in my ear. "But you're still a filthy Glut. You don't belong here."

I didn't belong in Canada either. *Where the hell can a Glut go, then? Where's my rightful place?*

Six feet underground, I guess.

Then, Mira's wide green eyes take over my vision. Forest green, like the trees that surrounded my former home. My getaway spot. Out by the coast.

Maybe together Mira and I could find a place to belong. A place where no one would dare call us Gluts, or surplus.

Or in my case, a Roth.

That's just another hallucination. I shake the vision away, knowing full well it could never be real.

The Guard shoves me into the back seat, and the door that must weigh as much as an airplane's closes with a bang as loud as a shotgun blast.

I nearly jump out of my skin.

Seated directly across from me, our knees almost knocking, is the man I haven't laid eyes on since he abducted me from the tunnels beneath his mansion. The man everyone keeps telling me I share my DNA with.

Governor Roth, the notorious ruler of Texas. Better known in my country as the superstar of the Lone Star state.

My not-so-dear grandpa.

He's not the governor anymore, I correct myself. He ran from his capital; he lost his army.

Roth's just a man, Mira's voice echoes in my memory.

Really? Then why does it feel like I'm staring into the voracious eyes of an immortal titan that somehow survived everything the Common could throw at him?

Even poison.

For days I've believed the whisperings of the Guards, swearing their leader was on his last legs.

But I should know by now. Everything about these people is a lie.

"You're lucky," Roth announces in his low, placid voice, "that I have the patience to keep sending my men to retrieve you."

Lucky is the last word I'd use to describe my situation.

Perched like a diminutive bird on the seat to Roth's right is Director Wix, a woman I thought I'd never cross paths with again. I thought I'd made sure of it.

Mira and I left you zip-tied in a cabinet, I wish I had the nerve to scream. *How are you not locked inside Guardian Tower?*

The recently installed, and I *thought* freshly *deposed*, Texas Family Planning Director removes an IV drip from a bulging vein in Roth's arm. She throws a little sneer my way. But there's no room in this moment to focus on her.

Roth is here. With me. He's never here on these hunt-down missions. This can only mean something's happening. A *big* something.

He's fully recovered. *We're moving to a new location.*

"Drive!" Roth suddenly commands.

The Beast shoots forward and the shock on the Guard's face is priceless. He hasn't yet made it into the limo tank, and it looks like he never will. His shouts don't penetrate the five-inch-thick windows, but I can see him scrambling for a door handle, for anything, even attempting a last-second leap onto the back. A loud *thud* tells me he didn't make it.

The rear window serves as a screen, and it's almost like I'm watching a far-fetched movie and not my real life. The Guard goes rolling, head over heels like a malformed tumbleweed, and I suddenly remember his name. Wheeler.

My blood stings ice-cold when I realize I'm smiling. *That's something a Roth would do.* Find pleasure in another's pain. I all but smack the grin off my face, trusting no one saw.

"Does anyone else have something they wish to say about my grandson?" Roth asks coolly. There's a force behind his voice that I recognize from snippets of old speeches I'd sometimes catch my dad listening to on the news.

Roth's strength is back. Redoubled. The others must feel it too.

Every soldier packed inside the luxury tank, including the Director, shouts, "No sir!" in hearty unison.

I can think of a million things to say about his grandson, but I keep my mouth shut. Halton. My half brother. Roth's first and *only* grandson, or so all of North America thought for eighteen years. So I thought too.

Why did you have your grandson killed? Will you kill me too? Your illegal second grandchild?

The Beast speeds to ninety clicks, and soon the abandoned Guard becomes a speck on the wide horizon. He'll be dead by tomorrow. We're hundreds of miles from civilization. From water, food. Help.

A fraction of me feels sorry for him. The bit that still clings to who I am. Or was. If I've kept my days straight, it should be the third Sunday of my captivity. And if I weren't caught in this waking nightmare, I'd be at my water polo match. Or safe, in my room, studying for a future I thought was mine.

Lies and ignorance, Mira would probably say to me.

My life was one long oblivious slumber before Mira came and shook me awake. Told me my truth.

Mira. You were the truest part of my life.

"I'm not your grandson," I choke out, massaging my sore ribs, scraping together as much nerve as I can muster. But I find it impossible to look Roth in the eyes.

"In time, you'll feel differently. Alexander left you too long in Canada. Both have brainwashed you."

"The most serious case of Stockholm syndrome won't make me call you Grandpa," I vocalize, in case he's under any delusions.

"That's a title I've never much cared for. You can call me Governor."

So Roth still thinks he's in control. Has power. If we're not retreating, what are we doing, then?

He unfolds and straightens his sleeves, buttoning his polished cufflinks with their distinctive logo of the Texas State Guard. Not a wrinkle or speck of desert sand spoils the striking effect of the military uniform that somehow still fits him like a glove. *How'd he find the time—or the person—to alter it?*

The man's grown nearly skeletal since his illness. A sharp suit can't cover that up. But any perceived weak point is made up for by his intensity. He emanates a severity that I assume comes from conquering death. Almost touching hell itself, then returning with a big middle finger.

He looks certain. Of what, I don't know.

His place in this world, I guess.

"You're strong," Roth says, all his intensity aimed at me. "Not just your body, but your will."

Something akin to a wistful expression brightens his clean-shaven face. It's incongruous, unnatural. I don't like it.

I know what he's about to say.

"You remind me of myself," he remarks, and I almost jam my fingers into my ears, start screaming, anything to blockade this stranger's lies.

He leans toward me, offering a fresh pair of combat boots that look just my size. I gaze down at my throbbing feet, my runners that are shredded to pieces.

I can't run in these. The desert floor is like lava, booby-trapped with plants armored in needles all across its pathless domain. But I'd rather attempt my next escape from the governor on my raw skin and bones than accept anything from him.

Roth grips my hand. "Your father and brother were weak by every definition."

I'm so depleted and numb, I don't even recoil. I look at anything but him. The scads of weapons on the walls, in soldiers' hands. The oxygen tank below Roth's seat, the bags of inky red liquid that must be his blood.

All armaments making the man harder to kill.

"I'm glad we've been reunited," he says after a long delay. *Was he waiting for me to speak?*

Ripping my hand from his, I knock the boots to the floor and cram myself into the farthest corner. A flashy piece of metal strapped to the nearest soldier's utility belt grabs my attention.

There it is. The knife Mira entrusted to me. The blade, with its ringed knuckle duster handle made of steel, was stolen from me the second I was taken captive. Now it's only an arm's length away.

"You will pay your grandfather respect," the Director snaps at me, but Roth holds up a quiet hand.

Peering down at my wrist, I outline my sad excuse of a tattoo. By only the light of the moon, I carved the symbol into my sunburnt skin with the sharpest rock I could find.

>

To me it means truth is greater than ignorance. Greater even than pain.

And fighting for truth is greater than my own well-being, because the cause is bigger than me.

I move my eyes back to my knife, then finally meet Roth's scrutiny. I hold his heavy gaze, calculating whether I have enough strength, in body and will, to shove the blade straight into his chest.

"There's not a single thing about me that's like you," I say.

Except my jawline, my height, my nose. My name . . .

And my sudden desire to kill.

"Get him ready, Director Wix," Roth orders the Family Planning Director. "Our arrival is imminent."

Get me ready for what? Where are we arriving? There's nothing out here to arrive *to*.

As the compact, hawklike woman eagerly makes her way toward me, one of those IV bags and needles in her slight hands, tornadoes of dust unexpectedly whirl outside the Beast's windows.

I didn't hear their approach, this tank limo is soundproof, but a pack of military SUVs with the Texas State Guard seal on their doors have formed a ring around us. At first, my optimism soars, thinking this could be the Common Guard here to finish what they started in Dallas.

But why aren't they firing?

¡Ponte trucho! *You idiot!* The State Guards are his.

Roth still has soldiers loyal to his side.

My elation drops to the floorboards that are stained his favorite royal purple, and I suddenly can't catch my breath.

Not because of the military reinforcements.

But because I just caught a glimpse of our destination.

I shake my vision clear again. No, this is not a mirage, as much as I wish it were.

The gargantuan fifty-foot wall we're speeding toward is very much real. The steel and concrete barrier blots out the entire horizon, as if right here at the edge of this wasteland we've reached the end of the world.

It might as well be.

Before I can even compute how we're supposed to make it through the indomitable blockade Roth calls his Big Fence, the bumpy terrain flattens out into a smooth dirt road. The vehicles all queue up behind the Beast and I feel us moving steadily downward.

Walls close in around us.

A tunnel.

We're going *under* the wall.

And straight into Mexico.

AVA

Sleep has no place in the aftermath of tragedy.

Rest is impossible when every part of my being desires to retaliate against a wrong so grievous, I'm certain there's no good left in the world. How can there be when my father, Rayla, Pawel—good, passionate people who were fighting for something greater than themselves—are all dead, while their murderer still lives free?

I don't even pretend to sleep anymore. In the midnight hours while the rest of the Common members are tucked into whatever makeshift bed they were able to find, I roam the ravaged Governor's Mansion, now the rebellion's new headquarters, searching for any secret clues to where Roth could be hiding.

I know he's still alive. Monsters don't die that easily.

The halls are dark—no wasted resources—but I can still see the torn-off wallpaper, the leftover pieces of glass from the shattered portraits. All the custom furniture—extravagant leather couches, costly American chestnut tables and benches—tailor-made clothing, and invaluable art, all the symbols of the governor's wealth and power, are gone. They've either been destroyed or stolen, the loot already showing up on the Black Market after the storming of Roth's gilded mansion.

The biggest trophy went to whoever took the governor's most prized possession: Stephen F. Austin's flintlock pistol. Owned and passed down in the Roth family for generations, the centuries-old piece of history—used in the Texas Revolution by the Father of Texas himself—has now disappeared into obscurity.

Out with the old.

It's time for the new.

I run my fingers along the deep knife marks that have been cut into the plaster walls, a small smile on my lips. I used to love history, always more than eager to honor those who came before. But now I know we can't build the future until we raze the past.

The former First Family's wing is roped off. There's a Common Guard standing at attention, gun on his hip, making sure no one enters. This section of the mansion barely survived the Battle for Dallas—Emery ordered soldiers to protect the Roth family quarters after a group of angry citizens attempted to light the wing on fire. *We must preserve all evidence,* our leader insisted, steady hand on my shoulder.

What about my family home in Trinity Heights? The basement where Mira and I successfully hid from the government for eighteen years? Father blew it to pieces.

The evidence of my life wasn't allowed to survive.

Why should evidence of the Roths'?

"Did you hear the news?" the young, recently enlisted Common Guard says to me. "The vice president has run off." His heart-shaped face twists in disdain. "The coward."

The president of the United States is dead. The day after Roth, his greatest ally, fled Dallas, a rush of stress hormones stunned the president's heart, causing rapid and severe heart-muscle weakness. His left ventricle stopped contracting and he never recovered. It's rare for the sudden condition to be fatal, but the president wanted an out—he knew he was no match to lead a country at war with itself—and his heart gave it to him.

Now that the vice president has fled, our country's highest office remains vacant. A special emergency election could spiral us into further post-rebellion turmoil.

Two people will likely throw their hats in the ring. Senator Gordon of Washington State—the man whom I thrust into the spotlight when I forced him to publicly resist Roth's invasion and align himself with the Common—and his opponent Millicent Cole, the autocratic governor of New York, a carbon copy of Roth and his ironfisted policies.

"If there's an election, we have to make sure our side wins," the Common Guard says, urgent.

I nod to the soldier but don't engage further. This Guard reminds me too much of my friend and former mission companion Pawel, and it hurts to even look him in his eager, wide eyes. They're the same steel blue as Pawel's were, before I closed them to the world forever after he died in my arms.

Instead, I motion wordlessly toward the blocked-off entrance. This is just a formality; I've paid nightly visits to this forbidden wing for a week straight. I know he will let me pass.

No one says no to a Goodwin anymore.

I don't even say no to myself.

Gripping my rucksack filled with paint thinner tighter to my side, I move past the Guard and into the First Family's wing. When I spotted the bottles of highly flammable liquid earlier this morning in a ransacked maintenance store, I knew exactly what I was going to do with them. Consequences be damned.

I'm living off pure reactionary emotion. Father wouldn't approve—all his lessons taught us to approach every situation in life with reason or logic. *That's the best way to survive,* he drilled into us. But my fury cuts through all rational thought like a red-hot blade.

Fury, the emotion eclipsing even my insurmountable grief, is the fuel that keeps me from drowning in a sea of my own bitter tears, never even bothering to kick myself back up to the surface again. My anger is giving me life.

I tread quickly through the windowless hall, my tunnel vision leading me to the door of the Governor's Quarters. It's open, like every other door in the mansion. Roth can no longer shut out the truth of what happened inside these walls. Although the Common has found enough evidence of high crimes and misdemeanors to guarantee a life sentence to almost every member of Roth's regime, they've discovered nothing at all on Project Albatross. And despite my nightly searches, neither have I.

When I told Mira of Father's twin-gene-mutation trial the day after the memorial service, the revelation that the Family Planning Division was working to eradicate twins was met with stoicism. It's like nothing can surprise my sister anymore. Her tolerance for family secrets has reached such a high level, she didn't feel the pain and disappointment that should have come with this new shock. But Mira immediately agreed that we have to keep our father's controversial gene-editing trials to ourselves until we find out more than merely secondhand information from Father's rivals.

He isn't here to defend himself, Mira contended. *For all we know, Father was working to sabotage Roth's plans.*

And if he wasn't, then we will. Mira and I will put an end to Project Albatross, together.

The lights in the governor's bedroom remain off, like the rest of the commandeered mansion at night. *Save power to gain power.* I don't bother to turn them on. The dazzling Dallas skyscrapers sufficiently illuminate my surroundings through the elongated one-way windows.

I shut the heavy door, then move to stand in front of the gilded bedframe, the sheets still coated with the governor's vomit. Evidence of Skye Lin's assassination attempt. Poison, her specialty.

She got closer to bringing down Roth than anyone else has.

Rayla was murdered in the tunnels directly below where I stand. This bed—this panic chamber—was the gateway to my grandmother's death. Suddenly it feels like I'm on fire, heat rapidly spreading through my limbs and stopping in my chest and fists. My arms begin to visibly quiver with my suppressed rage. *Take action,* it feels like my body's telling me.

I pull a bottle of paint thinner from my bag.

I twist off the metal cap and douse the bedsheets with the noxious smelling liquid. If I had thought through what I'm about to do logically, I would have come prepared with a time-delay device, something that would have allowed me to initiate the blaze remotely, for my safety. But I don't want to be safe. I want to be here to watch Roth's home burn down, in person, with my own eyes.

Reaching into my pocket, I take out a long strike-anywhere match and flick the stick into life by snapping my thumb across the match head.

All at once a brilliant orange pool of light surrounds me in the dark. Tears spring to my eyes, spilling down my cheeks. The first I've allowed myself to shed since my grandmother's death.

Emboldened by Rayla's strength—by her love—I don't hesitate. Standing back from the bed, I hold out my arm and am just about to let the match fly when there's a shout behind me.

"Ava, what are you doing?!"

Razing the past.

I drop the flaming matchstick to the lush carpeted floor, and instantly the trail of paint thinner that leads to the bed dances with bright-yellow flames. It happens so fast, the bedframe igniting like a funeral pyre, the fire hungrily spreading to the ceiling and walls. I don't recoil from the almost unbearable heat and instead stand transfixed by the indigo blue at the center of the blaze. Blue, the color that's supposed to represent stability and calm, is the hottest part of a flame, a color that I now see as a symbol of powerful wrath and destruction.

The entire Governor's Quarters will be reduced to ashes in a matter of minutes.

If only Roth's decades-long regime could be wiped out as efficiently.

A strong hand clutches my arm, dragging me away from the fire and toward an open, empty closet in the far corner. The hot, smoky air burns the inside of my nose and eyes, making it difficult to breathe and see, but I manage to shrug off the would-be hero and stumble down a set of stairs that leads to the underground tunnel on my own.

"My mom always warned me that redheads could be fiery," Owen quips, slamming the tunnel's fireproof steel door shut. "But damn. You just took that adage to a *whole* new pyro level."

Leaning against the smooth concrete wall, I surprise myself by laughing out loud. The light, carefree sound echoes throughout the mazelike passageway, unnerving me. I slap my hand over my mouth as if I just committed a grievous offense.

There can be no laughter where Rayla took her last breath.

"I was thinking of doing something similar, but my daydreams involved a sledge hammer," Owen says, pointing to the burning Governor's Quarters above. "Your method was way more efficient. Hats off to you." He feigns removing a cap in a gesture of respect.

Owen's natural cheerful demeanor has halved since the Battle for Dallas, but he hasn't lost all his charm. Not by a long shot. He's as lean as the top branch of an old oak tree, and his red T-shirt and the dark mahogany pants that match his skin fit snug, hinting at his toned body underneath. He looks relaxed and effortlessly cool—the opposite of the Kismet-uniformed boy I first saw in his wanted photo.

He moves away from the door and closer to me in the tight, dimly lit passageway. His golden eyes flare like two piercing flashlights in the dark.

I notice that Owen's body language isn't that of a panicked person ready to run and scream "Fire!" to a house full of sleeping Common members. He trusts that I have a plan to contain the blaze.

"Too bad Emery won't share your approval," I say, coughing from the smoke in my lungs. The Common's leader will be furious with me, not only for disobeying her orders, but for setting such a dangerous example for "appropriate" post-battle behavior. *The eyes of Dallas are upon you,* Emery has stressed again and again to Mira and me. *Your actions matter now more than ever.*

Owen bends down to pick up a scattering of items that spilled from my bag in the scramble to reach the underground escape tunnel. He stares at the bottle of paint thinner, then rises to meet me face to face. "But honestly . . . I think Rayla would have approved." Owen breaks into a sad smile, his wiry shoulders lifting in a resilient shrug. "That's gotta mean you did something right . . . right?"

My stomach clenches at the mention of my grandmother. Heartache threatens to burst through the carefully constructed dam I've built for myself, but if I give in to my grief, I'll be lost. *I must keep hold of my anger.*

"I miss her so much," I murmur, so softly that only Mira could possibly understand.

"I miss her too," Owen says surprisingly, mirroring my pain. His dimples shine with his tears. He wipes them away with a quick brush of his shoulder, an indication he, too, is keeping his own heartache at bay.

But somehow, sharing a small piece of my immense hurt out loud, with him, I feel lighter. Like we're carrying the impossible weight of Rayla's loss in tandem.

Owen places the silver bottle safely back into the bag that sits at my hip. I catch sight of his inked wrist, a twisted snake, just like mine, in honor of the woman who showed us both how to use our own strength.

He keeps hold of a clothbound book, a rare third edition of *Frankenstein* that bears the first visual depiction of Mary Shelley's Dr. Frankenstein and his monstrous creature, worth a fortune.

"I've never seen an *actual* book before," Owen marvels, running a finger over the gilded title on the dark-brown spine. He looks up at me, one eyebrow cocked. "Odd choice of story to be carrying around, no?" His face twists, thinking on it further. "Actually, it's pretty perfect," he says, smiling.

That gives me pause. *Has he read the book?* I look Owen up and down with fresh eyes.

"So where'd you get it?" he asks furtively.

He lingers close to me in a familiar, casual way—we've grown comfortable with each other's company over the past few weeks. So much so, I'm honest with him about the duplicitous way I obtained the priceless present.

"I stole the book from Strake's library," I tell him. All schools and universities in Dallas have closed until the capital regains its stability. With a war going on, the Guard isn't concerned about safeguarding an antiquated campus library filled with never-touched books—so I took the beloved story before someone else did.

"Gift for your sister?" Owen says without skipping a beat. "Must be a trip sharing a birthday with someone."

That gives *him* pause. I never told Owen our birthday was coming up. He flashes a sheepish grin, which I interpret as, *Hey, in all fairness, I'm a hacker. I know everything about everyone.*

"I don't know what it's like to *not* share a birthday with someone," I say. "I grew up sharing everything."

"Even your DNA," Owen observes, handing me back the book. "Is there *anything* you have just for yourself?"

We stand there, close enough to feel each other's breaths, both of us a little awkward and unsure. I know from the way Owen's looking at me that he senses it too, the thread that suddenly connects us. Pulling us together.

Is it more than just a bond that sprang up over losing someone we love? I don't know. I just know it's a relief to feel something other than sadness and anger.

In another move of pure reactionary emotion, I place my palm against Owen's wet cheek.

I've never kissed anyone before—I could never reach that level of intimacy with someone while Mira and I were playing the life-or-death game of sharing a single identity. I ignore the nervous lurch of my stomach, close my eyes, and lean my mouth toward his.

But my lips touch nothing but air.

I snap my eyes open to find Owen's no longer there. He's back on the ground, questing for more fallen books and paint thinner bottles, mumbling to himself that he thought the sonic fire extinguisher would have turned on by now.

He's attempting to play off what just happened.

His clear rejection of my advance.

No one says no to a Goodwin is my first irrational thought, my hands balling into fists at my sides. My nails dig into my palms, erasing the touch of his skin. My second fiery thought is cut off when a deep, heavy bass sound pulsates the ceiling above. The low frequency rumble is so intense, my chest rattles.

Owen jumps to his feet faster than a bullet, grateful for the booming excuse to change the subject. "Ah, there it is!"

Of course. He must've been alerted that someone time delayed the autonomous fire-extinguishing system and came to see if there was a problem. Owen's part of the Cybersecurity Team now. *That's why he's here.*

43

Not just to find me.

Up in the Governor's Quarters, wall-of-sound extinguishers have dropped from the ceiling, several large collimators focusing sound waves directly onto the fire. The burning material and all the oxygen that surrounds it are being manipulated and separated—eliminating the fuel for the flames. All public buildings are equipped with these high-tech sonic extinguishers, an innovation driven by the need to safeguard our country's water supply from being drained on unremitting wildfires.

Above us, the flames are dying out, just like between Owen and me.

"Crazy cool what sonic waves can do, right?" Owen says, his cheeks vibrating when he smiles.

I stare daggers at him, waiting for him to explain himself, or at the very least to remove that grin from his face. But all I get in response is a half-baked, "What?"

If Owen's playing games with me, drawing me close only to turn away the moment I make a first move, he should have learned by now that I'm the master of games. He won't win.

But this is one I don't wish to play.

Screw this. I carefully place Mira's birthday gift back into my bag, turn, and charge down the tunnel, toward the next-closest secret-passageway entrance. By the time my fingers wrap around the first rung of the ladder, Owen has caught up with me. One by one, we climb in tense silence.

The tunnel opening pops us out near Market Square in the middle of uptown's affluent shopping district. Half the well-to-do stores are closed and boarded up, fearing plunderers. It makes sense that Roth would place a tunnel entrance here—he has many allies in this district.

"Ava," Owen begins, standing two feet apart from me like he's afraid I'm going to jump him again. "It's not that I don't want to—"

But before Owen can finish his excuses, something much more distracting happens.

The lights of every single building around us suddenly go out, plunging the entire capital into darkness. It's so eerily pitch-black, for the first time in my life I can see the stars between the towering skyscrapers.

"What the hell?" I breathe.

"Uh, that's not good," Owen says, closing the gap between us in a hurry. Hand on his gun, he scans the shadow-filled Market Square, looking for signs of a threat.

But this is the hottest summer in Dallas on record, two degrees higher than the twenty-first-century average. Owen comes to the same logical conclusion that I do.

"The electrical grid itself must have gone out," he says.

Or is this something more? Did Roth just make his first counterstrike?

Either way, Owen is right, this is not good at all.

I have to find Mira.

"She'll be looking for Emery," Owen says, anticipating my thoughts.

Even in the dark, I can tell he's fidgety, bouncing on the balls of his feet like he's itching to take off. It's obvious something—*or someone*—is on his mind. Owen's popularity in the city is second only to mine and Mira's. He has his pick of eager admirers.

Who was his first thought when danger struck?

"If you have somewhere else you need to be, then go," I say, willing the jealousy out of my voice.

"Of course I don't," Owen answers too quickly. He locks his hands in front of his waist in an effort to stay still, a gesture I've come to know means he's holding back.

"Let's go find Emery," he says, simultaneously looking over his shoulder, the opposite direction of the mansion.

Owen can have his secrets. I've got my own to worry about.

"This is my hometown," I say, slipping away from his side and into the inky-black Market Square. "I don't need an escort." I've had my city's street maps memorized since I was six.

The gun at my hip is the only escort I need.

A quarter of Dallas shines bright again. Primarily the outer ring of the city, populated with the homes and businesses of the privileged class—the ones rich enough to afford their own solar-powered battery backup systems. That stored energy will only last a day at most, however. And gas generators were outlawed decades ago due to environmental conservation and shortages of the natural resource. But I'd wager Black Market models will be put to use tonight. Still, that's only a temporary fix.

All Dallas citizens—high ranking and low—are tied to the Texas Interconnection power grid. Every class depends on it for modern life. If we don't get the electrical grid running again, *and fast*, the repercussions will be catastrophic. No lights, AC, TXRAIL transportation, refrigeration of food, or means to charge communication and medical devices are just the hellish beginning.

"The governor's Guard is coming!" a wild shout rings out from somewhere in the crowd of citizens gathered in front of the mansion.

Huge solar-powered spotlights flood the front lawn, illuminating the rising alarm on the people's faces. They're kept back by a wall of armed Common soldiers, a tight yellow-tinted line that has replaced Roth's twenty-foot see-through wall that was torn down mere weeks ago.

"If the blackout was done by Roth, his soldiers would be here by now," I shout, trying to calm my fellow citizens' fears. "It's just the heat wave!"

"Return to your homes!" a bullhorn cuts over my assurances. "Shelter in place for your own safety!"

Then a thundering *whup-whup-whup* causes everyone's heads to snap to the sky, squinting to catch sight of an incoming helicopter.

Emery's leaving the mansion.

Suddenly in my own panic—I *must* get to the rebellion leader before she takes off—I attempt to fight my way through the wall of soldiers, to no avail. I'm shoved back roughly into the crowd.

Cursing, I throw down the hood of my lightweight jacket, exposing my disheveled telltale red hair, and push my face up toward one of the Guards. "I'm Ava Goodwin, let me through."

It comes out as a command, and the woman carries out my orders immediately, stepping aside for me to shoulder through.

Right as the chopper lands on the mansion's scarred front lawn ruined by thousands of storming feet, Emery dashes out the double-paneled French patio doors, surrounded by Guards carrying solar lanterns to light her way. Since she officially took on the mantle as the Common's leader, Emery's entire look has softened; all her rough edges that I had come to admire have smoothed out. She's now a more polished, camera-ready version of the woman I met at the rebellion's headquarters in Calgary over two months ago.

I sprint straight for Emery, catching eyes with the soldier that flanks her escort. The young Guard who was standing sentry earlier tonight at the entrance to the First Family's wing.

By the way he glares at me, I know he must've taken some heat for my actions. I quickly scan the Governor's Quarters to find it just as it should be: a ruined shell while the rest of the mansion remains unharmed. *Good—the citizens need to see some justice done, even if we can't find the man himself.*

Then I hear my sister's voice, and immediately a wave of calm washes through my panic.

"We won't be left behind," Mira argues fiercely. She walks close by Emery's side, eyebrows knitted together like two blood-red crescent moons. I smile, knowing the "we" means me and her.

"Where are we going?" I shout, crouching underneath the helicopter's blades to face the troop. Mira doesn't bat an eye at my sudden presence.

"The entire state has lost power—not just Dallas," Mira updates me. "And the Eastern Interconnection grid refuses to send power to Texas."

Forty-eight million people without electricity in the middle of this record-breaking summer heat. I can barely wrap my head around it. This statewide blackout has the potential to be the most catastrophic event in Texas history if we don't find a solution, fast.

"The superstation's controlled by the Loyalists, and New York's Governor Cole had the gall to say Texas is on its own, just like our state always intended to be," Mira seethes, pushing her blonde-tipped bangs out of her eyes.

Texas is one of the most powerful states in the country, not just because of its might, but because it *literally* has its own power. An entire power grid owned and operated outside of federal authority. But we've only shared that valuable capital three times in our state's history, and that was over a century ago.

It's no surprise the other states remain bitter. Texas repeatedly turned a deaf ear to their calls for help, and now that we're the ones crying out in need, they're returning the favor.

An eye for an eye will make for a blind world, Rayla told the country. But still no one's listening.

"What about the Tres Amigas station?" I say, guessing Emery's intended solution for the blackout. "New Mexico's not far; is that where you're going? To negotiate for the Western Interconnection to link their grid to ours?"

Or to force the link ourselves if they refuse.

"Yes," Emery shouts above the whirring rotor blades. "But I am undertaking the mission alone." She stops between me and the open helicopter door, wearing a formal deep-mulberry suit tailored to perfection, her hair tamed into a smooth bob. I miss her signature wild, Einstein-like coils and bold yellow coat.

Despite her own lack of sleep—the woman has been on her feet non-stop, making endless urgent decisions and continuously strategizing—Emery exudes raw energy.

Rayla taught her well—Emery's done the miraculous and led the shadowy underground rebellion from obscurity into a national movement that has captured one of the most important cities in the United States. It takes every available ounce of time and vigor Emery has and then some. It's like she has a deeper well to pull from than everyone else. I myself think it should be *her* running for president, not Senator Gordon, but I know she'll say her place is here with us, the Common.

Emery holds up her hand, stopping me before I can argue. "Governor Roth might have abandoned his post, but the Common is not recognized as the official government of Texas. Our leverage with Tres Amigas is precarious, and we cannot risk any *stunts* like the one you pulled tonight, Ava."

My cheeks burn hot when Mira exclaims, "That was *you?*"

"It wasn't a stunt," I defend myself, unfaltering even under the disappointed glare of my mentor. "I took necessary action."

Emery turns without further comment and steps into the cabin of the chopper. She gives Mira and me a firm look. "Your actions matter now more than ever. The surveillance cameras may be gone, but remember those who are still watching."

The landing skids hover off the ground.

Mira and I give each other a side-glance, knowing exactly what the other is thinking.

Apparently so does Emery because before either of us can take our first step to bulldoze our way inside, Emery slides the door closed, and the helicopter rises up into the heavy night air.

But then suddenly, I don't care that Mira and I have been left behind. The helicopter, the commotion of the blackout, all of it fades into the background as I narrow my focus onto an agile figure with long raven-black hair that hangs straight as rain to her waist. She moves closer, fighting to break through the wall of soldiers at the edge of the lawn.

I know that face.

Mira squeezes my hand. She sees her too.

"Let her through," I shout.

Our old friend moves toward us.

Lucía.

OWEN

Well, things are looking dark.

It's lights out for nearly all the skyscrapers in the cookie-cutter residential section of Dallas that I'm wandering through, and I'm lost enough to admit *I'm* the one who may have needed an escort.

No power's not good for the tenants who live above the second floors. Modern high-rises need electricity—air-conditioning, specifically—to keep them habitable. The higher floor windows don't even open, which means zero ventilation. In this heat wave, the buildings have turned into fifty-story ovens.

I bet there are even a few poor chumps stuck in elevators.

Since it's way too hot indoors, the nighttime streets are clogged with sweaty bodies stripped down to their underwear, which is a pretty fascinating sight. I've never seen so many people this naked at once before. Crazy-high UV indexes and the illegality of swimming pools kind of spoil any use for bathing suits.

Inspired, I peel off my shirt. Not in vanity, to be clear, but to make a headwrap to keep the sweat from dripping into my eyes. It works, and the nonbreeze actually feels quite nice against my bare chest.

Am I serious right now?

There's a statewide power outage, I completely botched Ava's first—and probably last—advance, I'm heading toward a secret I'm risking my neck and sanity to keep, and I'm distracted by moon bathing?

Get it together, man.

A loud *pop, pop, pop* fires off somewhere nearby.

I don't even flinch. Since the Battle for Dallas, looting has been a huge headache for the Common, but now that the grid's down and citizens have their own guns, it's going to be an outright free-for-all in the capital. People will always take advantage of chaos. It's like it's written in our DNA: *Now's the time to get what you think you're owed!*

High beams from a string of military SUVs suddenly barge their way through the jumpy crowd. The new and improved Common Cavalry.

Looks like I'm not the only one who's anticipating some serious damage tonight.

The SUV's headlights shine on a group of girls wearing lingerie with way too many straps for comfort. Their hair is all dyed blonde and chopped short like Mira's on the night she outed Roth's hypocrisy on top of the Capitol steps. That's the "it" style these days, for girls *and* guys. Doesn't hurt that the cropped cut also helps beat this crazy heat.

The girls carry clubs and empty sacks in their hands, which tells me they're about to inspire some trouble. Just like their idol.

"Join us?" one of them asks, raking her charcoal-lined eyes over my shirtless body.

I'm famous now, by Cadwell association. Rayla plucked me from mundane obscurity and brought me with her to the biggest fight of the century, and I was right there by her side until her bitter end. *Me*, some punk kid from an autonomous car factory in Detroit.

This guy must be something special, people think.

In the old days at Kismet, I gabbed out loud to myself like a dope, because I couldn't get anyone to talk back. Now anyone and everyone will talk to me. They are *honored* to speak to me, actually. I used to spend mindless midnight shifts at the factory, pipe dreaming what it would be like to bask in the limelight for doing something that mattered.

Now that I've achieved some fame in real life, it all feels a hell of a lot emptier than I ever imagined it would.

I don't have the skills to unpack that. A lifetime of ignoring any form of self-reflection has left me emotionally handicapped. Perfect for a Code Cog, sure, but I'm aiming higher for myself nowadays.

Ava Goodwin's a megahigh bar to meet halfway, yet I know that's exactly what she deserves. A partner who is her equal. Any person worthy of her has to be willing to put in the work.

And my work won't be done until I make sure Roth disappears, permanently.

"I've got somewhere else I need to be," I say to the Mira look-alike, shaking my T-shirt wrapped head. "Duty calls." She looks disappointed, but I don't have it in me to flash her one of my best grins.

Smash! Storefront glass shatters up and down the street. The girls laugh and move toward the sound of anarchy like it's a siren's song. Common Guards shoot out of their SUVs, guns raised, shouting for order.

"Return to your homes!"

"Shelter in place for your own safety!"

Those words are scary close to what Roth's Guards were ordering Dallas citizens to do, just three weeks ago. *Return immediately to your residence, or you will be arrested!*

Sure, the Common isn't locking the citizens up. *Yet.* But after tonight's lawlessness, it will be a different story.

Case in point: Just up ahead, a group of men in briefs starts a scuffle with the uniformed Guards. Punches are thrown. The scuffle turns into a brawl.

Okay, time to leave. I've got places to go and people I don't want to see.

A perimeter fence rings the Strake campus, one of the few orders Emery and Alexander agreed on after the Common's takeover. Something about safeguarding the places of higher learning justifies the nice, not-so-gentle *zap!* that will knock your butt to the ground if you try to climb the thing.

Even though I have no skin in the elite college game—Kismet recruited me out of school at thirteen for my prodigy-level computer know-how—I was all for the electric fence for my own personal purposes. The secured campus was a perfect stash house for my unwelcome guests. I took a two-pronged approach: trespassers can't get inside the weaponized fence—well, except for Ava, apparently, but she seems to be the exception to every rule—and most key to my needs, my self-labeled POWs can't bust free.

Now that the power's out, all bets are off.

They damn well better still be in there, or I'll go nuclear.

Turns out, there's no need to disable the fence with my fancy Cybersecurity Team fob, like I've been doing for the past two weeks, because the gate at the north end of the Great Lawn is wide open.

You've got to be kidding me.

We practically made a blood oath that they'd stay hidden inside the swanky Finn House dormitory when I'm not around to protect them. The idea that they're loose or worse, *discovered*, ratchets up my pace.

I blow past Stephen F. Austin and his limp Texas flag, zigzagging through an obstacle course of downed surveillance cameras and facial recognition scanners that litter the dark quadrangle. When I reach the purple ivy-covered building, in record time, I slow down. *Be cool, don't show them you're in a tizzy.*

But the dorm's oversized doors are wide open too.

I lock my hands in front of my waist, fighting to remain calm, and creep into the dark lobby.

The first thing I clock is how quiet the 3D-food-printing machine is, shut down from lack of power. Awesome. Going to have to come up with another food-supply plan. Not that they were ever grateful for my hacking skills that got them access to the fine-dining printer without a microchip in the first place.

The only thing that's edible is the pecan pie! Nothing tastes as good as the way they print it back home!

Who knew people could still be so critical, in wartime, while a huge chunk of the country goes hungry?

Trained in the art form of grinning and bearing it, I continue to inch my way through the ridiculously huge foyer, but before I can make the left turn that leads to the first corridor of dorm rooms, the high beams of a souped-up security golf cart cut into the unlit entrance hall, and straight into my eyes.

Instant blindness. Second "Who knew?" of the night: light can pierce as effectively as a blade.

Properly nettled now, I whisper a few choice curses and slam my body against the nearest wall a) to wait for my eyes to blink away the stars and b) to make sure these people are not Guards, looters, or ex-Strakers out for a joyride.

Before my eyes can catch up to the scene, I hear screeching tires and then a loud *crash!*

I rub my vision back into working order and initially think I must still be dazed. Seeing things, because on the floor in front of a stalled security vehicle are bits of . . . people?

Cut-off arms. Shattered torsos. A disembodied head.

Someone jumps out from the driver's seat and starts fumbling with a rogue leg.

Next second, my pistol is in my hand.

An argument, testy and snappish, echoes down to me.

"No, no! You're doing it *all wrong*!" a woman's voice screeches.

"Well, *dear*, if you're such an expert," a man counters, "why don't you get up off your—"

"I *told* you I should have been the one driving!"

"You're the one who *told* me to make a left!"

Holstering my gun, I mutter a few more curses and slap a hand to my sweaty forehead. Whitman give me patience, because I'm speedily losing my temper. Nope, it's flat-out gone. AWOL. And with these two under my charge, who knows when I'll get it back.

"What part of 'stay put,'" I chide, sounding way too much like my old Kismet overseer, "means nabbing a set of wheels and gallivanting across campus *in a blackout*?"

Life with my parents has never been easy. Why should it be now?

"You guys have *one* task. Stay hidden," I continue, stopping next to the driver's seat. I reach over to the control panel and kill the engine with a tap of the screen. "That means *stay put*. Do nothing."

It was easy enough for them to stay put and do nothing back home in Atlanta, while I plugged away and did all the work in Detroit, keeping them—and myself—alive.

"Oh, look dear, who decided to bless us with an appearance . . . ," my dad says, shaking a chipped marble hand in my face.

Right. Stone statues, *not* real people, are the victims of my parents' latest blunder.

I swat the severed hand back toward my dad. He's still wearing the same monochromatic baby-blue shirt and pants he's worn since I was a kid. Rolled at the elbows and ankles, never wrinkly, an ace color against his dark skin. Same hairstyle too. Clean, fresh, and sharp, like if he never changes his looks, maybe the world around him will stay the same too.

My attention jumps from my parents to the broken white limbs that are scattered across the corridor's floor like some ghostly crime scene. A line of Roths—from the supreme grandmother, Meryl Roth, to the beheaded face of Howard Roth—lie at my feet. I stick my steel-toed boot into one of the ex-governor's hollow eye sockets.

"Your day is fast approaching," I promise under my breath, so my parents don't hear. Best to avoid flaring up another argument.

"The lights went out," my dad accuses, like I'm somehow to blame. "Your dear mom has been terrified—we waited for you, but we couldn't just sit there in the dark! We thought it was an ambush!"

My parents have always had an inflated sense of self-importance, but impending civil war has really fine-tuned it, nurturing the idea of their global relevance to next-level.

"Breaking news: the lights are out across the whole capital, not just here," I say as coolly as I can. "And I was only gone for three hours. I sprinted here right when the power blew."

"And you've lost half your clothes in that time, I see," my mom says, frowning at my bare chest. Her pursed lips highlight the small dimples on her cheeks, the only feature I inherited from her.

"Is that the new Commoners uniform?" she continues in her clipped way. "Stripped of shirts . . . all decency and morals?"

Strike one.

I bite my tongue so hard I taste a mouthful of bitter blood.

Mom and I are about as opposite as two people can get. How we're both dressed—or *not* dressed—right now sums it up nicely. She's buttoned up all the way to her neck, reserved and uptight in her rigid, practical gray dress and leggings, whereas I'm shirtless—free and open to face the new and no doubt scary experiences that come with the admission price for a post-Roth America.

Comfort and consistency are Dedra Hart's brand. The road ahead—still under construction—will not be a smooth one for her. Or Dad. Change frightens the daylights out of them both.

My tablet starts vibrating in my back pocket for the tenth time since Dallas went dark, but whatever it is can wait. My plate is kind of full right now.

"If you'd both stop yacking and do something useful, we could get this done triple-quick," my dad huffs and puffs.

"I'm not the one who knocked the statues over," my mom states, crossing her arms into her favorite pose. "We should never have come to Dallas . . ."

Yeah, well, I really wish you two hadn't come here either. After the Battle for Dallas, I didn't think things could get any worse, until dear old Mom and Dad showed up one morning at the Common's headquarters. They saw their meal-ticket son all over the news and knew exactly where to find me. Well, not *exactly.* That would require a level of ingenuity *just* out of their reach. Turns out, I found them, wandering lost in the old state dining room.

To say it was an unhappy surprise is the understatement of the year. It's more than just that they're embarrassing parents. They're full-on pro-governors. Pro-*Roth.* Even after all that's happened. I've been killing myself for fourteen long days and nights, keeping them a secret from Blaise and Ava. Can you imagine what they'd think if they knew the people I came from?

Hey, I remind myself, *a Hart has to start somewhere.*

"We both *agreed,* dear," my dad says in his faux-calm voice, struggling to haul a full-figured bust upright. "We couldn't leave our son in the hands of *Commoners.*"

Strike two.

Yeah, go on telling yourselves you came here for me.

I wind back my leg and give a good kick to Roth's smug limestone face, sending his head rolling. "Just leave it. It'll all go to the landfill soon anyways."

"It's a disgrace," my mom says, giving the proverbial middle finger to our truce about sticking to neutral topics. "Commoners have no decency, like I said."

Strike three.

I did my best, but a day just wouldn't be over without one of our blowups. They're a ritual, like a lullaby before bed.

"Your observation is totally off target," I assert with as stable a voice as I can muster, but my *dear mother* won't look at me. "A disgrace is decades of unchecked rule by a governor who feels *zero* hesitation in pulling the trigger on his *own* citizens. Roth murdered Darren Goodwin—"

"Fabrications," my dad mutters. I round on him. His dull brown eyes bulge like he thinks I might sock him.

Calmly, so he'll listen, I place my trigger finger between his creased brows. "He shot Rayla Cadwell right between the eyes," I whisper, hoping my voice won't crack. "I was lying on the ground right beside her when he did it. Are you really so sick to think I could make something like that up?"

I still feel the dead weight of Rayla's body in my arms when I carried my leader—my friend—from the tunnels. She was so heavy.

"That woman was asking for it," my dad says, smacking my hand aside. His bony finger stabs at my chest, but I stand my ground. "She knew exactly what she was getting into," he presses, "and she had no business dragging a sucker kid like you down here with her."

"Kid?" I yell.

"Rayla the Slayer is no martyr," my mom spits, sitting pretty on her cushy passenger seat, arms crossed, mind proudly closed.

Rayla cared more about me in the week *I knew her than you ever have in my whole existence.*

Speaking my mind has long been my specialty, but when it comes to my parents, it's always been impossible. And heavier things, harder things, like emotions and love? Those don't fall under the category of "neutral topics." I'm the first to confess that I'm no good at admitting my deeper feelings out loud. Guess I inherited more from dear old Mom and Dad than I care to own up to.

Out of nowhere, Ava's fiery, disappointed eyes sear across my vision. But a guy can learn, right?

My tablet starts rattling away again—"Blaise" lights up across the glass—and I almost throw the damn thing across the hall. Instead, I mitigate my stage-ten irritation by powering the pest of a device off.

"Oh, so you only answer if it's Ava, huh?" a peeved voice reaches me from the doorway.

The man himself. Blaise.

Well, folks, the other shoe finally dropped, along with my stomach. I stop breathing and stand comically still, like Blaise somehow won't be able to track me in the dark.

"Owen, you know this . . . *person?*" my mom gasps.

To be fair, at first sight, Blaise is a lot to take in.

He's got on his trusty boogeyman bandana, smile of flames and all, and he's shirtless like me—great coders think alike—but his crazy-pale chest shines like a glowworm.

It might just be the battle bonds talking, but I've come to view his scary appearance as comforting.

"And who are these happy-looking people?" Blaise wisecracks, eyeing my glowering parents, no doubt double smiling underneath his fire-grin mask.

"You tracked me?!" I protest. "Isn't that treason now or something?"

Blaise shrugs. "Had to, man. You weren't answering my calls."

"What's so important you had to call me sixteen times and *then* stalk me?" I say.

"Two things. Alexander's making a mess of himself again at his favorite bar . . ."

Not good.

"A bad look for the Common's morale," Blaise chides, shaking his head so hard his detachable hood nearly slides off. "As I'm sure you know, you're the only one he'll listen to when he's drowning in his cups."

"Alexander and his tequila," I mutter with a prolonged sigh. I've stuck with the guy since I pegged him as my best shot at getting to his own dear old dad, the ex-governor. I trusted his thirst for revenge as a counterpart to mine, what with Theo being MIA and all. But it looks like his thirst for liquor and his quest for oblivion will be serious roadblocks.

Do all adults have to be taken care of?

"And the second thing?" I ask Blaise, more than ready for this night to be over. Fires, a blackout, my total meltdown of nerves with Ava, my ever-more-inconvenient parents . . . what else? Lay it on me.

"Oh. We got him."

"*Who*?" my dad butts in.

"You got the governor?" my mom asks, highly skeptical, slightly scared.

"Almost," Blaise answers.

He holds out the suspense, a twinkle in his eyes.

"We got the Whiz Kid."

This announcement is a major letdown for my parents. Their faces screw up in complete confusion.

But it's a mic drop moment.

"Roth's IT guy?" My jaw drops. "You should have led with that! *How*?"

Blaise's fingers make a steeple, his favorite triumphant gesture. Then, another milking-it pause.

I lean forward into his silence, my whole body buzzing with excitement like a wild beehive. This is *huge*.

"He walked right up to our front door."

The Cybersecurity Team has been searching nonstop for this elusive ghost for three freaking weeks. And now he's come to *us*?

Blaise and I bump fists in celebration, opening our palms and spreading our fingers to make it rain.

We knew a guy like the Whiz Kid had to be in Roth's employment; any Programmer worth his salt has been solicited to work for rich crooks at some point in his career. Luckily for the two of us, things never got so dark as to necessitate such a soul-destroying job. It's not a path you want to take unless you're dark and twisted yourself or you're flat-out desperate.

All right, enough self-congratulating, it's time to go. I fling my backpack off and shove it into my dad's hands.

"Here's food and water to hold you over until I come back," I say double-quick. "The last of all my rations."

"You're not leaving Dallas, are you, Owen?" my mom says, wringing her hands all concerned. Not for me, of course, but for their own preservation.

Am I being too harsh? She does seem clammy . . . out of breath . . . *The effects of the heat,* I tell myself, choosing to ignore her sallow complexion.

I turn away and give my dad a stern look.

"Just go back to your dorm room. Lock the door. *And stay put.*"

The Blind, Drunk, and Happy is popping tonight.

It's way past serving hour, and still there's a line down the block to get inside. Rules are meant to be broken during blackouts, it seems.

Blaise and I don't have to wait, of course—one of the few perks of being famous. We push our way through the open doorway and into the hot main room that's lit by red candles in long, skinny glasses. The retro lighting really classes up the joint, I have to say.

There's nothing classy, however, about more than two hundred sweaty bodies all packed together, most of them juiced up on so much warm beer, they've forgotten basic decorum.

I know the heat is getting everyone buzzed faster—but *come on.* That doesn't excuse the off-duty Guard who just decided to banshee scream utter nonsense directly into my face, immediately followed by an unidentified, uninvited butt grab, rounded out by an elbow to the temple by an elderly drunken dancer with two left feet.

Okay, we've just walked into a hotbed of Dallas's pent-up energy. All the hurry up and waiting we've been doing for weeks has been a massive citywide mood killer. Judging by the amount of stimulants floating around the room—the colorful square patches of Tape seem to be the local upper of choice—and the numerous couples taking full advantage of the shadows, people are in serious need of letting off a bit of steam.

Blaise nudges my shoulder and nods to the source of a ruckus at the back of the bar. He's easy to spot, since he's a head above the others.

Zero surprises here, it's Alexander, three sheets to the wind.

Even in his staggering state of belligerence, the ex-governor's son somehow keeps his rumpled uniform tucked in and buttoned-up. While all the other patrons in this sweatbox of a speakeasy are practically wearing birthday suits, this stubborn lieutenant's in a damn *sauna suit*.

I want to keel over just looking at him.

"Come on, put up a fight!" Alexander commands, slurring his words. Goading every citizen and off-duty Guard he teeters past, he juts out his square chin, begging someone to land a punch. "Hit me!"

"Oh, I wish I could," I mutter. "If only to put you out of your misery. And mine."

Usually when I come to collect the tormented man, he's sedate and alone in a corner, staring off into the middle distance, no doubt nurturing the most macabre of outcomes for his kidnapped son.

But tonight, to the delight of many—and soon to be thousands, judging by the various tablets I spot recording—Alexander prowls through the inebriated crowd, screaming his lungs out, "Hit me! Take a swing! I dare you."

Thank Goodwin all the onlookers think this is a joke. Even in the inky shadows of a power outage, no one would dare clock an officer. A fact that seems to rile Alexander, spurring him into a tantrum of rage. He gestures and postures, challenging any and all to take up his offer.

"Take . . . a . . . swing! You . . . scared?" Then a string of incoherence.

Why must he keep looking for trouble? Your fight's not here, bud!

Blaise and I start to jostle our way over to him, but Alexander has unforeseen agility for a blitzed forty-something man. He crashes into tables and dancers, spilling spirits and wine all over his would-be aggressors, snatching up shot glasses, downing each one indiscriminately.

"Come on! We're at war and no one's ready to fight?" Alexander hollers. "Hit me! Or is this city llena de cabrones con pocos huevos?"

No idea what that last bit means, but it doesn't sound like flattery.

"How's the guy still on his feet?" Blaise asks, sounding impressed.

In my peripheral vision, I see a hulking figure rise from his chair. My eyes dart to the enormous man with an eight pack and a scowl so dark there's a good chance he came from one of the governor's liberated prison farms. He steps forward, ready to take up the offer. When he holds up his fists, both as big as sledgehammers, I know it's time to panic. This guy was probably champion of some Warden's illicit boxing ring. Alexander doesn't stand a chance.

"He won't be on his feet for long," I say, rushing to get to Alexander first. "Buy me some time!" I shout over my shoulder, and Blaise darts to block the hulk-man's path.

Weaving through a pack of dancers, I reach Alexander and immediately have to duck because the bastard throws a punch at me. "Hit me!" he demands.

"Hey!" I yell, out of swinging range. "It's Owen. It's time to go, bud!" No use. The man is totally face blind right now. He gears up for another blow.

"This is for your own good!" I promise Alexander, pinning his arms down. I then toss him over my shoulder like a two-hundred-pound sack of potatoes. "You'll thank me later."

Safety over dignity. He gave me no choice.

"Back door," Blaise pants in my ear, at my side again. A quick glance to my right gives me a full view of the gigantic man splayed out on the floor.

"How the hell did you pull that off?" I ask, amazed.

Blaise's eyes crinkle. "All that muscle means nothing up against a weapon." He slips a taser gun into the pocket of his hoodie as a raucous crowd starts forming around the barrel-chested boxer, cheering for him to get up.

"Round two!" they chant.

All right, it's time to blow this joint and get Alexander to my car, ASAP. But before we can make it to the exit, we're cut off by a gaggle of teenagers.

"It's him! Owen from the Wanted List!" a girl squeals. They all start jumping up and down, and I swear I see tears in their eyes.

"Owen, you're my lionheart!" a boy screams.

"I love you!" some girl swears.

I take a step back at the sudden onslaught. There are too many of them to break through, and this attention is putting way too big a spotlight on us.

"This display is truly vomit inducing," Blaise says, laughing like he always does at my newborn popularity. "Maybe it's time for you to get a mask like mine." He then adjusts his demon-faced bandana, takes a step forward, and proceeds to scare the living daylights out of the teens, letting loose a wail that will haunt their nightmares for the rest of their young lives.

Well, that was effective. They scatter faster than if the roof was on fire.

"Emilia!" Alexander bellows as we finally make it through the back door and out into the alley.

"Who?" Blaise asks.

"His wife—well, soon to be *ex*-wife," I whisper. *Sore subject.* "Theo's mom."

Alexander's six-foot frame drapes all the way down my backside. Let's hope I can get him to my car before he has the chance to mistake me for Emilia and get handsy. One butt grab tonight was enough.

Ah, there's Duke. Waiting just down the street, right where we left him. Blaise opens the passenger door, and I heave Alexander into the back seat.

"Stay put," I say, strapping him in.

"She's stuck at the northern border . . . can't come here," Alexander blabbers on. "Emilia says it's my fault."

Alexander's crossed eyes suddenly snap into focus, staring straight at me. "I'm a failure," he whispers, his hoarse voice catching.

"We're all failures," I reassure him, making sure Blaise doesn't overhear.

I failed Rayla in the tunnels.

Alexander nods soberly and flails his arms around my neck in a sloppy hug. "I've lost . . . both my sons . . . to my con of a father."

"Theo won't be lost for long," I confide, smiling from ear to ear. "We've got Roth's Whiz Kid."

Alexander takes this in with a blurry, nobody's-home look, then proceeds to pass out on my shoulder.

Really? Tough audience tonight.

Well, he's definitely going to wake up to an eye-opening surprise. We're about to bag the most wanted man in America. By morning— hell, maybe within the hour—we could have the ex-governor Roth in our clutches. We could have Theo.

We could have victory.

All right, fine, we're technically two degrees of separation from victory.

But the Whiz Kid is our link.

An IT genius, he's the guy we think is responsible for setting up the ex-governor's encrypted messaging system, allowing Roth to communicate without fear of prying eyes.

An IT genius who just surrendered to the Common.

He's scared. Why else would he come running to us? I bet he's read every incriminating piece of communication Roth has ever sent or received.

With an adrenaline-fueled pep in my step, I hop into my driver's seat, downright giddy to hear the engine thrum.

"Right, where to?" I ask my copilot, peeling out onto the road.

Did Blaise stash the kid in the Council Room, the War Room, the Tower?

"The hospital," Blaise says.

"Um, wait . . . *what?*" I gasp, my eyes whipping from the mobbed streets to Blaise.

That can't be good.

"Yeah, I forgot to mention . . . ," he states, all nonchalant. "The Whiz Kid's kind of unconscious."

MIRA

I used to believe so many things in this world were impossible.

Once, I thought it impossible Ava and I would ever make it out of Texas alive. That we would even reach the first safe house on our father's map.

But we made it all the way to Canada, and back.

And so, it seems, did Lucía.

She was the first person I could truly call a friend, the first who knew of my existence and accepted me for who, and *what*, I am. The last time Ava and I saw her, we said our goodbyes in an underground safe house in the west Texas desert, certain our paths would never cross again.

We were all three of us unwanted and hunted, trying to achieve the unthinkable.

Come with us, I asked Lucía. But hers was a different journey.

"¿Encontraste a tu madre y hermano?" I ask her now. *Did you find your mother and brother?*

Lucía smiles. She's nearly unrecognizable. In the months since we parted, her thin, angular face and rawboned figure have rounded and softened, but that earnest gaze I so remember her for, that invariable tenacity in her eyes, remains the same. If anything, it's sharper. More seasoned. Ready for the new danger she sees ahead.

"Viajé por cinco estados y busqué veinte casas de seguridad . . . ," Lucía answers. *I traveled across five states and searched twenty safe houses . . .*

She brushes back the thick veil of her dark hair. "But I found them," Lucía continues in English, her accent making her voice sound labored, like she's speaking from the back of her throat. *She must have picked up a bit of the language on her trek north.* "They were in North Dakota. Waiting for me."

Relief floods through me. Ava smiles at this heart-soaring news. It's a novel sight, and I take a mental snapshot to carry with me for later.

Good news, I have a feeling, will only become rarer.

"We found the Common in Canada," Lucía reveals. "At a safe house in Winnipeg. Named Paramount Suites."

One of Ciro's hotels.

"But why . . . ," Ava asks, her voice trailing off in bewilderment.

"¿Por qué te irías?" I clarify. *Why would you leave?*

Knowing what it took for my sister and me to make it across the northern border and back, I can only imagine how difficult her own travels with her family must have been.

Hers was a greater journey, longer and crueler, traversing three countries, beginning in a notoriously unstable region of central Mexico. Climate change spared no mercy for Lucía's homeland. There, the war for life's most precious resource has been brutal and unending. Where in the States, governors rule, capos seized control in the southern republic. *Water lords.*

When I first laid eyes on Lucía, I thought it impossible that she had made it through the impenetrable Big Fence that guards the border between Texas and Mexico. It was an extraordinary feat. An amazing risk. Whatever would bring her back here to Texas—to us—must be equally extraordinary.

Why else would she risk being sent back to where she began?

"Aquí no," Lucía whispers. *Not here.*

She eyes the Guard standing watch beside the back entrance of the Governor's Mansion, lit by the dim yellow glow of emergency lights. *Not the Governor's Mansion,* I catch myself. It's now the Common's headquarters. Despite the fact that I currently live and sleep in the building, I still feel unsettled and unaccustomed to walking its once-corrupted halls, moving freely among the Guards beside my twin.

Judging from the pistol on Lucía's hip, on full display, it appears her deep-seated caution of others has endured, like mine.

"The gardens," Ava says, nodding toward a pathway walled with columned-shaped hedges, ten feet high. Perfect privacy.

Only moonlight illuminates the vast maze that forms the backyard of the mansion. The governor's gardens were once the green envy of all, styled after the luxuriant grounds of Versailles.

Howard Roth once boasted that he was a man with enough power to build an Eden in the middle of a wasteland. Now his spectacle of countless groves of rare trees and precisely pruned shrubbery is withered, dying, and bare.

Ava leads us left, then right, farther into the labyrinth, down a tunnel made of arched trellises wrapped in wilted ivy and clematis vines. Past a row of overgrown boxwoods, she motions to a metal bench beside a dried-up fountain, the wide mouths of the ornate water jets empty and silent.

"Here," she says.

Lucía shrugs off her rucksack and takes a seat at the center of the wrought-iron bench, which is still warm from a sun that set hours ago. Immediately settling at her left side, I briefly wonder how she trekked the thousands of miles it took to get here. Did she cover the distance on foot, the way we crossed Texas together? If so, she doesn't look it. Her vest and trousers, both the color of desert sand, and her black combat boots, Velcroed up to her midcalf, all appear new and unsullied. Cutting-edge, even. It almost looks as if she's wrapped in a suit of body armor.

Like she's primed for a mission.

Sweat clings to me like my nerves. Overstrung and restless, Ava paces the short distance beside the bench, her boots crunching the pebbles of the pathway as she waits for Lucía to speak.

Though the power is out all over our massive state, there's an electricity here. I feel it. Ava feels it too.

Change is in the air.

Lucía deftly cranes her neck toward the night sky, then over her shoulder, scanning for any unwanted eyes or ears. Satisfied, she grasps my hand and then reaches out for Ava's, pulling her close. Turning her head from my sister to me, she keeps her voice low, softer than a whisper.

"I came here to fight."

"¿Pero por qué te meterías en nuestra batalla?" I interject. *But why would you throw yourself into our battle?*

"I can't lose another friend," Ava murmurs, shaking her head.

Lucía presses her lips tight, her fingers working the wooden beads of a rosary. "Ahora se ha convertido en la batalla de todos." *It's become everyone's battle now.*

In the center of the garden, no sounds from the sleepless downtown streets reach us. No distant wail of sirens. I hear only my heart pounding and my heavy breaths.

"I know where your governor hides," Lucía tells us.

My head spins. I don't know how Ava stays standing.

I gape at Lucía, transfixed. She stares back, bold and sure. "Roth is in Mexico."

It's so implausible—inconceivable—it's ludicrous. Roth, fleeing into the territory of his greatest foe? Across his own impassable fence and into the southern lands he vehemently sowed so much bad blood and hostility against?

And yet, instantly, I believe her. I believe the impossible is true.

"¿Y tienes pruebas?" I ask. *And you have proof?*

"No," Lucía answers flatly.

"Then how?" Ava questions, taking a seat on Lucía's right. "Pareces tan seguro." *You seem so certain.*

A hesitation slips into Lucía's posture, but she keeps her steady gaze on Ava, then me.

"My last name is Salazar," she reveals, almost like a confession. "Me crié en Monterrey y serví al cartel allí antes de huir." *I was raised in Monterrey and served my family's cartel before I fled.*

Ava responds with wide-eyed curiosity. "The *Salazar* cartel?"

Lucía nods and my pulse beats faster, my mind racing with a thousand more questions.

Lucía is related to a water lord. The Salazar family commands a reign of terror all over northern and central Mexico. Is this why Lucía ran from her country? To get away from her cutthroat family?

I hold my breath, waiting for Lucía's next words.

"I heard things," Lucía continues. "Susurros de una alianza entre los Salazar y una poderosa familia extranjera." *Whispers of an alliance between the Salazars and a powerful foreign family.*

"The Roths?" Ava cuts in.

"Nadie pronunció su verdadero nombre," Lucía replies. *No one ever spoke their true name.*

I let out my breath. The alliance could be with any influential family on the continent. In the world.

"But they called them the Lone Stars," Lucía whispers.

Ava and I lock eyes. Only one family bears that nickname.

"Right," Ava says, popping up the hood of her jacket. "You can tell us more on the way." She lifts Lucía and me to our feet, spins on her heel, and marches back toward the garden's entrance.

"Where do we go now?" Lucía asks me.

"Para encontrar aquellos en quienes confiamos," I say. *To find those we trust.*

She gives me a solemn nod, then pulls her thin cotton scarf over her eyes, cloaking her face in shadow. She catches me inspecting her gun, the very pistol that got our ragtag trio across the west Texas wasteland.

A single bullet. That's all she'd had left. But it was all it took.

I blink and I'm back in the desert, the boy's hands all over my body, ripping me away from my sister and my future.

With her last shot, Lucía took a man's life to save mine.

And now here she is, saving me again. Telling me what I've ached to hear for the longest three weeks of my existence.

She can lead me to Roth. To Theo.

We can end this.

"Espero que hayas encontrado más balas," I say, pointing to her pistol. *I hope you found more bullets.*

"Yes," Lucía answers. "A donde vamos, los necesitaremos a todos." *Where we're going, we will need them all.*

I nod, a surge of exhilaration charging through my veins. I find myself smiling as we set off to catch up with Ava.

Recuerda. No tenemos miedo, Lucía and I once told each other before we faced a new danger.

Remember. We show no fear.

OWEN

"So . . . should we try slapping the kid awake?" I half joke after the doctor leaves us defeated in the hospital room. "Or maybe throw some water on his face?" Those tricks work wonders in the old classic films.

By the way, the Whiz Kid is an *actual* kid, it's not just a nickname as I'd assumed. With such a baby face, there's no way he's even hit his midteens yet.

A wolf in lamb's clothing. The whole innocent-looking thing—the rosy cheeks, soft auburn curls, and sweet smile, even while comatose—is one hundred percent a front. The kid's calling card. But I bet he had a rap sheet filled with cybercrimes as long as my arm before he left grade school.

Blaise, Alexander—a recovery IV inserted into his wrist to sober him up—and I have been standing over the unconscious kid's bed for the last half hour, impatient for a miracle.

The top reasons the doc said a person can faint: crazy high stress, overheating, exhaustion, or dehydration. No doubt the kid checked every one of those boxes.

Don't we all?

But instead of waking up after a few minutes like normal, he's totally lost consciousness for close to an hour.

He's going to kill me! were the boy's first and only words, according to Blaise, so I don't blame the Whiz for checking out. He's probably scared out of his mind that Roth is going to find him and lock him away. Or worse. It doesn't matter that he's just a kid. Pawel was just a kid too—didn't even get the chance to hit his twenties—and Roth's Guards shot him dead.

And Whitman only knows where this boy escaped from, and what it took for him to get to the Common's HQ—the odyssey couldn't have been easy.

I get that, I really do. Hell, most days *I* want to check out from all of this too. But we need the kid to snap out of it, ASAP, so he can tell us what he came here to say.

An entire army of search drones has nothing on this boy's ability to hunt down Roth.

"How long do you think the Whiz will be out?" Blaise sighs, pushing up his shirtsleeves.

We're both fully clothed again. There's something formal about hospitals that makes you want to put your shirt back on. *See, Common members have decency,* I think, happy to prove my mom wrong.

But I'm regretting it in this heat.

"Are we positive he's not faking it?" I press.

In answer, Alexander, dragging his mobile IV pole with him, shuffles closer to the Whiz and bends down to pry open the kid's left eyelid. He then straight-up pokes the boy's eyeball with his finger.

The Whiz Kid doesn't flinch.

"Nope," I say, shuddering. "It's the real deal."

With a long night of waiting ahead of us, I haul a chair over to the gurney and take a front-row seat to keep watch on the kid, monitoring for the slightest change that would indicate his consciousness returning from wherever minds go when they're lost. It's like waiting for water to boil.

So when the hospital room door slides open again, Alexander wastes no time rounding on the nurse before he can even step over the threshold. "I order you to revive him, now!" the newly restored officer barks, back to his usual bossy ways. "This is of national importance—"

But it's not the nurse who walks through the entrance. It's Ava and Mira, and they don't walk, they storm into the room, outrage clear on their faces. A dark-haired twenty-something girl in combat gear pops in next, shutting the door behind them in a hurry. Is she a new Common recruit? An old friend? She looks as fired up as the sisters.

"Seriously though, did someone put a tracker on me?" I ask, baffled by how they found our top-secret room.

"Your car is parked outside," Mira remarks, rolling her eyes with impatience.

"And your voice *is* louder than a bullhorn," Blaise adds, unsolicited. "You're an easy one to find."

"Who's that?" Ava asks, staring with raised eyebrows at the zonked-out boy in the bed.

"Who's *that*?" I ask in turn, pointing at the stranger with a gun holstered all brazen at her hip.

Something about the way the trio stands so close together, like they're protecting one another, it's obvious they share a battle bond. Now I'm even more intrigued. But before I can inquire further, Alexander butts in, his upper lip curling at the sight of the sisters.

"Why must you two always stick your noses into every situation?" he rebukes them. He shoots a particularly acidic glare at Mira. "I know it must be unimaginable for you, but your presence is not required here. In fact, it's likely you both will make things worse. That seems to be the trend."

"Hey, we're all on the same team," I interject, holding up my hands for peace.

The Goodwin's friend steps forward, and I'm caught off guard when she starts releasing a torrent of high-speed Spanish directed at

Alexander. Whatever she just said causes him to take a step back and shift his death-dealing look Ava's way.

"And you claim that *I* lack vision? You welcome disaster with open arms," he spits, rolling his IV pole between him and the new girl, blocking her from getting any closer.

Wait. Am I the only one in this room who's failing to keep up? Then my eyes land on Blaise, and I feel better. His second language is code, like mine.

Blaise spots me spotting him and moves to my side, whispering behind his Prince of Flames bandana. "The badass here is named Lucía Salazar, cousin to Lieutenant Salazar of Monterrey. She says she ran from her family just like Alexander deserted his."

I don't know what shocks me more, that Blaise knows Spanish or that this newcomer standing in front of me is a defected member of the infamous Salazar cartel.

If eyes could pop from their sockets, mine would be on the floor right now. *Ava and Mira are buddies with a Salazar?*

"That's not even the real kicker," Blaise says, all foreboding. "Lucía just told Alexander that their two families are in league with each other."

Hold on. Back up. Ex-governor Roth is somehow connected to *the Salazar water lords*?!

Alexander shakes his head. "My family is capable of many things . . . but building alliances with a nearly-century-old enemy—"

"Lucía knows where Roth is hiding," Ava comes in hot, flatlining Alexander's skepticism. "Your fugitive father is in Mexico."

"And if he isn't there already," Mira elaborates, "he'll be heading for one of the cartel's strongholds as we speak."

Uh, *what*? This has to be worst-case scenario. Not only is Roth no longer in the United States—I never took Roth for a border hopper—but apparently, he's being protected by one of the most dangerous and well-fortified organizations in the Americas.

Stay calm.

I turn to Alexander. "And you're really telling me you were clueless . . . ," I say. *Am I shouting?* ". . . that your dad got chummy with the current title holder for most homicides *on the planet*?!"

The cartel's capo is known the world over as the Heartless Butcher. And she's just the tip of her family's monstrous blade.

Ava puts a finger over her lips. "Not so loud—we don't know who might be listening."

"If this is true, it is a revelation to me as well," Alexander snarls, baring his teeth. Red blotches suddenly flare up all over his neck and cheeks. "I knew nothing about a Roth-Salazar truce—*alliance*—whatever it is you claim. I told you before, my father despised me. I was not groomed as the Roth heir—I was kept ignorant of the Roth family secrets. That role was left to Halton."

I've heard a lot about Halton since coming to Dallas. Ava shared with me late one night that she often wonders how things might have been different if Alexander hadn't left his first son behind. That maybe if Halton's dad had stayed, Halton himself might have been different. He might have felt loved and wanted and been less likely to seek out his granddad's attention the only way he knew how: by hurting people.

Then, just maybe, Ava and Mira wouldn't have been caught. Their dad would still be alive. And Rayla would still be here.

I see all of these thoughts flicker across Ava's face.

But then we wouldn't be on the verge of changing the world, I want to tell her. *And I* definitely *would never have met you.*

"Are you *drunk*?" Mira asks, accusatory, and for one purgatory-filled second, I think she's talking to me.

I've never been around siblings before, *obviously*, let alone twins. Mira's connection with Ava is something so deep, I could never hope to touch it. But I think Mira senses me trying. *She's mine,* her eyes sometimes say when they squint in my direction. It's like Mira can read me quicker than one of her books.

So thank Goodwin that right now her all-knowing eyes are on a glowering Alexander.

"Not presently, no," Alexander replies with a cool, I-don't-answer-to-you offhandedness.

"We're wasting time here," Mira says to Ava, holding her steady glare on Alexander. "Since they are your family, we came to tell you we found them out of respect."

"I don't need or require your respect," Alexander says. "You have none of mine."

Again, you're picking the wrong fight, bud.

Mira takes a step toward him, but Ava snatches the ends of her rucksack, keeping her back. *The last thing we need is for this conversation to end in fisticuffs.*

"I'm telling you we finally know where Roth is and you're just going to stand there?!" Mira challenges, struggling to keep her voice down.

Alexander sighs, pinching the bridge of his upturned nose like he's warding off an oncoming migraine. "And you received this intel how? From the madcap hunch of some outlander?"

"The way I see it, Alexander," Mira spits, "you're the outlander in this room."

"It's more than a hunch," Ava insists. "It's a fact you just don't want to believe. Lucía overheard the capo and the lieutenant speaking of a family they called the Lone Stars. It doesn't take a genius to reason out who that is."

"She thinks the capo has something Roth wants," Mira says, adding a cherry to our shit sundae. "And now he's going to collect it."

Shaking his scruffy head, Alexander looks down at Lucía, Ava, anyone but Mira. "I've had fifteen informers with *vetted* leads promising me they knew where Roth was." He holds out his empty hands, showing us what that intel got us. Nothing.

"Fifteen missions," he continues, "fifteen lost search drones. Fifteen failures. Tell me, what makes this one any different?"

"Because we ourselves are going on this mission," Ava informs the room. "Screw drones. Lucía will lead me and Mira into Mexico, where Roth will die by my own bullet."

Holy hell, is she serious? A fit of nervous laughter escapes my throat.

"Preposterous," Alexander scoffs. "Even if this insanity were true, it was one thing for the Common to track me down in Canada, but the idea of crossing the Big Fence into Mexico is absolutely out of the question. What you propose is a suicide mission."

"You can just stay here and keep doing nothing," Mira fires off to Alexander, "while I go and save Theo."

Alexander rips out his IV and slams the pole back against the wall. "That's what I've been doing Theo's entire life—*saving him*! Protecting my son!"

The outburst causes Lucía's eyes to dart out the cracked window. On high alert, she edges to the corner and shuts the glass, making an already-overheated room straight-up suffocating. She then zeros in on Alexander, releasing a series of words in Spanish that doesn't sound promising.

"Don't shout. You'll ruin us before we even begin," Blaise whisper translates for me, his voice more stilted than usual, like an agent relaying top-secret information. "The capo and governor will have falcons everywhere."

Falcons? I question with a look.

"Spies," Blaise clarifies for me.

Immediately, I snap my attention to Ava, but she won't turn my way. She has that serious, faraway look she gets when she's here but not here, like she's already off forging through the southern terrain.

"And if they learn we're coming for them," Blaise translates Lucía's next statement, "you can be certain they will find us first."

In an ominous gesture, Lucía covers her throat with her hand, and on reflex I follow suit.

You don't even have to traverse the deep Dark Web to read the crazy stories detailing how the Salazar cartel's enemies meet their end. No matter the elaborate, gruesome mode of death, one particular is always the same: their signature throat slitting, from ear to ear. *That's how they silence their enemies.*

"And why should I trust that *she* isn't one of those falcons?" Alexander accuses, scrutinizing Lucía. "Or a sicario, even? Sent here to lure us back to her family's slaughterhouse."

"Lucía isn't a hitwoman," Mira snaps. "She escaped her family and went north, just like you." She cracks all ten of her knuckles and bites back a mumbled curse. "Lucía left behind a great deal in Canada to come here and do what is right."

"Oh, don't give me that bullshit," Alexander bulldozes. "I did what you wanted of me, didn't I? I offered up my son and gave you a stage to publicly condemn my father. I did *what was right.*"

Alexander shifts his black eyes to Mira for the first time, in a complete stare-down. Neither of them blinks. "The last time I listened to you, Theo was stolen from me," he says. "So forgive me if I don't trust anything you or your Salazar friend have to say."

Mira's poker face collapses, exposing all her raw hurt and rage, and it suddenly feels pivotal that a barrier should be put between them, posthaste. I make a move, but Ava gets there first. She whispers something short in her sister's ear, causing Mira's eyes to shoot to her wristwatch, then toward the door. Without another word, the trio heads for the exit.

"Ava, wait!" I shout, earning an impatient glare from Blaise. He pulls his hood lower, tiptoeing to the thirtieth floor window like real falcons could be out there in the sky, listening.

I wouldn't put it past the Salazar cartel, actually—

"What, Owen?" Ava cuts in on my roving thoughts, fingers on the door handle. She finally meets my eye, and I spot that flash of disappointment again before she cements back into her inscrutable self. "I think you've said enough."

Which is next to nothing, and therein lies the rub. A huge part of me knows I should have already offered to go with her. But the smallest—and loudest—part keeps my boots glued to the floor.

There's not enough evidence—Emery would never sign off on a mission like this. And after defying her orders in the control room, I'm on thin ice. One more slip and it's goodbye inner circle for me.

"The Whiz Kid," I say, pointing to the comatose boy on the gurney everyone has managed to ignore these past few minutes.

"Keep it in layman's terms," Blaise encourages from across the room.

I take a big breath and let out all my thoughts in one go. "If Roth is bolting off to Mexico, do you think he could just show up unannounced? Yeah, the bastard has proved pretty unkillable so far, but he wouldn't last a *single day* in Salazar territory without some serious help. The runaway governor would have to send out a bevy of secret messages . . . plans . . . to *someone*. There has to be a designated meet-up spot he's heading for, and we can discover *exactly* where that spot is on the Whiz Kid's servers."

Ava's fingers slide off the door handle. She cocks her head slightly to one side, like she does when she's really listening.

"I know he doesn't look it," I continue, glancing at the Whiz, seeing what they must see. A boy with a body as narrow as a needle, his exposed wrists so thin they look like the small bones of a chicken's wing. "But this kid's the mastermind of the most sophisticated encrypted messaging system in the world. Entrusted to protect every single message and ghost call the ex-governor and the Salazars have ever sent or received and wanted no one to see . . ."

Like, for example, whatever the Salazar cartel has that Roth wants . . . *A weapon? A mercenary army to take back Texas?*

The servers could prove to be a greater gold mine than even Blaise and I first thought. As all good hackers know, information is power—whatever we find can be weaponized, put to spectacular use against Roth. A wave of jitters rushes over me, head to toe.

"When the kid wakes up—"

"If—" Blaise unhelpfully adds.

"*When* the Whiz Kid wakes up," I continue, "he can lead us to the servers—"

"How do you even know the kid still *has* the servers?" Mira interrupts.

Fair point. But something tells me *a coder's gut feeling* won't fly with her *or* Ava.

"Okay, *if* he still has the servers and *when* he wakes up, the Whiz Kid can give us our smoking gun. *Hard* evidence that pins down exactly all the whos, whats, whys, and *wheres*. Then we can go after the son of a bastard with no more guessing, no more failures, no lives wasted."

I hold Ava's eyes, but her fingers twitch like she's itching to throw open that door and set off to the heart of danger.

"I'm just asking you to wait," I say to her.

"You're asking me to wait on a kid that's in a coma," Ava replies, still skeptical.

"He's not in a *coma* coma—" I start to set the record straight, when the comatose kid himself proves me right.

Out of nowhere he catapults up from the bed like a possessed demon child arisen from a long sleep, cursing and screaming, "They're going to find me! They're going to kill me!"

No one in the room even flinches at the zero-to-one-hundred resurrection. We're all way too battle hardened.

The monitors start beeping like a crash warning and the door flies open, a disgruntled-looking nurse charging in, syringe in hand. "What is going on in here? This boy needs rest!"

Mira and Lucía have already disappeared into the hall, but Ava hovers for a beat, shaking her head at me before she yanks on her baggy hood. "Do what you think is right," she says. "See you soon."

Then she's gone, and the kid finally closes his *very* loud trap, and is back to being passed out, all angelic and silent, lost in sweet, numb oblivion. And I'm left with Blaise and Alexander, the latter shooing out the nurse, barricading the door after him with a chair. *My* chair.

"That went well," Blaise says evenly. My exceptional radar for sarcasm is subpar tonight, and I decide I'm way too wiped to spar.

It might take way longer than previously anticipated for this kid to return to a sound mind.

I take a seat on the floor, posting up next to the Whiz Kid, and mull over Ava's last words.

See you soon.

That means she'll wait, right?

I cross my arms, nodding stupidly in answer to my own question. *She'll wait.*

Then why can't I shake the nagging feeling that *see you soon* is just an easier way of saying goodbye?

AVA

Mira and I sit at Emery's desk inside Roth's commandeered office at the mansion, a ringing tablet held up in front of us on a sleek, heavy stand.

All calls—even old-fashioned video correspondence like this—require encrypted communications to ensure that neither party's identity or location can be traced. Ghost calls, Owen labels them. I have no clue how to set one up, but luckily, we didn't need Owen himself to follow us back to the Common's headquarters to facilitate ours. He and the Cybersecurity Team already outfitted Emery's new base for purposes just like this.

My thumb traces the half circles my nails cut into my palms to blot out the feeling of Owen's skin against mine. He's not here to have my back, fine. I don't need him when I have Mira. And now, Lucía again.

I still can't believe she's here. Her sudden arrival in Dallas was one of the best surprises of my life.

My eyes shift to our trusted friend leaning against a table at the opposite end of the industrial-style room. All of Roth's tables—including his vintage wooden desk with large steel I-beam legs—remain in the office simply by virtue of being too heavy to carry away. Lucía gives me an encouraging nod and I take a deep, calming breath, drawing courage from her fortitude.

With Lucía back on our team, I feel all my lost hope jolt back into my bones. Hope that Roth can and *will* be rooted out and defeated at long last.

When the ringing stops, Mira nudges my knee under the table, directing my attention back to the tablet. Mira and I square our shoulders just as Emery's face fills the screen. She looks notably grimmer than she did three hours ago when I last saw her boarding the helicopter for New Mexico. Negotiations at the Tres Amigas station must not be going well.

Obviously, or the lights would be back on.

"I have only a handful of minutes—what do you need?" Emery says.

"We've found Roth," I say, not wasting any precious time. "He's hiding somewhere in Mexico with the Salazar cartel, and Mira and I want your blessing to go and get him." I leave the details—the implied requests for funding, transportation, gear, and weaponry—unsaid.

Emery's thick brows rise dubiously. Mira follows up my extraordinary statement with context—a quick, careful explanation of Lucía, the source of our intel, and why we believe her claim is valid.

But the Common's leader shakes her head.

"I cannot give my consent to such a speculative mission based on one woman's unverified intelligence," Emery says.

For the third time tonight, Emery rejects my wishes.

My stomach drops along with my shoulders. I was confident Emery would say yes. That she would trust me like she did when she offered herself to my mission team to flip Senator Gordon to our side.

Has she lost all her faith in me?

"While I understand and admire your resolve to find Roth at all costs, it is my job to urge caution," Emery says. "The Common must not have tunnel vision for finding one man, a threat that at present has been neutralized. We must broaden our scope and look to the country's future."

"But Roth is *not* neutralized," Mira counters, heated. "Roth didn't run to Mexico just to hide—he's there for a reason—making plans *right now* to come back at us twice as strong."

"At the moment, that is just conjecture," Emery says, holding up her hand, calling for more caution. "There is no evidence yet for what you are claiming."

The Whiz Kid can give us our smoking gun. Owen's words snap back into my mind. *I'm just asking you to wait.*

But the time for waiting is over.

"We're not asking to go in with the Common army, guns blazing," I say, purposely not mentioning the possibility of Roth's servers. If Owen truly believes the IT boy is the goose that will lay the golden egg, it's on him to appeal his case to Emery himself. I won't let him slow down our mission in the meantime.

I spread my hands flat on the table.

Remain levelheaded. Rational.

"This would be another covert mission, a small group like last time—" I press.

"Is the station director ready to continue our talk?" Emery says, head turned away from her camera's lens, her attention divided among multiple important conversations at once.

Mira and I lock side-eyed glances. *We're losing her.*

"Yes, I will be right there," Emery says to someone off-screen before returning to address my appeal. She adjusts the thin silk scarf draped around her neck that conceals an old, poorly healed battle scar. Makeup now covers the holes left over from multiple eyebrow piercings, acquired in her younger days of rebellion.

Does Emery think a figurehead has to appear polished, perfect, in order to lead?

Screw that. It's not real. If Emery was here, sitting in front of me and not on a screen, I'm not sure I could stop myself from mussing up her camera-ready hair and wrenching off that useless scarf.

"Small, covert missions still require funding at the Common's expense," Emery says firmly. "Our adversaries and responsibilities at home are considerable and require our full focus and resources."

"We understand the Common's cause has expanded beyond Roth," Mira says, impatient. "But nothing is more important for the country's safety than preventing Roth from gaining back his power—"

An Elder appears in the frame and murmurs a message into Emery's ear. She shakes her head and rises to her feet, buttoning her tailored suit jacket.

"We cannot afford rash decisions right now," Emery says, giving Mira and me a stern look, then a direct order. "Remain in Dallas. We will discuss the matter further upon my return."

I throw my hands into my lap, balling them into fists. After everything we've been through together, I can't stand how distant and cold Emery's treating me now.

Rayla's murder shook Emery to her core. Instead of the loss bringing us closer together, she's put emotional distance between us, larger than a sinkhole.

It feels like a hard slap in the face. Like I lost more than just Rayla and Pawel that night in the tunnels.

"Emery, please—" I implore, but the screen cuts to black.

Mira and I turn to one another and have a whole conversation in just one look.

We don't have Emery's support. We don't have access to the Common's funding or military resources. Fine.

We will find another way.

"Interstate 35 will take us from Dallas all the way to Laredo," I say, dragging my finger from the starred capital on the map down to the border town.

Just touching a paper map again quickens my heartbeat. For weeks every part of me has been screaming, *Take action!* My nightly searches—in vain—for clues of Project Albatross and burning down Roth's quarters did nothing to alleviate my eternal desire for revenge. But poring over this map of south Texas and Mexico, strategizing routes and making plans, galvanizes me.

Maps have come to symbolize action. That I'm making real moves and advancing toward my goal faster than I ever would by standing still.

"There is a large supply warehouse in Austin," Haven says, standing close to Mira on the opposite side of the spread-out map. "The Common members know me there. We can gather food. Weapons."

Haven's once-colorless voice has taken on a melodic tone the more time that she's spent with us, her family. It reminds me of my mother's voice, at least what it sounded like in the hologram recordings I grew up watching, and it brings me comfort every time my aunt speaks.

Although Mira and I are not asking for open volunteers this time—our plans must remain top secret now that Emery officially disapproves of our mission—it was a given that Haven would join us on our latest undertaking. When Mira told Haven we found information on Roth's hiding place, she immediately started packing her bag, no follow-up questions asked.

"Good, our first and only pit stop will be in Austin," Mira says in English, then switches to Spanish for Lucía, who's positioned between us. "The drive from there to Laredo should take no more than four hours."

Mira hasn't put her feelings into words with me, but I see the tiny contractions in her skin muscles that are causing goosebumps to ripple across her arms and neck. Beyond her anticipation of getting Roth, Mira must be excited to see Theo again.

While the idea of the two of them touching still makes me see red at the edges of my vision—a leftover hang-up of Theo's blood ties to Roth—whoever Mira thinks is worth fighting for, I'll fight for too, every time.

I just hope Theo's still alive to fight for.

"Las principales fortalezas de Salazar están aquí," Lucía informs the group. *The main Salazar strongholds are here.*

She leans over the map, circling five of Mexico's supercities with her finger, moving from the southern region up to the northeast. "Each is led by a lieutenant."

Lucía's fingertip lingers on Monterrey, her hometown.

Every one of the capo's lieutenants is a Salazar—once born into the family business, there is no leaving it. And from what I've learned tonight, Lucía's branch of the bloodline rules Monterrey.

"How did you break free?" I ask her.

Lucía keeps her narrowed eyes on the map. Her tone dips to a guttural growl. "Mis padres se negaron a cumplir las órdenes de mi primo." *My parents and I refused to do my cousin's bidding.*

I know that look well. It's the look of unspeakable loss.

"The lieutenant had my father killed," she says haltingly, as if each word is poking at a festering wound. "Al día siguiente corrí con mi madre y mi hermano y nunca miré hacia atrás." *I ran the next day with my mother and brother and never looked back.*

Mira and I both reach out a hand to her. Lucía doesn't elaborate, and we know from personal experience not to press.

"You will not face returning home alone," I promise.

"We will take your cousin down, same as Roth," Mira vows.

Lucía nods, then slides her finger over to a small town outside Monterrey.

"Aquí encontraremos aliados," she says, voice as sure as the dawn. *Here we will find allies.*

But first, we have to cross yet another international border that's rumored to be impassable. How exactly we're going to do that, we haven't figured out all the way yet. But three out of four of us have done it before, more than once. Somehow, we will do it again.

"And transportation?" Mira asks, raking a hand through her red roots. "How are we going to steal a military SUV without detection?"

"I will do it," Haven offers without hesitation.

Our aunt wants to place the burden of consequences on her own shoulders if we're caught. But there's no need—I know exactly where we can get our transportation.

"I'll handle the vehicle," I say.

"We should leave tonight. Right now," Lucía says, adamant.

We all nod in agreement. She's right. We should take advantage of the blackout and leave under the cover of darkness and confusion before anyone can try to stop us.

The future waits for no one, Owen likes to tell me.

I'm living by his code more than he is.

My stomach twists at the thought of leaving Owen behind with no real goodbye. But where I'm going, there's a high chance I won't be coming back. Owen shouldn't have to risk his future just because I am.

But for me, there is no future when Roth's still in the present. There is no peace when there's so much rage in me, I can't even pretend to sleep, much less go on living.

May they rest in peace. And may we remain unrested, I said to myself at Rayla and Pawel's funeral.

If no one else is willing to go and do what needs to be done, I gladly offer myself.

I look at Mira, Haven, and Lucía in turn, grateful to have them with me for what lies ahead.

"We have to get him this time," I say, voice thick with conviction.

I don't know if my shattered heart can take another failure.

Then I'm suddenly struck by a thought so strong it's like a vision.

"There's one more person we need to recruit before we leave," I say, surprising myself as much as everyone else in the room.

Continuing my streak of living off pure reactionary emotion, I follow what my intuition tells me, and head straight for Guardian Tower.

Outside, the luminous glass ball at the top of Guardian Tower—the brightest star in the Dallas skyline—has gone out.

Here inside Level 102 of the Tower, where the high-risk inmate cells are, only the dim emergency lights remain on. It was child's play for us to talk our way in. Mira's a masterful liar; her whole existence relied on deception for eighteen years.

We're here under General Pierce's authority, Mira lied.

When the elevator—thankfully still running from solar backup power—opened on cell block seven, the first thing I noticed was the deafening racket. The inmates' desperate pounding on their metal cell doors and reinforced windows. The howls of "Let me out of here!"

The second was the suffocating heat. With no air-conditioning, it's a death trap up here.

Mira looks at me, conflicted, as we struggle to walk calmly down the long, hectic hallway. "Ava, they will all die of heat stroke," she says, her doctor's instincts kicking in.

"The Common Guards are handling it," I say, nodding toward the back of the cell block where the Guards shout orders to a group of cuffed inmates forming a line.

The Tower's top levels hold Dallas's worst criminals until they are relocated to supermax labor camps all across Texas, where they'll spend the rest of their lives working off their debt to society. The Common has now inherited these prisoners, as well as a fresh crop from Roth's inner circle. What exactly to do with them hasn't been figured out yet, but for now, I overhear a Guard say they'll be brought to the Tower's rooftop to wait out the power outage.

No one can escape from a balcony 120 stories in the sky.

At the front of the line, I see the hatchet-shaped face of Roth's former secretary of the treasury, the woman who helped members of high-ranking society grow fat as ticks while the rest of the citizens barely had enough rations to survive.

The red prison jumpsuit looks good on her.

All up and down the hall, Guards tear open cell doors using physical metal keys. By Emery's orders, the whole capital was fitted with actual locks after Roth's unprecedented citywide lockdown that trapped citizens inside their own homes.

Electronic lock systems are a thing of the past, as are corrupt and avaricious cabinet members, like Secretary Adair.

"We have to get to cell one-five-one before the Guards do," I say, quickening my steps.

Without another word, Mira and I split up. Divide and conquer, like we've always done.

Keeping my head confidently up like I'm here with an official purpose, I pass two stressed-looking Guards, hands on their taser guns.

I pause when I reach cell 148. The steel-reinforced concrete box my father was locked inside when he was murdered by Roth. I linger, closing my eyes and reaching out my heart, but do not feel his presence.

Wherever my father is now, he's someplace much higher, and free.

I move on to cell 151 and find the door is still closed—I got here first—but the Guard's only four cells away. I have to act fast.

Pulse racing, I open the small square window in the center of the solid door. Blackness. No emergency lights in the six-by-eight-foot room.

"This is Ava Goodwin," I say hurriedly, lips pressed against the fortified glass. "My sister and I leave tonight on a mission to kill Roth. No one has come closer to achieving that than you."

I hear a slow shuffling to the door. A show of resilience against the stifling heat, which makes every physical exertion feel like moving a mountain.

Good. She's still a fighter.

The dark outline of a willowy figure fills the window. I can just make out two unkempt French braids, sharp cheekbones, and long, sweeping eyelashes.

Skye Lin.

"You have fifteen seconds to decide if you want to join us or remain here," I say.

Three seconds of silence, then, "Emery is really letting me out?" Skye's voice is weak and hollow, like I'm the first person she's spoken to since her incarceration. "I don't believe she would forgive me."

Emery was Skye's mentor when she was young, and she took Skye's betrayal of the Common like a gut shot. An unhealable wound. Our leader hasn't set eyes on Skye since the night she ordered her arrest.

"No, *I'm* letting you out," I answer.

I'm not offering forgiveness for her past treachery, only the chance to finish what she started.

Skye smiles, but it's a gesture devoid of pleasure. It's heavy, mournful. Yet intrigued.

I will take full responsibility for Skye if she chooses to come with us. She isn't a danger to anyone outside of governors and Family Planning Directors, the same people that we are hunting.

Adding Skye to our team, a seasoned assassin with a murderous skill set none of us possess, was the brief vision I saw back at Emery's office. Left alone in this cell with nothing but her thoughts and regrets, the need for revenge must burn through Skye's veins.

And, I'm betting, the desire to avenge herself.

Guards close in on both sides, two doors away now. I wipe the sweat from my brow, ignoring the sudden rush of lightheadedness caused by the intense heat.

I stand on the balls of my feet, ready to move fast, whichever way Skye decides.

Just as I think it's too late, Skye presses her right hand flat against the window. I see cuts on her palm, slashes that follow the creases of her skin to minimize noticeability.

But I see them, and her pain.

Skye's last words in Roth's bunker come rushing back to me. *Please. Shoot me. I can't go back to Guardian Tower.*

"Yes . . . I will join you," Skye says. I wait for her to say more—to give an explanation, a declaration, something—but then realize nothing more is required. Locking eyes through the thick glass window, we understand each other without any extra words.

Right on time, Mira races up beside me, breathless and gripping a large metal key—her part in this break-out operation. She raises a questioning eyebrow. *Is she coming?*

I nod and Mira places the key into the lock. Together we pull open the heavy door.

"Skye Lin, General Pierce has asked me to escort you to the Common headquarters," I proclaim, loud enough for the nearby Guards to hear. "Place your hands in front of you and come with us."

People see what they expect to see. The Goodwin sisters are trusted Common members, so that's exactly what they see happening now. Ava and Mira Goodwin doing sanctioned work for the greater cause.

Skye presents her wrists for handcuffs, and just like that, Mira and I walk our final recruit across the hallway, down the elevators, and out Guardian Tower's front door.

And soon, clear out of Dallas.

PART II
THE SEARCH

THEO

I really am a puppet now. And the saddest part about that depressing fact is that I don't even have any strings. There are no zip-ties around my wrists. No taser gun pressed into my shoulder blades directing me to obey.

If I'm ordered to *wash up,* I do it.

Cut your hair, I do it.

Put this on, I do it. *Sit here,* I do it.

Keep your mouth shut, I do it.

And don't even think *about running again.*

That one, at least, I don't obey.

Escape is a desire that never leaves my mind. In any new room, hallway, vehicle, or *country* I'm hauled off to, I'm continually devising an exit plan. Daybreak to midnight, even in my rare moments of fitful sleep. Plot, scheme, prepare. Ready to make a run for it at all times.

Patience is an action of its own, I've begun to learn.

If Roth believes he's broken me, diminished me into his little marionette, I figure I will be given more freedom within my prison. If I act the role of a convincing convert, the cuffs will stay off. The number of my muscled and heavily armed entourage will dwindle down to none. I will be trusted.

Eventually, left alone.

Then the window of opportunity will bust wide open.

I will make a clean getaway. No obstacles barring my path but the miles between me, Dallas, the Common. Mira.

So far, this current tactic of biding my time and playing yes-man has won me greater mobility, and at present, a Pacific-blue leather chair next to Roth inside the reception room of a lavish palatial estate that could only have been designed for a king.

Or a lord, maybe.

A water lord?

If the dozen men dressed in expertly tailored designer suits posted throughout the room holding gold-plated rifles are any indication, I'd say yes. Each guy has on his own distinct colored silk shirt, elaborately patterned, but all have on identical crocodile belts fastened with a gold *S*.

The Salazar cartel.

Even all the way up in Canada, I've heard of them. Everyone has. Not only is their capo the tenth richest person in the world, her grisly gunfights with rival cartel and Mexican security forces make international headlines almost weekly. She became infamous when she had her cartel abduct and butcher the entire family of a police officer who arrested one of her lieutenants—his infant grandchildren, aunts, uncles, second cousins, in-laws, *everyone*. All to send a message.

I lean back and eyeball Governor, as he instructed me to call him, on the other side of a highly decorative, and frankly erotic, painting I suspect could be an actual Gustav Klimt. His formal blue service uniform looks drab in comparison to our ritzy hosts and surroundings, even with all its badges and ribbons.

On the Beast ride over here, I watched him hand polish each medal himself, and currently, they're blinding me.

The brightness bounces off the mirrored doors of the room we've all been waiting to enter. Both panes of glass are floor to ceiling, and as wide as they are tall, meaning it's more than difficult to hide from my reflection.

I can't bear to look at myself, knowing I'll see a sunburnt teen, dressed in an officer's State Guard costume, who fits right in with the bad guys. Perfectly assimilated into their ranks.

It's like the owner of this place wants his guests to take a long, hard look at themselves before they enter and face him. *Just what are you made of?* I imagine the glass asking.

Avoiding the question, I turn my attention instead to Director Wix, who gazes up with a contemptuous snarl at the four enormous satin-gold chandeliers that hang from the vaulted ceiling. The two-hundred-plus crystals sway from a strong draft of air that blows up from platinum-plated vents along the floors.

The entire palace is as cold as an ice fortress. The goosebumps that dot my arms and legs feel like a luxury of their own, each bump as extravagant as diamond cufflinks, when just outside these gilded walls is a sweltering desert.

Director Wix teeters over to Roth, making sure every clack of her six-inch heels on the marble floor can be heard. "The lieutenant should not make you wait like this," she hisses like a house cat about to strike. "It's intolerable. These *southerners* should take care to show more respect."

Roth moves for the first time since we made our grand entrance approximately one hour ago, curling his vampire-pale fingers around the armrest of his high-back barrel chair. He seems to be in some manner of hibernation, storing his energy. *For what?*

I haven't settled on whether he's still in recovery mode from his poisoning, or if he's simply a human rock, monolithic and steady, knowing he'll outlast any coming storm.

"Compose yourself," Roth says placidly, staring straight forward at his image in the glass. *What are you made of?* "Our dealings here will be brief."

Dealings. Is he here to make a deal with the Salazars?

The true purpose of my little field trip out of confinement hits me like a Guard's blow to the kidneys.

Is Roth going to trade me?

Sell me?

Leave me?

It was common hearsay in Canada that America's Family Planning Divisions shipped off their illegal second-born children to their southern neighbor to become laborers, servants, or even playthings for the wealthy. The rumors were so universal they became accepted fact.

Is Governor planning to abandon me here?

For one harrowing instant, my most basic instincts of self-preservation kick in, nearly driving me to my knees to beg Governor to please keep me.

I squash the impulse like the scorpions that invade my nightly sleeping quarters.

The thought was only a flash of desperation, a moment of weakness, but I hate myself for it. My hearty dinner of filet mignon jerky shoots up my throat, and I have no other choice but to swallow my humiliation.

I have to get out of here.

Before I can reassess my plan of action, a woman wearing a form-fitting dress and a face full of makeup appears at Governor's side. She tosses her long ponytail away from her bare, goose-bumped shoulder, not spilling a drop from the etched wine glasses she offers us on a silver tray.

When she bends to present us with the drinks, she speaks in lively Spanish, but her words are immediately translated into English by a cordial electronic voice. "Would you care for a glass of water?"

What I mistook at first for a gold necklace at her collarbone is in fact a translator device. I've seen them before in Vancouver, but none so stylish. The tech is imbedded seamlessly, a whole generation above what we used back home.

It's not just any water that's being offered; we're being granted a taste of the Salazar cartel's famed product. Allegedly, the best water in the world.

The Salazars control virtually the entire water supply in central and northern Mexico. No man, woman, or child gets a drop without going through them, not even if it falls from the sky.

I try not to think about the violence behind the clear liquid in these glasses.

Governor gives a hand signal, and one of his Guards, the taste tester, drinks the water first. When the soldier doesn't drop dead, Roth motions for the woman to bring him the tray. He picks up a glass and drains its contents in three large gulps.

"There really is something in the water down here, I'll give them that," Roth says. He taps the edge of the glass, producing a musical ring with a slight echo. Real crystal.

Governor takes the glass meant for Director Wix, hands me the other, and clinks them together in a toast before guzzling down his second helping.

Wix fails to hide her disappointment at the snub.

The pony-tailed woman slides open a compartment at the bottom of the silver tray, revealing more translator devices. She passes one to each of us with an encouraging smile.

"All guests are required to wear the necklace at all times," she informs us.

Governor glares at the "necklace" as if he has the choice to refuse. I quickly work out that the translator ensures everything anyone says on the property can be understood and most likely recorded. No secrets, nothing lost in translation.

Another form of the Salazars' security to go along with the gunmen and surveillance cameras I know must be clocking our every move.

"Let me help you," the woman says, gliding the ornamental chain over Roth's wide chest. He does not refuse her charms, and as soon as the translator snaps closed around his neck, the rest of his men follow his example.

Roth has his reasons to acquiesce, I guess.

He wants something. Shelter? Manpower? A new job? I haven't figured out exactly what yet.

Just after I clasp on my own gold necklace, the mirrored doors push open, letting in a man who has about a decade on me, and a good twenty pounds. In his flashy bronze tracksuit, our host gives the impression of a hefty walking statue. He moves as slow as one, too, a tactic that clearly riles Governor.

A low grumble vibrates from Roth's throat, and what would normally only be heard within intimate range is picked up by the translator and broadcast for the room. In his own power move, Roth stays seated in his high-back chair, making our host come to him.

"Lieutenant Salazar," Governor finally speaks, his words parroted back to him in a brassy Spanish. His thin lips disappear into a hard line, like the notion of him speaking the foreign language makes his stomach turn.

The lieutenant halts in front of us, his fists full of rings hanging stiff at his sides. No handshake hello, then.

"Governor Roth," the lieutenant says, smirking down at Governor, flaunting his four gold incisors. "Or should I address you as *Mr.* Roth now?"

Director Wix clicks her tongue sharply, no translation necessary. But Governor lets crack a smile, which somehow makes him all the more threatening. The leather of his boots stretches when he rises and marches the three odd steps it takes to stand toe-to-toe with the lieutenant.

A number of the Guard detach from the lineup to shield his left and right, hands on their loaded holsters. I was bewildered that the State

Guard were allowed to maintain possession of their guns, but I suppose that's what makes the lieutenant all the more threatening. He knows he has the real power here.

Not that Governor seems to accept this.

"I see you've replaced those front teeth I knocked out at our last meeting," Roth says, brazenly.

Did I just hear that correctly? Is his tech faulty? I rewind his words in my mind, both in English and in Spanish, fully interpreting their meaning.

This is not their first face-to-face encounter.

The lieutenant's smirk widens, his smile of gold bricks catching the light of the chandeliers. "And I see you've replaced your grandson," he retorts blithely, pointing one of his jeweled fingers in my direction. He flicks his hooded eyes up and down, appraising me and sneering.

Next thing I know, I'm pushing myself up from my chair, buttoning the jacket of my uniform, and squaring my jaw to stare him down. I have no pistol, no lineup of my own Guard, no business doing such an action, but whatever is about to go down, I want this Salazar lieutenant to know that I'm made of much more than he thinks.

I feel a pat on my back. Governor telling me he approves. He's proud.

The nausea returns. This time I have difficulty swallowing it.

"Let's get to business," Governor demands, the translator perfectly capturing the forcefulness of his words.

The lieutenant nods, his smirk disappearing. It's a small move that instantly transforms him into a severe and disquieting figure.

My goosebumps turn to chills.

He focuses his dark look on me. "Why don't you have your boy roam the grounds while we chat?"

Why? Because this is my new home? No thanks.

I'm hoping Governor, believing me to be his puppet protégé, will take me into the room with him. Then I can learn what he's planning not only for *me*, but for two whole countries, apparently.

Instead, Governor nods his consent, then marches through the mirrored doors alongside the lieutenant and Director Wix, leaving me alone with their army of henchmen.

¡Mierda! I almost curse out loud. *Shit!*

I linger in the reception room for a useless amount of time, paranoid this is one of those scenarios when the captive thinks they're safe but really, they're at the zenith of danger.

Ultimately, I decide to take up the lieutenant's offer and stretch my espionage legs. When I make my move for the exit, none of Governor's State Guards bother to look my way, but I can't take my eyes off the soldier by the window.

The guy is the definition of jacked, with a body built like a vault, and although he has about seven different weapons on his duty belt, I opt to ignore these deadly details.

Because sheathed next to his pistol is my stolen knife.

"Hand over my blade," I bark out like an order.

The Guard's thick neck rotates to meet my glare. He squints his unblinking eyes straight at me, two black pits that say, *Make me.*

"You dare disobey me?" I snap, playing my part of a high-ranking officer, reminding him who has the upper hand now. I spent weeks locked in a room with Guards like him beating away my resolve. It's time I got it back.

"No sir," the soldier replies, removing my knife from his belt. I yank it from his hand and turn to take my leave before the Guard can fully realize he just handed over a weapon to a prisoner.

I pocket the blade and walk down a wide hall decorated with Black Market art, bolstered by the weight of the steel and how comforting it feels to have a piece of Mira back with me.

Turning a corner, I wedge myself behind an ornate statue of a charro straddling a rearing horse. I down the last of my water and place the rim of the empty glass against the wall, then hold my ear to its bottom.

I'm looking for intel, anything useful to bring back to the Common. Emery and the Elders have no idea Roth's in league with the Salazar cartel. Someway, somehow, I've got to warn them.

But I need more first. And my makeshift listening device is giving me nothing.

Then I hear muffled voices, but they're coming from outside the room. I lower my spyglass, peer out from behind the statue, and spot two chatty cartel women posted outside a pair of open terrace doors.

Their talk is unintelligible to me, neither Spanish nor English.

What language are they speaking?

My translator device must be out of range, because when I switch it to external mode, it still doesn't translate their conversation.

Keeping my back against the wall, I creep closer. The two cartel women, sans necklaces, continue to talk in the fast, clipped language that my translator fails to interpret for me. Both have on crocodile *S* belts over their skintight dresses, and semiautomatic gold-plated pistols strapped to their curvy hips.

Are they speaking a code language?

Fascinated at the thought, I inch closer, running my fingers along the translator to see if there's a secret button I'm missing, when a silvery voice calls out to me from the balcony in flawless English.

"You won't find our language on any device, I made sure of that."

Splayed on a chaise longue, a third woman in an elegant snow-white linen suit beckons me to join her outside. I hesitate, wondering if I've reached the apex of danger, but then remember I don't have a choice.

At the door, the two cartel women ogle me with curiosity, reaching out to fondle my arms and chest. They banter back and forth in their code language, but I can guess what they're saying about me isn't chaste by any stretch of the word.

"Restrain yourself, ladies," the woman in white commands.

Reluctantly, the armed women unhand my body and allow me to pass through the doors and out onto the sundrenched balcony that overlooks a grove of grapefruit trees.

Up close, I realize the woman who summoned me is not a woman at all, but a girl of about fifteen. The low cut of her jacket, which bares enough skin to flaunt her huge amethyst necklace, her designer sky-high heels, and her painted face threw me off. She possesses such a domineering aura she appears way beyond her years.

"What were you doing in the hallway, Theo?" the girl asks.

I stare at her stone-faced, giving no reaction to the fact that she knows my name and potentially caught me snooping. "Nothing," I say, at ease with my lie.

Something about this girl feels familiar to me, although I've never heard or read on the news about Lieutenant Salazar having a daughter.

We take measure of each other, the outdoor fans blowing cool air at my back.

I bet this girl has never once broken a sweat in her life.

"Were you spying?" she asks me, her manner light, her voice playful, almost sweet.

"No," I say, the translator echoing my free and easy attitude.

The girl's bronze skin is smooth and poreless, her golden-brown hair long and straight. When I take note of her turned-up nose, my blood freezes. My hand shoots unbidden up to my face.

"You're right," she says. "We have the same nose. Which means we can both smell bullshit better than a Texas Scent Hunter."

I shove my hands into the deep pockets of my uniform. "Who are you . . . ?" I ask, looping my fingers through my steel-ringed knuckle duster.

The girl's mouth cuts open into a smile sharp as a knife. "Valeria."

I scour my memory but can't recall any noteworthy Salazar member by that name.

"Were you hoping to overhear the lieutenant's meeting?" Valeria asks me point-blank.

"I've answered twice already," I reply evenly, calculating whether I can whip out my blade before one of her guards can get a shot off. "Or do you not understand no?"

Her smile disappears. I'm sensing Valeria surrounds herself with yes-men and yes-women, and the word *no* is as rare as the gemstone at her throat.

"This will be my only warning to you," Valeria says, rising from her chaise longue. "Never lie to me again."

She glides toward me, looking me over. "I might be younger than you, but I am your aunt. And therefore, your superior."

Did I miss something?

Did I land in Oz? Or did I die already, and this is hell's waiting room? Or maybe I'm trapped in a night terror and I just need to figure out how to wake up. I start slapping my cheeks.

"Wonderful," Valeria says with a snide petulance. "You're not a quick one, are you?"

Her bodyguards' laughter bounces off the hard marble floor.

I must be staring at her dumbstruck, because Valeria rolls her umber eyes.

"The Salazars and the Roths made an alliance," she informs me, lifting her hand to present herself like a showpiece. She then turns inward, clutching at her purple gem. "I never believed this day would come."

"I'm not following you . . . ," I say, my brain boggled by what she might be trying to tell me. "What does all of this mean?"

"It means it's all happening. Tomorrow, my mother and father are meant to meet for the first time." Her smile's back. "The Lone Star is finally here."

"I don't understand . . . Governor Roth . . . is your *dad*?" I say slowly, waiting for reality to catch up. "And who exactly is your mom?"

"Everyone calls her the capo."

How is this even possible? I'm suddenly sweating bullets.

"You're blessed, nephew," Valeria says, reaching over to sweep my long hair from my eyes. "You'll be here to see it."

"See what?" I ask, terrified of the answer.

"The day everything changes."

MIRA

It's 4:38 a.m.

For the last two and a half hours, I've seen no other lights but ours. Only starless, near-complete darkness—town after town, mile after mile. It's like we're on an empty highway, driving straight into nothingness. The black abyss.

And Ava's making excellent time.

"This ride costs more than a low-ranker's life savings," Skye Lin says, breaking the silence that's settled inside the car since we set off from Dallas. "Did one of your admirers just *donate* their car to you?"

"No," Ava says back, her hands gripping Duke's steering wheel tighter. "I stole it."

"Even better," Skye answers, a smile in her husky voice.

I can only imagine Owen's fury when he learns his beloved car has vanished from its usual parking space. *He'll understand,* I told Ava as we packed Duke with our supplies and left our home city without a glance in the rearview mirror.

And to be fair, Owen's possession of the costly Kismet vehicle was the result of his own thievery, so he should understand our measures.

Nothing is given to you in this world. You have to take it.

And the five of us in this vehicle are taking our chances on each other.

From the back seat, Haven starts passing around a bottled water, reminding each of us to hydrate. Crammed between my aunt and Lucía, Skye, who has swapped her prisoner's uniform for black coveralls, accepts the offer, sipping the warm water and smacking her lips like it's vintage Napa Valley wine.

"Five years of solitary confinement . . . ," Skye says, staring at the clear bottle, "when you're stripped and deprived of *everything* . . . I found out all you truly crave is clean water."

"And revenge," I add, thinking back on my own short stint inside a cell. Put there because of a double-crossing mole on our team. Skye Lin.

We need to raze the past, Ava told me before we broke her out from Guardian Tower. *It's time to rebuild.*

Skye leans forward, her tone sincere but clipped, like it's difficult for her to admit mistakes out loud. "I'm sorry for betraying you and the Common," Skye says, holding out the bottle of water like an olive branch. "But I'm here on this mission with you, ready to offer up my life to make it right."

I take the water with a nod, accepting that Skye had her reasons for aligning with Roth. He gave her freedom and promised to give her back what the government took—her right to choose to have a child. A sterilization reversal surgery that could restore her autonomy, her power to control her own future.

But alliances built on hate never last. And theirs was quickly broken, betrayed. Poisoned.

Ricin, according to Skye. Perfect for close-contact targets.

Roth shouldn't have lasted an hour.

"What does that say?" Lucía asks, pointing toward the large green reflective sign ahead.

LONG LIVE THE GOVERNORS

On the last stretch of my dash to Canada, I would spy "Save the Twins" tagged on buildings along the country roads, three words that would lift my spirit and remind me the people were on our side.

I close my eyes to the Loyalist sign as we speed past, unable to speak the words out loud. "Graffiti a favor del gobernador," I tell Lucía. *Pro-governor graffiti.*

"Propaganda," Skye remarks. "Roth probably ordered the few soldiers he has left to spread these lies. Making it seem like he has numbers."

I rip my eyes open and blink out the image of the ten captive Common members drowned beneath the Gulf. "All Commoners will be exterminated," the message above them read.

Roth supporters are out there. Out *here.* The only question is, where are they hiding?

"Half of Roth's Guard can't just disappear," Ava says, sweeping her eyes across the crumbling, deserted highway, anticipating a soldier popping out from a pothole at any moment. Will she swerve, or slam the accelerator, undeviating, straight as an arrow, ready to take more lives if they stand in our way?

In this world, you have to take.

"Emery told me Texas has the biggest army in the country?" Haven asks, still trying to map out the borders in her mind. Growing up in the Camps, she was told Texas *was* the nation.

"Yes," I answer, keeping a fixed stare out my passenger window. All clear. "Even though a third of his State Guard flipped to the Common, he still has a powerful force."

The soldiers Roth sent north to "protect" the states from the Common never returned south to Texas. Tens of thousands of Guards vanished overnight, just like their leader. Emery operates under the belief that the bulk of Roth's army united with the other pro-governor states to continue the fight, abandoning their own governor after his downfall in the Battle for Dallas. But Ava and I believe his loyal Guards *did* return. They're just waiting on orders to make their next move.

Keeping a vigilant watch out my window, I reach over to the driver's seat and squirt a few sips of water into my sister's mouth, then toss the bottle to Lucía.

Another battered street sign approaches on our right. No graffiti this time, but the numbers are scratched and faded, forcing me to squint to make out the distance. "Austin: 30 miles."

"Half an hour," I inform the car.

Ava nods, her relief clear as she loosens her white-knuckled grip on the wheel, unclamping the tight muscles of her jaw. Despite this, I feel the car increasing speed as she weaves around the cracks and fissures that pit the neglected highway.

She must be exhausted. We all are. Sleep pulls at my eyes, my body desperate to tell me I've been up for twenty-one hours and it's had enough.

"Goodwins," Skye says from the back seat, stinging my nerves to high alert. I whip my chair around toward the back windshield—panicked she spotted a vehicle, soldier, *anything*—but find only Skye and Lucía locked in a glaring match.

"Could you tell your friend to stop eyeing me like I'm one of those falcons?" Skye says, a sharp edge to her request.

Lucía shakes her head, raking back her sweaty bangs. "¿Dices que esta chica es una asesina? Los asesinos trabajan solos. ¿Jugará bien en un equipo?" *You say this girl is an assassin? Assassins work alone. Will she play nice on a team?*

"What, are you afraid to insult me in English?" Skye bites back at her. "You're right to be scared of me, but not because I'm a spy."

Before I can answer and pacify either of them, Haven shouts the word every one of us has been dreading.

"Lights!"

My aunt points to the horizon behind us, seconds before two head-lights crest a slope.

"Ava, a vehicle, six o'clock," I whisper to my sister, much calmer than I feel. "Two hundred yards. I can't tell yet if it's theirs or ours."

There really is no "their side" or "ours" anymore. Not with this unauthorized mission.

Ava looks to me. *We can't let anyone stop us.*

"Faster!" Lucía shouts, slapping Ava's headrest to spur her on.

Skye throws off her seat belt, crawling toward the rear glass for a closer view. "How fast can this thing go?!"

We're about to find out.

Ava steps on the gas as I twist my chair forward, buckling myself in. The bright-blue numbers on the LCD speedometer rise quicker than I can blink. Eighty, ninety, one hundred and one. Ava fastens her eyes straight forward, unflinching and single-minded. *If this comes down to a chase, we're going to win.*

My instinct to shout for Ava to cut Duke's lights and use the dark-ness as cover is difficult to bite back. At this speed, and with only the faint glow of the moon to guide our path, Ava would never be able to navigate this minefield of a road without crashing.

But we're like a lighthouse. A damn beacon. A moving flare that signals *We're right here,* no matter how much distance we put between our pursuers and us.

"They are closer," Haven says, leaning forward in her seat, her hot breath on my ear. "We must do something."

"An exit, one mile!" I direct Ava, nodding toward the off-ramp. "Let's see if the car follows."

Earlier on the drive, I counted eleven cars dumped along the side of the highway like roadkill. Overheated batteries and engines that couldn't take the scorching sun. Nighttime travel seems paramount with these sweltering temperatures. So I cling to a quiet hope that the vehicle trailing us may just be a water truck en route to its deliveries, or an early morning commuter aiming to avoid the heat.

No luck. Not that I've ever believed in fortune. As Ava flies off the highway, veering onto the access lane, the spotlights of the stalking vehicle grow bigger and brighter, mimicking Ava's every move.

"It's a Guard SUV!" Skye yells from the back. "It must be going a hundred fifty, because it's coming at us like a rocket!"

"¿Cómo podemos perderlos?" Lucía asks, drawing her gun from its holster. *How can we lose them?*

"Up there!" Ava shouts, and I immediately see her plan.

I can just make out the shadowy silhouette of a giant five-level freeway interchange a few miles ahead. The massive structure looks like a neglected Texas-sized rollercoaster in the center of nowhere, with its fifty-mile-high loops and stacked roads.

It's dangerous enough to merely pass beneath these deteriorating interchanges. A piece of concrete as small as a fingernail could break off and kill someone from that height—no less the threat of *the entire* structure itself collapsing down on our roof.

But to go *up* on one of those decaying bridges, hundreds of feet into the sky? It's difficult to believe even a vehicle such as Duke could save us from the fall.

Rayla's voice cuts through my fear. *I won't tell you to be careful, because you need to be fearless.*

It's the only way to outrace them.

"Do it," I tell Ava. And she guns it.

We speed onto an on-ramp at 120 miles per hour, a curved two-lane road that takes us up and left.

"They're still after us," Skye reports, climbing back into her middle seat, strapping her safety belt over her shoulders. She eyes Lucía's gun. "Do I get a pistol?"

Lucía ignores her. With a seasoned swiftness, she checks the chamber of her handgun. "La pelea comienza antes de lo que pensábamos." *The fight is starting sooner than we thought.*

My fingers itch for the security of my own gun, but that would be admitting we might lose the chase. I turn my focus forward, out the windshield, to what's ahead.

What I see drops my stomach to my feet. *Brake!* Every instinct in my body screams. *Brake!*

A gap—an enormous chunk of missing pavement—cuts off our upcoming road. The empty space, a black hole, looks fifteen yards wide but it might as well be a mile. It's a death trap. A losing game. And it's thirty seconds away.

So is our tail.

"No way," Skye says, incredulous. "How the hell did they catch up?"

Then the Guard SUV is suddenly right behind Duke, bumper to bumper, flashing its brights at us like strobe lights. It's blinding, disorienting. Driving me mad.

We're going to crash any second.

Twenty seconds, to be precise, before we meet the black hole.

Ava doesn't hesitate. "We can make it," she says, as even as her speed.

We're going to jump.

We're going to make it.

"Not a bad way to die!" Skye shouts, the most animated I've ever seen her. "Better than a prison cell."

"¡Sin miedo!" Lucía cries. *No fear!*

Lucía and Skye let loose harmonizing roars, not from alarm, but pure lusty adrenaline.

The SUV's horns start blaring. *Beep! Beep! Beep! Beep!*

I wait for their bullets to start peppering the shatterproof glass.

Fifteen seconds.

I turn back to Haven, grabbing hold of her hand, as if our link could protect us if we plummet to the earth.

Ten seconds.

It's then I catch sight of the flicker of yellow. Like a flare, a small flag of truce waving above the SUV's roof.

Haven must see the color reflected in my eyes. She whips her head around while squeezing my fingers, hard. "Ciro?"

His buzzed blonde head appears above the hatch as the SUV skids to the side of the road, his long flagpole arms swinging desperately in the air for us to pull over.

"Ava, it's Ciro!" I relay, uncertain if this information will make her brake. Or if I even want her to brake.

We can't let anyone stop us.

For a brief moment I think she's going to go for it and vault us over the gaping divide, but in the final seconds, she slams the brakes, and somehow Duke comes to a screeching halt inches from the saw-toothed edge.

I don't dare look down.

As the dust and smoke from the tires settle, no one moves or makes a sound.

Then Ava unleashes a single low chuckle, audacious and infectious, and soon we're all releasing our tension in a bout of cathartic laughter.

I throw open my door, pressing my shaking fingers to my chest, trying to slow my still-racing heart.

"You are all crazy!" Ciro shouts down at us.

"*Crazy* is just another word for *brave*," I shout back, squinting to make out the faces of those marching toward me.

"I have to say," Kano's smiling voice reaches me through the dark. "My feelings are a bit hurt my name didn't make your mission list." The black metal studs in his ears glint off the headlights, so does his mischievous grin.

"You're not here to stop us, then?" Ava asks, the hint of a challenge spiking her words. She steps up to my side, Lucía moving to stand on my left, gun still in hand.

"We're here to join you," Barend answers, head to toe in black military gear.

"If you'll have us, of course," Ciro adds.

"Does Emery know?" Haven asks behind me.

All three men look to the ground, and I take their silence to mean no.

This must have been a grueling choice for them. To go against our leader's wishes, to follow mine and Ava's. Their allegiance feels heavy on my shoulders, but I can't help but smile.

Our old mission mates, back together and united.

We really can win. I feel my hope flutter and expand, powerful enough to ignite the blackness around me.

My elation proves short-lived.

The hulking figure of Alexander Roth slinks out from behind the vehicle, his glare aimed straight at me. He, too, wears all black, except his outfit appears hodgepodge, like he slapped on whatever he could find. Like his was a last-minute decision to come on this mission, and he's not sure if it was the correct one.

"We are standing targets up here," Alexander proclaims, like anyone asked for his opinion. "We must move if we want to find cover before sunrise."

He's already trying to take over.

I turn to Ava to see how she is taking Alexander's far from desirous presence, but her attentions are directed elsewhere.

Owen emerges from the driver's seat, a black hat and a checkered bandana veiling the majority of his face. He shakes his head, staring first at his stolen car, then at Ava.

"Act first, apologize later," Ava yells to him, lifting her chin as I cross my arms, narrowing my stare.

He'll get no apologies from me. Apologies don't belong in rebellions. *In this world,* I remind myself, *you must* take *what you want.*

I turn my back on Owen's sparkling golden eyes, which are still aimed at my sister, and move for Duke's driver's seat.

"I'll take the wheel now," I say, but Ava's not behind me. She's stomping toward Owen.

Toward the Whiz Kid, who has suddenly appeared at his side.

OWEN

"Seeing me sooner than you thought, huh?" I remark, all upbeat, making a point to keep on my black bandana and trucker-cap combo. I don't want Ava to know how pissed I am. Riled up, even.

Hurt is the right word, you could say.

Not about her stealing my car—that, I hate to admit, was a good move. Masterly, really.

Hurt that she didn't wait for me.

Second thing I hate to admit: Blaise was right. It's nice sometimes to hide beneath a disguise.

Especially where I'm headed.

"Nice driving skills," I say when Ava stops in front of me. "Must've had an awesome instructor."

Ava shrugs away the banter, moving straight to business. "You brought the Whiz Kid . . ."

I keep a secure handful of the kid's shirt, making sure he doesn't try to make a break for it, and tuck down his own black hat, covering his *extremely* wanted face.

We might be forty feet up on this bridge, but Guards and falcons could be anywhere. *Anything.* I throw a suspicious glare at the jumbo mosquito winging its way toward me. *Drone or insect?*

"You brought Skye Lin, looks like," I say, taking a detour from my inner dialogue to watch the members Ava had deemed worthy getting back into *my* car.

I'm fine about it all. Really.

"What's that saying?" I ask before I can stop myself. "Fool me once . . ."

The mosquito flitters between us for a beat before Ava slaps her palms together, solving my debate. Her hands pull away to reveal blood and goo. *Definitely insect.*

She gestures to the kid, wiping the entrails away with one clean flick. The Whiz, dressed in one of Blaise's oversized hoodies, stares up at her with his newfound zombified nonexpression. If he recognizes her at all, he doesn't show it.

"I'm assuming you didn't come here to join with us?" Ava asks like a mind reader.

I wish, I want to say, but my pride gets the better of me. "No," I reply instead. "My gut is pulling me to take a different course."

"He told you where it is, then?" she asks, knowing not to say the word *servers* out loud. She eyes another mosquito flapping in our direction.

"In a way . . . ," I answer.

It was more like I did all the talking and he shot me a few telling looks. But a look is worth a thousand words, right?

And the look Ava's shooting me right now is piercing. It's laced with disappointment. Whether it's aimed at my particular self-appointed mission or my stubbornness to see it through is open to debate.

I tug the kid closer, patting his shoulder like he's the one who needs reassurance.

Standing next to the four-foot Whiz is like hanging around a nuclear reactor—the info this kid's storing in his mind is powerful and dangerous and everything could all blow up in a flash—but there's a job to be done and I know I'm the one to do it.

I have to locate those servers before a falcon locates us.

Find the servers, find Roth.

End of story.

"Sorry to interrupt this private tête-à-tête . . . but it's go time!" Blaise comments from the SUV's passenger window.

I become aware of the fact that Ava, the Whiz, and I are the only ones left loitering on the road. Ava nods a welcome to Blaise before she turns away, scanning the highway below with those cat eyes of hers, like she can see everything in the dark.

"Transients," Ava says, jutting her chin to the two dots of blue LED lights moving at glacial speed on the highway under our bridge.

On instinct, I shove the kid back into the front cab of the SUV, crossing all my fingers and toes that he doesn't start up his shrieking again. "Stay put," I tell him. I'm *mostly* positive those trekkers down there aren't sicarios or Guards—they wouldn't be kind enough to let us *know* they're coming—but at this point, everyone is suspect.

"Haven knows a safe house in the old capital," Ava says, turning away from the walkers with their bulky turtle-shell silhouettes, rucksacks so thick it looks like they've got everything they own strapped to their backs.

I wonder if Ava's musing back on her stint as a wayfaring transient, or if it's more that she's picturing the hellish trek that awaits her down south.

Which city are you searching for Roth first? I want to ask. But I don't, of course. Not here.

"We should all get some sleep before we break off and head out," Ava says, fiddling with the folded paper map tucked inside her waistband.

Looks like for the next few hours at least, Ava's course and mine are headed in the same direction.

And I could definitely use a serious power nap right about now. I'm either woozy from this height, the heat, or the comedown from catching up to Ava.

A thought strikes me, not for the first time tonight.

"Hey, you were totally planning on sending Duke back to me, right?" I ask, tightening my bandana. "Maybe with a little goodbye note telling me where you were going?"

"Who has time for goodbyes?" Ava answers.

Duke's brake lights start flashing—Mira, signaling Ava to move. *Let's go!*

My next words fly from my mouth without my full authority. "You really couldn't wait?"

Ava's bow-shaped lips curl up into the ghost of a grin. "You always say the future waits for no one."

And with that she disappears into my car.

The side entrance of a multistory warehouse finally opens, and a man with a stubble goatee steps out, throwing up an okay signal.

"Thank Goodwin," I say, relieved. While the gang—which I've dubbed Team Takedown—has been outside resting and waiting for Haven to sway her Austin contact to help us on the quiet, I've been wrangling the Whiz.

I left my parents behind in Dallas only to continue my unenthusiastic role as babysitter.

Now that the kid's awake—and whatever drugs the nurse gave him have worn off—he loves to move. I refuse to cuff him or anything like that, he's not a prisoner, but damn, he's trying my patience. Every time I turn my head for one second, I whip back around to find him at the riverbank twenty yards away. The Trinity River is basically all dried up, a rocky wasteland. But for some reason the kid just wants to stare down into it.

He's either a) got ideas to throw himself off the bank or b) has some serious psychological trauma with the water lords and craves to be near it.

"Hey, kid, it's not safe to be out in the open," I say each time, luring him back to our hiding spot behind an old hotel high-rise. And each time he stares at me with vacant eyes, then follows me, coltish, without a word.

He's so scary silent now I kind of wish he'd start screaming again. Not just for our sakes—he could let slip more intel—but for his own.

Haven leads the way into the building, at least I'm pretty sure that sturdy figure is hers. We're all practically duplicates of one another with our faces cloaked in military shemaghs.

Indistinguishable is the word of the night. *No one can know we're here.*

I'm the last to enter the Common's Austin nerve center, guiding the Whiz inside and quickly down a series of window-lit hallways. When we reach a dark stairwell door, the goatee man has us line up single file.

"Follow the light," he says.

He flicks on a solar-powered flashlight and heads down four flights of stairs, then the line stops when we reach a yellow cellar door that requires a key to open.

What do they have locked up down here? Loyalists?

Stupid question.

Haven said this building is a Common supply warehouse, and we're currently experiencing a most inconvenient power outage. A smarter question: How did people store cold foods before there was such a thing as refrigeration?

Basements. The coolest part of a building. And the best place to sleep away the blazing daylight hours before heading back out on the road come sundown.

I'm handed a small flashlight when I get to the bottom of the rickety steps and cross the damp threshold. Yep. An unfinished basement, borderline dungeon-like, with low ceilings and a hard concrete floor, crammed full of wooden crates packed with all kinds of fruits and vegetables.

"Impressive stockpile," I admire out loud.

But before I can snatch a super rare avocado—I haven't had one of those in *years*—a sleeping bag is shoved against my chest.

"I grabbed us a spot over in the dairy section," Blaise says. "Figured we could kind of hem the kid in with the giant waxed cheese wheels."

Blaise and I have come a long way from being adversaries, fighting over positioning in Rayla the Slayer's esteem, to first-class teammates. I like to think Rayla's proud, wherever she is.

The others start dividing into bunkmate parties.

Ava, Mira, Lucía, and Kano set up camp in the opposite corner, laying out their sleeping bags next to the chest freezers. Skye opts for a solo arrangement in the middle of the room near the root vegetable boxes. Unsurprising when you think about it, since the jailbird is probably used to having only her shadow for company. Ciro and Barend roll out their sleepers side by side near the stairs, their backs to shelves of canned goods. I mentally dropkick myself when I see Alexander moving a cheese wheel to make room for his padded bag in my section.

How does it happen that Ava and I seem to always be on opposite teams lately?

Ava and her team leave for Mexico in ten hours—the basement's lively with muffled chatter about tactical plans and still-needed supplies. The word "weapons" reaches me from Lucía's area, "proper gear" from Ciro's.

It's going to be hard for everyone to fall asleep, forcing our circadian rhythms to flip their sleep-wake cycle double-quick. But from now on, both of our missions require us to travel by night—not just for stealth, but to move easier in this excessive heat.

By virtue of the Whiz, my path is leading me elsewhere. Back in the Dallas hospital room, Alexander threatened to use an AI lie detector on the kid, military interrogation style, if he didn't spill his guts, stat. Scared for the boy—Whitman only knows what the hell that drone was programmed to do if it detected he was lying—I stepped in while

Alexander left to make good on his promise, and tried my own more *human* method.

After thoroughly searching the kid's clothing and person for any hint of where he ran from—dirt under his nails that might home in on a specific region, a tablet or company badge stuffed into his pockets, a microchip still imbedded inside his wrist, et cetera—I ended up finding the Whiz's stash house location by good old process of elimination. I drained what was left of my tablet's battery to pull up a map of Texas, and then pointed to every city in this beast of a state.

I knew I'd hit the jackpot when the kid's amber eyes rounded bigger than two supermoons.

Turns out, the goods are hidden in some place called Enchanted Rock, a pink granite mountain ninety-five miles west of Austin. Sounds mysterious, right?

The kid must've copied the data from Roth's servers onto a hard drive before he cut and ran, and then squirreled away the drive somewhere on that peak. Tonight, Blaise and I are going to play a game of high-stakes hide-and-seek.

But first I need to say a proper goodbye to Ava.

Rolling out my sleeping bag, I keep trying to catch her eye, hoping for a private moment, but she's dead focused on scheming with Mira and Lucía. For twenty minutes, she doesn't even glance in my direction.

I feel my window of opportunity slam shut when Haven announces, "Lights out!"

I'm more than tempted to shout *Ava!* before all the lanterns switch off, but I crush that knee-jerk impulse, knowing Ava would hate having the spotlight thrown on us. Plus, I'm pretty sure one glare from Mira would put a serious roadblock on a private conversation between her sister and me.

Bide your time. Play it cool. Wait for another window.

I tell myself I'm going to just rest my eyes but keep on the lookout for movement, in case Ava gets up to find a glass of water or something and I can follow her. But in a rookie move, I must've fallen asleep, because next thing I know, I jolt awake.

Shit.

I raise myself up on an elbow and scan the room.

By a single lantern's light, I clock the crown of Ava's red head sandwiched between Mira and Haven in her sleeping bag. Awesome. How am I supposed to get her attention when she's fast asleep?

Over by the stairs, Barend's passed out but appears to be cuddling a . . . *Is that a pillow? Wait, where's Ciro?*

My eyes search the basement high and low, but nope, he's nowhere to be seen. Ciro's gone.

Inspiration hits. I shimmy out of my sleeper, careful not to wake Blaise, who snores so freakishly loud it sounds like he's sawing wood, or Alexander, who's got a firm grip on the Whiz's bony leg, and tiptoe over to Ava's side of the room. I stand there next to the freezers for a few winks, thinking Ava might sense my presence.

I know back at the mansion, Ava never slept. Most nights, we'd meet up at her favorite lookout spot on the fringes of the capital. We'd sit inside the burnt-out shell of a high-rise, dangling our feet. We wouldn't even talk most times—it was more to not be alone in the night.

We helped each other avoid the nightmares.

It's highly possible she's awake now, waiting for me to make some kind of move.

I pick my way to the exit door, hoping she'll follow.

I hang around the hallway outside the basement door, praying to Whitman it opens.

Ava makes me sweat it out for what feels like an eternity, but then suddenly my heart's in my throat when I see the door handle twist and her svelte figure emerge.

I break into a smile, dimples and all, and move toward her. *Maybe I didn't blow it after all.*

"I don't know what you're grinning about," Ava says nonchalantly. "I just came out here looking for the bathroom."

My smile dies, along with my confidence.

"Oh . . . ," I sputter, taking a step back.

Ava smirks, all sly, then ties on her camouflage shemagh, heading for the staircase labeled "Roof Access."

She's suddenly got jokes. Am I somehow rubbing off on her?

I pull my bandana up just shy of my eyes and follow Ava to the stairwell.

On the climb, a sense of finality drops on me like the heavy blade of a guillotine. I bite down on my lips, keeping my thoughts strictly to myself.

I don't want Ava to know I'm terrified.

Terrified that I've got it all wrong . . . The Whiz kid is just a regular kid and I'm just a *punk* kid who's bound to mess it all up. I'm terrified that I'm going to fail, let everyone down, and these are our last minutes together because I'm choosing to launch my own mission and, after this, I'll never see her again.

Ava throws open the metal door to a sky ablaze in the light of magic hour.

Good, I could use a bit of magic.

We move to the edge of the roof, savoring the view. The entire skyline is an eruption of neon orange that casts a soft light across Ava's face, making her eyes glitter like emeralds.

Last I checked, Ava's bounty was hovering around five million, but what Ava has is priceless. Don't the Loyalists realize that?

Hope shines from her like a power source.

Just standing next to her as we bask in the peaceful sunset, I feel calm, yet energized. Neither of us says a thing. Usually silence makes me skittish—quick to fill in the dead air with the sound of my voice—but with Ava, when we're together like this, alone, it's different. Like I don't have to speak a word and she understands me.

The fiery sun melts below the western horizon when Ava finally whispers, "Goodbyes feel too final."

She takes her eyes off the downtown skyline, a quarter the size of Dallas, to face me. "Back before all of this, when we were still in hiding . . . every time Mira and I would separate and face another dangerous day, we would always tell each other, *See you soon.* Never goodbye."

Before I can stop myself, I reach out and graze the tips of my fingers against hers, wondering if there will ever come a time when her hand itches for mine instead of some weapon.

Not for the first time in my life, I question whether hate is stronger than love. Will Ava ever feel anything other than the drive for retribution while Roth is still out there alive? *Will I?*

She doesn't pull her hand away.

"I still don't agree with your choice to not come with me," Ava says, staring straight into me. "But I'm trying to respect it."

"Ava . . . ," I say. "I just have to."

I swallow a deep breath and start to tell her all the details of my mission, but she slips her hand away from mine, holding up her palm to stop me.

"No—don't tell me anything. Not where you're going. Not even exactly what it is you think you're searching for."

My mask and cap do nothing to hide my hurt at her sudden detachment. This close up, she can see it in my eyes. *It's like that, then? You really care so little about me?*

"Of course I care," Ava says, quick to decode my thoughts. "Of course I do . . . It's just, once we cross the border, I don't know what will happen to me or my team. If the State Guard or the Salazars' sicarios get us—"

"That won't happen—"

"If they do, I don't want them to learn about your mission from me."

I shut down the terrible thought of Ava being tortured by the cartel.

"If Mira and I go down," Ava continues, dropping her voice to a whisper, "and if you're right about the Whiz Kid, and what could be on those servers . . . then at least one of us can succeed. One of us can stop him."

For the love of everything Common, I better be right.

Ava cracks every one of the knuckles of her right hand, a habit of hers that makes the snake tattoo on her forearm slither—on the move, like she wants to be.

Dodging my eyes, she whips out a folded chunk of paper. I'm glad once again for my bandana, because I can't help but smile. *Is this the goodbye note?*

"See you soon," Ava tells me.

Before I can reciprocate her words, twin bombs explode three blocks away. The blast nearly blows my eardrums.

Holy Whitman, is the Guard here?!

Like second nature, my hand goes for my gun, flicking off the safety.

Boom!

Between the sounds of explosions, I think—*just for a split second—*of myself. *Why does bad news—disaster—always seem to follow when Ava and I are together?* Two nights in a row now. Might be a good thing we're splitting up.

Boom!

Next thing I know, we're both knocked flat on our asses, and I see stars.

AVA

A blast wave slams Owen and me to the rocky rooftop.

Splayed out on top of Owen, I jerk my attention away from him to the sky but find no airplanes with the five-pointed Lone Star on their tail wings. Just cotton-like cumulous clouds drenched a goldenrod orange by the setting sun.

This isn't an aerial attack. *Has the State Guard penetrated into Austin's city limits on foot?* No, the Common Guard would have sounded an alarm.

Untwisting our tangled limbs, Owen and I scramble to our feet and rush to the rooftop's ledge. *Boom! Boom!* Two smaller blasts erupt simultaneously a block away.

"They're taking out the cell towers!" Owen shouts. "Shit, and the backup generators, look!"

From our 180-degree vantage point, he gestures across whole districts whose emergency lights have suddenly gone out. All of downtown and West Austin, and presumably every neighborhood in the whole city, is now completely without power.

"Is this the State Guard?" Owen asks, voice taut with anger.

My attention snaps to the commotion in the street below. While most citizens shelter on the ground, hands over their heads in protection, a group of people dressed in plain clothes with bright-yellow kerchiefs around their necks run shouting toward a street corner. I watch, helpless, as one of the attackers pulls a pipe bomb out of a bag and launches it on top of an artificial treescape that hides a cell site.

"Run!" I scream to the bystanders within range of the blast wave, but it's too late.

Boom! The cell tower blows, sending shrapnel flying, crueler than bullets. The sharp fragments of metal find their targets, slicing indiscriminately through bodies and building facades.

From my medical training at Strake, I know the gruesome damage shrapnel can cause. Awful, life-changing injuries, shattered bones. Death.

I pull my gun from my hip and start rapid firing.

"Ava, what are you doing?" Owen shouts beside me. "They're wearing our colors!"

Though the attackers wear the yellow mark of the Common, these are not our people. We do not senselessly kill our own.

The yellow kerchiefs are a ruse.

This is Roth's doing.

"I'm aiming to wound!" I shout. "We can capture and question them!"

Bullets ricochet off the roof's ledge. Owen and I crouch down, gasping breaths pounding in sync. "Our own people would never return fire on a Common base," I tell him, certain. "It's Roth."

"They could be a rival faction vying to usurp Emery," Owen conjectures. "Or crazy anarchists who want to throw the world back into the Dark Ages."

Words that Roth spit at my grandmother on national news come flooding back to the surface of my mind. *Your criminal gang is on a rampage that will soon spiral out of control.*

A part of me now worries if our rebellion inspired *too* much change. What if these attackers aren't the State Guard? What if they're Common members who seek to subvert the past, just like me, but are willing to take it a hundred steps further? Wipe out *all* technology, power, communication, modes of transportation, news. And government rule.

A total reset from which to rebuild the world.

Screaming from the wounded reaches us in the growing dark. After the initial shock of being hit, it took a few minutes before the first signs of pain kicked in. The cries are so gut-wrenching, I want to cover my ears.

Instead, I grip my gun tighter. Before I can rise to fire off another round, Owen shouts, "Cover me!" and surges to his feet.

I charge after him, protecting his flank until we both run out of ammunition.

"To the basement!" I yell, leading the way back to the stairwell door. Fear clenches my insides, all at once terrified that Mira or one of my teammates could have taken a sunset walk out on the streets.

Everyone was accounted for, in their sleeping bags, when I sneaked out of the room. Except for Ciro. His sleeping bag was empty.

Oh God.

Owen and I race down the stairwell and shoulder our way through the now-crowded hallway, packed with Common members gathered around their leader, the man with the goatee who gave us shelter in the basement.

"The Common Guard has set up a perimeter to capture the assailants," the man shouts, coolheaded under pressure. "Our focus is on helping the wounded. Our medics will administer care under fire, then we will evacuate the victims to Barton Hospital."

His leadership style shows a people-first mindset; he's empathetic, a servant to society, much like a pastor. He opened his doors to Haven and the other former Inmates after they were liberated from the Camps. When we arrived early this morning, I watched as he gently informed my aunt of her friend Cleo's death, the woman who freed her from her prison farm. Haven never stopped searching for news of her after the Battle for Dallas. But Cleo never made it out of Guardian Station.

She was shot on the rail platform fighting soldiers who were dragging citizens without microchips away to the Tower.

I almost freeze when I see a familiar face I've been hoping to avoid since arriving in Austin. "Duck!" I tell Owen, and he does so immediately.

Throwing myself behind him, I bury my face against his shoulder before I can be recognized by Kipling. The hardened but jovial cowboy was assigned by Emery to help the Common hold Austin, along with Xavier and his son, Malik. When I feel Owen's muscles tighten against my cheek, I know he's spotted his friend.

After the combat he and Malik went through together, they're more like brothers, he told me.

"We can't talk to them." I tilt my chin up to whisper. "No one can know we're here." I squeeze his arm to encourage him to keep moving forward.

Even a quick hello could jeopardize our entire mission.

It feels like a betrayal, purposely excluding friends who have been there for Mira and me time and time again since our initial escape from Dallas. They would join our new mission in a heartbeat if they knew of our plans.

But they are most needed here, and they will be safer.

I can't risk more people dying on my account.

We reach the door that leads to the basement, and I pull away from Owen's shoulder, his earthy scent of sandalwood and pepper lingering on the cloth of my headscarf. But when I turn the door handle, hard, it doesn't budge.

"It's locked," I say, my fear returning. *I will not be separated from my sister.*

Owen attempts to bulldoze the door open with his body, to no avail.

"Allow me," Ciro says, appearing out of nowhere. He produces a nickel key from his pocket. *Where'd he get a copy?* Futile question, the man is a master of keys.

I scan the large stuffed duffel bags he's carrying. *Is this why he disappeared? To gather supplies?* Ciro's shemagh outlines his glacial-blue eyes. There's a clarity in them I haven't seen since the day we first met at Paramount Point Hotel.

The door opens, and my focus quickly jumps from Ciro to my sister. I see her, bathed in lamplight, trying to fight her way up the stairs, but Kano stands like a wall in her path.

"I can help," Mira argues, heated. "I have medical training. Ava is probably already out there, giving aid, instead of standing useless in a basement like I am!"

"They have their own *real* doctors; you're not needed," Alexander says, stepping into the orange pool of light.

"Attackers wearing Common colors are blowing up cell towers and backup generators!" I inform the team, hastening down the stairs. Mira rushes to my side, ignoring Alexander.

"What?" she says, face twisted in confusion. *Mira's gut reaction is the same as mine: this isn't the Common's doing.*

Barend barrels past Mira and me, racing to get to Ciro.

"Where have you been?!" he reproaches. "What are these bags?" He takes two off Ciro's narrow shoulders and places the heavy load onto his own.

"Please, everyone draw in quickly," Ciro says, locking the basement door before taking his place at the center of the room. He motions for Barend to set the duffel bags at his feet, and for all of us to line up around him.

"There's a five-minute window before the Common Guard will have the entire city perimeter sealed and the mission's secrecy will be at great risk. If you're going to get out, you must go now."

Ciro didn't say *we. He's not coming with us either.*

Does Barend know?

Judging by his shell-shocked face, no. While Mira translates what's happening to Lucía, Barend steps out of line. He tries to keep his testy voice low, private, but we're twelve bodies packed into a small basement; there is no privacy.

"I couldn't *make* you remain in Alberta, no matter what I did, and now you *volunteer* to stay behind. Why?"

Ciro places his steady hand inside Barend's.

"We both know I'm no fighter—my talents lie elsewhere," Ciro hastily explains. "Attacks like this will continue, and Emery will need my help stabilizing the chaos. While she's away, my place is in Dallas."

Barend shakes his head, clearly loath to separate, but before he can argue, Ciro presses, "When your mission is successful, you'll need a country to return *to*." He smiles, lifting their linked hands up to his heart. "I'll be here, 'holding down the fort,' as they like to say here in Texas," Ciro jokes, attempting to defuse Barend's worry, but it's clear his decision to stay remains firm.

With a reluctant nod, Barend appears to accept Ciro's choice, but he doesn't fall back into line. He remains close by his partner's side while Ciro unzips the first duffel bag.

"I hope most of you know, I would never let any team of mine leave for such an important mission without top quality supplies," Ciro says, inviting us to come claim his offerings. "Everything you'll need is in these bags—food, the latest weaponry, state-of-the-art desert apparel and boots, translator devices, night vision goggles, and non-tech navigational tools."

Kano lets out an elongated whistle. Skye steps forward to take a closer look. One corner of her mouth quirks up, impressed.

"Where'd you get all this stuff?" Owen asks in wonderment, not fully understanding who exactly he's talking to. Owen wasn't there at the Common's headquarters in Alberta before we left on our original missions. He didn't get to see Ciro's impressive Offering Room.

"Ciro can get ahold of *anything*," I tell Owen.

Then Ciro reaches out to clasp my sister's shoulder. "Mira, as I am no longer a member of your mission, when you find our friend Theo, he can happily have my gear." He places a charcoal-gray field uniform—a garment I know must be as advanced as the Blackout Wear he supplied last time—into her hands. "I believe we are about the same size."

Gratitude washes over Mira's face. She places her hand over Ciro's, and it's clear Barend isn't the only one who will miss him. *Battle bonds.*

Boom! The basement shudders from another explosion in the streets above.

"Let's move out!" Haven says, zipping up one of the bags and throwing it across her shoulders.

"Ciro, please tell Emery . . . just tell her I had to," I say hurriedly. She'll be angry, but deep down, I know she will understand.

Act first, apologize later. My new mantra.

I feel a pang of guilt for leaving, but my unbridled energy is best served out in the field, giving full rein to Emery and the Elders to shepherd the country into the future. The last thing Emery needs is more distractions like my pyro outburst, which truthfully would have been just the beginning if I was forced to stay put.

"I will, but you can tell her yourself when you return," Ciro says.

If I return. I squeeze his shoulder, the Common's farewell.

"Alexander, grab our duffel bag; Blaise and I will fetch the Whiz," Owen calls out from the corner, hauling away large cheese wheels to release the docile kid.

But I see Alexander hesitate. *Is he backing out of the mission too?*

Coward. Owen needs him more than Emery does.

Then Alexander surprises everyone by approaching Mira.

"I'm going to Mexico," he declares without asking. "If this is truly the last chance to find my son, your team will need a seasoned adult as leader."

That role is already filled by Haven, but Mira springs to our aunt's defense first.

"Your leadership didn't help your dozen other search missions," she snaps.

But we can't physically stop Alexander from coming with us. If he follows, he follows.

Mira and Lucía glare daggers at Alexander, but there's no time to protest further. Another *boom! boom!* rattles us all back to the task at hand.

We need to get out of here, *now.*

Owen and I lock eyes, hovering by the stairs, as the rest of the team files out of the basement.

"Will your mission be okay with just you and Blaise?" I ask. For the first time I feel myself worry for someone the way I do about my sister. *A taste of what Mira's been feeling for the last three weeks without Theo.*

Owen flashes me one of his confident smiles, a bulky duffel bag strapped across his chest. "We're the two best black-hat hackers in cybercrime, *and* the heads of the Cybersecurity Team . . . Those servers don't stand a chance."

He holds my gaze, his golden eyes as deep and forbidden as my favorite Black Market whisky.

"Ava, let's move," Mira says urgently.

I think about pressing Owen's lips to mine—it might be my last chance—but I stop myself, and pull back. *My heart must remain hard.* I can't allow emotions to weaken me on the mission I'm committed to seeing through until the end.

"See you soon," Owen says, squeezing my hand.

"See you soon," I say, pressing back.

We climb the basement stairs two at a time, and then break apart to join our separate teams. As I race down the crowded hallway beside Mira, I don't look back.

Divide, and conquer Roth. *One of our missions will succeed.*

"I told Blaise we had to trade vehicles—Duke is too small to fit us all with our new additions," Mira updates me as we burst out the side door of the warehouse.

Pandemonium hits me like a sharp punch to the face.

Everything is a blur around me—the smoke-filled sky, the blown-out buildings, the frantic people running in the streets, the unmoving bodies lying on the ground—all sound is one loud static whir.

My head spins, swirling my thoughts into doubt.

Are we wrong to run from this fight? Do I really have tunnel vision for one man like Emery said, blinded by personal vendetta?

I'm snapped back to my senses when I feel the cool weight of a gun pressed into my hand.

"Ava, did you hear me?" Mira says.

We've somehow already made it to the Guard SUV, and Mira's holding open the driver's side door. The whole team waits for me inside.

My sister looks at me, steady.

"Are you ready for this?" she repeats. The same question I asked her two months ago, right before we stole onto a railcar and barreled into the unknown.

Clarity washes over me. *No, we're not running. We're making moves for the future.* Ciro's right. These attacks will keep happening across the country as long as Roth is still alive.

Things are only going to get worse unless we take action.

I draw a deep breath, steadying my racing heart, and nod.

"I'm ready," I say, taking my seat behind the wheel.

Time to win the game, once and for all.

THEO

Where is the governor?

I imagine this is the exhaustive question on the minds and lips of half the world.

I've stayed awake most of the night asking myself the same thing.

Roth never returned from his meeting with the lieutenant. I've mentally drawn up a list of the possible reasons why. None of them bring about a positive outcome for me.

And that's only a fraction of it.

I ponder the fate of Texas, Dallas, the Common. I wonder where Mira Goodwin is in this exact heartbeat. *I bet my Wright fortune that Roth is wondering the same thing.* The Goodwin sisters' names are on half the Guards' lips.

I brood on whether Mira is safe, if she's happy. If she's forgotten about me.

I puzzle over my mom and dad, my messed up family, and its preposterous recent addition. The new raw fact that I have an aunt, my dad's half sister, who is currently enjoying the springtime of life, three years my *junior*.

There are so many unresolved questions as to how *that* precisely came about, my head starts pounding. One thought hits the hardest.

Did my dad know? Or was he just as ignorant of his own old man as I was of mine?

I feel the hooks again, the lies that I so obliviously swallowed whole, wrenching at my gut. At least one thing isn't in doubt. Tonight, I'll find no shut-eye.

With all the pacing I've done, the fresh boots I accepted with begrudging reluctance from Governor have already been broken in. I've inspected every inch of my spacious rooms, hunting for a getaway route. So far, I haven't found any handles that turn or windows that open. No bookcase that pops out and leads down a secret passageway.

I flick my scrutiny to my untouched bed. One of the soldiers, I think it was my erstwhile personal guard, Wheeler, told me that was how Roth made it out of his mansion. An escape bed, he called it.

With a shrug, I step toward the gaudy upholstered bedframe, contemplating where a switch or button might be cleverly concealed, then the door opens.

"I'll sleep when I'm dead," my alleged aunt says by way of hello. "I'm pleased you live by this adage as well."

She wears the same bone-white suit from our earlier encounter, as sharp and flawless as she is. Not a wisp of her shiny hair is out of place, and her face glows with vivacity. Despite the hour, she looks fit for a gala.

Or her quinceañera, more like. *Isn't it well past her bedtime by now?*

"Want to have some fun?" Valeria asks, a villainous twinkle in her eye. I'm guessing her idea of a good time is completely unlike mine.

Don't be a fool. Water polo, soccer, getting lost on pebblestone beaches, the things I used to love, are entertainments for the boy I once was. The boy with the wool safely covering his eyes. I've no idea what fun is to me any longer.

Still, I hesitate. This causes Valeria to approach me, her unhurried gait as dignified as a tiger's.

She embodies the meaning of her name: strength.

"¿Dónde está el gobernador?" I ask her in Spanish, trying to bypass the redundancy of the translator necklace. But this proves futile, as the device around my neck repeats my question in English. *Where is the governor?*

"You speak Spanish? You might be more than just looks after all," Valeria says, seeming pleased. "The Lone Star is still with the lieutenant."

She then surprises me by reaching out to touch me, laughing when I pull away.

"So jumpy," she jeers. "Stay still."

Cross at giving her the upper hand—*Tigers can smell weakness*—I force myself to stand unflinching.

She traces a finger along my translator to the back of my neck, then presses a series of buttons, disabling the device. "Let's test if I can trust you."

She doesn't drop her hand. Instead, Valeria curls her long fingers around my throat.

I remember our earlier encounter and her warning. It was more like a threat, clear as Salazar crystal.

Never lie to me again.

That's going to be difficult. Everything about me is a lie.

"It's useful having someone here to practice my English with," she says. "Even if you *are* a boring northerner . . ." The tips of her sharp nails dig into my skin, drawing blood. "Is that why the Lone Star brought you? To be my companion?"

Not on your life.

I say nothing, but don't break from her inquisitive gaze.

Big cats are predators that prefer to ambush prey. If I show no fear by looking her in the eyes, announcing myself as a predator too, she will be less likely to attack.

"Follow me, nephew," Valeria commands, releasing my windpipe.

If I'm not going to rest, it's a better use of my time to go with her and scope out more of the fortress. *I'll sleep when I'm dead* is right.

"Después de ti," I say, not conceding *everything* to the girl. *After you.* I extend my arm toward the open door.

She smiles, approving of my stubbornness.

"We're going to be friends, aren't we, Theo?" she declares, like it isn't really a question. She has an eerie, wistful expression on her unnaturally symmetrical face, similar to the one Roth had when taking stock of me in the Beast after my final runaway attempt.

I don't like it.

But I answer her delusional assertion with a coy smirk and an impish shrug. Better to play the puppet. Let her believe she is the master. Like with Governor.

I follow Valeria out of my room and down a long corridor that ends with a glass elevator. We walk slowly, quietly, and alone. The armed cartel women who I saw guarding her earlier today are nowhere in sight. From what I can tell, she has no weapon either.

Valeria scans her ringed thumb and the doors immediately ping open. As we enter the see-through compartment, I eyeball the gurgling water fountain in the entrance lobby three floors down, the two cartel men at the front door holding semiautomatics, then Valeria's choice of statement footwear. I'd install an elevator too, if I had to walk around this mansion in those torture devices.

"Doesn't the capo run the cartel from Mexico City?" I ask, breaking the silence. "Why do you live here, and not with your mom?"

Get her talking. Gather intel. Keep a look out for an exit plan.

"I don't live *here*," she scoffs, as if this sprawling estate is beneath her. "I left the Salazar property in Mexico City to be a part of the Lone Star's welcoming committee."

She orders something in the clipped code language, and the elevator dings closed. We drop smoothly to ground level.

"Did you really invent the cartel's language?" I question. "Impressive." *What is she, a wunderkind?*

144

"That's just a taste of what I'm capable of," she answers, strutting out into the lobby.

Valeria keeps her leisurely pace as we head into another extensive corridor, giving me adequate time to scour future break-out options.

Double windows flank the back entrance, no obvious locks. Four armed cartel men pace the grounds outside. No windows in the hallway.

After we make a series of right turns, we reach a doorway blocked by two armed cartel men whose biceps are as thick as my waist. When they see Valeria, they break into smiles and quickly step aside. She rattles off something to the men in their secret language, and I guess it must have been a wisecrack because all three of them snicker.

This girl can make scary men with guns laugh.

I wonder briefly if I was the butt of the joke.

We walk through the door and straight into an after-hours club scene. A full-blown indoor grotto, picturesque and humming with bathing-suit-clad men and women dancing to bass-heavy music and drinking champagne. A boy in sea-green trunks screams, wild, before cannonballing into the pool, soaking a group of girls in tiny bikinis and stilettos. Every single one of them has Tape on their chests, the rich kid's drug of choice.

I'm disappointed by my aunt's cliché idea of fun.

But Valeria doesn't stop to join in on the late-night revelry. Our path clears, and every head turns to watch as Valeria and I, a stranger in a Texas State Guard uniform, walk down the rocky pool's edge before disappearing into what looks like a small cave entrance.

We're met by a heavy door that requires her fingerprint scan to enter.

"Another party?" I ask, skeptical of what's on the other side. A VIP section? Still not my idea of fun. But maybe I can get her to talk more if she partakes in the flowing champagne.

"It is," Valeria says with a smile.

The door slides open, we step inside, and my heart jumps into my throat.

This is not a VIP party room. This is a torture chamber.

The four walls and ceiling are mirrored, as if the cartel takes pleasure in having pain reflected back at them.

What are you made of? the glass asks.

My eyes land first on a woman in her underclothes, strapped to a steel table, a wet piece of cloth clinging to her face. Her red-painted toes curl in agony as a cartel man in a designer suit pours water over her nose and mouth. She gags, fighting to breathe.

The woman and floor are both drenched. I avert my eyes from the bloodstained drain at the center of the concrete floor and see a young man wearing a slim black leather eye patch over his right eye. His swollen hands are cuffed behind his chair, which gives him a front row seat to the torture table.

He's being forced to watch the woman drown.

The man's stubble-bearded face is twisted in pain, his golden skin and dark curls dripping with water. *He was waterboarded too,* I realize with a sinking horror.

Did they pluck out his eyeball first? Is that his blood in the drain?

No. It's an old wound. The Salazars would never cover up their work. It's like art to them.

His single red-rimmed eye spares me a quick glance, and I see it fill with hate as he takes in my uniform.

He thinks I'm the enemy. My skin crawls underneath my costume, and I have to stop myself from shouting to the man, *I'm not one of them!*

I can feel Valeria's sharp gaze on me, dissecting my reaction.

Am I the sort of guy who will yell for them to stop? Am I the sort who will try to run? Will I shrink from the screams, or will I laugh like Valeria?

Am I a Roth or a Wright?

What am I made of?

I pick my words carefully. She might just strap me up on that table next.

"What did they do wrong?"

With a simple lift of Valeria's smooth hand, the torture stops. The woman beneath the cloth spits up a torrent of coughs and gulps for air.

Valeria breathes deep, enjoying the sounds of a woman struggling for her life. "The better question would be, *What have they done right?*"

I feel guilty even breathing while this woman drowns, bound to a table. *Am I really going to just stand here and do nothing?* Why aren't I whipping Mira's knife out from my boot, chopping off my pathetic puppet strings, and putting an end to all of this?

Concentrate. Think smart.

There are two of them, one of me. One heavy-duty gun to my knife, and whatever Valeria has up her silk sleeves.

And like the captive staring daggers at Valeria, I've learned that pleas for mercy are wasted breaths. They only make things worse.

The woman on the table suddenly goes silent. Her frail body falls slack against her ties, and for a painful second I don't see her chest rising. Then a muffled gasp escapes from below the cloth. "Andrés . . . no puedo . . ." *Andrés . . . I can't . . .*

The one-eyed man, who I assume is Andrés, finally cracks. "¡Tienes que pelear, mi amor! ¡Respira! ¡Lucha!" he screams in broken cries. *You have to fight, my love! Breathe! Fight!*

Valeria moves to the tormented man. Every one of his muscles strains as he battles to get to the woman beside him. The sight is unwatchable. His restraints are so fixed, he doesn't move an inch. Valeria examines him, unmoved herself.

"They are always whining they don't have enough water," she says cruelly with a shrug of her slender shoulders, a familial gesture that shoots an ice-cold shudder down my spine.

"You disapprove," Valeria surmises. I keep my mouth sealed. I'm petrified of what will come out, or *in.*

"I'm only giving them what they asked for . . . ," she teases, signaling for the water to start again. "How is it my fault they don't understand they want more than they can stomach?"

My own stomach turns.

"These two are thieves," Valeria continues calmly, standing over the thrashing woman. "Falcons reported barrels of illegal rainwater hidden in their pathetic town. They thought they could steal from the capo . . . but she owns everything that touches this land. It's amusing, really, imagining these *mice* trying to fight back."

She switches her fixation to me. "Have you heard of the People's Militia?"

"No," I answer, using my voice to muffle the sounds of the woman's smothered heaving. *I'm going to crack any minute now.* I clear my throat. "I'm guessing these two are members?" I say unfazed, almost dismissive.

Valeria nods, her dangle earrings swinging like Guard's batons. "My family loses an obnoxious amount of time and resources making sure the People's Militia stays a dead cause."

These two are going to die. It's a fact I have to swallow without flinching, but it goes down like shattered glass.

"Our sicarios work to make sure the outside world never hears their name. Their members hide and scatter, but there's an infectious nest of them, aiming to plague the capo's territory." She saunters over to me and brushes back the strands of hair that block my eyes. "They're not unlike your Common."

She must've heard me stop breathing. "The Common isn't mine," I exhale, hoping it's not my last breath.

She flashes that cutting smile. "You don't think I saw the videos? I know your part in the Battle for Dallas."

I stare Valeria square in the eyes, letting her know I'm made of steel as well, and we can cross swords all night and I won't bend.

"Then you saw I was a prisoner of the Common. All I did that night was tell the city I'm a Roth. Call me selfish or arrogant, I wanted to come out of hiding and take my place next to my grandfather."

"And what a night to do it," she presses, trying her best to suffocate the truth out of me.

"Mira gave me the stage. She thought I was in league with the Common," I lie and shrug. "Her fatal mistake, my opportunity."

"And here I was thinking Mira was your girlfriend," Valeria says in mock disappointment.

"Mira Goodwin better be prepared for the day she sees me again," I spit, like it's a threat and not my greatest pipe dream. I clench my fists for better effect.

Valeria titters, looking pleased again.

Finally, she lifts her hand for her goon to stop the water.

I brace my nerves for the woman's cries for air.

They never come.

She doesn't move.

This sends Andrés's screaming into overdrive, the man's heartache pouring from his chest in one shrill wail.

Somewhere to my right, Valeria says something in her code tongue.

I level my eyes on the Texas State Guard leering back at me in the mirror. *She died while I just stood here.* In the reflection beside mine, the cartel man's hands tear the cloth away from the woman's empty face.

I make myself look.

She was young. Only a few years older than me. Her big chestnut eyes had so much left to see in this life.

Is no one going to close her eyes? I think.

I say nothing.

Andrés's shrieking turns into a raspy curse. "Algún día tus fortalezas arderán y tu familia no tendrá suficiente agua en el mundo para apagar las llamas. Te lo prometon." *Someday your strongholds will burn, and your family won't have enough water in the world to put out the flames. I promise you.*

Valeria pounces, unsheathing Mira's knife from my boot. *How did she . . . ? There must be cameras in my room.*

She's been surveilling me. Does she know I've been trying to escape too?

Reaching her prisoner, Valeria twists a fistful of Andrés's damp hair and yanks back his head. His exposed throat glistens with sweat.

She drags my knife's blade teasingly across his bare chest. The razor-sharp tip hovers above an artery just below his left ear.

"My mother doesn't approve of me getting my hands dirty," Valeria says, "but I'm not the kind of girl who likes to just sit and watch."

Breathing hard through his nose, Andrés bravely faces his imminent death with his wide eye boring into his executioner's. He must know she wants a struggle, and he's refusing her the satisfaction.

He's a fighter.

And what am I? Think fast or this guy dies.

I take a step forward before she starts to cut.

"I have to say, it's not how *I'd* do it," I sneer. "Is this really how you stop a plague? It's all just so . . . underwhelming."

Amazingly, my dig halts the blade.

"If you want to show Governor—the Lone Star as you call him—just what his progeny is capable of, you'll have to think bigger than this."

"Are you seriously referring to that stupid catchphrase? *Everything is bigger in Texas?*" she scoffs, clutching at her purple gemstone. *Did Roth give her that necklace as a gift?*

I want to choke her with it.

"Show the capo and your future lieutenants that you won't just cut down militia mice . . ."

I take a step closer, pulling her in with my strings. "You'll burn them."

Valeria purses her glossy lips, pondering.

"*You* will be the *start* of the flames," I press, drawing from the captive's threat. "It's not how you'll end."

She lowers Mira's knife, then points the blade at me instead.

My blood, a quarter the same as hers, freezes. *Did she sniff out my bullshit?*

"I *knew* we were going to be friends," she says, lively, like she's not standing next to a woman she has just made a corpse. "What do you have in mind?"

"Oh, I've got some ideas," I reply, exaggerating this half truth. I can learn to think like a murderous villain. It's in my genes.

If I play this right, I can create an opportunity to break not just myself free, but a captured militia member as well.

It's not just my life on the line anymore.

I try to make eye contact with Andrés. Give the broken man some hint of hope that I'm on his side. But when he looks at me through one glaring slit, it's clear that to him, I'm a monster in a Guard's uniform. No better than my diabolical aunt standing next to me.

But that's not my truth. Hands behind my back, I trace the rebellion tattoo carved into my right wrist, reassuring myself of who I am.

I'm a Common member, burning yellow underneath this facade. Rebellion in my heart, just like him.

I told myself in the south Texas desert that fighting for truth is greater than my own well-being.

Now's my time to prove it.

Resist much, obey little.

MIRA

The debate about which crossing to choose was heated and tedious. During the three-and-a-half-hour car ride, it was nothing but border maps, strategies, and minor blowups, but in the end we took a vote.

Seven to one.

I couldn't help relishing the outcome. The last time Alexander and I sparred over the best game plan to cross an international border, I was outvoted.

Now it's Alexander's turn to lose.

Tonight, I'll take the wins where I can get them.

Northeast of our position, a mile up the road, a string of lights appears, cutting across the darkness like a fuse caught on fire.

Headlights. Moving directly toward us.

I flick my eyes to my wristwatch: 2:54 a.m.

Right on time.

Pulling down the visor of my new ballistic helmet—one of the many gifts I found in Ciro's offering—I throw Alexander a look. *Told you.*

He scoffs, yanking up his night vision goggles.

Theo's father argued for our mission to take us to the Gulf and travel by boat. Avoiding the wall. No surprise there, considering he spent his newfound life in Canada as a shipping magnate.

But Lucía's plan is far better; it's shorter, and if everything proceeds as designed, faster.

Besides, Lucía's pulled it off before.

"You're a genius," Kano whispers, adrenalized, shaking the mastermind's shoulder in lieu of applause.

Lucía readjusts the translator device that hugs her upper ear like a silver cuff. *Another offering from Ciro.* The tech translates languages seamlessly and discreetly, and is disguised as a simple piece of jewelry.

"Or crazy," Lucía mutters to herself, but my device picks up her whisper.

"Just another word for *brave*," I remind her and everyone listening.

Skye approaches Lucía's side, hiding her translator under her tight jet-black braid. "Maybe now we can better understand each other."

Lucía purses her lips.

On my right, Ava folds and puts away her map, staring out at our target.

We're ninety yards from the Big Fence. And the bridge. *The Unmapped Passage*, Lucía calls it, the crossing that will lead us over the Rio Grande and into Mexico.

Our only cover is the natural cloak of darkness. *We must be quick and quiet.* We abandoned our SUV miles ago, and if this ends in disaster, all we can do is run.

The plan will work, I prod my nerves.

I turn my gaze from the oncoming trucks, south toward the bridge's towers and gate, and feel a rush of power as I watch the Border Guards staring directly at me. Seeing nothing.

Clueless as to what's about to happen.

"Let's not get overly excited," Barend warns. "The trucks arriving is only step one." He sets his jaw and cocks his gun, rolling a black mask over his forehead and mouth, all the way down to his uniform's collar. The high-tech materials absorb the starlight so expertly, he disappears right before my eyes.

"See you on the other side," Kano says to Ava and me, flashing his bright smile before securing his own mask.

The line of trucks is five minutes away now.

They're moving fast.

We'd better move faster.

Ava slips her helmet over her red hair and squeezes my hand.

No fear.

"I've always wondered what it would be like to be a twin," Lucía says, looking at the two of us. She tugs a Goodwin mask over her slicked-back ponytail, covering her chestnut- brown eyes, her dark rose-bud lips. Vanishing behind the face of Ava Goodwin.

"So have I," Haven mutters beneath her own 3D-printed face that looks identical to mine.

Her statement isn't despairing or bitter. Just her truth. The reason she's out here fighting.

My mother. I tug at my sleeve and expose my right wrist, taking a last look at the ink stained into my skin. I trace my gloved fingers along the yellow petals of a black-eyed Susan, my mother's emblem, which hug the curve of a radiant eye.

It's my mother watching me. My father. Rayla.

Not the Guard. Or surveillance. Their power's about to come to its end. *We're here to see to that.*

"It's time," Lucía announces. She grabs Skye's arm, pulling her close. "Remember, stick to the script."

Skye grins. "That's not how I work." She yanks Lucía's gun from her belt. "I'll be needing this," she says and sets off first, throwing up her chin like a woman in charge.

"All eyes," Ava says as Kano and Barend disperse, stealing into their positions.

Alexander lingers, shaking his head like he has a mind to desert. But finally, he turns and follows the soldiers into the dark.

"Do not hesitate. Be forceful," Haven instructs Ava and me as she moves into position. "That is how the Guards will know you are one of them."

She bends her knees and shoulders to even her height with Lucía's. They stand side by side in front of us, placing their hands behind their backs. Ava and I hand them guns.

"Do what you need to sell it," Lucía says.

Ava nods and grips Lucía by her ponytail, making her intake a sharp hiss of pain.

"Good," Lucía murmurs beneath her mask.

"If they open fire," Haven whispers, "stay behind me."

I nod, but I have no intention of staying behind in any capacity. Ava shoves Lucía forward, and with a deep breath, I grab a fistful of Haven's collar and push her ahead.

With their baggy jackets and matching boots, the pair looks near enough like twins.

Twins worth a substantial bounty.

This plan will work, I repeat to myself right as Skye shouts.

"Guards!" she yells. Her voice projects across the empty terrain dividing us and the two surveillance towers.

It's dead silent out here on the edge of nowhere.

"Disable the weapons and speak with me!"

Skye stops her advance and toes the line that splits dark from light. One more step and she will walk into the blinding perimeter of the spotlights. One more step and she will activate the automated guns. The lasers. The drones.

One more inch and she's in the kill zone.

"I have captured Ava and Mira Goodwin!" she shouts, waving the gun in her hand, gesturing for us to move forward.

My sister and I drive "Ava" and "Mira" the last few steps to stand beside their captor.

"Open the gate!" Skye commands, like someone accustomed to being obeyed.

The harsh beam of a searchlight flashes on our gang of five. For an instant I shift my weight to the balls of my feet, hankering to run, but I dig in the heels of my boots and stand my ground.

We're still sixty yards from the two towers that sandwich the stainless steel gate.

And on the other side, the bridge.

From this distance, the Guards will fall for the Goodwin masks. They'll have to trust their facial recognition cameras to be their eyes and judge.

Exactly what the prosthetic masks are designed to do. *To trick surveillance.*

"Identify yourself!" a cold voice orders through a loudspeaker.

"The name's Skye Lin!" our posse's leader shouts. "Might have heard of me?"

"Stupid," Lucía whispers hotly.

We were to give away no names. But maybe it will help. Her reputation might persuade them that this setup is real . . .

"That assassin's in Dallas, locked in Guardian Tower!" the hostile voice returns.

"Aw, are you guys left out of the Loyalist dispatches?" Skye digs. "I escaped! Took the Traitorous Twins with me. I couldn't find the State Guard anywhere to hand them over, but I knew the Border Guard would be here . . . you always are."

Silence.

"Do you want a piece of the reward, or not?" Skye yells with a biting impatience. "Open the gate!"

Nobody moves. And neither does the gate.

To my right, Ava kicks the back of "Ava's" knees, sending her to the rocky ground. Lucía releases an echoed cry.

"Mira" mocks a fight to escape her bonds. "Use force," Haven whispers urgently behind her mask. "Make them believe."

Steeling myself, I jab my boot into her leg and snatch her red mane as she drops to her backside. "Stay down, you filthy Glut!" I shout, the words like acid in my throat.

"It's your own heads, then!" Skye calls out. "I'll be sure to tell Governor Roth his Border Guard let his twins get away." Her warning rings across the dead air.

Still, the metal gate doesn't stir.

I feel Ava bristle beside me. *All of this shouting's leading nowhere.*

A deep line creases Skye's forehead, her eyes narrowing beneath her thick lashes. Her trigger finger taps against Lucía's pistol.

No. We can't outgun them. Our only chance is to outwit them.

Does the promise of riches and arresting the infamous twins really hold no power over these Guards?

Did we overestimate our value?

"I'll take my bounty to another unit!" Skye shouts, her final rehearsed lines. "And yours will end up in a prison cell!"

She doesn't wait for a response. Signaling for us to leave, Skye flicks up her middle finger to the towers in a bold show of insolence.

I expect the cries of sirens. Or the first rounds of machine-gun fire.

But it's the Guard's electronic voice that responds, halting our faux retreat. "We could just take the prisoners from you. And the reward—"

"You could try!" Ava challenges, unable to stay silent.

Ava can't ever keep her mouth closed.

The plan was for neither of us to join in on the exchange, evading any chance the Guard might realize the true Ava and Mira really *are* here.

Hauling "Mira" up by her hair, I flick off the safety of her pistol, then mine. I press my helmet against Haven's ear, pushing out a barely audible whisper. "Do you see any drones? Scent Hunters?"

Haven shakes her head. "Look . . . the gate . . ."

It's opening.

It's working.

Skye lets out a brazen laugh. "Finally!"

Before she can take a victorious stride forward, Lucía stops her with a warning.

"Wait. Test it first."

Skye bends to pick up the nearest rock. She tosses it a few feet in front of our line and I hold my breath as it lands.

No bullets, lasers, or hidden landmines sound off.

Skye doesn't wait another second before charging into the kill zone.

"Step two," I whisper, invigorated.

This plan will work.

I steal a glimpse over my shoulder and see the column of trucks has gained significant ground. Almost two minutes away now.

Ava and I strong-arm our captives into the spotlights, Haven and Lucía both feigning admirable attempts to break free.

The effort to make my feet walk and not sprint to the wide-open gate drains the last of my willpower. With every step I think the Guard will enable the automated weapons, but our posse makes it to the opening unscathed.

Right as our boots stomp over the threshold and hit the bridge, every light in the vicinity cuts out.

Step three.

Alexander, the sharpshooter, I think, reluctantly impressed. It's a rare skill for a soldier, as high-precision targets are left for autonomous weapons. But he found his bulls-eye: the bridge's standby generator, poking out from the base of the west tower.

"It's a trick!" a Guard shouts.

In my mind's eye I see Kano and Barend racing through the darkness for the gate.

"Mow them down!" another Guard screams.

A bullet sings past my ear. Then another.

"East tower!" Lucía cries, ripping off her Goodwin mask, darting toward the limestone structure.

Haven shoves down her own mask, wrenching on her night vision goggles. As we rush after Lucía, she elbows me back, shielding me with her body as she returns fire.

"Aim to wound," I remind her. "Not kill!"

Haven gives no sign she heard me.

Ava and Skye set off for the west tower where the shouts of a Border Guard echo down from the ten-story staircase. "Stand down immediately!"

I can only see six feet in front of me in this blackout. My own goggles bang against my collarbone as I run, useless around my neck.

Useless like my gun. *I can't shoot blind in the dark.*

But it's either night vision or concealment; I can't have both.

I almost make the decision to rip off my helmet.

No, I chide myself, *keep your head. Keep your face covered. Stick to your part of the plan.*

No one can know I was here.

When Haven and I reach the east tower, we find Lucía crouched against the wall beside an open door.

"How many?" Haven asks.

Lucía holds up her trigger finger in answer.

Only one.

That's all the information Haven needs before she barrels into the tower.

Two shots. Hers or the Guard's? Six. Ten. Then I lose count.

I rip off my helmet to bolt to her aid, but Lucía grabs my arm. "Wait!" she says, pinning me to the wall.

It's gone silent.

"Haven?" I yell into the surveillance tower, my heartbeat pounding in my ears.

"I'm here!" Haven's gravelly voice reaches me. "He is dead!"

She appears like a ghost in the doorway. "All clear."

Lucía nods, sprinting to provide backup for the other groups.

"We agreed not to kill," I whisper.

She answers simply. "He was a Guard."

I wonder fleetingly if the rest of the team will stick to the plan.

"All clear!" Ava cries from the west tower.

My muscles unclench and I loosen my white-knuckled clutch on my gun.

"All clear!" Kano and Barend shout simultaneously from the direction of the bridge.

"We passed," Haven says, waving for me to move with her to the gate.

Her way of saying we lived. We won.

"Ah!" an unmasked Kano exclaims, appearing out of nowhere by my side. "Here's our step four, pulling right in."

The front truck's headlights so overwhelm my eyes, I have to turn away. When I do, I spot three bodies. One slumped over the metal stairwell of the west tower. The other two splayed out on the concrete near the center of the bridge. A Guard, and likely two cartel men.

I should be glad none of the bodies are ours. Still, I look to Ava, who stands on the opposite side of the gate, holstering her pistol.

Was it her bullet or Skye's?

The plan was to zip-tie the Guards and cartel men, unmask Haven and Lucía, show them the twins were never here. We're just a band of raiders, after whatever's in the water tankers. Not Common members seeking to cross the border.

But that plan was just shot to hell.

160

Ava avoids my gaze, shoving her helmet into her rucksack. "Are we all here?" she shouts as the line of five autonomous tanker trucks rumble past.

The massive cylindrical tanks are a dull coal black, not white, and carry no label like real State Guard water trucks.

But there's water in there, or at least there *was*.

Lucía hid inside one of these on her first crossing. She almost drowned, but she made it to the other side.

While the team starts a roll call, I speculate on what could possibly be inside these tankers now. *If there's anything at all.*

"Marley!" I say when it's my turn, making sure to use my code name.

The trucks slow to a stop along the bridge and park one after the other like a small-scale railcar. Instantly, the pavement below their tires glows an electric blue.

They're charging. Just as they should be.

"You did well," Lucía tells Skye, holding out her hand for her gun.

"Was that a compliment?" Skye replies with exaggerated shock, relinquishing the borrowed pistol. "It has a nice kick to it. Oh, and you'll definitely need to reload . . ."

"Let's move!" Alexander yells, marching for the last tanker in the line. He wrenches off his goggles, his narrow black eyes looking past me, over the bridge.

South. Toward his father and son.

"Good shot," I say, offering the smallest twig of an olive branch. I expect him to plow right by me. Which he does. But he graces me with a response.

"The governor trained me well," he says tersely over his shoulder, not slowing his pace.

"I bet Roth never expected that training to be used *against* him," Kano observes, falling in by my side.

Just like Roth didn't expect my father to move against him.

When we reach the trucks, Haven runs her calloused fingers along the stainless steel. She waves Ava over, pulling us close. "I know these trucks," she says. "Camp 11. We filled them with biofuel."

Ava and I lock eyes. *So Roth* was *illegally engaging in international trade.*

"In the final trucks," she continues, climbing the three-rung ladder affixed to the tanker's flank, "the Inmates loaded gold."

She presses open a hatch, plunges in her hand, and brings up a single golden brick.

"There's movement on the other side of the bridge," Barend informs us, binoculars pressed against his jutting brow.

"The cartel men were your marks!" Alexander rebukes, shaking his head at Barend and Kano like they're amateurs. "If he called us in . . ."

"We took out both of them!" Kano insists, gesturing to the bodies on the pavement.

"A woman," Barend reports. "In the south tower. She's in plain clothes. No confirmation of a weapon."

Kano starts to move toward the bridge, but Lucía grabs his arm. "No, let me," she says.

It takes two seconds for Kano to get the message in English, and he nods, holstering his gun.

Lucía looks up to Haven. "A brick, please. Quick."

Haven descends the ladder, passing Lucía a bar worth a whole year's tuition at Strake.

"I'll meet you across the bridge," Lucía tells me, and sets off at a sprint.

"Our tactics are to pay for silence now?" Alexander admonishes under his breath, before barking orders for the group to scale the ladder and squeeze into the truck's tank.

But Haven leads Ava and me to the front. "There's room for two in the cab. Stay together."

We nod and she helps us clamber through the high door to cram ourselves on the floor below the navigation panels.

As my sister and I sit inside the immobile truck, I count every excruciating second of the five minutes it takes the tanker's battery to recharge.

When the wheels finally start turning, I grip Ava's hand. *This is it.*

Our view is marred by the truck in front of us, but I imagine the south gate is about to open as scheduled, allowing the first of our line to pass through without complication.

Step five.

The illuminated tower comes up fast on our right.

We made it across the bridge.

And we're gaining speed.

"Do you see Lucía?" Ava asks urgently, crouching beside me. "We can't leave her!"

"Ten o'clock," I say, pointing out my window to the blur of white running south from the border wall. I see a flash of the golden brick clutched between two hands.

It's the civilian woman Barend spotted in the tower.

Not Lucía.

"I don't see her!" Ava says, panic punching every word.

"We have to stop the truck!" I yell, scouring the panels for how the hell to halt an autonomous convoy.

Then a *bang!* outside Ava's door.

Lucía's face slams against the glass as she struggles to gain ahold of something—*anything.* Ava flies to the door and from a selection of bright neon buttons, manages to choose the right one. The window lowers and I lunge to help Ava pull Lucía into the cab.

Exhaustion weighs down my legs and arms and we all lie where we fall, listening to the screaming wind.

There's barely room to move. But we don't have to. The trucks are doing that for us.

"The woman will stay quiet," Lucía whispers, and I believe her.

The less death we can leave behind the better.

I don't know if giving the woman the gold was a bribe or a mercy. Who knows what led her to this isolated border crossing.

All I know is the plan worked.

Step six.

We made it into Mexico.

AVA

We fly down Mexican Federal Highway 85 at eighty miles an hour, straight as a bullet fired toward Monterrey, smuggled inside the final tanker truck in a line of five.

We're surrounded by a blanket of darkness—the trucks' headlights cut off the moment we left US soil. There's not even the gleam of the stars or moon to light our way tonight.

Mira, Lucía, and I huddle around our autonomous vehicle's intricate dashboard, studying the ultraprecise, high-definition Live Map. We're taking full advantage of the high-tech navigational system before it's back to strictly paper maps as our guide. For the last hour, it's been just small towns and sweeping deserts with low mountain ranges edging the desolate highway.

Wearing tactical gloves, Lucía uses her thumb and forefinger to zoom out on the digital map, looking ahead to our destination—a small town forty miles outside Monterrey. The headquarters of the People's Militia.

Lucía sought shelter there with her mother and brother for six months until the Salazars' sicarios found them and they were forced to flee again. I wonder how she gained the militia's trust, given that Salazar blood runs through her veins. How did she prove she wasn't a falcon sent by the cartel to take the unruly rebel group down? Whatever the case, I'm piecing together that not only did they believe her, they accepted her into their ranks.

She points to the town on the Live Map, chin lifted, shoulders strong and straight in her sleek charcoal-black uniform.

"The People's Militia will join us on our mission," she says steadfastly, her words translated through my ear cuff in English, making her vow feel all the weightier with the repetition.

And if they refuse?

They won't. Lucía will make sure of it.

Mira opens a small window that divides the truck cabin from the cargo hold. "Fifteen minutes," she says to Haven, crouched on the other side.

"Fifteen minutes," I hear Haven echo to the others cramped in the back among the bags filled with gold.

Dirty money Roth stole from his own state.

Lucía's finger moves farther south, hovering over Monterrey, the capital of Nuevo León, Mexico. Are memories flooding her mind? Thoughts of her family, her upbringing?

The industrial city lies in the foothills of the Sierra Madre Oriental and, according to the map, isn't choked with skyscrapers. In a different time, when I didn't have eyes only for completing my mission, I would have loved to tour Lucía's hometown streets and see how she lived.

Lucía ran from her city just like we ran from Dallas. Monterrey can't be that much different from our hometown. Violence, class warfare, not enough of anything to go around.

She just had better views.

"Trouble," I say, alarmed, pointing to a series of blinking red dots that just appeared out of nowhere on the map. They converge right where the highway exits the long roadcut we're driving through, blocking our path.

"An ambush!" Lucía warns the team through our ear cuffs. "A rival cartel who dares to raid a Salazar transport."

The worry that creases her brow tells me she didn't foresee this happening. Who would risk challenging the most powerful cartel in Mexico? The payback would be unimaginable.

"I thought no one could stop the trucks once the transport was underway?" Barend shouts from the cargo hold.

As if to answer Barend's question, the autonomous machine guns atop all five tanker trucks suddenly open fire. *Bam, bam, bam!* Rapid and ruthless.

"The vehicles are programmed to never stop, yes," Lucía says. "But that doesn't mean there aren't those who will try to *make* them."

The cache of gold and biofuel in these trucks is enough to change the lives of entire cities—whole regions—if stolen by the right person. But the rival cartel will most likely use it to further their own violent means.

I feel an angry vein bulge in my neck, matching the one on Mira's.

"Uh, team, what's happening?" Kano calls out from the back of the truck.

"Is this a highway robbery?" Skye asks Lucía, shoving her head through the window divide.

"The trucks are under attack!" I shout, answering them both. "Get ready to jump!"

That was always the plan: when the transport slowed outside a remote Salazar territory checkpoint fifty miles from their stronghold, Haven would force open a hidden emergency door she knows exists because she once installed one herself at a Camp, then we would all jump out onto the rocky desert floor in relative safety.

I've escaped from a water truck before, back in Montana, on my way to the US-Canadian border. Jumping was my idea. But that autonomous truck wasn't driving anywhere close to eighty miles per hour when I bided my time for a slow left turn.

This fall will kill us.

So will these bandits if they manage to stop the transport and find us still inside.

"We're moving too fast!" Alexander insists.

"We know that!" Mira snaps.

"Is there some kind of Crisis Mode we can enable?" Barend asks, urgent.

Lucía listens to his question through her ear cuff, then shakes her head, rattled. "There is nothing," she says, although I see her mind desperately racing for a solution.

A bitter thought flicks across my own mind. *If Owen were here on this mission,* he *could have programmed the truck to stop.*

"Maybe that will stop us," Skye says forebodingly. I see the orange cloud of destruction reflected off the window's glass before I hear the explosion.

All at once I'm slammed against the side of the cabin, hard, colliding foreheads with Mira. Lucía crashes against my stomach, knocking the air out of my lungs. My diaphragm spasms, and I groan as I struggle to breathe, my head pounding from ramming against my sister's.

Just as Mira helps pull me to my feet, the three of us pitch forward against the windshield, smashing violently into the bulletproof glass as the truck recovers from the blast wave.

The transport continues to whirl forward.

"Lockdown Mode enabled," an automated voice warns over and over, red lights flashing.

Every door lock on the truck seals with an audible *click!*

"They blew up the road!" Mira exclaims, her knee jammed into my back. "We're penned in by the hills—will the transport turn around?"

Still painfully winded, I have to take slow deep breaths through my nose and exhale through my mouth, stretching my diaphragm, before I'm able to lift my cheek from the glass to face our latest challenge.

A mile ahead, it looks as if a huge bite—from some angry and greedy beast—has been taken out of the road. Blackened orange-red flames lick the starless sky, plumes of smoke billowing off into a windless night. Slabs of concrete from the blasted road lie strewn across our path.

But the transport does not retreat. It does the opposite.

Giant flat metal plates bust out of a compartment at the front of the armored vehicles, turning the trucks into bulldozers. The lead truck rams a busted chunk of concrete the size of a bus tire head-on, dragging it forward into the fire. Then the truck drops, disappearing from sight.

Are we driving straight into the bomb's crater? The second truck plunges into the fiery hole, then the third.

A suicidal game of follow-the-leader.

Before the fourth truck initiates its death drop, I scream, "The cargo hold!"

The sentry guns on our roof have never stopped firing. The metal floor of the truck vibrates with each automated pull of the trigger as I make my way to the back of the cabin.

That's when I fully notice the cartel robbers are not returning fire. *Why?*

The biofuel.

A small mercy. For a single rapid heartbeat, I'm relieved Roth traffics in such explosive goods.

"You first," Mira tells Lucía, then clasps her hands together to form a ladder. Lucía quickly steps onto Mira's palms and shoves her way through the narrow window that leads into the cargo hold.

"Hurry!" Haven shouts from the other side. She reaches out her gloved hands, urgently trying to grasp hold of us.

She needs to open the emergency door at the back of the truck. Time is running out.

"Now you," I rasp to Mira.

But as I help lift my sister into the window opening, our truck plunges into the crater at a forty-five-degree vertical angle, sending Mira and me flying back onto the dashboard.

Somehow this latest body slam gives me my breath back.

Unable to find anything to hang on to, Mira and I slide roughly back and forth while the truck bulldozes its way across the blasted hole.

"Ava, come on!" Barend yells. He battles his way to the window and reaches out his muscle-roped arm.

But every attempt at grabbing hold of his lifeline sends me hurling to the hard floor.

Exhausted and running out of options *and* time, I feel the truck begin to clamber up the other side of the crater, and I know what has to be done.

I just don't know if my aunt will let me do it.

"Haven, get everybody ready to jump, *now!*" I shout. "Mira and I will find another way!"

"I will not leave you!" Haven argues, pushing Barend aside. She grips the window's edge hard for balance.

She means it, down to her very bones.

But she has to, or we will all be trapped inside this truck and the mission will die before it ever really began.

"I know a way out," I lie as I'm thrown helter-skelter against the passenger door. "Owen taught me, in case I ever got into trouble. Now go!"

Haven's hard-lined face pushes through the window, each deep crease around her eyes and forehead earned from a lonely life at a labor camp.

She can't be captured by the raider cartel. She deserves a better death than that.

"Please, Haven, you have to get out," I beg.

"We'll be right behind you, Haven, go!" Mira urges.

"You heard them, they're fine," Alexander grunts, pulling Haven away from us. "The ideal time to jump is *right now!*"

"Let's not get handsy," Kano warns. He pushes Alexander, forcing him to release my aunt.

But then the truck levels out, back on solid ground, causing everyone in the cargo hold to lose their footing and tumble on top of each other.

The tanker truck has yet to accelerate after its climb. *This is the slowest speed the truck will ever hit.*

It's now or never.

I pull myself to my feet, hissing with pain from the nonstop blows my body has taken.

"See you on the other side!" I shout through the window, then slam it shut, silencing further challenge.

One look to Mira, and she knows I was lying.

I don't know a way out.

We give our team a ten-second head start, hoping that one by one, they're leaping out of the truck's emergency door.

Then, together, we start pounding wildly on the vehicle's control panel. I don't believe in luck, but maybe our frantic efforts will trigger something to happen. Maybe we'll get lucky.

Don't be a fool. No amount of button pushing will shut off Lockdown Mode. We're trapped.

I watch helpless as the truck's speed ramps back up to fifty miles per hour . . . sixty . . . seventy. Even if a door magically opened for us now, we wouldn't survive the impact of the drop.

I smash the speedometer with my fist, crying out in frustration. "This can't be how it ends!"

It can't all be over now.

"Ava, look," Mira gasps, pointing out the windshield.

What now?

Battle tanks. Four of them.

Each sixty-ton armored vehicle flies a flag marked by slate-gray skulls and has a gun big enough to fire either high-explosive anti-tank rounds or a guided missile.

And they're all pointed directly at our transport.

Dread washes over me, raising the fine hairs on the back of my neck. Our tanker trucks can't bulldoze their way through this blockade.

Maybe I was wrong about the bandits. Maybe their intention is to *eliminate* the trucks, not steal them.

If they can't get their hands on the goods, then neither will the Salazar capo.

Just as I'm about to grab Mira's hand, thinking all might be lost, each truck in our transport simultaneously discharges missiles into the blockade. Before the tanks can retaliate, the trucks make a unanimous hard right, careering into the desert.

Is the cartel going to give chase?

"Keep trying!" Mira cries, spurring me back into action.

She takes the butt of her pistol and starts ramming it into the control panel. I take out my own gun and thrash the right side of the panel while she takes the left, ignoring the deep ache each blow sends across my battered body.

It doesn't work. The doors are still sealed shut.

My God, what now?

Suddenly the red lights stop flashing. There are two panicked seconds filled with nothing happening, then both doors of the cabin slide open. My heart soars. "We did it!"

The transport slows, moving in a snake pattern across the pitted desert floor, making us a harder target. *We can do this.*

Mira and I approach the passenger door and wait for the truck to swerve left, away from our landing zone. The harsh wind whips the tips of our hair against our faces as we stare out into blackness. We'll have to jump blind.

"Remember to tuck and roll," I say, squeezing her hand.

I feel Mira nod beside me. "You first," she says, pressing back. "I'll follow after you."

Just like we came into this world, I think as I cross my arms over my chest and leap from the vehicle, backward.

I push my legs up, my body forming a tight ball, aiming for the center of my back to take the hit on the ground. Right when I feel impact, I roll, dissipating the force of the fall.

Something large and sharp stops my frenzied spinning.

A cactus. The padding on the uniform Ciro gifted me took most of the spikes, but an exposed part of my neck stings like a legion of assassins threw tiny daggers into my soft flesh.

"Aeron, where are you?" I hear Mira call out my code name, twenty yards away in the dark, somewhere to my left. She sounds more anxious than hurt.

"I'm here," I answer, breathing fast and hard as I shift into a crouch position. "Keep talking."

I follow the sound of my sister's low voice, careful to scan our surroundings for any pursuing cartel men or signs of our separated teammates. I find nothing of either.

"Are you injured?" I ask when I reach Mira, thinking of the sprained ankle she suffered when she jumped out of our bedroom window back at Trinity Heights a lifetime ago.

"I'm good," Mira says hurriedly as I help lift her to her feet. "You?"

"I just lost a fight with a cactus, but I'm fine," I answer, slipping my night vision goggles onto my face.

All at once I can see in the dark. My field of vision is flooded with hyperrealistic images, all tinted green, the color the human eye is most sensitive to. The goggles' image-enhancement tech collects all available light—including infrared that isn't visible to the naked eye—and amplifies it, allowing me to easily see what's happening in a four-hundred-yard radius around me.

Which, right now, is nothing but stoic cacti and mountains standing their ground.

"It could take until sunrise to find the others. Even with the goggles," Mira assesses our situation, fast. "We could be miles from their jumping point."

Before setting off on our border-crossing operation, the team agreed that if someone got lost or separated, we would all meet inside the church at the People's Militia's headquarters.

I pull out my paper map from my waistband. Mira pulls out a simple compass from her vest pocket. Apart from my night vision goggles—Mira's dangle broken around her neck—and our guns, they're our only survival supplies.

We left our packs in the back of the water truck.

My stomach sinks—Mira's birthday present was in mine.

There are more important things to worry about right now.

Like staying alive while traversing a hostile Mexican desert with no food or water.

Two minutes out of the vehicle and I'm already cold and thirsty. Without the searing sun, the nighttime temperature has dropped drastically. *How long can we last in these conditions?*

My best estimate is that we'll need to withstand at least ten miles.

Oh God, is that even possible?

"We've got at least a three-hour walk ahead of us to the town," I inform Mira, keeping the worry from my voice.

Through my goggles, I see Mira's green arm lift a compass and point it south, toward a huge expanse of barren wilderness.

"Maybe more, factoring in the rough terrain," I add, thinking about the cactus-strewn desert floor. My neck feels swollen, the little barbs I couldn't pull out myself still lodged painfully in my skin.

And what about accounting for other dangers? Sicarios? Exposure? Wild animals? The possibility that we just screwed up our mission and ruined our last shot at getting to Roth?

You both must focus on the task at hand. My grandmother's words come rushing back to me, all the way out here in no-one's-land.

And what is *the task at hand?* Mira replied angrily to Rayla in the Montana grasslands on our way north to Canada.

Making it across this prairie.

I take a deep, powerful breath.

Focus on making it across the first mile, Rayla tells me now.

"Task at hand, Ava," Mira says beside me in the dark. *Rayla's giving her strength too.*

"Task at hand," I repeat.

Side by side, we set off into the night, hoping to beat the sunrise.

OWEN

Since awakening from his semivegetable status, the Whiz has become somewhat of a motormouth. Sure, it's a victory that Blaise and I even got the kid talking, but the issue is, he just keeps rattling away the same mind-numbing pleas from the back seat of the car.

"Let me go! . . . They're going to find me! . . . They'll kill us! . . . They will slice you open!"

"If you'd tell us the location," I hiss through gritted teeth, "we could all keep our throats and guts intact!"

My patience is thin. Tightrope thin. It's only hour two of our mission, and I already feel like I'm about to fall and crack before the Whiz does.

Tell us where you stashed the drive, you crufty runt! I open my mouth to shout. But I bite my tongue. Blaise and I are playing good Guard, bad Guard, and I'm supposed to be the one with honeyed words.

I take a few deep breaths, like I've seen Ava do in moments that seriously try her patience.

"There's a reason you came running to the Common in the first place," I say, switching Duke into autonomous mode so I can turn my chair around to have a little heart-to-heart. "You trusted us. And now, we're trusting you. Help us end this."

The Whiz doesn't even glance at me. He twists his head left, right, and behind him, monitoring every window with those huge eyes of his. His slight fingers twitch, like he's trying to write code to fix his current situation. Or his fingers are itching for the door handle, but I have Duke on lockdown.

His only way out is to give us information.

"The capo . . . she'll have sent out her sicarios by now!" the Whiz whisper screams for the twentieth time tonight. "The governor . . . his drones!"

"So you've said—"

"They're coming! They'll find me!"

"Tell us something we don't already know!" Blaise snips. "Like the location of the *gov*damn hard drive!"

Blaise is trying to make *govdamn* a thing. So far, his clever expletive has only caught on with himself.

"Arriving at destination," Duke's gruff voice informs us.

I whip my chair around as the beams of Duke's headlights hit Enchanted Rock's welcome sign, and let me tell you, the thing's seen brighter days. The wood is so rotted and sprayed with graffiti that the only legible word is "wild." Well, that's what tends to happen when a state's government abandons wholesale the parks and wildlife department.

Maybe that's for the best. Humankind did a pretty lousy job as stewards of the earth. Time to let nature take back control.

"Warning, rough road ahead," Duke gives us an unhappy heads-up.

More like the pavement just stops existing at all. The road continues for about fifty more yards before it's utterly swallowed up by a woodland of mesquite trees.

Awesome. As if hiking four miles up and down a granite dome in the dead of night searching for a needle in a haystack wasn't hard enough, we now have the added challenge of accomplishing the feat with no clear path.

Can't be mad at the kid. He did well. Anyone undertaking the scavenger hunt of finding out what's on Roth's servers has to *really* want it.

Good thing I do.

"Well, guys, looks like we're continuing this field trip on foot," I say, taking the wheel to park Duke out of sight behind an old restroom facility with a caved-in roof.

The Whiz starts breathing at high speed—short wheezing pants that sound like he's on the brink of a hyperventilation meltdown.

Not ideal.

I counter with slow, exaggerated breaths, aiming to subliminally calm the Whiz, and I really think it's starting to work when Blaise ruins it all by butting in with his boogeyman face, growling burning threats.

"Listen, genius boy, the sooner you show us the location, the sooner we can all get out of here. If you keep up this helpless act, we're going to find the hard drive on our own and leave your ass on top of the govdamn rock."

The kid stops breathing outright. Whether it's out of fear, protest, or acceptance is unclear. But he finally says something worthwhile.

"I was never supposed to come back here."

Blaise flings himself back in his passenger seat, flicking off his safety belt. I throw him a mental high five, betting my smile outstretches his ear-to-ear fire-toothed grin.

We finally cracked him.

The Whiz just confirmed he's been to this place before.

"Well you *are* here, so why don't you do something about it?" Blaise dares the preteen. "You dubbed yourself the Whiz. Now earn that alpha title and finish the job you set out to do." He straps a headlamp over his forehead, shuts off Lockdown Mode, and pops open Duke's door. "Hackers are foot soldiers now. Let's go end this war."

Well, *I* feel inspired by Blaise's talk. Revved-up, even. Capitalizing on the energy, I dig into my pack and smack a creased map onto the Whiz's lap, a paper printout of the old park.

"For the last time, will you point to where you buried the treasure?"
The hard drive. The answers.

"Please," I add for good measure.

The kid responds by adopting a thousand-yard stare, and then proceeds to rip the map into confetti.

Deep breaths, I coach myself, muting my blue-ribbon curses.

"You're in control here, bud," I tell him, flipping my black cap backward and slapping a headlamp on. "It's up to you how long we're out here."

"I am the controll*ed*," the Whiz whispers. "Always."

His words poke at the Code Cog that's still squirreled away somewhere inside me. My whole life, before I joined up with Rayla, I was the controlled too. The programm*ed*. And considering who this kid worked for, I bet he had it a thousand times worse than a Kismet Programmer. He must've been invisible chattel to people like the ex-governor and the capo.

I've had zero scruples dragging a twelve-year-old into a hotbed of danger. My blinders have been up: *Do whatever it takes; we're at war.* But suddenly my conscience wants to come out.

Not a good time! I tell my moral compass.

Blaise looms over the Whiz's chair and grabs the kid's hand, pulling him out of the car and into the pitch-black night.

"You're in control," I maintain. Whether to the Whiz or to myself is up in the air.

A quarter of a mile into our hike, the tree line ends, and our steep climb begins.

While I can't see much of the 425-foot pink granite dome rising out of the land in front of me in the dark, I can feel its massive presence. It's unnerving.

Before I left Dallas, I did some digging on this place and read that the local indigenous tribes believed the rock was haunted by spirits and regularly saw ghost fires flicker at the top of the dome. Thus, the name *Enchanted* Rock.

I'm hoping those legends were spun to keep away enemy tribes and settlers, because I'm in no mood to deal with supernatural energy right now. I've got enough on my hands. Literally. The Whiz's sweaty paw is interlocked with my left, while my right grips my gun in case we run into mortal foes like the cartel or the Guard.

Not taking any chances, Blaise has the boy's other hand locked inside his. Humane zip-ties. I won the brief heated argument with Blaise for human cuffs instead of the real plastic ones. *He's our informant, not our prisoner.*

I know what it's like to be cuffed, and the last thing it inspires is collaboration.

"Okay, kid," Blaise says, totally winded. The famed coder's natural element is not the great outdoors. "At least tell us if what we're looking for is on the summit. If I slog up that thing and you've really hidden the treasure at the base of this humungous rock, you won't have to worry about any sicarios slicing you open, because *I* will."

"He doesn't mean it," I assure the kid.

"Do you hear that?" the Whiz says in terror, aiming his big eyes at the dark sky above us. "Drones! We have to hide, *now!*"

"Nice try, kid," Blaise says, unconvinced. "You're going to have to do better than that to dupe the likes of us, genius boy."

"Stop calling me a boy!" the Whiz spits.

"Well, you're certainly no man yet," I begin my retort—hell, I'm not sure if *I've* even crossed that threshold myself—but then get cut off with a sudden sharp stab to my left shin. Then another.

"What the—?!"

"You little ankle biter!" Blaise exclaims, voice turned murderous. He must've gotten pricked too.

"I'm a girl, you slow hacks!" the Whiz declares and then hauls ass up the rock, leaving us in her dust.

I'm pretty sure the Whiz just pulled a Joker knife on us. The old blade in the shoe trick. I'm impressed.

Blaise, however, is not.

"I'm going to toss that kid off this rock when I get my hands on him."

"On *her*," I correct him.

Now we have to find the hard drive *and* the Whiz. I take another one of those deep, calming breaths. This time, it doesn't work.

"I think the kid took the 'you're in control' bit to heart," Blaise growls at me. "Hope this was part of your plan."

I swallow a fiery admission that *there is no plan! Don't you know I'm winging it, and this could all turn out to be a complete waste of time?!*

Ava and Mira's team could be facing off with Roth in Mexico already while we're out here in Nowhere, Texas, chasing our own tails.

"Nothing to do but follow," I say instead, continuing our ascent up the granite rock.

Hours have wasted away. Still no Whiz. No hard drive.

All I've gained so far: an infestation of cacti barbs on my boots and shins, buns of steel from that *serious* incline, and a cranky, incensed Blaise who mutters truly pioneering curses with each one of our plodding steps.

"All right," I huff, winded to the point it feels like I'm breathing out of a straw. "I swear we've passed this same megaboulder three times."

Blaise wheezes behind me. "We're walking in circ—!" His observation cuts off with a *gfft!* He must've tripped again over one of the gazillion potholes that pit this humankind-forsaken rock.

I stop our slog to take a breather and find my bearings. Enchanted Rock covers over six hundred acres. The park, over a thousand. I divulged none of these discouraging particulars to Blaise, of course. Best to keep the "indoor" rebel ignorant.

Because, really, I'm starting to think we can search all we want, and all we're going to find is a mountain-sized slice of humble pie.

But what I *do* see is the Milky Way. With no light pollution out in this dark zone, the image is striking. Straight-up mystifying. That white-as-milk swath of light is our galaxy.

Blaise lumbers up by my side, and we both click off our headlamps to better stargaze.

I wait for him to call it. To tell me the mission is over. He's had enough.

I expect him to say that we're small, inconsequential, not only in the universe, but in the fight.

What we do doesn't matter. Couldn't matter.

Instead, he breaks into a sprint. "Get moving!" he yells at me, finger shooting to the sky.

A shadow zips across the horizon. Is it a spirit? A bird? A Scent Hunter?

Inhaling a long, ragged breath, I kick into a gear I didn't think I had in me.

Blaise gets there first.

"Holy . . . ," Blaise breathes beside me.

"Shit!" I finish the sentiment for him.

A mutant drone—a nightmare-inducing mix of bird of prey and spider—has hold of the Whiz. The kid's wrists are bound by some kind of super-rope attached to the drone's belly, while one of the demon-robot's claws forces the kid's protesting face up and still. My stomach flips when a blue light flashes.

A facial recognition scan.

The Guard. *They know we're here.*

All hell breaks loose when the drone's spider hand releases the kid's face and then straight-up takes off, lifting the Whiz into the air by her wrists.

The drone flying away with *our* teammate is a terrifying sight. It stuns me to a standstill.

Her screams bring me back to action.

Nope. Not on my watch.

"Let her go!" I shout, lighting the mutant drone up with bullets. Blaise charges forward and wraps his arms around the Whiz's legs, weighting her to the granite ground.

"Don't let go!" she cries out.

Bet you wish you didn't run from us now, huh, kid?

Lucky for her, this isn't my first time wrangling a drone.

Double-quick, I pull out a net gun from my bag, aim, and fire. A snare launches from the barrel, and just like the Killer Drone I took down with Blaise and Malik, I don't miss.

The wide netting wraps around the drone's four propellers, entangling its blades. The mutant robot struggles to stay in the air, but with its rotors snared and Blaise pulling it down via the captured Whiz, it doesn't stand a chance.

The propellers falter, and the drone, along with the kid, comes crashing down on top of Enchanted Rock.

The Whiz starts hacking at the net with the tiny blade attached to her boot tip, scrambling to unsnarl the drone.

"Whose is it?" Blaise asks, crawling on palms and knees to get to the downed UAV.

"PZH Orion," the Whiz reads from the metal base. "A civilian model."

I swear I hear a collective sigh of relief.

But the short recess from "we're all about to be flown away to die" proves short-lived.

Lights. The size of fireflies, four hundred feet below. The beams of headlamps. Five of them.

"Could be bounty hunters," Blaise calculates.

"Or just *extremely* territorial drifters," I propose.

"The drone scanned my face," the Whiz says, oddly composed as she cuts the ties that bind her wrists. "What if I'm already on the Wanted List . . . as a traitor . . . a squealer . . ."

"You're not a squealer," I try to embolden her, meaning it. "You're a hero."

"They'll know where to find me now," she responds.

We all know the "they" she's referring to. She starts to get that shell-shocked look in her eyes again.

"The Common will protect you," I swear. "We just have to get the drive and make it off this rock first."

I don't know if she believes me. Or if I even do. Emery didn't sanction this mission. And no one can really promise a govdamn thing—none of us have any *real* control. But we have to try to act like we've got the wheel sometimes, right?

"My parents were government," the Whiz reveals, continuing to chop the rope entangling her with the drone. "I was seven when they gave me away to work for my tormentors." It could be sweat or tears that streak her ruddy cheeks. "They made me hide who I really am, hate my own skin."

When she rubs away the drops with her shirt, she mumbles a bitter phrase. "Born a boy, always a boy."

She throws off the last netting that traps her feet, and stands, her eyes meeting mine for the first time in our brisk acquaintance. "Thank you for seeing me. And saving me."

"You saved yourself by getting to Dallas," I tell her.

"I don't mean to interrupt our team bonding here," Blaise says, getting to his feet, "but those hunters aren't slowing down."

The band of lights that's hightailing it our way is way too close for comfort now. Not good.

Time to go. *But not before we get what we came here for.*

I take a step toward the Whiz. "Please, can you just tell us—"

"Stop!" she yells, holding up her hands. "Don't take another step!"

All the hairs on my arms stick up, and I sense imminent danger.

"Did you booby-trap the treasure?!" I ask, standing as stock still as possible for my dear life.

The Whiz smiles. *Smiles* that Blaise and I were *this close* to being blown to kingdom come.

Thank Goodwin I earned her trust and she saved *me.*

She walks in a wide arc in the direction of the giant rock wall at the back side of the dome, crazy careful where she lands her steps.

I watch from my safety zone as she steps over a nest of spiky bushes, crouches down, and disappears into a narrow cave opening, just big enough for a child-sized body to crawl into. Ten seconds later, the Whiz returns, signaling to us with a thumbs up.

A chunky rectangle box is in her hands.

The hard drive.

The three of us sit huddled around a makeshift hacking station Blaise set up in the back of my car, parked in a dark alleyway somewhere in Crabapple, Texas, five miles outside Enchanted Rock.

We've got the drive connected to our home network, but we just ran into a major roadblock.

Of course. I mean, so far, it's just been *too* easy, right?

I wish.

All the data the Whiz copied over from Roth's shadow network servers is AES encrypted. Unintelligible without an encryption key to unscramble it.

"Son of a governor," Blaise curses, troubled eyes glued to the computer screen. "We'd need a quantum computer to break this cipher." He turns to the Whiz, thick brow raised in hope. "Unless you have the key written down somewhere . . . ?"

The Whiz shakes her head.

"This whole operation means diddly-squat if we can't read the damn messages," I say, wanting to dropkick myself in frustration. I knew the kid didn't have an encryption code stashed on her person—I searched her in the hospital—but I was betting on the key being taped to the drive itself or hidden somewhere on the rock. *Stupid.*

My knee bounces up and down, and I take massive deep breaths, fighting to not lose my composure. Or my head. "The closest supercomputer is all the way back in Dallas at Guardian Tower," I say.

It'd be another half day at least before we could unlock Roth's location. By that time, it could be too late to help Team Takedown.

In wartime, every wasted minute could mean life or death.

The Whiz puffs out her chest and clears her throat.

"Good thing I memorized the private key."

My jaw drops to the wood floor.

"No way," Blaise says, turning to face her.

Committing to memory a sequence like that would be impossible for practically anyone. Hell, I don't even think *I* could do it. The key to that level of security encryption involves a mind-boggling amount of random letters and numbers. It's genius level.

"You want to do the honors?" Blaise asks the Whiz, handing her control of his keyboard.

She nods, her fluffy curls bouncing with an energy that matches her newfangled spunk. *She's lost all her fear.* Her fingers dance across the keys like a maestro at work, breaking down the encryption's initial wall in a matter of seconds.

Next thing I know, folder after top-secret folder pops up on the screen.

"Holy Whitman, you did it," I say, smirking like a pirate who has just unburied the mother of all treasure troves.

"You *are* a govdamn Whiz," Blaise says, tipping his black hat to her.

Seeing Roth's server files right in front of my eyes—*It's real; I was right*—shoots adrenaline straight through me, buzzing me into overdrive.

It takes all I've got to not sprint back up that rock and shout from the mountaintop: *We're going to get you, Roth!*

Calm, deep breaths, remember? We have to see what we've unlocked first.

"The Salazars are hosting an international trade meeting . . . ," the Whiz paraphrases the message exchange. "At their stronghold in Mexico City . . . Roth confirmed his attendance. The capo looks forward to the deal tomorrow night . . ."

What are they trading? Nothing good for anybody.

"Wait," she says, sifting through the files. "I found some folders that require a secondary password to open . . ."

Roth's most valuable secrets have got to be on those. Like what he's planning to get ahold of in the southern capital.

The Whiz looks up at Blaise and me, shamefaced. "I was never given the code . . ."

"We'll break it, no problem," Blaise says, clapping her on the back. "You've done more than enough." She cracks a smile, a wobbly one at first, but then it sticks.

While I'm pumped that we're now dead sure of Roth's location, my immediate follow-up thought is, *Where's Ava headed?*

Mexico is a massive country, and the Salazar cartel has a whole slew of strongholds. If Team Takedown's first stop isn't slated for the capital, they're going to risk the mission—and their lives—for nothing.

And they're going to miss the trade.

We can't let Roth get his hands on whatever destructive goods the cartel is trafficking. If it's a weapon like I'm guessing, it could be catastrophic. Apocalyptic.

We could lose the war in a single day.

"You're going to Mexico, aren't you?" Blaise says to me. "You've got that look in your eye like you're about to do something crazy."

"I can't let the others chase after Roth blind," I say to myself as much as to Blaise.

"Mira said *crazy* is just another word for *brave*," the Whiz points out.

"Right," Blaise says with a reinforcing nod, wasting no more time. He grabs a flash drive from one of his pockets and sticks it into the hard drive, syncing the still-passcode-protected folders. "You go find Alexander and the Goodwins. The Whiz and I will get to Emery."

"But—"

"You can brute-force attack the locked files on your way to Mexico," Blaise explains as he plugs the flash drive into Duke, downloading the data onto the car's computer system. "And we'll keep trying to crack these files in Dallas."

Blaise and the Whiz disassemble the hacking station in no time flat and are suddenly out of the car, standing at the edge of the road.

"Two birds, one stone," Blaise says, shouldering his jam-packed messenger bag. "As your girl likes to say."

Ava's not my girl, I think, but I keep it to myself.

The Whiz hugs the hard drive close, holding her spindly body with a dignified hardiness that makes me think she really is going to make it out of this all right.

"When you find my old bosses," she says, "tell them Tess said goodbye."

Tess grins, looking at me through the window with those full-moon eyes of hers. They glow yellow against the night. "I think you're just crazy enough, Owen Hart, to vanquish them."

Brave was Rayla Cadwell's middle name. Maybe it can be mine now too.

"Wait, I can't just ditch you two on a deserted highway—" I start to protest, but Blaise cuts me off with a dismissive scoff.

"I'm afraid you've been too habituated to my talents."

True. The world-famous black-hat hacker can steal any autonomous car, even one hundreds of miles away, with just a few taps of his fingertips.

He'll have a new ride delivered to them in no time.

I turn my focus to the Whiz. Tess. "The Common will repay you for what you've given," I say. "Blaise will keep you safe."

She nods, like she finally believes it.

"My parents . . ." I sigh, suddenly remembering their existence. There's a high probability they're hiding in a Strake dorm room in the dark. Empty stomachs, frantic minds. Two Loyalists in a city full of the Common. A seed of guilt buds wherever my conscience lives. "My mom . . . she's sick . . ."

I've never said that out loud.

"I'll look after them," Blaise promises, his fire-toothed boogeyman mask grinning wide. "Besides, I think they liked me."

Mom and dad could warm up to him, I tell myself. Like I did. *They'll have to.* He might be all they have left if things go bad for me and I don't come back.

The notorious enigma hermit pulls off his mask, showing me his face in a gesture of respect. He trusts me.

And I trust him.

"Let's get cracking," he says, stepping back from the car with the Whiz.

"What we live for," I reply, repeating the line he lectured to me the night our forces aligned. "Subvert the powers that be."

"Don't die," Blaise says, his eloquent way of saying goodbye.

"You too," I reply. "Either of you."

Before I can analyze what's ahead of me or dwell on what I'm leaving behind, I start Duke's engine and hit the gas.

"It's just you and me now," I say out loud to Duke, happy to not be completely on my own.

We're pulled over on I-35 South, the road to Mexico. Where exactly in Mexico we're headed, I'm not sure yet. I figure I need to worry first about crossing the border wall without dying.

Five minutes, then it's go time. But I've been waiting for a moment to be alone with Ava's words, and now's my chance.

I pull her goodbye note from my pocket.

Maybe she'll say something rousing and encouraging. Maybe she'll tell me she's started to fall for me the way I've fallen for her.

Maybe she's better at expressing herself with a pen, because in person she's unreadable. She keeps her cards close.

I settle into Duke's cushioned front seat, ready for the letter to shed some light on Ava's cavernous inner world.

Unfolding the creased paper, I break into a smile.

Ava didn't write me a goodbye letter. It's even better.

She gave me a map.

And it leads me straight to her.

THEO

It's not real.

The realization fires my mind awake, and I'm wrenched out of my sleep, away from the flames.

I'm burning up, soaked in sweat. My shirt and boxers stick to my skin like I popped the water mattress in my flailing attempts to run from the blaze.

Andrés, the militia captive, was screaming inside the inferno. And I was standing with him, *next* to him, my whole body consumed in red and orange and blue.

In the night terror, Valeria found me out. She unmasked me and saw plain as day what I am. A Wright, a rebel, who should meet his end in flames.

Chills rack down my spine, the goosebumps on my thighs and arms almost painful.

It wasn't real.

The grand execution she has me planning will never happen.

Andrés and I are going to make it out before then.

This will all end in escape.

I keep those words on my lips, whispering it like an ASMR podcast as I close my eyes, forcing myself to shut down and get some rest.

The clock says I've only been dozing for an hour. *I'll need more than that to stay sharp.*

But before I can drop off, a door opens, followed by a brusque voice.

"Get up."

The Family Planning Director.

"Lights on," she commands, and every lamp and chandelier in my dark cave ignites at once. I slam my eyes shut, rubbing out the sting of the flash.

When I open my lids, I find Director Wix standing over my bed.

I get up slowly, aiming to show her I might be a puppet with strings, but she's not the one pulling them.

My heart skips about three beats when I reach for the crystal glass of water on my nightstand and see my knife. *Mira's blade. Did Valeria put it here while I was sleeping?*

"Who said you could have your weapon back?" the Director questions, her hawkish face knotted with outrage.

"I did," I answer, grabbing the knife before she can get her claws on it.

With a doctor's clinical gaze, she scans my half-naked body. *What does she see? An athlete? A Roth? Or just a second-born Glut she still can't wait to eradicate?*

A memory of the laboratory below the Governor's Mansion tugs at me like a fisherman's hook.

Mira went white as a sheet when we found the place her own dad must have created.

What were in those smashed refrigerators? What happened on that cold surgical table?

Darren was an expert at building secret rooms belowground. He had been brilliantly successful in concealing twins for eighteen years; what else was he capable of hiding?

The lab was something to do with Project Albatross, I'm guessing.

Wix threatened that the program or whatever experiment the Family Planning Division developed had already gone global.

Is that why we're here in Mexico?

You won't win, the Director promised Mira and me.

We'll see about that.

I flex my forearm, both to show off the strength she failed to defeat and to make sure she gets a good look at my Common tattoo.

She clicks her tongue in disgust. "We'll have to get rid of that. It will be painful." She tries to whisper the last part in my ear, but she only reaches my chest. "I'll make sure of it."

"Careful," I warn her, "you saw what happened to the last person who threatened me."

That Guard is probably dead by now. Or has one foot in the grave from thirst in the south Texas wasteland.

Tú eres el próximo, Wix. You're next.

We stare each other down for a moment, then I brush past her to the mahogany wardrobe in the far corner to get dressed. But my State Guard uniform is gone. Pleased with that development, I grab a navy terry cloth robe instead, wrapping it around myself before turning back to face the Director.

"Where are we going?" I ask, dropping my knife into my robe's front pocket for safekeeping. I won't let anyone take anything from me again.

I wrap my fingers around the knuckle duster hilt, imagining the curved grooves to be the steadiness of Mira's hand.

I'm going to stop them, Mira. Even if I go down trying.

The Director beckons for me to follow her to the locked door that flanks the right side of my bed. She scratches the wood in what I guess is a knock, and immediately the door snaps open.

"I trust you are well rested," Roth welcomes me from the other side, arms stretched out like a cross. A petite servant with a plump, meek face is busy meticulously brushing his freshly laundered uniform, which now includes a sharp military cap embellished with a shining five-pointed Lone Star.

He looks healthier than I've ever seen him. And cheerful. Too cheerful for anyone's good. He doesn't even appear bothered by the translator mirroring his words back at him in Spanish.

"The meeting with the lieutenant was a success?" I ask, poking around for intel. "Knock out any more teeth?"

Governor's thin lips crack a smirk. The chills are back, a shudder down my limbs, but luckily, it's easy to hide my aversion to making the devil laugh beneath my plush robe.

"Not tonight," he answers, sounding regretful of the fact. "The Monterrey lieutenant is a pawn, and therefore wasted energy."

When the translator device parrots his snide remark in Spanish, the servant crosses herself, head to chest, shoulder to shoulder.

I'm guessing nobody insults a water lord and lives to keep their vocal cords. *But Roth is not a nobody.*

Right now, in his imposing uniform, the way his eyes brim with vim and vigor as he stares at his reflection, he looks like the most powerful *somebody* in the world. Once again.

He's just posturing, I reassure myself. Putting on an act like I am. The man was usurped. Humiliated and stripped of his title. The Common wrested his state and country from his iron hands, and he ran south to his mortal enemy with his tail between his legs. He's not governor of Texas anymore.

Then why are my palms sweaty? It's sixty-four degrees Fahrenheit in this room.

"We leave on the hour for Mexico City," Roth reveals, breaking eye contact with himself in the glass to stare fixedly at me.

"For a meeting with the capo?" I ask.

Roth nods, seeming proud that I can keep up. I contemplate whether I should let on that I met his secret daughter, but I determine that I should save it.

I bet my own second-born life that his Glut-hating Director doesn't even know of her existence yet.

And the trade? What does the capo have that you need? I want to press the topic while it's hot, but it would be an oafish, rookie move. He won't let slip such bombshells in the presence of foreign servants.

"Don't just dawdle," Roth orders me. "Get dressed."

His servant bows low to him before she turns to usher me toward my own dressing station.

My State Guard uniform waits ready for me, sparkling clean with two new additional medals on the right breast. I step onto the platform, but instead of mirrors surrounding me, I'm met with a wall of screens.

All stream American news. All of it a detrimental blow for my side.

In a dizzying overload of information, I take in what's been happening outside my bubble of captivity: bomb explosions in Austin, Chicago, New York, and Detroit—all linked to the Common—riots and disorder have shut down major cities across the US, and Texas is battling a simultaneous heat wave and power outage, woefully losing on both fronts. The state's death toll has already climbed into the thousands.

Mira. Where are you in all of this?

I comb the news scrolls for any sign of the Goodwin sisters. Nothing. Only more alarming headlines that claim Emery Jackson has abandoned the Common and fled the capital of Dallas.

Our leader hasn't been seen in over twelve hours.

Suddenly on tenterhooks, I jump when Wix's grating voice commands the volume to turn on, blasting a juiced-up newscaster's breaking news announcement, loud and clear as cartel crystal.

"Governor Millicent Cole has been shot outside New York City Hall. We've just learned the presidential hopeful is now in critical condition, fighting for her life. Reports indicate the still-at-large gunman has direct ties with the Common."

Hovering beside me, the Director grins like a Cheshire cat, not surprised in the least at a development that should distress both her and Roth.

I don't believe for a second that the Common is behind the assassination attempt. Governor ordered that hit.

He wanted Cole dead.

But why? What's his angle? Isn't the New York governor on his side?

Roth wanted to get her out of the way, I judge.

To make room for himself. For his return.

He wants turmoil to fill the void of his absence.

I can feel Roth studying me. It seems crucial to use this moment to continue the role of bootlicker and smile along with the Director.

He's waiting for praise, a congratulations on the Common turning out to be everything he warned his citizens against all along.

Criminals on a rampage that will spiral out of control.

I can't seem to choke out the words I know he wants to hear. I want to scream the truth:

You're a liar, a hypocrite, and a murderer.

"You were right," I utter instead. "You predicted chaos."

Roth nods again, approving. "This is what anarchy looks like, Theo. *The people* brought this upon themselves."

His country's misery incites an exultant energy in Roth.

"Commoners cannot rule," he asserts before marching out the door.

"Long live the governors," Director Wix chants, following after him.

And I'm left alone with the now-muted screens filled with panic-inducing headlines, and the servant girl who refuses to meet my eye.

It's still dark out. The only thing I can see is a row of parked State Guard SUVs. I assume Roth's leading us to the Beast at the center of the squadron, but he stops our regal party of three a few feet from its closed doors.

One of his soldiers materializes at his side, standing at attention. Roth covertly slips the Guard a piece of paper—blink, and I would've missed it, but lately my eyes have been wide open.

A note? Instructions? How in the hell did he find that spare bit of paper? The only thing I know for sure is Roth doesn't want his translator to pick up his orders.

The soldier salutes, then marches back to the vehicles. We stand and watch while the SUVs file out one by one down the stretch of pavement as long as a runway, and I notice the tiny flags affixed above their headlights have a new addition. Beside the starred Texas flag flies the red scorpion banner of the Salazar cartel.

A symbol that will assure them safe passage through their territory to Mexico City.

The fleet's departure opens my field of view and reveals our actual means of transportation to the cartel's main stronghold.

A private jet.

All gold, jumbo-sized, with an elongated red carpet leading up to the airstairs.

Valeria waits for us on the tarmac, clothed in her elegant white suit that I now realize is her own style of uniform, except she's added a crimson dahlia flower to her long, lustrous hair. Lieutenant Salazar stands at her right side in a loud ensemble that probably matches the cost of my entire wardrobe back home.

"Governor Roth," Valeria says as we approach, her smile gleaming brighter than her violet gemstone, which she clutches like a talisman. "We are pleased to have you in our territory, but it seems your country misses you."

Triumphant and grinning in his private rooms, Governor now cools and stiffens into cold formality, offering Valeria a quick and curt nod as a greeting in place of a handshake.

Is no one going to address the elephant on the runway? The obvious truth?

Because their relation is evident, even in the moonlight.

Roth and Valeria have the same upturned nose, the same angular cheeks, the same measured, unnatural quietness about them. Seeing them together raises every hair on my skin.

But if the lieutenant and Director see it, too, they opt for a deadpan mug, giving nothing away.

"I've been anticipating this meeting, Governor," Valeria says. The plane's engine powers on and she's compelled to shout. "You're every bit the man the headlines claimed." Her pointed, claw-like nails keep tapping at her gemstone, like she's hoping he'll notice and say something.

With her ivory pants and blazer, and her jeweled purple embellishment, she looks like a glitzy Strake student. The university the Roth family founded. How did I just put that together?

But Roth gets right to business. "The lieutenant explained to me the capo has been unwell. I trust this does not delay the meeting?"

"I assured the governor everything is moving as planned—" the lieutenant starts, but Roth plows over both him and his translator.

"I don't take assurances from subordinates," he bites, belittling the guy with the enormous gun on his belt. "You're the doormat in my welcoming committee. I came here for the capo."

The lieutenant slides his tongue over his gold teeth, cracking his knuckles like he's calculating where's best to land a punch.

"In our final communication, there was no mention of a problem," Governor continues, his voice simmering with repressed impatience. "The capo was to meet me at her northern stronghold and escort me on her private jet to the capital."

I lean a few inches away, wondering if this will be the moment he finally explodes.

"Where is the capo?" he demands. The question is so quiet it's disturbing. "If she is playing with me, I do not like games."

Unless he's the one controlling them, of course.

Valeria unsheathes that cutting smile.

"It pains me to say my mother has in fact been unwell." I expect her to elaborate. She doesn't. "But the Salazar capo *is* greeting you here. In *my* northern stronghold."

Valeria lifts her hand, displaying a thick ring that covers half her finger. Gold scorpions make up the outer band, their claws wrapped around an enormous blood-red ruby.

Director Wix, still shorter than Valeria, even in her high-heeled boots, shifts her weight backward, away from the girl who wears the emblem of the Salazars. The ring that marks her as their capo.

The sight strikes me dumb. "¡De ninguna pinche manera!" I let slip. My translator trumpets my horrified shock for the entire tarmac to hear. *No fucking way!*

How? When? What, did she murder her own mom to claim the title? A woman called the Heartless Butcher can't have gone down easy . . .

The lieutenant bows to Valeria, kissing the ring. "I declare allegiance to your rule," he says.

Valeria keeps her wide eyes on Governor, her dad, like she covets his approval even more than her new power.

Roth holds back any reaction behind his stalwart veneer, like he's neutral to the news.

Like Roth's neutral to anything.

Most especially to news that his secret daughter now has, or has *taken*, the role of capo.

He removes his military cap in a form of salute. "Congratulations, Capo. I look forward to our meeting."

Movement under the belly of the jet catches my attention.

A slew of servants, including the girl who dressed me, is loading the Salazar's luggage into the cargo bay. I spot Andrés, Valeria's caught mouse, escorted by the two cartel women I saw when I first met my aunt. They banter back and forth, laughing, one of them wearing the captive's black leather patch over her own eye.

Hands cuffed, shoulders sloped, Andrés looks like a beat-up shell of a man, like his soul died right alongside the woman he called his love. All his fight is gone.

But he's still alive.

That's one piece of good news tonight.

Valeria looks pleased, jubilant even, as she leads our party to the airstairs.

When I enter through the jet's oval door, I can't even properly take in the wildly extravagant cabin interior, because seated on one of the five white leather couches is a man I recognize. He's the pride and hero of Canada and my own former leader.

President Moore.

"I must say, I did not expect to see you here, Theo," he remarks, the gold translator necklace popping against his beige suit.

So he recognizes me too. From the Battle for Dallas, I'm guessing.

I bet he wishes he could arrest me right now. Not only for being a foreign Glut who dared to live in his sacred lands, but for my freshly minted status of "legitimate grandson" to his foremost rival.

"Your new country is treating you well, then?" he says, eyeballing my uniform and medals.

The president's chestnut hair is as glossy as a thoroughbred's coat, and when he runs his hand through it and smiles, he oozes his famous I'm-a-good-guy charm, like he would never detain and torture asylum seekers like Ava and Mira in black-site prisons. My fingers clench into fists at the thought of feeding tubes forced down Mira's throat on his orders.

I take a step toward him, half-sure I want to blow my cover just to sock Moore's perfect, dishonest face, but the president rises to his dapper feet when Roth and Valeria enter behind me.

"I see you've decided to come after all," Governor greets the northern president. "Good." His downturned lips lift into a grin.

Did I miss something? There's little chance Governor's forgotten about Moore's botched deportation of his Traitorous Twins.

He despises Moore. Why is he pleased to see him?

"Well, gentlemen, should we engage in pleasantries?" Valeria asks in her silvery voice, inviting Roth and Moore into a conference room at the back of the cabin.

This is the first time in decades the leaders of these formidable countries have met in person. All three have immense, expensive borders with the sole purpose of keeping each other out. And now, here they all are, on their way to making secret deals that will affect hundreds of millions of lives.

All of North America's leaders seem to be in on this alliance. *But what is Moore doing here?* Canada has more influence and riches than its two southern neighbors combined, making Moore the most powerful person on this jet. Why do dirty dealings with the likes of governors and water lords?

The only thing I *do* know, and what Moore is most likely ignorantly blind to, is that no matter what they're set to negotiate tonight at the capital stronghold, the balance is skewed.

There's more than one Roth taking a seat at the power table.

The scheming leaders disappear behind the mirrored door of the conference room, and soon the Monterrey stronghold starts diminishing as the jet's engines speed our party down the tarmac and up into the air.

Director Wix lowers herself onto the nearest couch, slipping off her heeled boots with her toes. She sighs in pleasure, then tucks two stainless steel briefcases I've never seen before beneath her swollen feet.

She catches me looking. "You either have a foot fetish or an emboldened curiosity that needs to be stifled."

I take a long look at myself in the pristine glass of the conference door. *What are you made of?* my reflection asks again.

"Are you trading whatever's in those briefcases?" I ask.

They seem too small to carry a weapon . . .

Wix laughs, a delicate airy sound so incongruous with her person.

"Don't you have an execution to plan?" she answers. "It will be a nice send-off before we head home."

"Home?" I say, taking pains to keep the fear from my voice. "To Dallas, you mean?"

She laughs again. "Yes. What will be left of it."

MIRA

"We're not lost," Ava asserts, stubbornly.

But we've been walking—or what feels more like meandering—around the desert for fifty minutes.

No sign of anything. Or anyone.

"Highway 85 should be right here," Ava stresses, stopping abruptly without warning, causing me to collide violently with her backside and lose my carefully placed footing.

I've been following Ava's lead, literally, since we made our hasty retreat from the runaway truck. My own night vision goggles broke in the jump, cracked in two by a rock and my breastbone.

So I took to shadowing Ava's footfalls, step for step.

Yet now I find myself on the ground, staring up at the stars, having fallen head over heels.

Ava spins around, the two tubes of her night vision goggles jutting outward like their own form of weapon.

"Shit, are you hurt?! You fell right onto a cactus!"

"I didn't *fall*," I answer, short fused. "I was blindsided."

I see her hand hovering an inch from my nose, and I take it, wondering why my rear was spared the sharp pains that usually follow landing on a plant with three-inch spines for armor.

Back on my feet, Ava inspects me, her gloved fingers coming away with dozens of knifelike barbs.

"Your uniform caught them," Ava says, relieved. Even in the pitch black, I can make out the angry crimson welts on her neck from her own rumble with a cactus. "Thank Whitman for the high-tech padding."

Thank Ciro. He's helping, even from afar.

Unlike us. Ava and me stumbling lost in a desert helps no one. My frustration forms as an icy burn in my chest, a weighted panic stored just below my heart. A cold sweat drips from my skin when I instinctively reach for my rucksack and remember it isn't there.

We have nothing but our pistols, our wits, and each other. We're northerners, outsiders, *enemies*, roaming the highly controlled Salazar territory, clinging tight to our ebbing conviction that we will make it to the People's Militia's headquarters.

Before the sun rises. Before we faint from exhaustion and dehydration.

Before the sicarios detect us.

Ava pockets the compass, tucking her map between her arm and ribs. "Keep going?" she asks.

Always keep going.

We found the highway.

Ava makes sure to maintain a wide distance from the road, although so far we've been the lone travelers in this isolated terrain.

"Seven more miles," Ava announces up front. She picks up the pace.

I look at my watch, squinting down at the barely visible hour hand.

We're making terrible time. There's still more than a two-hour trek ahead of us.

"We'll run into the team soon," Ava says, more as an encouragement than a certainty. "We can't be *that* far behind. No question Alexander's slowing them down . . . He might be a Guard officer, but I know he hasn't marched a day in his life."

I nod, though I realize Ava can't see me. My tongue sticks to the roof of my mouth like sandpaper, all my saliva dried up and long gone. I can't waste my breath.

And Alexander is the last person I want occupying my mind. I feel lost enough as it is without that man veering me off course.

It's all your fault.

I shake my head, clearing away his condemning words. Doubt and blame only misguide me, I've learned.

Besides, I'm on my way to make things right.

"Seven more miles," I hear Ava repeat to herself.

She starts marching faster.

For an instant I consider yanking up the needled pads of the prickly pear cactus that surround our path. *Nopals, for hydration,* Lucía taught us in the west Texas desert.

I have no knife. No blade to scrape away the large spines. My gloves could work, but the act would feel desperate. Defeatist. Time-consuming.

I keep walking.

"Only two more hours," I whisper out loud to make it feel real.

Two hours and we'll find the town, the others, water.

It's grueling, having to keep my eyes lowered on my feet, on Ava's footsteps, when every urge and impulse in me craves to look up, around, behind me.

What's out here, concealed in the dark?

To distract my thoughts from turning as bleak as this stretch of land, I think of Theo.

We're on the same side of the border now. The same country, territory. Every step shrinks the miles between us. My fear, like a weight threatening to crush my chest, suddenly lightens.

I imagine Theo's amber eyes, shining with life and hope. His fingers, soft and strong, wrapped around mine.

I can still feel his touch. The memory's seared onto my palms like a tattoo. His right hand in my left, pulling me toward him.

If I could find him once, I can find him again.

I'm going to get you out, Theo. Save you, like I couldn't save my father. Or Rayla.

Without fail, my thoughts flash to the man who took them all. Pure, unbridled hate courses through me, hot, like the blood in my veins.

What are you scheming, Roth? Did you really think you could run and hide behind a cartel stronghold?

Did you really think we wouldn't come for you?

It's not enough to merely take Roth's title, his state. His country. *We must take his life.*

And I know, like I have since the moment I watched my father leave this world, that I'm going to be the one who takes it.

"Six more miles," Ava updates me over her shoulder.

I allow the hate to take hold of my heart in an iron grip. With every beat I harden. Strengthen.

We're getting closer.

For two thousand footsteps I've managed to keep my mind an empty vault. So I'm as surprised as Ava must be to hear my voice over the monotonous silence.

"Are you and Owen—"

I seal my lips before I can finish the question. The accusation.

"No," Ava says loud and quick like she wants to cover up the lingering unsaid word. *Together. Are you and Owen together?*

"No," Ava repeats, quieter this time but just as forceful. I hear the catch in her whisper. A strained guilt, like I caught her cheating.

My sister and I were born soul mates. Where—*how*—do Theo and Owen fit into that inseparable bond?

I never speak to Ava of Theo. And she keeps Owen from me like a secret.

"We used to tell each other everything," I whisper.

"We had to," Ava says. "To stay alive."

"And now?" I ask.

It's all so different now.

Before she can answer, a light wind picks up, shifting the air, and I catch the smell. A strong, musky odor that sears my nostrils and flips my stomach.

It reeks like something died here.

"What's that *stench*?" Ava asks, tugging her uniform over the lower half of her face.

I cover my nose with the ends of my scarf. It does nothing to block the foul stink.

"What's that noise?" I ask, the more dangerous question.

It's a sound like building thunder. No, more like a wall of water hurtling straight for us.

Ava whips her head left and right, scanning the night with her goggles.

I slam my back against my sister's, in fighting position, and draw my gun. Before I can ask if she sees something, I spot a billowing dust storm and its wild cause.

Javelinas. An entire herd of them.

"It's a stampede," Ava breathes.

"My six o'clock!" I shout, and Ava springs to my side right as the first boar-like animal charges.

Ava and I leap in opposite directions, and the short, fifty-pound javelina strikes thin air. Ava pivots and gets a shot off before it can round for a second charge.

The accompanying screech tells me she found her mark.

"I don't understand," I say between ragged breaths. "Javelinas don't attack humans!"

Yet ten more rush straight for us, the coarse salt-and-pepper fur on their necks bristling in alarm mode.

"Just keep shooting!" Ava yells above the pandemonium of their tiny hooves. "Scare them off!"

It's when I feel the biting stab of a tusk tearing into my calf that I register this must be the sick work of the Salazar cartel. Their sicarios.

They must feed the javelinas. Make them attracted to humans who encroach on their territory.

This is a game to them. They think using wild animals to weaken their prey is much more fun than using drones.

But Ava and I fire again and again, refusing to go down easy.

Four or five of the small beasts scurry away, but the rest remain, frenzied and persistent.

A second stab to my left calf sends me to my knees. My uniform's padding is no match for strong, clamping jaws.

I try to swallow my scream, but it's useless. The shrieks from the animals will attract whoever's out there listening. Lying in wait.

Next thing I know, Ava's flat on the ground beside me, a jaw fastened around her thigh. She grunts in agony as she bangs the butt of her gun into the javelina's snout.

It lets go and lunges for her neck, but my bullet's quicker. The carcass drops stiff on top of Ava's chest, it's putrid musk mixing with her sweat.

Finally, the last half of the herd barrels off. And silence settles.

The ominous kind.

No time to nurse our wounds or formulate any real plan.

A single light materializes on the eastern horizon, deviating from the highway. Right toward us.

With one look Ava and I vault behind the nearest rock and collapse to our stomachs. Backs to the barrier, we each hastily unlatch a secret pocket in our uniforms. We throw cape-like blankets over our bodies and stay as still as possible, hoping we just disappeared.

Like me, Ava must be betting whoever is after us, almost certainly a Salazar's sicario, is combing the dark with his own form of night vision optics.

But the aluminized plastic fabric of our capes should camouflage our body heat from his thermal energy goggles.

This will work. Just like the Scent Cloaks outsmarted the hummingbird drone.

The hitman's motorcycle emits no sound. Beyond the hammering of my pulse, I only hear the cracking of cacti as the fat tires plow effortlessly over the three-foot plants.

The rider shouts while he searches for what he thinks is easy prey, his disembodied voice toneless. "Ustedes, estúpidos ratones, creen que son valientes . . ." *You stupid mice think you're brave . . .*

His taunts echo across the mute desert, hitting me twice. Once in Spanish, and once translated through my ear cuff, making it feel like he's right up against me. The wind is his breath. The rocks are his nails, digging into my throat. "If you're so brave," he mocks, "then stand up, militia mice!"

He thinks we're members of the People's Militia.

And I'm wagering he doesn't think we have guns. I mentally send out a hasty thanks to Ciro for our pistols' high-tech silencers.

The sicario circles our perimeter with his bike, the constant *crack, crack, crack* of the snapping cacti our only marker for his position.

One o'clock, twelve, eleven.

"Stand up and run! Show me what you're good at!"

Crack, crack, crack. He's getting closer.

My mind clears, and my pulse slows.

"Whoever runs fastest can die first," he goads. "And when my blade kisses your throat, I'll make it quick."

The *crack, crack, crack* of tires tearing a path through the cacti grows louder. Nearer.

It's only a matter of seconds before his bike's headlight finds us.

Crack. Ten o'clock.

Crack. Nine.

"Now!" Ava whispers beside me.

Leaving no time for doubt or fear, I tear off my cape and surge to my feet. Standing, like he was calling for us to do. But instead of running, we fight.

Trailing the barrel of my gun on the moving gray shadow, I pull the trigger until my chamber empties.

One of our bullets lands, and the sicario flies backward into the air, his speeding bike racing forward without its driver.

After a few suspended heartbeats, the motorcycle crashes to the ground. The man, who I see only as an inanimate shadow, lies crumpled on a prickly bed of cacti.

"He's dead," Ava says. "Let's move." She holsters her gun, its silencer muzzle dipping below her belt. Just above her flesh wound.

My legs start throbbing, worse than the pain in my head.

Ava and I just killed another man.

I look down to see dark stains—*My blood,* I realize, dazed—soaking the uniform above my calves and shins.

"Can you keep going?" Ava asks me, but it's a waste of breath.

There's only ever been one option.

Always, forever, move.

AVA

It feels good to ride a motorcycle again.

All my senses are hyperfocused on the road in front of me, wholly attuned to my environment. The dusty, sweet, earthy scent of the desert fills my nostrils, stripping away the smell of blood. The wind simultaneously caresses the sweat off my body, kissing the stinging wounds on my neck and thigh, and screams nonsense into my ears, drowning out the memory of Mira's cries.

The perfect balm after what we just survived.

The final stretch of Highway 85, before we reach the People's Militia's headquarters, is pure straightaway. I pull the electric motor's throttle and everything speeds up as if I just hit a fast-forward button.

Mira wraps her arms tighter around my waist.

For the next five minutes it's quiet. Hypnotic. Almost peaceful.

Then I hear them.

Church bells. Ringing loud and urgent.

At first, I think the haunting melody is heralding daybreak. But when we get closer to our destination, Mira squeezes my arm and points upward.

Freefall parachutes drop from the awakening sky, slow and eerie like umbrella-shaped jellyfish in the plum-tinted light.

An airdrop delivery?

From whom? We're still too far away to make out the symbol on the chutes.

Just as I veer us onto a cavity-ridden exit ramp that leads to the small town ahead, fireworks explode inside the center plaza. Brilliant greens, pinks, and azure blues blast between the stucco buildings, not ten feet off the ground, like beautiful, luminous bombs.

These pyrotechnics aren't aimed at the open sky like the lavish reelection celebrations Father would take me to at the Governor's Mansion.

These fireballs are meant to do damage.

Is the People's Militia using fireworks as weapons?

Bam, bam, bam!

A rain of gunfire breaks out, the rapid pops echoing off the mountains.

"Do you think our team's in there?" Mira cries out behind me.

I don't know which sides are battling—cartel versus militia, Roth versus militia, our team versus Roth *and* the militia—but I don't hesitate.

I gun the motorcycle faster.

Mira and I shelter under a cathedral's arched colonnade. The agreed meet-up spot if anyone gets lost or separated from the team.

We peer out into the square that's distinguished by a tall pale-blue clock tower. The bells, which I now know are a warning siren, are so loud they rock my very core.

On a normal morning, I imagine this zocalo, lined with multihued buildings with a vaulted kiosk at the center of the square for concerts, is bustling with people from all walks of life, busy with their shopping or socializing with friends under the arcades.

But right now, it's a battleground.

From what I can glean from our position, the parachutes that litter the cobblestone streets are the objective.

Gunmen with red-and-black bandanas pulled over their faces load the large cargo boxes into a squadron of pickup trucks, spraying bullets mercilessly all across the plaza.

I manage to make out the symbol on the containers—two shaking hands that form a heart—before Mira pulls me back to safety behind a column. Bullets ricochet off the stone where my head was just moments before.

"It's the Salazar cartel—there's a scorpion on the truck doors," I inform Mira. "They're stealing a humanitarian aid drop from the town."

From the other end of the colonnade, two men brandishing Roman candles scream "¡No más!" and run into the open square. *No more!*

They fire their weapons straight at the cartel, blowing two Salazar gunmen to the ground. The men thrash about screaming, clutching their stomachs, trying to put out the flames. The militia members race for one of the cargo boxes but are easily mowed downed before our eyes by three separate bandana-clad men wielding automatic rifles.

Here it seems, just like back home, civilians are denied true weapons to fight back.

The ones with the guns always win.

I grip the handle of my pistol.

"Ava, no," Mira cautions, firmly taking hold of my arm to keep me back. "We need to find our team."

Haven. Lucía. Did they make it here? Are they bunkered down, or did they join in the conflict?

The gunfire ceases. *They're reloading.*

"Let's move, now!" I tell Mira, and as one we push away from our columned shelter and scramble through the church's arched doors.

We're greeted by shafts of early morning light through bullet-ridden walls and the potent smell of spicy cooking.

Then the threatening sound of guns cocking followed by hostile demands in Spanish.

"Who are you?" my ear cuff translates.

"Don't come any farther," another half-panicked voice orders.

Mira and I freeze in the center of the lobby, reluctantly lowering our weapons so they won't shoot.

The armed man and woman are concealed somewhere in the shadowy far right corner. No way I'd be able to shoot my gun before one of them fired a bullet straight into my chest. But maybe if I charge them . . .

"Somos amigos de Lucía Salazar," Mira declares, loud enough to make certain she's heard. "¿Está ella aquí?" *We are friends of Lucía Salazar. Is she here?*

Silence, but for the violent din of battle raging outside.

I shift my weight to the balls of my feet, ready to attack. We can't be certain the People's Militia even still operates from here—it's been months since Lucía left this town. *These could be cartel gunmen.*

On the point of making my offensive move, the cathedral doors burst open behind us. Mira and I hurtle out of the way, pressing ourselves against the stone walls, poised for another threat.

The cartel would steal from a church? The town's humanitarian aid isn't enough?

But it's not a cartel gunman that charges into the lobby. It's a stocky middle-aged man wearing a wide-brimmed straw hat and a double-holstered belt weighted with two pistols. There's a limp to his gait, and he clutches a wailing child in his arms.

Blood smears the girl's forehead.

"Two more injured by the clock tower, go now!" my ear cuff translates the man's shouts as he runs for the sanctuary.

"At once, Matías!"

Matías Villarreal, the People's Militia's leader.

The militia man and woman, who moments before had their pistols aimed at us, emerge from their hidden guard position, their mettle returned at the sight of their commander. They dash out into the fight, screaming, "No more!"

Pressed into the shadows and scarcely daring to breathe, Mira and I watch Matías kick open the sanctuary doors, revealing an improvised field hospital. A woman in a white doctor's coat rushes forward to take the wounded child.

Arms unburdened, Matías turns from the sanctuary and unsheathes a four-foot Mexican white oak walking stick from a scabbard across his back. He leans his brawny weight on the twisted wood with a large square hand.

"You are not the cons or you would have already fired your weapons."

The cons. Los contras.

His name for the Salazar cartel.

The look in his hard-as-nails eyes is lethal. *How did he sense we were here?*

"Who are you?" he asks, voice gruff. Threatening.

Making sure the cloth of my shemagh covers my telltale red hair—would Matías or his militia even care about a foreign wanted criminal?—I step out from the wall and repeat that we are friends of Lucía Salazar.

"¿Ella está aquí?" *Is she here?*

Surprise flicks across the man's face; he's clearly caught off guard. His free hand moves to one of the gold-plated pistols at his waist. *Did he commandeer his weapons from the cons?*

"There has never been a Lucía Salazar here," he says, a clear warning hanging in the smoky air.

He's protecting her, even now.

But did our team make it, or does he truly believe Lucía's still out of the country, on the run with her family?

The screeching sound of retreating tires—the cartel leaving with their booty—causes Matías to sheathe his walking stick. He draws both his pistols, but his aim is not on us.

"No more!" he bellows, charging out into the perilous plaza, guns blazing, synchronized firework blasts from the rooftop covering both his flanks.

A leader willing to get his own hands bloody. Like Rayla.

I see why Lucía followed this man.

"Do you think our team ran into sicarios?" Mira asks, anxious. She steps forward and searches the chipped sanctuary booths turned hospital beds for a familiar face. "Should we go looking for them?"

"Listen," I say, holding up my hand for quiet.

The gunfire has ceased. The supply raid is over.

A nurse who attends a patient on a nearby pew quickly examines Mira and me from afar, his trained eye instantly spotting the damage to our bodies.

"You're hurt, please come inside," he says.

Instantly Mira and I fall back, away from his gaze.

I forgot that I was even injured. Staying alive and reuniting with our mission team has been my sole focus since the convoy attack. Now, having been reminded, the pain from the wild animal bite in my thigh pulsates through me like a white-hot wave.

So does the concern.

The bite wounds on Mira's calves have formed bloody pools at her feet. *Javelinas can carry rabies.* Mira and I will both need immune globulin shots as soon as possible.

Then all thoughts for my sister and myself die when Haven and Barend storm into the church carrying a stretcher with a writhing body between them.

Oh God. Who is that? One of ours?

I can't see their face.

"Kano!" Mira screams.

She runs to him and immediately applies pressure to his bleeding chest, leaning hard into the wound.

"Don't worry about me . . . ," Kano wheezes, voice weak, trying but failing to smile. "It's just a flesh wound."

It's a hell of a lot worse than a flesh wound.

If we don't act fast, he's going to bleed out.

But this is a church, not a hospital. What if he needs surgery or a blood transfusion?

"Doctora!" I shout, pressing my hands on top of Mira's, slick with blood.

The woman in the long physician's coat hastens over, immediately—and thankfully—taking charge. Her soft white hair blooms around her head like a dandelion cloud, tempting me to press my lips together and blow. *Please let Kano live,* I'd wish.

"Bring the man into the office!" she directs Barend and Haven. The doctor's orders translate into their ear cuffs, and they hurry Kano across the sanctuary's altar and into a priest's office turned OR. They carefully place him on top of a high table fitted with a green cotton bedsheet.

The doctor, and the nurse who offered to help Mira and me earlier, inspect Kano's injuries to see if there's an entrance and exit wound from the bullet.

Mira and I hover close, desperate to help but unsure how to step in. Our skills are limited—we never made it to medical school. Our advanced biology classes are no match for this real-life trauma.

"Did the gunshot damage any organs or blood vessels?" I ask, fearing a yes.

The doctor furrows her brow, taking her focus from Kano to scan me instead, her keen eyes inquiring, *Who are you?*

The question Mira and I have yet to answer.

In my distress for Kano, I spoke English as my default, giving myself away as an outsider.

"Out, now!" she demands.

Haven and Barend place a hand on each of our shoulders, urging us out of the room. Their uniforms torn, faces scratched and dirt stained, they must've had as long and hard of a night as we had. *But where are the others? Are they injured too?*

Mira gently brushes Kano's sweaty forehead, whispering, "Stay strong," before allowing herself to be pulled away by our aunt.

"Your friend is in good hands," the nurse assures us as he shuts the door.

Clustered in the cramped altar outside the priest's office, Mira rounds on Barend. "What happened?!"

"Voices down," Haven warns, wary of our curious audience from the pews.

We're drawing way too much attention to ourselves.

"We should move," I say. But Mira stands in front of the OR door and crosses her arms, making it clear she's not going anywhere.

Barend rests his bloody hands on the altar table, clearly exhausted. He sighs deep before answering. "We made it to the town right as the firefight broke out," he explains. When he sees he's soiled the holy cloth, he jumps back, rattled, and attempts to wipe his hands clean against his chest. "We saw that the Salazar cartel was raiding the town's supplies—killing civilians—and Lucía and Kano joined the battle."

"And everyone followed?" Mira asks.

"Not Alexander," Haven rebukes.

"Where are Lucía and Skye?" I question.

My first thought was, *Are they injured?* Now I'm questioning whether Skye took the opportunity to cut and run.

"Where's Alexander?" Mira demands, suspicious.

"Out there," Haven says, nodding her head toward the open cathedral doors. Sure enough, Alexander's tall figure paces back and forth along the colonnade, impatient. He's here to help his son, not a town full of strangers.

He'll never lift a finger for anyone but his own.

Skye saunters past him, wheeling a dolly stacked with huge barrels of water. One of her braids is undone and her fair face is splotched with soot, but she's beaming, triumphant.

"Saved this lot from being plundered," she says when she reaches us at the front of the sanctuary. "Can't accuse me of not being a team player now."

When Lucía storms into the crowded sanctuary, Skye sits on top of the rescued water barrels, trying to catch her eye. But then Matías enters the room, surging down the aisle toward us, somehow managing to overtake Lucía despite the lack of his hardwood stick.

"Matías, wait!" Lucía implores.

The People's Militia's leader does the opposite of waiting.

Livid, the man jumps onto the altar and points his thick finger first in my face, then Mira's. "You cannot be here!"

Brimming with adrenaline, I stand my ground, lifting my chin. I've come too far to be intimidated now. *Make me leave.*

Barend moves to stand between Matías and me, gun firmly in his hand.

"Back away," Haven advises the militia leader, shielding Mira.

Matías pulls out his walking stick, raising it in a defensive stance. I'm not the only one willing to stand my ground, it seems.

This showdown is going to end with more people in the OR.

Mira sidesteps Haven and falls on Lucía. "You said the People's Militia would help us!"

Lucía lowers Matías's staff, then leans into her leader's ear like an old confidant.

"We all want the same thing," Lucía explains to him. "The cons have one of their people."

Matías Villarreal appears unwavering.

She pulls out an extra ear cuff from Barend's bag, prompting Matías to put it on. Five beats of stoic resistance before he nods his assent.

"You want the capo, we want Roth," I say immediately after Lucía turns his device on. "Our enemies have united."

"We can go after them both together," Mira promises. "We are all stronger if we join forces, like they have."

Based on what Lucía has told me, and from what I've seen of the man's actions so far, the militia leader is a true polymath, possessing both Emery's gift of logic and the warrior spirit of Rayla.

He must know a good deal when he's offered one.

But still, Matías appears impassive.

"My son," Matías finally says, his voice faltering.

"Andrés?" Lucía cries. Her dark eyes glitter with fear, and she reaches out to clasp Matías's arm. "Did the cons take him?"

All the muscles in Matías's thickset body suddenly appear as tight as a primed crossbow.

"I will accept an alliance if you help me bring back my son."

"Done," Mira and I agree in unison.

"We will strike this afternoon," Matías says, sheathing his oakwood staff. "Ready yourselves."

But Mira and I have been ready for this moment our entire lives.

OWEN

"Wake up, Owen," Duke's gruff electronic voice announces. "You have arrived at your destination."

I bolt upright from my reclined seat, still half in my dream world and reluctant to leave it. Usually when I sleep, it's lights out, nothing-to-see-here blackness, but this time Rayla was with me. We were back on the front porch swing of the Colorado ranch house, and instead of me standing lookout while she rested her eyes, she was watching over me.

"Thanks for the ride, Duke," I say, grateful for once that I didn't have to manually drive the 250 miles to Laredo from Enchanted Rock. I hadn't zonked out in over twenty-four hours, and I needed the recharge, bad.

First things first. I stretch and power on Duke's operating system to check on my password-busting status.

Please tell me the decoding program was able to unlock another info gem. It's been going at it for four hours.

But nope. Nothing useful.

The highlight is a file that contains an embarrassingly personal audio conversation between Director Wix and a much younger male employee of her Division. I did *not* need to hear that.

Looks like Roth installed spyware on his inner circle, giving him access to not only their GPS locations, call logs, and text messages, but the microphones on all their devices. He was creepily monitoring his subordinates' private conversations from afar. No surprise there, really, that Roth's a paranoid bastard.

I wonder if there's saved data on Ava's dad, Darren.

Not sure I want to step on *that* potential landmine—the guy was the right-hand man of the devil himself for decades.

But Ava loved him more than anything. Darren must've been one hell of a dad, raising and protecting Ava and Mira the way he did, under such insane surveillance.

I wonder if he'd like me. I know a thing or two about security . . . I can keep his daughter safe too.

Even in Salazar territory?

A Hart can try.

I double-check that my heavy-duty mission gear is all in order. Not antisurveillance Blackout Wear like Ava's team wore on their mission to Dallas, but just as cool and illegal. Designed for battle, my charcoal-black combat uniform is more sophisticated than what the military's elite commandos use. Definitely not approved for civilians.

Ava wasn't overselling it when she said Ciro's a man who can get ahold of anything.

"Duke, activate Image Magnify Mode, a hundred yards south," I say.

I wasn't going to let my car autonomously drive me right up to the infamous Big Fence without due diligence, was I?

While I'm sure Ava would never lead me here without good reason, that doesn't erase the nineteen years' worth of "you will die if you even get close enough to *see* the wall" indoctrination. So I instructed Duke to take me close to the map's X coordinates, but not *too* close, and to hole up out of sight before sending me a wake-up call.

I squat in front of the wide control panel and get a close-up view of the last thing I expected to see.

A wide-open gate that leads directly through the fifty-foot border wall and into Mexico. That's just too good to be true.

I call bullshit.

"Duke, magnify the east and west towers flanking the bridge," I command, expecting to find troves of Border Guards. Maybe even one of those notorious gray wolves rumored to sniff out and attack would-be border hoppers.

But there's zero activity.

Not possible. Border Guards never leave their posts.

Something scratches at my brain.

Unless they were forced to . . .

"Duke, zoom in on west tower, sixty feet up," I say.

The screen switches to a large-scale image of a very dead Guard lying folded over the tower's limestone battlements.

Did my team do that?

"Duke, pull back camera," I say, still not fully believing that the crossing could be Guard—or cartel—free. I press my face an inch from the screen and scan for any hint of movement.

Still nothing, except a vulture that flies parallel with the Big Fence. This is my first time seeing the beast wall in person, and I swear it looks like the protruding back of a thousand-foot dragon that's trapped below the hellish desert landscape.

Will it come alive if I make my move?

"What do you think, Duke?" I ask, rising to my feet.

After a lifetime of freewheeling on my own, packless, I've grown accustomed to having another person to pro and con decisions with me. First with Rayla, then Blaise.

Now I'm riding solo again.

I know what my parents would say. Dad would tell me I'm just a sucker kid who got dragged into something I can't handle. Mom would tell me not to go. That I might not be able to come back.

What they don't understand is, I've already come to terms with my one-way ticket.

But who will take care of us? my dad would ask if he were sitting in the passenger seat next to me. *Of your dear mom?*

I can't think about that now.

Right now, I have to relink with my team. I have to get them the vital intel that Roth's in Mexico City, *not* Monterrey—that something major is scheduled to go down.

And we all have to stop it.

"What if they've already gone to the wrong stronghold?" I ask myself out loud, preying on my worst fears. "What if they're already hurt?"

There's nothing for it, really, but to go forward.

Even if there are still enabled autotarget sentry guns guarding the border gate, Duke is bulletproof.

Which means so am I.

I move to the driver's seat, pull down the emergency steering wheel, and floor it.

Mid–bridge crossing, the body count doubles. More unmoving shapes litter the road.

Cartel, not my side. Shots to the head.

I mentally block out the gruesome image and keep my eye on the south tower, prepared for a machine-gun welcome to Mexico.

But again, zero activity.

Team Takedown did it! They pulled off an extraordinary break-in. And by all accounts, lived to tell the tale.

Exhilaration rushes through me as I leave the Big Fence in my rearview mirror.

I made it through.

I'm in Mexico, one step closer to Roth.

My fingers dance across the steering wheel. It's a small victory. But it's progress. Eyes on the road, I dig in my bag for Ava's paper map and clutch it tight in my hand. My thumb traces and retraces the *town* she circled a hundred miles south of the border.

"Ava, I'm on my way."

This can't be the town.

At least, I hope this isn't the town Ava circled on the map. Four times, in blue ink.

Its dusty streets are deserted, and every vibrantly colored building appears unoccupied. The windows that aren't boarded up with bullet-cratered sheets of metal are empty, both of glass and suspicious eyes.

It looks like nobody's home.

Not good.

But most distressing of all is there's no Common Guard SUV in sight. *Did they already leave for Monterrey? Did they even make it here?*

"Where are you, Team Takedown?" I say out loud, like this helps me not be alone with my bleak thoughts. And fears. "Don't tell me I'm too late."

I park Duke a block from the cathedral—where Ava drew a star with the word "safe house" in her sharp, slanted scrawl.

"Please be in there," I pray to whoever will listen.

I confirm Duke's computer system is still running the decoding software, triple-check my gun is stuffed with ammo, then pop open the door and make for the cathedral.

Duke can handle himself. If anyone dares to lay a finger on my car, he's programmed to jolt them with the shock of their life.

Five steps into my dash across the plaza, I spot piles of cardboard shells on the rutted pavement. *Are those M-1000 casings?* Those firecrackers are all kinds of illegal in the States.

But they're evidence I just missed a fight. *Between whom?*

Maintaining a wide berth from the blood broiling on the concrete— *It didn't belong to anyone I know*, I tell myself—I question if my sudden appearance will scare the locals. *If there still* are *any locals,* I think, spying more dark splatters of blood.

Something tells me it takes more than a masked stranger to scare this town.

"Best to stay covered," I say, sliding up my bandana and fixing the bill of my cap lower over my eyes. I don't know which side I'll run into, or if an undercover falcon will recognize me and call in sicarios or Roth's Guards.

Either one would be seriously bad news.

I bound up the stone steps and approach the cathedral's doorstep with zero hesitation. Churches are sanctuaries in wartime, right? That's why Ava called it a safe house.

Forgoing the civility of knocking—because, again, we're in wartime—I go for the old copper handle that looks like a collector's item, but the door swings open for me.

A man, both his hands wrapped in bandages, shuffles past me without even a glance. The heavy wooden door almost slams closed, but I shoulder my way in, to the surprise of a woman in a white coat.

A doctor.

"Lucía Salazar?" I say straightaway, following the instructions Ava wrote on the map.

The doctor looks drained. She takes me in from hat to boots, and I gauge from her shaking head that I'm the last thing she wants to deal with.

She says something quick in Spanish, and my ear cuff translates instantaneously. "You're an American with the Common."

I nod and she shakes her head again.

The knot that's been forming in my gut yanks tighter.

I've never told anyone this—especially Ava, seeing as how the medical field is her family's *profession*—but I have an aversion to doctors. One too many nights spent in a hospital waiting room, I suppose, doing exactly what that room of torment is named for. Waiting. Waiting for my dad to stop complaining about how the cafeteria printers got his order wrong, just so he didn't have to focus on why we were there. Which was waiting for the doctor to come in and tell us if mom's breast cancer was back.

I shake it all off.

"Tell it to me straight, doc," I state, the opposite of what my dad would say. "What's the prognosis?"

Am I too late? Is my team gone? Did they never even make it?

I realize the doctor doesn't speak my language, but she must understand what I'm asking. She starts moving, speed walking across the vaulted entrance hall lined with shattered stained glass. "A member of your team is here."

"Who? Where are the others?"

She doesn't answer, and the knot in my gut mutates into a time bomb.

I am too late.

The doctor impatiently waves for me to follow.

In an exercise I've never been any good at, I keep my mind blank. No speculations or pre-visions while I jog after the doctor, past a solemn file of wounded women and men waiting to be seen.

When I get to the side room the doctor vanished into, I'm not prepared to see Kano buried under wires and tubes.

They removed his uniform. His right forearm dangles from the bedsheets, looking paler than the koi fish tattooed on his wrist.

The zippy soldier, always one to grin at death and danger, is not smiling now. His colorless lips are pulled over a breathing tube, a ventilator acting as his lungs while he sleeps.

But I know he's not just sleeping. I told the doctor I wanted the truth straight, bitter with no sugar.

"The tissue damage is severe," the doctor says, via my ear cuff. She examines Kano's chart. "When it's safe at sundown, I will order that your friend be moved to a proper facility in the city."

"Safe from who—what happened here?" I ask, forgetting our language barrier.

The bomb that's been ticking—waiting—inside my gut finally triggers, blowing all kinds of feelings to the surface.

I feel scared. Full of dread. I feel like I failed already, and I only just got here.

I was too late.

The doctor puts her hand on my shoulder, the way Rayla would to bolster morale. "Your Common and the People's Militia are heading for Monterrey now. If it's your friend's fate, his passing will be avenged."

Roth and the capo aren't in Monterrey!

I'm losing precious minutes just standing here.

If Ava and the others—*who are the People's Militia?*—get to Monterrey before I can catch them, odds are high there will be more needless casualties in our ranks.

I can't let that happen. We've all come too far.

I make myself look at Kano one last time, waiting for him to open his eyes, knowing full well they'll stay closed.

"Gracias," I tell the doctor, and remove myself from the room.

Before I race hell-bent for Duke, I make a quick stop in the sanctuary. Keeping my head down, I move to the altar where there's a long table overloaded with candles.

I've never been one for religion, and I don't know if this act is some sort of blasphemy, but I light one for Kano.

It's the least I can do.

"Please don't die," I whisper. "We'll get Roth, I promise. It's all about to be over."

I feel Rayla's last words wash over me like a baptism.

It's over.

I'm going to make sure that it finally will be.

THEO

"I was once an idealist like you," Roth proclaims.

We stand alone at the railing of an extravagant balcony, the length of an Olympic-sized pool, staring out at the stronghold's utopian grounds. The famed Salazar Reservoir is in the distance, its placid waters the crown jewel of the cartel's holdings.

In Mexico City, water has always been a source of power. Since arriving here, I've learned that its ancient Aztec capital, Tenochtitlan, was built on an island surrounded by a vast lake system, before the city was conquered and then drained by the Spanish conquistadors.

And now, centuries later, the Salazars have found a way to control what's left below the sinking ground, and what falls from the sky, as if it's their divine right.

The reservoir would make a fitting stage for the grand execution, I think, suddenly inspired.

Sixty feet from the Arabian-style mansion, a long line of cartel lieutenants is positioned in front of a bed of manicured dahlias flanked by insanely tall Mexican fan palms. Valeria greets each lieutenant, her pet white tiger by her side, sufficiently drugged into compliance.

Each deputy kisses her ring, pledging their alliance to their capo.

Where's the old capo, Valeria's mom?

I'm guessing Valeria probably drugged her into compliance too.

"I thought all Roths are born realists," I say, aiming to ride Governor's suddenly talkative wave. I fiddle with the gold necklace around my neck, which was switched back on the moment I stepped foot on the capital's soil.

Roth seems unconcerned about the cartel listening in on our conversation through our translators. But I follow his lead, eager for every morsel of information I can get.

"At your age, I was wide-eyed and callow," Roth grumbles, staring down at all those shiny medals on his stately uniform. "Convinced that humanity as a collective could save our dying world. I believed in the power of the people. My predecessors cured me of my ignorance."

Mira has already cured me of my own kind of ignorance.

"By predecessors, do you mean parents?" I ask.

Roth turns to me, clasping his strong hand on my shoulder. His grip feels heavy. Inescapable. "When my grandmother held the governorship of Texas . . ."

I feel my skin shiver and my blood curdle, realizing he's referring to my great-great-grandma. *Of course she has so many greats to her name.* "Meryl Roth the Great," the history books christened her.

". . . she instilled in me the importance of endurance," he presses on, centering all his focus on me. "She trained me the hard way. Governor, as I called her, dropped me and my fantasist notions outside her walls and protection, and into London."

"London, England?" I ask, gobsmacked.

His lips twist in an impish smile, like this nightmare trip somehow holds a pleasant memory in his diabolical mind.

"A once-thriving, preeminent nation that tried to rescue the world and became its own sinking ship. I quickly learned the sea wasn't all that pulled it under. The leaders allowed too many in. Disease, lawlessness, and war killed the empire."

My thoughts flood with visions of Roth keeping me here in Mexico, of airplanes and parachutes dropping me into London. Beijing. Berlin.

Hard lessons.

Great-great-grandma Meryl was a hard-ass. She trained a maniac who now wants to train *me*.

"Governor made me find my own way back," Roth continues, pulling me to the here and now. "And when I returned to Dallas, I finally understood our family legacy. The Roths are stewards of our land, Theo. Our duty is to make sure it endures."

And I guess personal power—a Roth empire—has nothing to do with it?

"You will soon learn like I did," he imparts to me. "I see it's in you, unlike Alexander and Halton. You will grow into your role as heir, and thrive."

I hold back my shock. *He really believes I'm his heir?* "How?" I let slip. "How will you make the American public accept me, a second-born?"

"Fear, Theo. It always comes down to fear." His grip tightens. "When the future is dark, blind panic sets in. And when people become terrified, realizing they've lost their way, they look up for guidance."

They look up to the Lone Star.

The chaos that's happening right now in the States. I now know, *for sure*, it was by his design.

"My citizens will forgive my choice in welcoming a second grandchild after the Traitorous Twins took my first."

Roth tells the lie so well even *I* almost believe him.

He was the one who took out Halton. Rayla. Darren. Why? So his legacy can better endure?

"They will accept my weakness so they can prosper from my strengths. They fear a country without my leadership. My guidance."

"And Valeria?" I dare to ask. The girl was clearly raised to rule. She's precocious, beautiful, and ruthless. Everything Roth acclaims. And yet, he remains unimpressed by her. "What is your daughter's role in the Roth legacy?"

His eyes narrow on my aunt. "She told you, I see."

Below us on the lawn, a barrel-chested lieutenant refuses to kiss the capo ring on Valeria's outstretched hand.

Her head cocks dangerously to the side as if she's asking, *Are you sure?* Just as the man begins to turn his back on her—publicly spurring Valeria's claim as his new lord—she snaps her fingers twice. Quicker than a skipped heartbeat, her tiger comes alive and pounces on the lieutenant. He mauls the man's thick thigh, driving him to his knees.

Again, Valeria holds out the scorpion ring. The lieutenant crawls to her, his whimper reaching us on the wind.

"I declare allegiance to your rule," he swears, pressing his lips to the blood-red ruby.

Satisfied, Valeria turns to face her dad on the balcony. She instructs her line of lieutenants to raise their arms in salute to Roth. When the tiger raises its massive blood-soaked paw alongside them, she smiles with delight.

Was that display of violence for him?

If so, I'm guessing she didn't get the reaction she was hoping for. Governor offers only a paltry nod in acknowledgment.

"The alliance was my father's doing," Roth explains. "In his time as governor, he did not believe Texas could stand on its own."

"So you and the former capo . . ."

Roth withdraws his hand from my shoulder. "I was never unfaithful to my wife."

It was against his ethics to cheat on Mrs. Roth, but he was totally fine with murdering her? *My grandma . . .*

Governor's face puckers into a grimace.

"Valeria was an experiment."

Experiment? What exactly does that *mean?* Before I can wring out any more details, Director Wix interrupts.

"We're ready for you, sir," she announces from the balcony's sliding doors.

Governor straightens his wide shoulders—whatever Director Wix has him on appears to have completely restored him to his full strength—and as quick as a blink, he's shut himself off, his hard veneer has returned.

"It's time to save the country from itself, my boy." He takes in a final glower of the impressive Salazar compound, his secret daughter Valeria, born not out of love, but to ensure an international alliance, then spins on his heel and walks toward what he's convinced is his destiny. His birthright.

Roth is about to come out of hiding, live on national news. What's more, he's doing it by announcing that he's reentering the presidential race, taking the late Governor Cole's place. Painting himself the hero.

And he will be, if I'm right about what he's trading for at tonight's meeting with the capo and President Moore.

I can't get the Director's threat out of my head. She said we're returning home. Or more ominously, *What will be left of it.*

It's one hundred degrees out here on the balcony, but goosebumps sting across my entire body.

Roth's here for a weapon. Something powerful enough to cause mass devastation, so that he can be the savior who swoops in to clean up the mess.

It's time to save the country from itself, my boy.

I don't want any part of this. But now's not the time to stop playing the willing protégé.

Turning to follow Governor, I take in the complicated 3D-capture technology that will project a 360-degree hologram of Roth into the nation's living rooms. President Franklin Roosevelt's fireside chats on steroids.

I will escape the family legacy, I promise myself again.

Soon. Tonight, after the execution of Andrés, the People's Militia rebel.

The mouse, as she likes to call him.

I promised Valeria flames. And I'd better be able to deliver.

Before Roth reaches the balcony door, the timid servant who dressed us in Monterrey approaches with a clothing brush raised, prepared to get the potential US president camera-ready.

But Governor keeps marching forward, plowing through the girl like she isn't even there. She trips trying to jump out of his way and tumbles to the ground, her kit flying across the terrace to land at my feet.

Without thinking, I gather her tools and reach out my hand to help her up. She doesn't take it.

A second-rate version of my translator necklace hangs around her throat, made of twisted silver instead of gold. The device relays her words in a subdued whisper.

"I'm sorry," she says, staring at my boots like she's waiting for me to wind back for a kick. "I didn't mean to get in the way, Sergeant Roth."

I flinch. "My name is Theo," I say, still holding out my hand. She takes it this time, and I lean in close. "Theo Wright."

Why did I just say that? What if she's one of Valeria's falcons? It just seems worth the risk, vital even, that someone knows my real name. *I'm* not *a Roth.*

The girl collects the clothing brush from me and feigns wiping dust from my uniform jacket. The handle pushes up the starched sleeve, and she stares at the cuts marking my right wrist.

Mierda. *Shit.* Does she recognize the mark as a Common tattoo?

I shove my sleeve down and try to take my leave with a nod—I don't trust myself to say anything further—but the girl grabs hold of my arm. A bold look stirs behind her eyes.

"What will you do with Andrés?" she asks.

This girl's more than just a servant.

I hold her gaze, hoping to see through her, right past whatever role she's playing. Is she a puppet? A falcon? A militia mouse, maybe?

A rebel, like me?

"I'm going to do with him just what he deserves," I say carefully, knowing my translator will project my words to anyone listening.

Valeria probably has surveillance on me from a dozen different angles.

"Would you like to assist me?" I ask, a normal request to a servant.

The girl studies me, then nods, a brisk, forceful gesture.

She's a member of the People's Militia. I feel it in my bones and blood.

I've just found my means to pull off tonight's show.

"Good," I say, motioning for her to follow. "Then let's get started."

MIRA

Ava drapes the soiled layers of my infinity scarf over my shoulders and forehead, taking minute care to ensure all strands of my red and blonde-tipped hair stay hidden.

I help my sister pull on a long, loose duster and wide hood, covering her charcoal-black uniform and fiery head. Despite washing every stitch of cloth and leather on us, we both still stink of javelina. That sharp, musky scent that's meant to mark territory.

Salazar territory.

I exit the back of the transport, a beat-up cargo van belonging to the People's Militia, and gaze out in the direction of the cartel's northern stronghold.

The lieutenant of Monterrey's mansion. Lucía's former residence.

Her prison, she called it.

Roth, are you in there?

Theo. Please be in there.

The puncture wounds on my lower legs pulsate with a dull ache, made worse by every one of my footsteps. I found Ciro's cutting-edge surgical glue in our packs to seal the swollen gashes, and before we left the small town, Ava and I accepted the doctor's rabies vaccines. But we staunchly refused the pain medications.

We must keep our minds clear. Focused.

No pain, no gain, I imagine Kano would say.

It felt impossible to leave Kano behind. Wrong and disloyal. *There was no choice,* I keep stressing this point to my conscience. We could do nothing for him. *The doctors will save him.*

The only thing I can do for Kano right now is make certain our side wins.

"We'll return for you," I whisper, looking at each member of our team, trying and failing to stop my mind from contemplating which of us will make it through this.

Stay focused. The endgame is within reach.

Lucía and Haven throw on scarves and loose coveralls identical to mine, while Alexander, Skye, and Barend cloak themselves in ankle-length jackets and hoods like Ava's.

In this harsh afternoon sun, our black uniforms stick out like crows against a pale sky.

You look like police, Matías told us.

And neither the federal nor state law enforcement have set foot in Monterrey in over a decade, he further explained.

The water lords paid them all off, Lucía said, her voice taut with tempered fury as she handed us our civilian disguises. *Everyone has a price.*

I think of the woman at the border bridge running off with Lucía's offer of gold. *Hush money.*

Ava always said those with the guns always win. But maybe it's money that holds the most power.

Tightening the straps of my shoulder holster concealed beneath the folds of my baggy scarf, I set off to join the line forming behind Matías.

Two steel platform carts piled high with bags of soil and mulch wait beside him. Today, rebels are disguised as gardeners, workers who tend to the lieutenant's prized grapefruit groves.

The militia leader's plan won in a unanimous vote, after only a minor grumble from Alexander.

"Father to father, I'll trust you," Alexander told Matías, finally accepting that this was our only strategy and we were wasting precious time. "Help me bring back my son and I will fight with you for yours."

While I'm glad to have Alexander's sharpshooting skills for the mission, a selfish bitterness festers inside of me like an old wound. *He tells a stranger he trusts him, but he'd never trust me.*

And I know Alexander would happily throw me into his father's arms if it meant he could get his son back.

Why do I care if I've earned his confidence? I chastise myself. The task at hand. Focus.

Once we're through the gate and on the stronghold's property, we're to break into two teams. Team One will be led by Matías and Alexander to locate the captives, their two sons. Most agreed Theo would be locked with Andrés, somewhere in the interrogation chambers.

But I think Theo will be somewhere near Roth.

I'm convinced Roth will be keeping his grandson, his presumptive heir, close. And if my gut is correct, I'm mere minutes from confronting both of our objectives, because Team Two, led by Ava, Lucía, and myself, is going after the former governor.

Lucía knows every nook of this mansion like the grooves in the beads of her rosary. *There are only so many places you can run and hide, Roth. Your time is up.*

Matías's whispered warning repeats through my ear cuff. "Remember, stealth is our greatest strength."

Deep wrinkles crease the militia leader's eyes. Before he took the role of a fighter, Lucía said he was the owner of a fruitful plot of land. *He must be used to planting seeds and waiting for something to grow.*

Well, today is reaping day.

"Do not break the line," he says, leaning his weight on his oakwood staff. He scrutinizes the teams and the gardening bags filled with explosives, then lowers the wide brim of his palm straw hat over his brow and waves the line forward.

Ava walks at my front, Haven behind. Our procession moves in a slow, leisurely pace toward the mansion's side entrance, but I feel far from relaxed.

"The streets were supposed to be empty," Barend whispers.

Just like in Texas, people here normally choose to hole up indoors in the oppressive heat of the daylight hours. But right now, the street in front of the stronghold is teeming.

Something draws a crowd to the gate of the mansion's main entrance.

Or some*one*.

A militiaman, a bareheaded teen who doesn't hide beneath a hat or scarf, breaks from the front of our file. He elbows into the crush of onlookers and umbrellas to get to the copper barrier with its spiked golden tops.

A body. A young woman. Clothed only in her underwear. She hangs impaled from one of the gleaming tips.

The teen screams, loud enough for the entire block to feel his hurt. "Rosa!"

The name incites a domino reaction down our fifteen-person column. Two women directly behind Matías set off in a sprint, stumbling into the press of silent spectators.

"Rosa!" they cry in unison.

Lucía crosses herself, her head snapping to Matías. Tears track his cheeks, pooling in the hard lines of his mouth.

They knew this girl.

"She was Andrés's girlfriend," Lucía reveals, my ear cuff picking up her hushed words muffled beneath her scarf.

"Is this the work of your cousin?" Skye whispers sharply, moving to Lucía's side. Is that concern in her piercing look, or judgment?

"The lieutenant will have tortured them, yes," she answers. "But this is savage, even for him."

The work of the Heartless Butcher, then?

The capo must be here.

And that means *Roth* must be here.

Lucía sighs either a curse or a prayer, keeping her steady stare fixed on Matías.

Quick and covert, Matías directs three from his militia to protect the gardening bags, then gives Lucía an imperceptible nod. They detach from the group and move to the entrance in tandem.

"Stay," Haven whispers to me, gripping the back of my coveralls.

The teen and two women have reached the gate's entrance by now. They throw themselves onto Rosa's body, desperately trying to lift her up off the golden spike. In the struggle, the girl's neck tilts back, displaying the terrorizing sight of her slit throat.

One of the women wails "Rosa!" again and again until she faints, falling against the metal bars.

I didn't notice before. The mice. Stuffed into the girl's stiff hands. Strewn about on the pavement below her dangling feet.

"Militia mice!" a cartel gunman taunts from behind the gate.

"Savage *cons*," Skye spits.

She's the first of our group to step out and follow after Lucía. Then Ava.

I jerk forward to move after them, but Haven's grip is strong. And Alexander appears on my left side.

"Don't," he warns. Orders. He locks his hand around my arm.

"Let. Go." I can't wrestle away. I can't cause attention. A scene.

"Do you not see?" Alexander breathes hot in my ear. "The perimeter is chock-full of armed cartel men."

"Did you think those guarding the capo and your father would be holding *flowers*?" I hiss. "I'm not scared."

"Oh, I forgot," Alexander throws at me patronizingly. "You're not scared of anything."

"I am," I admit, the truth catching painfully in my throat. "I'm terrified Theo's next to be strung up on that gate."

Alexander unleashes my arm. He tears away from me like he wants to get as far as possible from the image I just conjured, and moves to hover near the steel platform carts. Near the concealed explosives.

I make a second attempt to go for Ava, but Haven holds me tight. "This is a message," she whispers. "The lords will not let the message be taken down."

Matías and Lucía make it to the front. With gentle hands, they pull their friends away from the girl and move back toward our line.

Barend huddles close to Alexander, muttering something that makes Theo's father shake his head in protest. Under his oversized hood, I see Barend's jaw tighten as his commanding eyes bore into mine: *We're leaving; stand down.*

"No, we *must* go through with the plan," I say, reckless, way too loud, needing Haven to listen and let me loose.

The time is now. We have to strike; we can't let Roth and the water lords just get away with this. With *everything*.

If Matías calls this off, I need to figure out a way to get that gate open myself.

A wild idea flashes into my mind, dangerous as lightning.

I could rip off my scarf, tell the cartel gunmen who I am. They would arrest me. Take me into the stronghold—straight to Roth.

And then what?

You're going to get yourself killed, I argue with myself.

No, you're just scared.

What happened to doing whatever it takes?

More gunmen emerge from the stronghold. They swarm the lawn. The roofs.

Matías hoists his staff into the air, the signal to return to the vans.

"No," I protest. I will not retreat.

I yank myself free from Haven's grip and march for the arsenal of mortars and M-1000s waiting inside the gardening bags.

My aunt's hot on my heels, and Alexander sees me coming, but neither makes another move to stop me. *They won't retreat either.*

Alexander shields the cart from the cartel cons with his body while I peel open the top bag with one hand and flick the switch of an e-lighter with my other.

As I reach for the first explosive, I look to the front gate to calculate where best to strike.

I let the flame die when I see Ava halt in the center of the crowd. Her head turns toward a figure dressed in all black. My eyes rake over the dark cap and checkered bandana. The dusty combat uniform.

It's Owen.

Speeding right for her.

Haven darts forward with me, and side by side we push into the crowd's center.

We get to Owen at the same time as Ava and Skye. Alexander comes up a few paces behind, a Roman candle and his gun both stashed in the folds of his long linen jacket.

The five of us form a protective circle around Owen as he throws his hands over his head, fighting to breathe.

His words come out in sputters. "He's . . . not . . . here . . ."

I think he might faint before he gets the rest out.

Ava takes the cooling strip I gave her off her neck and places it onto his.

"Where is he?" she asks, more patient than I've ever seen her.

"Roth's in . . . the capital."

Mexico City.

"There's . . . a trade meeting . . ."

"When?" I press, the baking sun melting away the last of my composure.

"Tonight . . ."

My hope shrivels and disappears. Sweat drips into my eyes, stinging me to tears.

We'll never make it.

PART III
THE FIGHT

AVA

He did it.

Somehow, Owen uncovered where Roth is hiding. The location's been verified—his team found the hard evidence.

No more guessing, no more failures, no lives wasted, he promised in the Whiz's hospital room.

And he came through.

I felt a sudden flare of joy when I saw Owen running toward me, safe and whole. Despite his dark hat and bandana, he stood out like a strip of radiant sunlight in the crowd.

Owen found his way back to me. To our mission.

He had my paper map clutched in his hand. A love letter, not a goodbye note.

The kind I learned how to write from my father.

We've got six hours before Roth's meeting with the capo, he told us as we hurried back to our vehicles. *And the high rollers will no doubt be dealing big.*

Is Roth trading Project Albatross? From my time in President Moore's prison, I know Canada was attempting to exchange Mira and me for the "twin gene" editing therapy.

But what does Roth want from the Salazars?

A weapon? Tonight's trade meeting will have more on the bargaining table than tanks of water and biofuel.

That alarming thought spurs me to urge, "Drive faster!"

Mira sits practically on my lap, squeezed in Duke's passenger seat, Owen at the wheel beside me, the rest of our five mission teammates crammed in the back. We follow Matías and the People's Militia's vans as close as a shadow.

Any faster and we'll crash, but Owen indulges my request.

After weeks of doubt and agonizing, Roth has finally been rooted out. No more running or hiding, for either of us.

Tonight, at last, one side will win.

It will be you who falls, I send out a promise to Roth. Rage returns to my veins, hotter and more bitter than the fire I set to the Governor's Quarters. I feel ready. Dangerous.

Lucía must sense my eagerness.

"Almost there," she assures me.

Hands drumming on the steering wheel, Owen drives us skillfully down a remote dirt road, straight for the saddle-shaped profile of the Cerro de la Silla mountain.

"You are positive this leads to an airfield?" Alexander challenges, skeptically scanning our surroundings through the window. Even though Owen, his only ally within our team, has returned, Alexander has become more high-strung than ever.

"Lucía already said this is the route, didn't she?" Skye bristles. "So sit back, shut up, and enjoy the ride."

"I will not *shut up*," Alexander spits back. "It bears repeating that Matías himself said he's uncertain of the amount of stolen biofuel the militia has left in their stores. We should be *driving* to Mexico City, not taking this risk."

"No, bud, I think the risk is ten hours of driving on Mexican highways," Owen says. He manages to keep his tone light, ever the mediator.

Before Alexander can argue further, Mira, far less patient, snaps, "Do you want to get there in time or not?"

"Remember: same team, same goals," Owen presses, holding up his arms for peace.

"Hands on the wheel," Haven says.

"Right, of course, safety first," Owen responds, immediately grabbing the ten and two positions, before shifting a quick glance at me.

I wish he'd take off his hat so I could see his eyes. Maybe then I'd know what he was trying to tell me with that look.

"The militia are signaling to us," Barend warns from the rear of the car. Ahead, the lead van's taillights flash on and off twice.

"On it," Owen says, slowing the car as we curve around a series of twisty hairpin turns that take us deeper into the jagged desert mountains.

Seated on the floorboards behind our passenger seat, Haven has turned pale. Sweat shines on her high forehead and she clutches her stomach.

"Look out the windshield," I advise her. "Pick a stable object—it will help with the motion sickness."

"There's nothing stable about this drive," Owen quips happily. He's in his element. Out on the open road, his team by his side, adventure ahead.

I've never seen him more excited than when Lucía told us about the People's Militia's small fleet of Cessna airplanes. Our ride to Mexico City.

But my sister didn't look nearly as thrilled as Owen. She still doesn't. I cover her hand to stop her from cracking her knuckles.

"You traveled across the sea in a shipping container at the bottom of a boat to cross back into the States," I remind her. "This will be nothing compared to that."

"A ship, not a boat," Alexander clarifies. I feel Mira tense, hankering to throw out a barb about Alexander becoming a wealthy shipping businessman after fleeing his life in Dallas. But I squeeze her hand in caution: *Let it go.*

Owen turns down a final bend in the dirt road, and then all at once we've entered a sweeping desert valley, edged on all sides by serrated cliffs. The flat, V-shaped floor is covered in white-tipped Mexican feathergrass.

The perfect place for an unregistered airfield.

"Uh, not to ask the obvious . . . but where exactly is the runway?" Owen questions.

"You're looking at it," Lucía answers, pointing to a long strip of dry desert wash that's been cleared of vegetation.

Four twin-engine planes make their way out of a camouflaged hangar to the start of the runway, dust billowing in their wake like earthbound thunderclouds.

"These are drug planes," Barend says, reproachful.

We take in the sheet-metal birds in uneasy silence.

The seven-passenger aircraft have high, modified wings so they can take off from short strips, and metal plates attached under their engines to protect them from gravel. I note the extra-large tires, ideal for landing on rocky terrain, and the homemade fuel tanks peeking out from behind the seats.

Barend is right. These are smugglers' planes.

I remember hearing Roth brag at one of Father's work parties about how many drug planes his Texas State Guard had shot down at his Big Fence. He relished in comparing his legacy fleet of Golden Eagles to the inferior Cessna planes in fanatic detail. Every guest listened with rapt attention, a requirement if the person wanted to keep their position in his cabinet.

Now I know that was all a cover-up. A show for the public. Roth was really in alliance with the Salazar cartel all along. I bet he let them fly their Cessnas straight over the border and into Texas without ever firing a single shot.

"Where did you get the planes?" Owen asks Lucía, fascinated.

He lifts the bill of his cap, gaping at the small aircraft with a machine-buff's appraising eye. "They're old models, yeah, but anything with wings still costs a fortune."

"The capo has a fleet five times larger than the entire Mexican air force itself," Lucía says.

Owen shakes his head in awe as he parks Duke beside the militia's vans outside the hangar.

"Over the years, the militia collected the cons' scraps," she continues, "and raided their smaller bases for the parts they still lacked."

Skye's head pops up beside Lucía's. "Impressive."

Alexander grunts. "Rebellions require an exhaustive replenishing of funds to stay alive . . . and not all have a Ciro Cross at their disposal," he says, suspicion in his voice.

"Keep Ciro's name out of your mouth," Barend advises Alexander, pressing a finger into his chest.

"Tell me, Lucía, is the People's Militia really a proxy outfit for a rival cartel?" Alexander pushes, unfazed by Barend's threats. "Did Matías strike a deal with a lesser evil to fight a shared enemy?"

He thinks the People's Militia is funded by cartel money. My own counsel comes rushing back to me, ideals I told myself in the War Room after I escaped prison. *It matters how we get our power . . . We won't be able to wipe off the blood if we compromise.*

Lucía lets the accusation hang in the air. She watches, silent, as Matías shepherds his people out of the vans, splitting them into groups for the planes.

"Murder, kidnapping, starvation, thirst. That is daily life for the people who live in Salazar territory," Lucía says, hot-blooded. "Matías was tired of hearing the people's cries for help go unanswered."

She turns to look Alexander square in the eye. "If the government can't protect us, then we have no choice left but to protect ourselves."

She rises to her feet. "The People's Militia is true to its name. We have no other master but the people."

"Satisfied?" Skye challenges.

As if answering on Alexander's behalf, Owen opens both of Duke's winged doors.

Everyone files out except Mira.

"Are you sure this is safe?" she whispers, trying to conceal her hesitation. She cracks her knuckles again.

"Have we ever had a 'safe' day in our life?" I say, nudging her shoulder.

Mira pushes out a long breath, then surges from the car. "No fear, right?" she says.

Then I notice that while the rest of the team has already joined Matías and the militia by the planes, Owen hangs back, staring apologetically at Duke.

"Do you two need a moment?" I wisecrack.

"I know it's just a car, but I don't want to let Duke go," he says, eyes glassy. "We've been through a lot together."

Duke is the catalyst that changed Owen's future. The reason he crossed paths with Rayla, and his guardian during the Killer Drone attack. The car has saved his life more than once.

I know firsthand how hard it is to leave something you love behind.

"I'm sending Duke back to Dallas," Owen tells me. He plunges into the car and starts pressing buttons on the dashboard's screen.

Duke can navigate himself, but can he make it on cartel-patrolled highways and through the border wall?

"He can make it," Owen says firmly, as if he can sense my doubt.

"Ava, we need to go," Mira says. She grips her rucksack in one hand, holding out mine with the other. Thanks to Haven, our bags weren't left behind in the tanker truck after all.

Mira, Owen, and I make our way to the final Cessna, its pilot garbed in a lightweight bomber jacket and aviator shades. She nods a confident greeting as I ascend the short airstairs to join our team in the tight cabin. Owen lingers at the door, pausing to watch Duke speed across the valley and disappear behind a bend in the road.

When Owen takes his seat beside me, the pilot secures the door, then turns to face her nervous passengers. The cabin vibrates so bad my teeth rattle, and the vacillating roar of the engines sounds like they might fizzle out at any moment.

The opposite of my first flight experience aboard Senator Gordon's government-funded jet.

I grab hold of Mira's hand and squeeze. *No fear.*

"I will see to it my plane lands safely," the pilot says, our ear cuffs translating her promise. She places a closed fist over her heart. "Justice by our own hands."

Their version of the Common salute.

All of us, even Alexander, press a hand to our chests.

"Justice by our own hands," we vow.

OWEN

Before I sent Duke back to Texas, I established a remote-access VPN connection that links my tablet to Duke's operating system. Not just to keep tabs on my code busting, but to catch up with the outside world.

And guess what I just found out?

Roth is back in the race.

I mean, I knew he was running, but not for *president*. The bastard is at large, on the lam, fleeing from *us*. He's gone AWOL, abandoned his country for a hotter southern neighbor, and he expects the States to just welcome him back with open hearts and arms?

Site after site, poll after poll, indicates yes. It's a spirit-crushing twist—the public's susceptibility to a Roth revival.

And the headlines don't look good for our side.

"A Common Catastrophe"; "Chaos Heading for Ruin"; "Real Leadership, Right Now!"; "To Survive into the Future, We Must Forgive the Past"; "Howard Roth, the Dark Horse, or the White Knight?"

"More like the front rider of the Four Horsemen of the apocalypse," I scoff.

The Goodwins have said nothing since we saw the breaking news.

Ava takes all this in, stone-faced, stoic, except for the *pop, pop, pop* of her cracking knuckles. For a second, I think of grabbing her restive hand, telling her she can use my own as a stress ball, or as a steady grip to hold on to in this whirlwind, but Mira gets there first.

Then another headline catches my eye: "Common Leader Emery Jackson Unaccounted For. Twenty-One Hours Since Last Seen."

Did the State Guard get her? Or did Blaise? Is she locked in a Loyalist dungeon, or covertly on her way south, to us, as backup?

I'm on the verge of asking Ava what she thinks, but I decide it's best to avoid stirring the alarm.

The scrappy, claustrophobic plane suddenly dips, jostling half my body into Alexander's lap. The guy doesn't even notice. He's too busy staring out the murky window watching for the first glimpse of Mexico City.

"Still another hour, bud," I say.

I don't blame Alexander for wanting to keep his head in the clouds.

His dad is running for the presidency. Again. And there's a high chance Roth could get the public back on his side.

Roth could win.

A second dip and my focus shoots to the pilot. *We're going to crash; we're too heavy.* Eight passengers is one too many. I mull over which of us we could have culled, when my winning choice speaks up from the overcrowded row behind me.

"Are you sure your device is secure?" Skye asks cynically.

"Hi, I'm not sure we properly met," I snap, locking my eyes back to my screen, "but I'm head of cybersecurity, handpicked by Emery, recruited by Rayla Cadwell. I know what I'm doing."

I know what I'm doing.

"I'm good at my job too," Skye threatens, her temper as hot as mine. "So you should watch your tone." She rises from her seat, which happens to be Lucía's lap. I couldn't help but notice Lucía's arms were wrapped around Skye's waist . . . a human seat belt? Or is there something more happening there?

The infamous assassin leans over my headrest, reaches out, and glides a finger across my neck.

Um, did she just poison me?

No way, we're on the same team. I force myself to not wipe off my skin with my sleeve. Skye laughs, relishing in my squirms.

"Play Roth's announcement again," Mira demands, reminding us who the true enemy is here.

Taking a quick beat to calm myself, I enlarge the video to full screen and pump the volume.

The ex-governor's opening line is a real doozy.

"Did you miss me?" Roth asks the country, all smug and righteous, like he's not the culprit of all the chaos.

His whole state's gone dark; his Loyalists are blowing up cell towers *and* people, drowning "Commoners," assassinating rival candidates, and who knows what's coming next. Yet he can sit there in front of his Lone Star flag, look the camera in the eye, and say that he's the remedy and savior.

When the speech gets to the part where Roth promises to "cure the nation of the Common disorder," Haven slams her palms to her ears and screams, "Enough!"

I mute the bastard.

But in my mind, I hit replay again and again, on those first four words. *Did you miss me?*

No, I answer. *I've thought about you round the clock since our encounter in the tunnels.*

The ex-governor never leaves me.

Out of nowhere I'm trapped in flash memories of the worst day of my life: Roth shooting Rayla in the head, point-blank. Slipping away in his escape tunnels. Me lying wounded on the rocky ground, doing jack to stop him.

Do not run away, coward!

But he did run. He got past all of us, and took two lives on his way out.

Rayla. Pawel.

Three, including Mrs. Roth. The man's cold-blooded enough to kill his own wife. *And his grandson.* Even if Halton's murder wasn't by Roth's own blade.

I sneak a glance to Mira, who has her eyes locked on the ex-governor on the screen. *I hope to Whitman that Theo won't be added to that number.*

Fury coils inside my gut. Venomous, like the openmouthed rattlesnake tattooed on my wrist.

The coward won't escape this time.

Tonight, Roth doesn't stand a chance.

There's a plane full of dangerous rebels headed his way—an ex-soldier, three Gluts, a convicted assassin, a most wanted fugitive, a patricidal-minded son, and a Programmer turned battle-hardened Common warrior—every last one of us committed to go down fighting to rid the world of Howard S. Roth.

My tablet peals *ding, ding, ding* and notifications fill the screen.

Looks like we just got multiple hits.

It must be a big file—the unlocked folders have only been ringing in solo chimes until now.

Hope bubbles up inside me.

T-minus four hours until our long-awaited showdown with Roth. Now's the time to root out one more cannon-sized knowledge bomb to help us shape our battlefield.

Someone grips my arm, stirring me back to my seat.

I'm trembling.

"Got something?" Ava asks, cat eyes eager.

Play it cool. Don't get her hopes up.

What if it's a data gold mine on her dad?

I suddenly rise to my feet, hiding the screen against my chest. I mumble something about a bug and make my bumpy way down the aisle to the back of the plane.

Before cramming myself into the tiny cupboard that's generously labeled a "restroom," I throw a furtive look over my shoulder. Ava must have called bullshit on my hasty withdrawal, because she's homing in on me with a laser focus.

I spring into the restroom and slam the door, quickly discovering there is no lock. *Of course not.*

Better start scanning, fast.

Immediately I see we've hit pay dirt.

The subject line reads: "Project Albatross."

Before I can double tap the folder and uncover the goods, there's a pounding knock on the flimsy door.

"Occupied!" I say stupidly.

Ava and Mira barrel right in, the former ripping my tablet from my hands.

Mira shoves the door shut behind her, blocking it with her body, and I'm slammed against the metal wall and sandwiched between the sisters. Ava's so close I can see the golden flecks in her green eyes.

"Project Albatross *is* more than just a technology to eradicate the 'twin gene,'" Ava says, snapping me back to the task at hand. Her uniform's unzipped, the sleeves pulled down and tied over her waist, exposing her lean arms. Every one of her fine hairs stands on end.

"It's bigger than I ever thought possible . . . ," she says. "The Family Planning Division has unlocked the key to human genome editing."

Her finger flicks my tablet's screen, scrolling further.

Somehow I'm the only one in this joke of a restroom whose jaw just dropped ten thousand feet to the ground.

"I'm sorry, what now?" I say, awed.

"Was Father involved?" Mira whispers.

"Father was the locksmith," Ava answers. "He made the discovery."

"Okay . . . ," I barge in, trying to fully understand. "So Roth's making designer babies?" I attempt and fail to keep my voice down. I can't help but think about the positive. "Could the tech help correct errors in DNA . . . and cure people who suffer from genetic disorders?"

People like my mom.

Decades ago, the government outlawed biotech companies and independent scientists from even *reviewing* research involved with the modification of human embryos. Let alone actually *running* human test trials.

But it looks like the Texas Family Planning Division was operating their own experiments in secret labs.

And I thought *I* was a coder. Their dad was trying to rewrite the code of life.

"Wait, is Roth attempting to make *superhumans?*" I ask, my brain running a mile a second. "Trying to get a leg up militarily?"

"The tech is capable of all of that, yes," Mira answers quickly, "but that's not the most dangerous possibility . . ."

"Genome editing can be used as a bioweapon," Ava says, shifting her eyes from the screen to me. "The technology opens the door to create pesticide-resistant bugs that could wipe out an entire state's staple crop . . . or even drug-resistant strains of diseases."

"With Albatross, you could exterminate whole populations of your enemies," Mira contemplates, terrified.

"And you could come away with clean hands," I pick up her chilling line of thinking. "No fingerprints left behind."

"Roth has Director Wix, I know it," Mira says, eyes turning into daggers. "She has Father's technology."

I mentally slap my hand to my forehead.

Project Albatross is what Roth's offering to trade the Salazar cartel.

Roth has always considered himself above the law. I mean, the man has the gall to run for the country's highest office even *after* his catastrophe of a governorship *and* his recent crowning as top fugitive on the Wanted List.

But it looks like Roth wants to be more than just the president of the United States.

He wants to play God.

The goosebumps haven't left Ava's arms. "This discovery is huge," she says. "With global repercussions. If Roth trades this technology . . ."

"The world could end?" I finish for her.

No time to dig further into *that* terrifying thought.

The pilot's voice crackles over the busted-out speakers, and my ear cuff repeats her welcome announcement in English.

"Buckle up and prepare for landing."

I grab my tablet from Ava—for a split second I didn't think she'd give it back—and the three of us split up with the unspoken pact to keep what we just learned to ourselves.

Team Takedown has enough to worry about already.

Back in my seat, I look out the plane's small window and see the crazy sprawl of the largest and most crowded city on the continent. Over fifty million people, the population of the state of Texas, live inside this megacapital that's surrounded on all sides by huge, rugged mountains.

I've never set eyes on anything like it.

The Salazar cartel controls *all* of this territory, and Roth is hiding somewhere inside of it, behind their stronghold, which is doubtless harder to penetrate than any border wall.

We've got this, I give myself a pep talk. *I've got this.*

Resist much, obey little.

Justice by my own hands.

All of it.

AVA

Lucía sticks her arm out into the bustling street, hailing a pesero. The bright-green-and-gray microbus immediately pulls over to our congested street corner that's jam-packed with food vendors and distracted commuters. The hordes of people I'm familiar with, but the tacos? They smell like heaven.

Even a Texan who lived a heavily sheltered existence knows that Mexico City is a world-famous food paradise. *For those who can afford the cuisine, at least.*

Skye's nostrils eagerly inhale the delicious scents of sizzling homemade tortillas and mouth-watering carnitas, like a vulture sensing a fresh kill. All my teammates' stomachs growl, but none of us dares to order the legendary street food.

Not only do we not have any means to pay—but from here on out, we're forbidden from speaking at all.

It's too dangerous. Any hint of our American accents will flag us as outsiders. We'll be reported by an undercover falcon and then targeted by sicarios. Our mission lost.

The overpopulated capital is probably crawling with falcons, patrolling the streets like the State Guards did in Dallas. Except here, they pose as pedestrians, just like my team does.

To blend in, we wear civilian plainclothes over our combat uniforms.

I glance at Owen by my side, dressed in a pair of the long-sleeved coveralls Matías gave him. With his black cap and checkered bandana tied across the lower half of his face, he manages to pull off the incognito look with much more style and flair than Barend or Alexander.

The pesero opens its door, and my ear cuff translates the friendly driver's shouts of "Come in, come in, make room!"

He doesn't flinch when he sees that every inch of our bodies is covered and only our eyes show. Protecting one's identity is not out of the ordinary here in the center of Salazar territory, where kidnappings and murders are an everyday occurrence.

Lucía's words come back to me. *If the government can't protect us, then we have no choice left but to protect ourselves.*

I know that plight well.

Lucía leads the way onto the already-stuffed microbus, Skye following close behind. The driver waves them through, just like we planned. *He's one of the militia.*

Barend and Haven enter next, clearing a small space for Mira and me to take our places at the center of the bus, away from the windows. Owen and Alexander bring up the rear, scanning the other passengers for any signs of danger.

Right now, all across the supercity, Matías and his people are recruiting Mexico City's numerous civilian autodefensas to join him in tonight's battle with the Salazar cartel. Come midnight, he plans not only to liberate his son Andrés, but to end the Salazar reign for good and for all.

When we landed in the mountainous outskirts of the capital, Matías bellowed *No more!* as a rallying cry. *Tomorrow will dawn a new day for our country,* he vowed.

According to Owen's intel, the clandestine trade meeting begins at approximately eight thirty p.m. Just after sunset, Matías will assemble his forces outside the Salazar stronghold's gates.

We strike at nightfall.

My heart pounds in my chest like my own private war drum. *It's happening.* Soon, the final move will be played in our eighteen-year game with Roth.

Tonight, the king will fall.

Mira elbows my arm, covertly nodding to a sliver of exposed window between two sweaty men locked in a lively conversation about bullfighting. Truck after truck passes by, masked sicarios standing on the beds holding gold-plated automatic rifles. On patrol. Looking for an excuse to fire.

I'm supposed to keep my head down, stay hidden, but there's too much to see. Mounds of plastic water bottles piled on the streets and walkways, the Salazar scorpion sigil on every red label. At a traffic light, a frantic group of people lines up with buckets in their hands or stacked high on carts, fighting to get to a cartel man who distributes water from a tanker truck. Money changes hands.

The deliveries only come once or twice a week, Lucía said. In poor districts, the cartel cut all other distribution lines, including plumbing in homes and businesses. The citizens' only source is through the water lords.

The Salazar cartel controls life's most vital resource. The capo's monopoly of power is staggering.

I watch as a woman, dirt stained and rail thin, steals a bucket of water from a teenage boy. Even from where I sit inside the bus, I can see the desperation—the fear—in her actions. The wild, last-ditch effort to stay alive. But before she can flee with her spoils, she and the teenage boy are both shot dead by the cartel man.

Horrified, I think of the riot that almost broke out in Dallas when the State Guard tasered and arrested a woman for stealing a bottle of water right before my eyes. Here, the citizens re-form the line around the unmoving bodies, holding out their buckets, clamoring for them to be filled at any cost.

If they return home empty-handed, they won't survive.

Five microbus stops later, the passengers thin out, leaving just our mission team. The most multisensory experience of my life comes to an end when the driver turns off from the traffic-clogged streets, entering the garage of an unfinished skyscraper.

What was meant to be a forty-five-story bank tower is now one of the largest vertical slums in the world, home to thousands of squatters, all living without basic services like power and running water.

For the next two hours, this will be our safe house.

When we exit the pesero and are again alone and free to speak, Alexander corners Mira and me before we can follow the rest of the team up the garage stairwell.

"What else did you discover from the servers?" Alexander asks sharply, struggling to master his temper. "You may have been able to deceive my father for all those years, but I see right through you both. You're lying. You know something more."

He's right. We're lying by omission.

But Mira, Owen, and I agreed that we should keep the enormity of what Roth's trading on a need-to-know basis. Everyone must focus on the mission at hand, getting to Roth and the capo and saving Theo and Andrés.

Alexander is the last person I want to explain my father's culpability to right now.

Ever since we landed in Mexico City, a verse from "The Rime of the Ancient Mariner"—the poem Father used to read to us before bed—keeps echoing inside my skull like a penance bell.

> Ah! well a-day! what evil looks
> Had I from old and young!
> Instead of the cross, the Albatross
> About my neck was hung.

When I first learned of the secret project, I willingly took the burden—the shame—of what my father did upon my own shoulders. I swore I would stop what he started.

Together, Mira and I intend to keep that promise.

Project Albatross cannot spread. Father's technology and all its immense ramifications must be taken from Roth. The future itself depends on it.

Mira keeps her lips pressed in a hard line and attempts to sidestep Alexander. But he bars our way up the stairs and bears down with a cold fury.

"Owen will tell me nothing," he seethes. He points a threatening finger an inch from my face. "That boy has become putty in your hands. You're going to get him killed."

I take a step back, wounded.

"Just like what happened to my son because of *you*," he spits in Mira's face. He looks shaky, sweaty, like he's hankering for a stiff drink.

"Move," Mira says, holding back tears.

Anger sweeps over me. When Alexander pins Mira into the stairwell, demanding, "Tell me, now," I surge toward him, half-blind with rage, ready to unleash all the fire I've been storing in my belly. Without a second thought, I pull back my right fist and swing.

I hear a satisfying *crack!* Then blood bursts from his nose.

"Finally," Owen says, almost laughing, making his way back down the stairwell. "Alexander's been begging for someone to hit him, haven't you, bud?"

My knuckles sting, but from the way Alexander's eyes water, I know his face hurts worse. I can't hear his furious rebukes through his palms, which hold what I hope is his broken nose.

Owen claps Alexander on the shoulder, stepping between the two of us to prevent further confrontation.

But I'm not finished.

"My sister's the best thing that's ever happened to your son," I snarl. "Her loyalty is what will save him. But if he's already dead, it's because of you. Roth is *your* father . . . This is *your* family's mess."

Mira pulls me back. "Don't waste your hate," she whispers in my ear. "Keep it for tonight."

She's right. Alexander is just a distraction. *He's the wrong Roth.*

When I see Haven barreling down the stairwell, I move past Alexander without another glance, making my way to my aunt.

"What happened?" she asks, scowling at Alexander, her hands balled into weapons.

"Nothing worth our time," Mira assures her.

"Let's go," I say, continuing up the steps.

Haven and Mira follow close behind. Two floors up, we reach ground level. Through the stairwell landing door, I hear the tower buzzing with life. I turn to give Mira and Haven a warning look. *No more talking.*

Haven points up, then uses her fingers to relay that we're heading to the forty-fifth level. Even with my wounded leg, I practically run up the stairs. The stitch in my side and the burn in my thighs draws my focus, and I'm grateful for the respite from my mind.

When we reach level forty-four's landing, I stop, out of breath but enlivened by the exercise. Mira and I have always been able to communicate with just a look. She knows what I'm asking for without a word.

A moment to myself.

She nods. *See you soon,* our eyes say, then she continues up the stairs with Haven, leaving me to roam the deserted floor alone.

It has started to rain.

The unfinished top floors of the tower don't have walls or windows, leaving them totally exposed to the elements. I stand at the ledge, eyes closed, letting the water droplets wash over me, cooling off my temper.

I count my breaths, centering the strength of my body and soul for what comes next, until I hear my name being called. Softly. Slowly. Pulling me back from my meditations like a siren song.

Owen.

My eyes snap open and I turn to him.

He's there, right behind me. Without his mask. I hadn't realized just how much I missed that charming smile, punctuated by those dimples. His face is open. Eager.

"Happy birthday," he says.

My preoccupied mind completely forgot about my birthday.

Owen pulls a flower from behind his back.

It's the most alien-looking flower I've ever seen, an exquisite combination of yellow and electric pink, with a fringelike crown that looks like its thin tendrils are frozen in a slow dance.

"Lucía said it's a Mexican passionflower," he says with a sheepish shrug, handing it to me. It smells pungent, like a storage closet filled with mothballs. It's unexpected. Strange.

Like my growing feelings for him.

"I love it," I say.

When did Owen find time to remember birthdays and pluck flowers?

Our eyes meet, and all at once the butterflies floating in my stomach are set on fire. Heat flies through my limbs, reigniting my temperature.

I step forward, closing the gap between us.

"You came back," I say.

I slowly trace the curves of his face with my fingertips, leaving rivulets of rainwater in their wake. The heat between us grows stronger.

"I'll follow you anywhere," he promises. He grabs my hand, places it in his, gently caressing my bruised knuckles.

My heart broke at Rayla's funeral, fled its cage in my chest at the death of her, Pawel, and my father.

I never thought it would return.

But right now, standing here with Owen, so close, body vibrating, aching, I feel as if he's given back a piece of my heart to me.

It beats like the wings of a hummingbird.

"Ava, I want you to know—" Owen starts to say, but I press a finger to his lips.

"Show me," I breathe, drunk on his whisky-colored eyes.

We smile, then wrap our arms around each other, crushing the passionflower between our chests.

Our mouths don't part for the next twenty minutes.

And he shows me everything.

MIRA

I look down at my wrist and watch the time tick to 7:44 p.m.

The hour and minute my father pulled me into this world. And thirty minutes before my mother left it.

Father would always try to make this day feel special. Normal. A celebration of life, ritualized with cake and gifts and music.

Ava would get the "real" birthday party topside, a lavish show for our classmates and Father's coworkers, meant to cloak our family secret and keep our lie alive.

The lie, meaning me.

Afterward, Father and Ava would bring the festivities downstairs, singing, laughing, pretending that my own private basement after-party was fine, normal, *better*.

VIPs only, Father would make-believe.

Ava would end the night in a toast, wishing us a happy day of birth and hearty congratulations.

Birthdays are meant to be mile markers, and it was a tradition of mine to end the night singing, to myself, my own untraditional "Birthday Song."

Congratulations to you!
Another victory lap around the sun.
Another year of being alive.
Another year won.

Another year I survived as a twin, an illegal second-born. Another triumphant year in the game that's life.

This is the first time I can tell someone that on this day, this very minute, I was born. *I exist.* But being alone like this, staring at the hazy orange sun setting on a horizon of skyscrapers, another year won, it feels right, *normal,* to be on my own.

It's better this way, I tell myself.

And there's still the night, the battle, ahead.

I move closer to the edge of the unfinished room, to the wall made only of air. I let the tips of my boots hang off the floor, forty-five stories high, and gaze out at the bloated metropolis.

A steady shower of rain falls from low scattered clouds. I watch the water pour down from the slanted rooftops all across the district, collecting and funneling into bright-red gutters. I follow the invaluable water's route in my mind's eye, as it feeds into the network of aqueducts and pipelines, every drop leading to the Salazar stronghold.

It's a shadow on the distant skyline, but I see it. The blinding lights of the Salazar Reservoir and its adjacent mansion. If I squint, I imagine I can see inside, the meeting place, the players gathered around the table.

The capo. Director Wix. And the potential *President* Roth.

Theo, are you seated by his side? The visual turns my stomach, but it's better than accepting the alternative. *We're too late. Theo's already suffered the same fate as his brother, Halton. And he's lost to us for good.*

Every year, Ava gave me the best gifts for our name day. She invariably found the most elusive items on the Black Market; foreign liqueurs, sweets, flowers. The gifts were always perishable, illegal items that could disappear, cease to exist and show no evidence they were ever really there. Kind of like me.

But today, I'm going to give myself a present that will last.

A dead Roth.

And a living Wright.

Congratulations to me.

I hear footsteps echoing from the back of the room. Then voices lift in a soft song.

"Happy birthday to you . . ."

I turn to see Ava, Haven, Owen, and the rest of my teammates— my friends—moving toward me, tiny colorful sparklers raised high.

"Happy birthday to you . . ."

My eyes sting, joy welling up, coming out through tears.

"Happy birthday, dear Mira . . ."

Ava offers me my own firework. It sparks green and blue, the little streaks of light landing on my skin, burning as bright and fierce as my soul.

"Happy birthday to you," I join in the last line of the quiet song, locking eyes with my sister. "Thank you," I whisper, wiping my salty cheeks, all at once overwhelmed, humbled, heartbroken.

Scattered thoughts cut through my glowing warmth like a bitter, cold knife.

Father, Project Albatross, the poem, his guilt.

Father found a way to direct evolution. His discoveries have the potential to alter the course of human history.

And a ruthless, ironfisted man—*Roth*—has that technology. The immense power he could wield is unimaginable. *He could engineer our entire world if he wanted.*

The most personal implications hit me the hardest when I gaze at Ava.

We could be the last generation of twins.

I pull my sister into a hug. I can't recall the last time we embraced like this, but Ava wraps her arms around me tight, like she needs an anchor just as much as I do. We hold each other until the sparklers grow faint, then burn themselves out.

The room darkens and the moods shifts, an earnest, unified energy fanning out from every member of our team.

I glance at my watch: 7:50 p.m. It's almost time.

Ava and I pull away as Barend approaches, holding down his right wrist in the Common salute. The two black lines of a V mark his skin, symbolizing either victory or peace. I've never asked him which. But I suppose the two are interchangeable.

The soldier clasps his hands on our shoulders. "For Ciro and Kano," he says solemnly before moving for the stairs.

Skye steps forward next, traces of a cruelly removed tattoo hot pink against her pale skin. "For all those labeled 'undesirable candidates,'" she says. "The governors' control ends tonight."

Then Lucía moves toward us, her rosary coiled around her wrist. "Our paths were meant to cross," she says. "For this moment. So two tyrants can fall by our hands."

"No le tenemos miedo," I tell her. *We show no fear.*

Owen advances as Lucía follows Skye to the stairwell. He tugs his bandana down from his mouth, rolling up his sleeve to display his rebel mark. A silver-and-yellow rattlesnake poised to attack, shadowed expertly to make its rattler look as if it shakes in warning.

"For Rayla," he whispers, the muscles of his forearms tensing, flexing, ready to reach out and strong-arm whoever stands in our way. "Let's make today a govdamn holiday."

Ava folds her hand into his, and Owen smiles down at my sister in a way that pangs my chest. A painful tug that reminds me of the tie Theo has around my heart. And the strong, unabating pull I feel toward him.

I told you I'm with you, and I meant it, Theo said to me before storming the Governor's Mansion. Before he was taken.

I will do everything to get Theo back. To find him, protect him, keep him safe.

A weight on my shoulder eases, a burden I realize I've been carrying with me my entire life. *Owen feels the same for Ava.* I see this. I accept it. *Ava has three of us watching over her now.* Me, Owen, and Haven.

My aunt wraps her sturdy arms around my sister and me. What's left of our family.

The bottom edges of her tattoo peak out from her uniform, the roots of a tree, the symbol of her Center. "For us," she says. "Tonight, I fight for us."

With a deep breath, I close my eyes, thinking of my mother, my father. Of Rayla.

And then, inevitably, of Roth.

When I finally open my eyes again, my tears have dried, hardening over my skin like armor.

I see Alexander standing before me. He must have been hiding in the back—I didn't register his presence until now. He looks like a high-speed rail has smashed into his nose. I crack the knuckles of my left fist, ready if Alexander seeks to ruin this moment with another petty clash.

But to my disbelief, he holds down his right arm in salute.

When did he get his tattoo? I think fleetingly. *On one of his drunken nights in Dallas?* Black ink marks his wrist over his bulging veins. The number 2.

For Halton and Theo, I realize. His two sons.

Brothers who will never meet.

Alexander looks to Ava, then me. "You're both extraordinarily lucky to have each other."

Before I can say anything in return, he disappears after the others.

Haven squints at my watch. "Five minutes," she tells us with a nod and a smile, leaving the room with Owen to give Ava and me some time.

"I got you a gift," Ava says, digging into her rucksack. She pulls out a *real* clothbound book. That in and of itself is a sublime surprise.

But it's the gilded title that makes me exclaim, "Impossible."

Though I know full well nothing truly is. Especially when it comes to my sister.

"*Frankenstein* by Mary Shelley," she says with a grin, handing me the perfect present.

I flip through the yellowed pages, reveling at the surreal feeling of my favorite story in my hands.

"You carried it all this way?" I say.

"For your bookshelf. When we return home."

The idea of making it through this fight—*of making a home again*—is almost too much for me to take in.

I reach for my backpack and pull out my own nonessential baggage that I carried with me all these long miles.

The extra uniform for Theo.

I wrap Ava's gift carefully inside the padded material and store the bundle between my water bottle and ammo.

Ava nods, her grin spreading. "Look, it's stopped raining."

Our mission won't be starting in a downpour now.

Good news. I thought we'd had the last of that.

I set down my bag and we move to sit on the ledge. As our feet dangle in the breeze, Ava leans her head against mine, and we stare out at the last traces of the sunset disappearing below the winking skyline. We don't say a word and I let my mind clear.

This is our *day,* I think.

And the night will be ours too.

OWEN

Roth hid his tunnels. The Salazars show theirs off.

Our team's microbus followed the North Line for two miles, just one of the hundreds of watercourses that make up the cartel's ingenious network of aqueducts. Aboveground steel pipes as wide as a whale's mouth that eventually lead straight into the belly of the beast.

The Salazar Reservoir. Their main stronghold, and our main event.

We just have to make it *inside* one of those invincible pipes first.

Their source of power will prove to be their weakness, Mira promised when Team Takedown agreed on our master plan.

Govdamn right it will be, I vowed then, and promise again now as I excavate a pair of binoculars from my coverall's deep pockets and slam them to my face.

Scanning our target—a stumpy one-story concrete building, *very* low-key considering the owners—I catch sight of the three cartel men standing watch outside the isolated pumping station. Their shiny pistols pair well with their snazzy gunmetal-gray suits, and the *S*'s—*are those diamonds I'm seeing?*—on their bigger-than-my-fist belt buckles are a nice added touch, in case you forget what side they shoot for.

But getting past three guys with guns is a hell of a lot better than facing the scores of automatic rifles that would have greeted us if we'd tried to breach the main gate.

Let's move! I want to command the team and lead them away from our ditch of a hiding spot and out into action.

I feel all keyed up, on edge, on the outer limits of my self-restraint. It's vital I breathe, tell my jitters to *cool it*. But how can I chill? I'm sweating my skin off, packed under the dual layers of my civilian disguise and combat uniform.

And it's still T-minus twenty minutes before the major trade meeting starts. Scratch that, we're going to crash Roth and the capo's let's-end-the-world swap before it even begins.

It's the final countdown before I send the ex-governor to his big sleep.

The thought is selfish, but it feels like a competition to be the one to pull the trigger.

Re-pocketing my binoculars, I eye the competitors: Ava, Mira, Haven—hell, I'd even throw Alexander into the running. It will be a fight for who gets to Roth first.

"I'm moving in," Lucía announces via the placid translation of my ear cuff. "Follow on my signal."

Standing from our crouched position inside the trench, she slips off her scarf and threadbare coat, uncovering a fancy getup. A gold suit paired with gold spiked heels.

Dressed to kill.

Matías kept a few items of Lucía's old clothes—probably worth a month's stock of water—for occasions such as this.

Espionage. Infiltrating the cartel's ranks.

The militia has their own falcons.

"Final touches," Mira says, staining Lucía's lips a bruised plum before shadowing her eyelids a glittery gold.

"Rich looks good on you," Skye whispers to Lucía, her normal barbed tone now smooth. Flirtatious.

"I'd rather be poor and free than live by the blood on my cousin's hands," Lucía answers, shoving her coat into Skye's pack.

"I know, and I'll make sure the lieutenant *has* no hands after tonight," Skye says all amorous, like this offer is the height of romance.

"The lieutenant is *mine*," Lucía asserts, as if they've been arguing about it for hours. She squeezes Skye's hand and then she's off, sauntering toward the pumping station like she owns the place.

Those two have been getting close, fast.

I steal a glance at Ava. *Battle bonds.*

No, our attraction—connection—*has moved beyond the fight.*

I smile, thankful, as always, for the cover of my bandana. The memory—the *heat*—of Ava's touch burns up and down and sideways along my body. My bare skin. I feel a flash sensation of Ava's far from delicate fingers trailing down my back, where the scars from the Guard's bullets still hurt, across my chest, where my heart raced faster than a car could ever take me, to my lips, to make me stop talking, blabbering, confessing to her how much I have wanted this.

I suddenly feel Mira's eyes on me. *Can she read my thoughts?* Taking zero chances, I quickly veer my line of thinking back to the here and now.

Lucía's five yards from the cartel gunmen. And let's just say they don't look like they're about to roll out the red carpet for her.

Are they not falling for the flashy getup? Or do the men recognize her as the runaway Salazar from Monterrey?

No way. That makeup job made her look nothing like the face on every hit list across this territory. It's crazy what a little paint can do.

Though the cartel men point their guns at her, Lucía just keeps walking forward. She lifts her own weapon, a nabbed gold-plated cartel pistol Matías gave to her, and when she finally halts her approach and speaks, her command comes out in a tongue that sounds like a guttural form of Elvish.

"What the—? Is my translator malfunctioning?" I ask.

"I can't follow anything she's saying," Ava whispers to my right.

"It's not Spanish," Mira confirms.

"A code lingo, then?" I reason, my ears perking.

Did the Salazar cartel invent their own communication?

It seems so, and Lucía speaks the language.

She volleys out a few more terse words that make all three men holster their guns and lift their hands in the air in a show of submission.

Damn.

With her gun hand, she motions to their truck.

I can understand that much. She's telling them to leave. But before they vacate the premises, they watch her approach the pumping station's door.

Good thing we have the keys.

With the confidence of a high-ranking Salazar, she scans her thumbprint—really the capo's stolen prints, thanks to Matías—and the concrete door drags open.

We're in.

Lingering suspicions satisfied, the cartel men kick off toward their truck. Beneath my bandana I crack a grin when the engine starts and the truck speeds down the muddy road.

"This is it, bud," I whisper to Alexander, barely able to keep my adrenaline in check. "Lucky sixteen, our final mission. Theo's coming back with us."

Alexander gives me the cold shoulder, not even looking my way. He just stares straight forward, ready for Lucía's signal.

He's still peeved at me for not downloading the servers' latest intel to him. Unfair, seeing as we're all here only because I chased after the servers in the first place. And do I get a "thanks" from him? A "hey, sorry I jumped ship to another mission and abandoned you"? Nope.

But none of that matters now.

The floodlights flash off and on.

The signal to move.

In rows of two, Team Takedown hustles across the twenty yards of exposed Salazar territory.

We burst into the station to find Lucía, gun still raised, taking stock of the single room. She freezes when she spots a pair of flood boats stacked beside one of the sealed pipes.

The cartel watchmen were part of tonight's program. *Those*, however, were not.

"Something is not right," she says super uneasy. "The cartel never stores boats in their pumping stations."

I have to admit my spider senses are tingling, too, and it's not just because the floors are vibrating from all the pumps operating around us.

The purpose of this remote booster station is to help the water that's flowing inside the pipelines get to the Salazar Reservoir faster. There's no need for boats. Right?

Maybe to manually inspect the pipes for corrosion or damage from the inside? Questionable. I'm no water engineer, but I know there must be machines for that kind of work. Joyrides? Also doubtful. Then again, I've no clue how the cartel gets their kicks.

Mira either didn't hear Lucía's misgivings over the incessant noise of the pumps, or she just doesn't care. She holsters her gun and proceeds to the massive main pipeline in the center of the station. She pulls back the seriously heavy-looking latch, sliding open a section of the steel pipe with a loud grunt.

"Let's go," she says, dragging one of the small flood boats across the ground.

Ava and Haven rush to help, lifting the other end of the transport. Barend and Alexander begin to pull over the second boat when Lucía cautions, "We should rethink the plan."

"No," Mira argues, shaking her head. "We are the first wave of the assault—everyone is depending on us. We have to push forward."

"When something seems too easy," Skye says, "it usually means it is . . ."

"We are *not* turning back," Alexander growls.

No way the man's retreating now. We've all come too far and lost too much not to see this through.

There's only a ten-mile track of pipeline between us and Roth. It's go time, to whatever end.

That's my focal point—not the question of why boats are in this station. My view is that it's a good thing because a) we won't get soaked now and b) I'm a city boy who can't swim to save my life.

As I see it, it's a win-win.

"We show no fear, remember?" Ava says to Lucía.

That settles it. Lucía nods, then moves to complete the next task on her checklist: changing back into her battle uniform.

The rest of us huddle around the giant pipe, which has to be at least twelve feet in diameter. The good news is the water flows super fast—we won't even need an engine to propel us toward the Salazar Reservoir. The only drawback is we'll have to lie down flat or risk a premature death by decapitation.

"We have to slow down the water or we won't be able to load the boats," Barend says, popping his head back out from inside the pitch-dark pipeline.

Luckily for us, Lucía is already a step ahead of that particular problem. A word in that odd, clipped code language, then there's the loud *whoosh!* of a gear shifting. Just like that, the speed of the gushing water cuts in half.

Wasting zero time, Haven joins Barend to haul the first inflatable boat into the pipe. They keep it steady while Ava, Mira, Alexander, and I carefully clamber on, packing ourselves like sardines on the floorboard.

"Look for the red flashing light," Lucía reminds us.

The emergency hatch that leads into the water treatment plant. Our stop on this perilous water ride.

That building will officially put us onto the stronghold's property. I'll cut the power, then it's out onto the pitch-black grounds and into the mansion where Lucía and Matías predict the meeting will take place.

"We'll follow close behind," Barend says. Haven hops on before he lets go, sending us traveling toward one of the most dangerous places on the continent.

My mouth hangs open in a silent scream. I can't quite manage to convince myself that the boat's not going to flip. Then I feel Ava slide her hand into mine and my panic quickly disappears, and the rest of the twenty nail-biting minutes it takes to reach our port of call feels like smooth sailing.

"The light," Haven announces from the front of the boat.

I lift my body and shine a solar flashlight on the emergency ladder fused to the pipe's wall.

"It's coming up quick!" Alexander warns.

Haven lunges for a rung first, but misses. Mira dives for it next, manages to grip the bottom bar, then crashes back into the boat, landing hard on her knees. I take my shot, thinking third time's the charm, and slip on the slick floorboard before I can even touch metal.

Not good at all.

When Ava tumbles over me on her attempt at the ladder, the panic sets back in. I start to have visions of the boat flying out the tail end of the pipeline and plunging into the depths of the reservoir where we'll all meet a watery grave.

Bullshit if I'm going to go down by *drowning*.

Then in a move straight out of a VR action game, Alexander launches himself from the back of the boat and clasps hold of the ladder with one arm while clinging to the edge of our boat with the other.

"Grab the ladder and pull!" he yells. He hangs in midair, straining to keep his grasp.

Ava, Mira, and I leap to do as he says, each of us seizing a rung of the ladder for dear life. We drag the boat back toward the hatch with all we've got.

Haven pops onto the ladder first, attempting to twist the door open while we hold the boat in position.

But the hatch won't budge.

"Hurry!" Alexander yells. *He's losing strength.*

Ava and Mira race up the ladder to help their aunt yank the emergency door free. As they disappear through the opening, I secure myself onto the steel bars, leaving enough space for Alexander on the bottom rungs.

"Jump!" I shout.

He releases the boat to the will of the current and swings onto the ladder, his full weight crashing against the lower half of my body.

"Start climbing," he says, all calm, like he didn't just save the entire mission.

I follow his orders and then scramble out of the hatch door at the top. Ava has her hand out, waiting to lift me to my feet. Surprisingly, Mira does the same for Alexander, and he actually *accepts* her offer.

"I will help the second boat," Haven volunteers, crouching by the emergency door. "Go, we will catch up."

Ava and Mira nod, and Alexander and I follow the sisters into a museum-sized room teeming with pipelines and massive filtration tanks painted a shiny blood red. The Salazar symbol crawls all over the treatment equipment like an incursion. Not just a lone scorpion, but a whole nest of them.

It's like the cartel's version of those old epic war paintings. A crude depiction of the Salazar takeover of the water stronghold from the Mexican government.

The effect is so sinister and disturbing, it makes my skin crawl.

"You're up," Ava says to me.

Right. Time to take the Salazars' power. Literally.

The main electrical room should be near the back of the building. *Get inside, hack into the system, cut off all electricity, communication, surveillance for the entire stronghold.*

Easy.

Matías and hundreds—let's aim higher, *thousands*—of the People's Militia should be surrounding the stronghold right now, waiting in the wings for our cue.

"Let's make all hell break loose," I say. Ava smiles, her green cat eyes sharp and bright like a hunter's.

The rest of Team Takedown scrambles up through the hatch, and then I take off down a narrow hallway. I make it only about twenty steps when I hear an ominous *beep!* accompanied by a gear shifting.

A shout from Haven echoes off the metal walls. Then Skye's voice cries out, then Lucía's.

What the hell is happening?

I tear my way back to the filtration room just in time to see the galvanized steel floor drop out from under Barend.

"Run!" Alexander screams, but he's the next victim. Another round of *beeps!* and he plummets down into the pipes along with Mira.

"Mira!" Ava yells in horror, throwing her body onto the metal ground, scrambling on her hands and knees to follow the path of her sister's screams.

Mira's cries sound distant now. The water's rushing her away. *To where?*

I leap onto the edge of one of the tanks, managing to get a slippery grip, and reach out desperately for Ava.

"Grab my hand!" I shout.

But it all happens so fast. *Beep!* The floor where Ava crawls opens out from under her like a trap door.

She plunges into the pipelines.

"Ava!" I scream, over and over.

I slide along the side of the tank to where she fell and thrust my free arm into the water. *Please, please, let me grab hold of her.*

I was supposed to keep her safe.

But I keep coming up empty-handed.

This was *definitely* not part of the plan.

AVA

I'm drowning.

A powerful pull keeps me underwater. No matter how hard I fight, the current drives me forward like a rag doll in a dark, flailing dance with death.

Swim, swim, swim! I tell myself. *You have to fight.*

You can't die.

Not now. Not like this.

Then it hits me. My breaking point. Sixty seconds of struggling for my life underwater, and I'm suddenly overcome with the agony of running out of air.

My lungs burn. Begging me to take action.

Panic grips my throat, and I want to scream out loud to not be alone with my suffocating terror, but if I scream, I'll waste what little air is still left in my lungs.

Stay calm. You can't give up.

Tread water, my instincts urge. *You can't win against the current.*

That's when I stop fighting.

I let go, allowing my slack body to float slowly upward in the rushing water. Astonishingly, all at once, there's no longer any pain. Just a sense of comfort.

And then I surface, sucking in gulps of air and water.

Three breaths of respite, then I'm pulled back under.

The nightmare hasn't ended.

This time, in my panicked confusion, I inhale a lungful of water.

The pain returns. So does the terror.

Just when I think the end is near—*Mira, I'm sorry*—I feel myself shoot out of the giant water pipe, landing hard on a concrete surface.

Immediately I roll over onto my hands and knees, racked with a fit of violent coughing and retching. Utterly depleted, I collapse, heart pounding, mind racing.

Did the cartel know we were coming?

Where's Mira?

She can't swim.

Oh God.

I snap my eyes up to the pipeline's exit, but the rushing water has turned into a drip. *Mira, where are you?*

"Don't worry about the others," a silvery voice says, close by. "You will see them later."

My energy is all used up—it takes several tries for me to heave my body back upright. When I do, I'm given only a moment to absorb what, or *who*, is my latest adversary.

A teenage girl in a pristine white suit that reminds me of my Strake uniform. There's even an amethyst necklace that mimics the bold purple sash.

"You look like any other drowned mouse," she says, her disappointment sharp as a knife. "Nothing special."

My stomach clenches when I blink her face into focus. Her dark, cunning eyes. Her sneer, her privileged aura. Still groggy, I start to fit the fuzzy pieces together. *She reminds me of someone.*

Halton.

Who is this girl?

"I had hoped to capture the both of you together," the girl says. Her glossy bottom lip lowers in a pout. "I thought twins always came in a pair. But one will have to do."

When I try to demand where Mira is, my throat seizes. I'm hit with another outburst of frantic coughing that must make me sound like a wounded animal.

That sneer. I want to rip it from the girl's face.

She lifts her jeweled hand, and two cartel women in tight-fitting suits rush up and haul me roughly to my feet. Too exhausted to fight, I hang limp in their grasp.

The girl stalks toward me. A long finger, weighed down by a monstrous blood-red ruby, reaches out to brush my drenched hair from my face. *Is that the scorpion ring of the capo?* She laughs at the confusion in my eyes.

"Red hair, you must be Ava," she says. "Good, the Lone Star should be pleased."

Roth.

"Not as pleased as me," I manage, strong and intense as a feral growl. I'm alone, without the support of my team, but I am not helpless.

I'm about to face Roth. Our entire mission has led me to this moment.

And I will see it through, no matter the cost.

The girl smiles.

"Ah, bravado to the end," she says, clapping her hands together. "This is going to be fun."

With that, she turns, and the two cartel women drag me in her wake, out the door and down a concrete hallway. Two left turns and then I'm outside again.

At first, I see nothing but bright-white light. Spotlights. Then I hear moving water and feel wind on my cheeks.

I'm someplace high.

Then I see it. The Salazar Reservoir, fifty feet below. The wellspring of the cartel's power. A sprawling estate dominates its outer bank like a glittering citadel, as hard and beautiful as a diamond.

I'm on the dam.

And there's a cluster of people waiting for me at its center.

When I draw closer, I almost don't believe my eyes.

President Moore is here. He stands beside Director Wix and a Salazar man with a gold smile. Both men grip silver briefcases.

The bioweapon?

We're too late.

A wave of fury crashes through me when I spot Theo standing at Roth's side.

No cuffs. Not resisting.

Did he become a turncoat to save his own skin?

He betrayed my sister.

The Common.

Then a stranger catches my frenzied attention. A man with only one eye, strapped to a wooden chair by the dam's edge. Mouth gagged, his bent body resigned to his fate.

It must be Andrés. Matías's son.

He's drenched in a shiny liquid.

Gasoline?

A girl in a servant's uniform brings out a second chair and places it beside him.

An empty chair, meant for me.

THEO

The sight of Ava strikes me like a rogue wave.

The Common found me. Us. *Roth.*

And if Ava's here, Mira must be somewhere close by.

My exaltation lasts less than half a second before reality sets in, freezing my blood and stiffening every muscle. *Ava's been caught.*

All hope just died.

Is this Roth's work or Valeria's? Did they go all the way to Dallas to abduct her? Or was she captured trying to break in?

I flick my eyes past Ava, desperate to see—and not see—my dad, Mira. Kano. But there's only empty air.

Before I can fully grasp what the *hell* is happening, Valeria's two cartel women drag Ava forward, flashing smiles and six-inch blades at Ava's throat.

For a blink, I consider unsheathing my knife and knocking out their teeth with my knuckle duster, but that would help nobody.

Mierda. *Shit.*

Rally.

Concentrate.

In one sweep of her lethal glare, Ava tells me what she thinks of my State Guard uniform and my presence at Governor's side.

She then spits at my feet.

"Now, Ava, don't be a sore loser," Valeria admonishes, raising her jeweled finger. The women let Ava drop.

Ava takes the hard fall in silence, but she doesn't stay down long. She battles to her feet and unleashes a choked curse. "Theo, I *knew* you were a goddamn Roth—"

The rest of Ava's words get cut off when the cartel women throw her back to the ground. They dig the tips of their knives into her neck.

Coward, Ava's look screams up at me.

I stare down at her, unaffected, trying to match her hate, frown for frown.

"You found more fuel for the fire," I praise the capo, like a seasoned puppet, molding my lips into a grin.

Valeria bows her head to Governor, the purple amethyst swinging from her neck like a hypnotic charm. "A gift for you on the twins' day of birth."

I rip my eyes from Ava to look at Roth. This grand show, this entire escapade, was designed to impress and dazzle him—her estranged dad, the Lone Star.

He looks anything but pleased. With his hardened facade fixated on Ava, he puts up a good front, but from this close, beneath his stiff, regal uniform, I can see he's sweating bullets.

Roth detests surprises. Unless he's the one wielding them, of course. And odds are high he's recalling what happened the last time one of his family brought him a Goodwin as an offering.

Things didn't end well.

"I lay at your feet what your boys could not," Valeria says, her silky voice triumphant.

My dad. My half brother.

All failed to give Roth what he wanted.

The twin thorns in his side, the traitors, the catalysts of his downfall.

"Where is the other one?" Roth asks, his black eyes boring holes into Ava's.

Valeria's grin widens, devilish. "What is a show without an audience?"

Like a grand master of ceremonies, she directs our attention to the reservoir below with a dramatic wave of her arms. A powerful spotlight illuminates her stage.

Right on cue, a large pipe spits out what looks like bodies, one after the other launching into the pitch-dark water. Six splashes. I hold my breath, waiting for heads to surface.

Common members? Militia rebels?

Ten seconds pass, and then faces and floundering arms emerge. Frantic screams bounce off the water. Valeria titters.

The group, all clad in black uniforms, struggles to help each other swim to a gravel embankment on the east shoreline of the lake. When they make it, weak and coughing, one girl gets to her feet. She sways, lifting her head up to the walkway.

Mira.

My heart soars before it falls.

My dad appears at her side, then Haven, Barend. Two other girls I don't recognize stand with them.

Valeria has trapped them all.

Mira, run! I want to call out.

Y huiré contigo. *And I will run away with you.*

But a dozen cartel men clutching automatic rifles move in to meet the new arrivals on the embankment.

"Did you really think you could enter my territory and I wouldn't notice?" Valeria sneers to Ava. "The capo sees all."

But they're not the only witnesses she's gathered. More armed cartel arrive, herding at least fifty additional captives onto the bank and into the floodlights. *The People's Militia.*

Director Wix and the lieutenant share lost looks, gripping the metal railing. President Moore clutches his briefcase tighter to his chest and puts several steps between Valeria and himself. It seems they weren't privy to tonight's program either.

"What is this?" Roth asks, calm as the reservoir's surface. But I catch the hesitation in his voice, the same way my dad sounds when he's trying to project that he's still the one in control.

"Ava!" Mira's voice reverberates across the dam.

Another gruff cry rings out. "Andrés!"

Strapped to a chair by the dam's ledge, Andrés fights against his restraints, Ava against the cartel women's hold.

"My mother's rule will be humble compared to the power I will wield," Valeria says, face glowing with excitement. "This is how our new alliance begins . . . forged with the flames of our enemies."

She glides over to me in her daggerlike heels and places a familiar hand on my shoulder. "Theo helped inspire this little show. You were right to spare him."

"I hope you're pleased, Governor," I say, forcing my eyes level with his.

I coerce myself to remain still, silent, to not prematurely show my hand.

Roth just shifts his glare back to Ava.

My aunt leans in close, whispering velvety-toned words in my ear. "Your part's not done yet, nephew. Our family's rivals have to learn. Choose the lesson. Ava and Andrés, or the crowd of people below. Two lives or many? Your choice."

She gives a cold, dismissive shrug. It's no matter to her who lives or who dies. Because really, for Valeria, it's just a matter of who dies first.

And who is forced to watch.

On the embankment below, the line of cartel men lifts their guns. They aim their barrels at Mira, my dad, Andrés's people.

Everything about Valeria is poison.

The power-hungry capo isn't going to allow either group to leave her stronghold alive.

She just wants to see what hand I'm holding.

"Ava or Mira?" she presses, relishing in her grand scheme. Right now, she's outplaying us all. Myself, Governor. The Common and the People's Militia.

But I have my own master plan.

Concentrate, puppet. It's show time.

The moment has finally come to cut my strings.

"Ava," I choose.

With a nod from Valeria, the cartel women drag Ava to the empty chair next to Andrés. Inwardly, I smile when she manages to land a kick to one of their kidneys before she's thrown into the chair. Outwardly, I screw my face into a scowl.

They zip-tie Ava's ankles and wrists, then the woman wearing Andrés's eyepatch cuts a lock of Ava's famous fiery hair. *Keepsakes of her victims.* They laugh as they fall back in line behind Valeria.

I feign tightening Ava's restraints, trying to get her to look me in the eyes. I need to tell her what my voice can't.

"Don't worry," I say when Ava won't meet my gaze. "It won't hurt."

The translator distorts my assurances into a taunt.

Valeria and her women laugh.

"How vicious of you, nephew."

Don't waver now.

I snap my fingers to Roth's servant. The girl comes forward holding cans labeled "gasolina." Quiet and unassuming.

The perfect spy.

"Help me prepare the prisoner," I order.

I take one can from her, and we start dousing Ava.

Ava begins to shake uncontrollably. "Theo, please don't do this," she begs. Tears mix with the shiny fluid that drenches her cheeks.

"This is the way it has to be," I say, struggling to keep my face cold.

I'm going to be sick.

Nausea burns my throat, and I have to step away.

Valeria takes my place. She holds out her hand for the gasoline. I almost choke on my rising panic.

I'm not the kind of girl who likes to just sit and watch, she warned me.

The militia spy hesitates, then surrenders the can to Valeria. Looking the happiest I've ever seen her, Valeria dumps the entire contents over Ava's sodden head. Her face splits into a smile.

"If you want to guarantee the best results, it's better to do things with your own hands," she says to Ava. "Even if it means getting them dirty."

Valeria tosses the empty can to the ground. "Justice by your own hands," she says, turning to Andrés. "Isn't that what you mice like to say?"

She straightens the lapels of her pure-white jacket, toying with the amethyst. Governor eyes the gemstone, the ghost of a snarl on his thin lips.

Valeria must see it too. His implicit disapproval.

Or is she deluding herself?

"Any last words?" she asks.

"Mira, *run!*" Ava screams, her powerful cry desperate. "Haven, get her out of here!"

A diamond-hilted knife appears in Valeria's hand, pulled from her silk sleeves. She glides the blade across Ava's neck. Just a flesh wound, but blood trickles down Ava's trembling throat as she fights back a hiss of pain.

"Not *you*," she scolds Ava with a steely growl.

She turns to Governor. "Would you like the final word, Father?"

Gasps ring out all across the walkway.

If she was going for maximum shock value, she achieved it.

Valeria just revealed that she is Roth's daughter.

The public might forgive *one* second-born Roth, but Valeria *Salazar*?

Director Wix takes a backward step from Governor, her face reddening in outrage. The lieutenant's shark eyes turn to slits, and Moore orders his assistant to get the jet ready for his departure.

I expect Governor to snap, releasing all the hazardous energy he's been storing. But he stays stoic, just a single clench of his fist.

Governor slowly turns his attention to Ava. He marches over to her chair, shoulders straight as iron rods, and scans Ava's bound ankles and wrists, her sopping red hair.

His translator magnifies a sonorous grumble, then his final words to the girl whose family almost cost him his rule. His legacy and empire.

"After I killed Darren, I burned his body to ashes. Like your father's, no one will find your grave."

I can't see Ava's face from where I stand, but I imagine it's wrenched in heartrending agony. In unimaginable fury.

"Burn," Governor says, "knowing your sister will follow."

He returns to the walkway, and I see him attempt to slip Director Wix a folded piece of paper. At first, the Director hesitates—*is her loyalty faltering?*—but she slyly reaches out her claw hand, tucks the missive up her sleeve, and withdraws.

Does Governor have his own play?

No time to second-guess myself.

I nod to the militia spy for us to move into position, but before we can reach Ava and Andrés, Valeria scrapes twin fire-starter sticks against the dam's barrier and tosses them at the bases of the two wooden chairs.

Instantly, Ava and Andrés ignite.

It's the most horrific sight I've ever witnessed with my own eyes.

For three wasted seconds, I'm frozen where I stand, trapped by the terror-filled screams of Ava and Andrés, mixed with the harrowing wails from Mira and the People's Militia below.

Mira thinks I just burned her sister alive.

She'll never forgive me.

"¡Ahora!" I yell to the militia girl. *Now!*

Heedless of the flames, we kick the burning pyres off the ledge of the dam, sending Ava and Andrés tumbling down toward the reservoir below.

"No!" Valeria and Roth release unified roars, realizing my betrayal. The militia spy and I step onto the concrete ledge. I feel hands reaching out for me, trying to pull me back.

But they're too late. My strings have already been severed.

With a deep breath, I fall—free—into the water.

MIRA

My sister is a flame. A streak of burning light.

She plummets toward the inky-black water of the reservoir, Theo a hurtling shadow above.

Oh God.

What did he do?

Ava! my heart screams before it shatters into a thousand sharp pieces. Pain cuts through me. I'm hollow. On my knees. Choking on my cries.

Time slows.

It takes what feels like ages—insufferable minutes, *hours*—before Ava and Andrés hit the water. I blink back tears. Close my eyes. Their fiery bodies searing across my lids.

Ava, my soul reaches out. *Stay with me.*

When I pull open my eyes, my sister has disappeared beneath the surface.

A single dragonfly appears before my bleary vision, hovering where she fell.

And then everything goes dark.

The lights. The power.

Owen must have made it to the electrical room. He pulled it off.

Then, quick and brutal as gunfire, time shoots forward.

Alexander yells an unintelligible cry, diving back into the water after Theo.

I can't swim. Only Ava mastered the lessons.

But I can't just stand here.

I can't breathe until she resurfaces. Reappears. Comes back to me.

Theo. What did you do?!

Lucía plunges into the reservoir, Barend rushing headlong after her. Both tear through the water toward the ripples where the four bodies landed.

"Save them!" I scream so hard it feels like my throat rips.

Haven hurls my body behind hers, shielding me from the army of cartel men that trap our group along the embankment. The gunmen lift their pistols. Waiting for the order to shoot . . .

From the corner of my eye, I see Matías. *They captured him too. Oh God.*

In a single fluid movement, he raises his staff, yanking loose the top of the oakwood handle. A secret cavity opens and he wrenches out a long, thin firework shaped like a rocket.

With a wild shout, he lights the fuse and it launches into the air, the explosive force throwing his bulky frame to the ground.

The rocket sets off a shrill, soul-piercing shriek, flying higher and higher until it detonates over the concrete dam.

The signal.

The blast illuminates a crowd of silhouettes gathered on the walkway above the curved dam that looks every inch a stone fortress. I narrow my eyes on the towering figure at its center.

Roth.

Raw, uncontrollable hate fills my hollow chest. I feel no fear. Only certainty.

I'm going to take him down.

I expect Roth to run, but he doesn't. He waits.

And watches.

The faint shouts of a thousand militia rebels echo across the reservoir.

They've invaded the stronghold.

With one last look to the placid water—*Ava, where are you?!*—I reach for my gun. Flicking off the safety, I aim the barrel between the eyes of a cartel man who looks up to his leader, his capo, impatient for the signal to fight.

Look to me, I think savagely.

I feel my anger surge through my veins. Hot, violent. Crazed.

I'm in control here.

"Fight!" I scream until my lungs burn.

Haven picks up the rallying cry, our voices harmonizing with a terrorizing energy.

"Fight!"

I didn't want this. To win by leaving a trail of bodies behind.

But it's the only way forward.

I let go of all forbearance and self-restraint.

And pull the trigger.

Owen

I try to look at the bright side of my situation.

I hacked in and shut off the stronghold's power grid, easy. This place will be under a blackout for the next solid hour.

The dark side? Now I'm on a solo mission with a hell of a lot more on my to-do list.

Get to Ava. Find the others.

Get to Roth. Find the weapon.

Save the govdamn day.

I just don't know which I should go after first.

Crouching low to the metal floor—crossing all fingers and toes the panels don't drop out from under me—I sneak down the hallway in search of an exit.

Exit, exit, exit. Where are the damn emergency exit signs?

There! To the left.

Sprinting now, I hoof it to the corner and ram open the steel double doors.

Of course an alarm triggers, yowling to everyone: *I'm right here!*

But no one's listening. The sound's a blip on no one's radar.

It's a full-blown war zone outside.

And I'm blown away by what I see. Literally.

An aerial shell explodes six feet off the ground in front of me, and I'm blasted backward, my skull slamming pavement.

My head feels like it just split open. I have less than a second to check if all my pieces are intact before another shell detonates in yellow and green sparks. This one whistles and crackles, raining down flaming death stars.

And this one hits a target.

An arm drops on the sidewalk, right next to my feet. It's clothed in a suit sleeve, it's jeweled fingers still clinched around a gun. It's an "it" now, right? Because the cartel guy "it" belonged to is sprawled facedown over the hood of a truck.

A truck that's speeding my way, packed with a band of his buddies.

Swallowing a tirade of curses, I scramble back into the filtration building and bang the door closed with my boot.

Well, at least two things are going to plan.

Matías rallied his militia.

I unlocked the stronghold's doors, and now they're invading.

The battle has begun.

I gather all my wits and reach for my bag. Night vision goggles, check. Blackout mask, check. I pull both on and feel myself turn invisible in the dark. Drawing my pistol from my hip holster, I check the chamber. Locked and loaded.

I take a few of those deep breaths Ava likes.

"The future waits for no one," I spur myself, and charge back through the door and out into the fight.

I take in the scene. My green phosphor vision conveys a mash of insanity.

Bullets fly across the sky like deadly neon-green fireballs. More fireworks burst in the air and on the ground, wreaking their havoc. Thousands of green bodies race around in the pitch black, fighting half-blind.

I slip under and past the bombardment and charge in the direction of the loudest ruckus, figuring that's where Ava and Mira will most likely be. The center of the action.

Weaving through an obstacle course of slain bodies, I reach what looks at first like a well-organized miniforest, but then I work out that it must be some kind of orchard. Branches shatter from stray firework shells, sending wood shrapnel hurtling in all directions. I throw my arms over my head and neck and push on.

Fallen fruit litters my path, and I'm forced to kick every bullet-ridden green bastard out of the way so I don't trip.

I'm moving too slow!

Where's my team? Where's Roth?

Right or left?!

To my right I see something stalk through the stunted trees. It's shaped like an extremely large cat with vertical stripes like a tiger's.

Wait, is that an actual *tiger?!*

A gunman in a suit stumbles right toward the beast, blindly spraying bullets in the wrong direction. The tiger pounces, striking the guy to the ground before he even knows what hit him.

Definitely a hard left, then.

Chasing the escalating *booms!* and *pops!* I make it to a roadway. I follow the single paved lane for a few yards, picking up speed, then I run into my next problem.

And it's a big one.

The Texas State Guard is here. Like *a lot* of them.

A whole army's worth. And they're firing at the Salazar cartel—turning on them.

What the—?

Is Roth vying for a takeover?

All alliances appear to be off.

State Guard SUVs and military tanks choke the road ahead, obliterating anyone in their way.

I weigh my options.

To my right, a green sea of militia members swoops down on the soldiers, their cries drowning out the teeth-chattering *pop, pop, pop, pop!* of the State Guard's gunfire.

To my left, I spot a stray Texas Guard in riot gear. The temptation to shoot is powerful—retribution for the cowards who shot me in the back in the Dallas tunnels—but I strong-arm the urge.

I need to get to Ava. Or Roth.

I'm on the verge of slipping past him when I immediately regret my decision to shelve my revenge, because the son of a governor lifts a Scream Gun and fires.

The auditory assault drops me—along with the entire militia wave—flat to the ground, squirming in agony in the dirt. My brain feels like the worst migraine on steroids. I try to roll away, but the shrill, lethal shockwave just gets louder.

Then I remember Ciro's offerings.

With trembling hands, I pilfer my bag and dig out two items I could kiss him for.

I shove in a pair of high-tech earplugs, and the relief is instantaneous.

But I waste no time savoring the small victory. I snatch an abandoned firework from the ground, light the fuse by the flames of a burning bush, and launch the shell at the Scream Gun.

The explosion takes out both the sonic weapon *and* the Guard holding it. Two birds, one stone, like my girl would say.

Ava, where are you?

The militia surges back to its feet, redoubling the charge on the Guard's SUVs and tanks.

Bullets whiz past me. I raise my gun and return fire, booking it toward a metal fence. I scramble up and over, then put as much distance as I can between the road and me.

I end up at a raised footpath that overlooks the Salazar Reservoir.

All up and down the dam and the embankments, it's straight-up pandemonium. I've reached the center of the battle zone.

"Ava, where are you?" I shout, even though I know she'll never hear me.

On the east bank, a militia group blasts a round of M-1000s into a whole troop of Texas Guards, knocking them down like bowling pins. But an armored helicopter with a Lone Star on its flank converges on the rebels from above, spitting machine-gun fire.

They drop like flies.

"That's not a fair fight!" I yell, like anyone can hear my protest.

Then a pixie-haired figure charges into the heart of the clash.

Mira. *She made it out of the pipes.* Thank Goodwin.

I zoom in with my goggles, heart leaping, expecting to see Ava by her side. But I only spot Haven. Skye.

Ava's absence is a gut punch. Worse. Like the concrete has been ripped from under my boots, and I'm spiraling downward.

I think of Rayla lying on the tunnel floors. Dead.

No, no, no. This isn't happening.

Ava, I can't lose you too.

I only just found you.

Setting my sights on a warpath, I'm on the verge of jumping down into the reservoir and swimming my way into the fray, but then I hear shouts.

Somewhere nearby, to my left.

More like death wails, actually, or screeches from the devil herself.

"You dare betray me?" a furious voice howls over the gunfire. "Your own blood and equal?"

The voice belongs to a girl in a low-cut suit, standing on the dam's walkway. She has a diamond-crusted pistol in her hand, aimed right at the ex-governor.

Holy Whitman. Is a Salazar about to end this war for us?

But what did she mean by *own blood?*

I close in on Roth with my goggles. He sneers, then lifts his own gun.

"This territory is mine!" the girl seethes, firing a warning shot in the air. "Speak!" she bellows on repeat. Her screams become pleas. "Speak to me! Answer to your betrayal!"

Roth's only response is a gunshot in her direction.

Shrieking what I can only imagine to be first-class curses in their code language, two cartel women and an entire line of men in suits break from the girl's side and charge at Roth, gold-plated guns blazing.

Roth and his soldiers start picking off the Salazars who rush at him, one by one.

A man with a blinding snarl I recognize as the lieutenant of Monterrey grabs hold of the girl. He tries to drag her from the dam, but a bullet lodges into his thigh and he stumbles.

Is that a briefcase in his hand?

It falls to the ground. Swallowed up by storming feet.

How can something so small carry such a world-altering weapon?

Without a second thought I start sprinting toward it.

Toward Roth.

I'm still forty yards and a battlefield away.

I'll never get there.

But a Hart has to try.

AVA

I'm falling through the darkness, strapped to a chair. My body feels battered, bruised, like I just hit a wall of concrete.

Hands claw at me—tugging at my ankles and wrists. Just like the nightmares Mira would have in the basement back at Trinity Heights.

But unlike my sister, I don't hear my mother's voice singing to me, soothing me.

Only my own drowned screams.

I was set on fire. Burned alive.

And now I'm sinking again. Headed for a watery grave.

Then my wrists and ankles are suddenly free to kick. To fight for life.

But they feel as heavy as lead. Useless.

An arm wraps around my chest, then another, pulling me to the water's surface in a chaotic whirl of bubbles and limbs.

When I emerge, I gulp down air, still screaming.

Someone has hold of me, keeping me afloat. A lifesaving grip, swimming me to the shore, past pieces of the shattered wooden chairs. Voices shout at me over and over, but all I hear are my own cries.

I'm alive, I'm alive. I didn't burn.

When we reach solid ground, I frantically search my body, expecting to find blackened skin, severe burns. But I see only minor holes in my uniform, minimal damage to my hair and exposed skin. How? I was set on fire. Ciro's high-tech uniform couldn't have saved me so wholly from those flames.

Stunned and disoriented, I take deep, shaking breaths to try to stop my cries.

I'm alive. I didn't burn.

My eyes sting from the gasoline, but through blurry tears I see something small floating in front of me.

A dragonfly. Electric blue and yellow, buzzing peacefully. Its four paper-thin wings glide over a bag lying discarded on the embankment.

Mira's.

I pick it up and cling to it like an anchor.

Suddenly I notice what's happening outside myself.

Loud bangs resolve into gunshots. Shouting into words. Whirling shapes into people.

"Ava, are you all right?!"

Theo.

He reaches out his hand, attempting to help me to my feet.

I jump, rising on my own, searching for a gun.

My sister was wrong about Theo. He's a Roth.

A liar.

Dangerous.

He set me on fire.

I find a pistol on the ground, lift it, and take aim.

"We switched one of the cans with a fire-retardant gel!" Theo spits out, desperate to explain. "It was part of my escape plan . . . The servant girl helped me! She's really a militia spy."

My head's spinning.

The bottom of Theo's pants are scorched, and he grasps Mira's knife tight, his knuckles cut and bleeding. *He must've been the one to cut my cuffs—he's the one who saved me from drowning.*

Beside us, Alexander and Barend unload their weapons, holding back a cartel assault. My old instincts come rushing back to me. *We have to move.*

The man who was ignited alongside me is unharmed too. He fights back to back with Lucía, bullet shells dropping to their feet like a golden hailstorm.

Boom! Boom! Firework explosions go off forty yards away, brighter than the Fourth of July, lighting up the battlefield.

It's chaos. The Salazar cartel and the People's Militia bitterly fight all across the stronghold's vast property. But it's not just the Salazars that our side's combating with now—there's a second enemy at play.

Roth's State Guard.

This is where the bulk of his soldiers must have been. Hiding in Mexico. All at once it hits me that Roth's making a play to seize control of the cartel's water supply.

If he controls the priceless resource, he can rebuild his empire twice as strong.

This is the real reason he fled here—not to trade weapons—he already has the most powerful one of all.

"¡Tenemos que seguir adelante!" Lucía warns. *We have to press forward!*

Then there's a short break in the gunfire.

Alexander takes advantage of the reprieve and falls on his son. "Mijo!" He embraces Theo so tight it's like he never plans to let go. Another *boom!* causes him to finally pull away.

"You have to remove your uniform!" Alexander appeals. He starts pulling off Theo's officer's jacket, desperate to make his son less of a target.

Our team or the People's Militia could confuse Theo for a State Guard and kill him by mistake.

When Theo's left standing there in his shirtsleeves, half-naked and vulnerable, a translator device fastened to him like a gold collar, I remember what Mira brought all this way just for him. I quickly tear open her bag and pull out the extra battle uniform.

"Hurry—put this on," I tell him.

Lucía rushes over to unlock his necklace with an expert tap of her fingers. When two rapid firework bursts illuminate the casualties strewn across the war zone, the wounded crying out for help, my head starts spinning again.

"You're bleeding," Alexander says. My hand jumps to my throat, tracing the gash the vicious capo cut into my neck. Leaving her mark on me.

Alexander strips a piece of cloth from the cast-off State Guard uniform, presses it to my neck, then resumes unloading his weapon into the onslaught of soldiers and cartel gunmen.

Firing round after round, Barend withdraws to my side and crouches. "We're easy marks standing here, we need to move," he shouts. "Can you run? Roth's still on the dam."

All at once my focus zeros in on our target, the reason we're all here: Roth.

I take Barend's night vision goggles, press them to my face, and look up just as Roth raises his pistol and shoots President Moore in the chest.

The most influential leader in the world falls to the concrete, dead, splayed out like a rag doll. Roth steps over his body and grabs hold of the briefcase, continuing to volley bullets at the advancing cartel, surrounded by his Guards.

This time, Roth didn't run from the fight.

And neither will we.

Then my heart jumps to my throat when I zoom out my goggles' field of vision.

Mira.

She's sprinting for Roth, with Haven and Skye at her side.

Theo, now in his charcoal-black battle gear, sees her too. I feel his body tense next to mine.

We raise our weapons.

"To the dam!" I shout.

We can't let her face Roth without us.

MIRA

There are just too many.

The Salazars, the Guards, they keep coming in waves.

My team's pinned against the grove of palm trees that lines the outer banks of the water, the tall stems providing little cover.

"We'll be fertilizer for these trees if we keep standing here!" Skye yells between gunshots, three stems over.

Beside me, Haven tosses down her empty gun and plucks a pistol from a dead Guard to continue firing, all in one swift motion. "Mira, don't stop shooting!"

But we're running out of ammo. And time.

I watch Matías, ten yards away, blasting off Roman candle launchers and artillery shells, keeping a wide perimeter. His militia rebels are swarming the stronghold, coming to our aid, but will the numbers be enough?

We have two enemies to fight. The Salazars, and now the State Guard army.

It's just too many.

We're surrounded.

And I've lost sight of Roth.

Ava, did you make it out of the water? The flames?

Smoke from the explosives thickens around us like fog, burning my throat and eyes.

I see no way forward.

Yet I hear myself shout to advance. "Let's move!"

Haven and Skye fall in close, and we push through the nauseating haze behind our raised guns.

Our line makes it ten steps before bullets zip overhead. Five, maybe six gunmen. The Guard or the Salazars?

For the ninth time since I washed ashore, I reach for my rucksack that isn't there. *Dammit!*

All I have left is my gun. And three bullets . . . two. One.

No. Save your last one.

"I'm out!" I yell to Haven and Skye.

"Get behind us!" Skye shouts, and Haven pulls me behind her. They maintain a steady stream of firepower, trying to clear a path.

I search the ground for a fallen pistol, knife, firework—a *rock*—anything I can use to take up arms and fight. But I find nothing.

"Haven, on your right!" I scream, pointing to a shadow storming toward us.

Two *pops* and the shadow collapses into a dark heap.

"More on our left!" Haven shouts.

"Shit!" Skye curses. "I'm out of ammo!"

She falls back behind me, and Haven leads us forward.

To where? We're blind, and there are too many.

"Mira?" a muffled voice shouts.

I whip around, almost triggering my last bullet, before I recognize the night vision goggles and checkered bandana that emerge from the smoke.

"Owen!" I yell, a second too late. Skye's already kicked his legs out from under him, and he drops to his knees.

"Really?" he cries.

"The one time I'm glad I'm empty-handed," Skye apologizes, helping him up.

With no spare second to dust himself off, Owen lifts his gun in my direction, and I duck, hearing two ear-piercing *pops!* followed by a loud *thud*.

"This way!" he cries, waving us on. I step behind him, Skye moving in after me, Haven covering the back of our line.

"Where's Roth?" I shout at Owen.

"Where's Ava?" he shouts back.

Our mirrored silence is as deafening as the battle raging on around us.

Skye shakes my shoulder, pointing skyward. "Are those ours?"

Planes. Helicopters.

I didn't hear the rumble of their arrival over the uproar.

Owen looks up, fiddling with the control screen on his goggles. He yanks down his bandana as his lips split into a beaming smile.

"It's the Common!" he laughs, lifting his fist into the air. "Blaise, bud, I knew you'd get to Emery!"

Reinforcements. We stand a chance, then.

My fleeting sense of security proves short-lived. More Guards—*or are they cartel?*—have spotted us. Bullets pierce the palm trunks left and right.

"Owen, twelve o'clock!" Skye warns.

He aims his gun and then I hear twin *pop, pop, pops* in stereo.

Skye found a weapon.

I search, desperate for my own, but I feel a hand on my arm. "Mira, follow me," Haven says quietly, for only me to catch.

She races off, and I sprint after her.

Did she find Ava? Roth?

Theo?

Thirty yards away, the smoke clears.

A lone figure stands next to a military helicopter, blades spinning, chopping at the air. A mist swirls around my father's killer. My grandmother's murderer.

The destroyer of my world.

Haven doesn't hesitate. She lifts her gun. *Click, click, click.*

Empty.

"No!" she screams.

Roth doesn't move. And no soldiers move in to protect him.

Is he really alone? Where are his Guards?

Roth must realize he is finished. The Common will tell the citizens what was done here. What was planned.

There can be no cover-up, not now.

And yet he doesn't run.

Roth's eyes find mine, and we stare each other down. Even from this distance, I can decipher his glare. He may have lost the larger game, but he thinks he can still win a prize.

Me. The second-born Traitorous Twin.

The Achilles' heel of his rule.

I hear Owen shout my name behind me.

But I run forward.

Because there is only forward.

And I have one last bullet.

THEO

It feels good to have finally shed my puppet's costume.

And all the lies.

If the mirrored walls asked me now, *What are you made of?* I could face myself in the glass and confidently answer.

Truth.

"How much farther?" Ava asks.

Barend's the only one with night vision goggles, but he's having trouble seeing through the melee of bullets and smoke.

"The sensors are malfunctioning," he says, "but we're close."

We march in a line along the reservoir's east bank, toward the dam, with Barend at the lead beside Ava. The militia spy and the woman called Lucía jog ahead of me and Andrés, my dad securing the tail end of our team.

"Remember, mijo," my dad yells to me. "Aim for the chest, the largest target."

I nod, half-amazed he's not trying to hold me back from the fight like he's done my whole life. I've gone through too much—seen too much—for him to think he can protect me with ignorance ever again.

Wild gunshots fly past us, the bullets popping through the dark water like death-dealing skipping stones.

"Get down!" Barend orders.

We fall to our knees and scour the darkness for the shooter. *Where are you?*

I fire in the direction that Ava aims. My shoulder rears back with the recoil, sending my bullet flying uselessly into the night sky. But I don't waste time feeling discouraged with my first ever shot.

I'm a quick learner.

I've proven that.

More bullets whirl into our line. This time one hits more than just water.

The militia spy—she never told me her name—jerks rapidly in a grotesque dance, then drops hard to the gravel. She doesn't move again.

"No!" I scream.

I can't rip my eyes from the girl's bloody body, the reality refusing to sink in. Mere minutes ago she helped me pull off our grand escape. And now here she is, lifeless.

After so much courage. It doesn't seem right.

Lucía crawls over, a rosary in her hand. She closes the girl's eyes and mutters a rapid prayer. Then her head flicks up.

"Cousin," she growls, rising to her feet.

The lieutenant of Monterrey stumbles toward us through the smoke, sightless in the dark. He's limping from a gushing wound in his thigh. He's frantic. And alone.

Valeria despises weakness, just like her dad. *She must have abandoned him.* Left him to his own fate.

Crack! A loud shot from beside me. Lieutenant Salazar lets loose a high-pitched shout and tumbles across the gravel path.

Lucía. She blew out his kneecap.

The lieutenant writhes on his side, hands pressed in a steeple of appeal as Lucía and Andrés approach. His gold teeth gleam in the firecracker light as he begs, "Primo, por favor. Misericordia." *Cousin, please. Mercy.*

Does a man like him deserve mercy?

Lucía answers for me.

"No quitarás más vidas." *You will take no more lives.*

She lifts her gun.

"Me ocuparé de eso con mis propias manos." *I will see to that by my own hands.*

She fires a bullet into his heart.

"Justice by our own hands," Ava whispers.

"Did anyone else hear that?" Barend asks, cocking his ear toward the embankment behind us.

At first all I can make out is more gunshots and the loud whooshing of helicopter blades. But then . . .

"Resist much," a familiar voice rings out, checking to see if we are friend or foe.

"Obey little," I answer. My pulse begins to race.

Emery reveals herself through the thick mist, like a vision in a bright-yellow coat.

She's every bit real, though. Ava shoots forward into her arms, happier even than me to see our leader's face again. "You came after us!"

So the Loyalists didn't catch her after all.

Materializing behind Emery, a lean skyscraper of a man with a shaved head rushes straight for Barend. When he pulls off his night vision goggles, I realize it's Ciro Cross.

If the top Elders are here, so is the Common Guard.

That means this is now an even fight. Two armies against two.

"We feared we would be too late," Ciro pants, folding his hand over Barend's.

"We all still might be," Ava corrects him.

"You were right, Ava," Emery says. "I should have sent our Guard here when we had the first clues. Did the trade go through?"

"Where is the bioweapon?" Ciro presses.

Bioweapon?

After being his prisoner, I've learned what Roth is capable of. *Anything.* He would do anything to get his country back. To restore his power.

But a weapon of mass destruction?

Fear, he told me. *It always comes down to fear.*

"The briefcases!" I say.

"Roth took them," Ava pants.

If Roth slips through our hands, he could take down millions.

We have to take him down first.

Then a crazed shout cuts through the heavy smoke.

"Theo!"

It's Valeria.

She screams my name over and over until she emerges from the dark as a succession of fireworks ignite the sky.

The capo is barefoot, her white suit caked in dirt and blood. And the two cartel women flanking her aren't laughing now.

They're outnumbered.

"Theo!" she howls. "I warned you what would happen if you lied!"

Then everything breaks into turmoil.

"¡Por Rosa!" Andrés shouts.

A blind shoot-out ensues. Ava and Emery charge out ahead with Andrés, Valeria's duo blasting off shot after shot in return fire.

"Theo!" Valeria screams from the darkness.

"Aim lower!" Barend advises me from somewhere to my right.

On my other side, Lucía grabs a souped-up Roman candle off a fallen body, sets fire to the fuse, then points the blast of fireballs right at the Salazar women. They scatter.

Like mice.

"Theo!" Valeria cries over and over.

But where'd she go? Gray shapes dart left and right in the thickening haze, but I can't find her.

"Theo!"

"I'm right here, Valeria!" I shout, unwilling to hide anymore.

"Theo, stay back!" my dad urges, yelling over his gunfire. He grips my arm. "Why is she after you?"

"Because she's my aunt. And your half sister," I shout at him, and his hold on me loosens. I can't see him in the darkness, but he must look like I felt when I learned the secret of my own half sibling.

When Valeria calls for me again, I take full advantage of my dad's distraction and bolt toward her voice.

It sounded near the water.

But she finds me first.

Out of thin air, Valeria's on me, tackling me to the slick ground. Her hand locks around my throat in a viselike grip, her dagger nails digging into my skin.

Trying to squeeze the life out of me.

Then a blade appears above my head, shining red from the fiery explosions in the sky. With a ruthless jab, Valeria attempts to plunge the knife into my neck, but I manage to clamp hold of her wrist before she can bury the blade in my throat.

I yank back her fingers until I hear the *pop!* of each one breaking. She releases the grip on her knife's hilt with a scream.

I hook my foot around Valeria's right ankle and buck and roll, flipping her off me and sending her flying.

We both get to our feet at the same time. I realize the only weapon I have left is Mira's knife, and I hold the blade out in front of me, ready for Valeria's next attack.

I expect her to unsheathe one of her cutting smiles, enjoying the fight. Battling with her own hands. Getting them dirty.

But she stares at me with a terrible sadness.

"Nunca fuimos realmente Roths," she says. *We were never really Roths.*

"No, no lo fuimos," I tell her. *No. We weren't.*

She clutches her knife with her unbroken hand, and I squeeze the steel rings of mine.

Valeria charges, all her fury directed at me, but I stand my ground, knowing I've trained for this.

At the last second, I spin on my heel and Valeria's blade slashes only air.

She topples over the embankment wall, sliding down the concrete spillway. Before she reaches the water, her amethyst necklace catches on a protruding steel bar.

Valeria hangs there, choking, her fingers fumbling uselessly at her throat.

I don't wait to watch her take her final gravelly breath. I turn my back on her, pulled by an overwhelming need to find Mira.

Gripping my knife, I start sprinting.

I need to be there to witness it.

The moment Roth's empire dies. For good.

AVA

Mira reached Roth first.

Ten yards in front of her, the untouchable governor of Texas, former military general and presidential candidate of the United States, stands alone, his eyes dark and empty as an open grave. No soldiers or armaments to guard him, just a mortal man.

His pistol lays useless at his feet. Out of bullets.

Vulnerable, at long last.

He's surrounded by Common members, on the ground and in the air, and he knows there's nowhere to run this time.

I move to take my place by my sister's side.

Haven, Skye, Owen. They all look at me like I just came back from the dead. And it feels like I have.

But now is not my moment.

Now is the moment for our game with Roth to finally end.

I hear Director Wix before I see her. Her voice is shrill, twisted with fear and desperation.

"Governor!" she wails from inside a State Guard helicopter. Dead men in suits hang out the side. "You can still save yourself! Get inside, now!"

She clutches two silver armored briefcases.

"Wix has the bioweapon!" Emery warns.

When Emery and I raise our guns at her, the cries for Roth to save himself cease. The massive, autonomous chopper takes off. Rises into the sky, fleeing the battlefield without him.

But within seconds, a Common helicopter blasts a high energy laser at Wix's chopper, sending it crashing to the ground, setting fire to a grove of palms. Emery signals, and Barend and Ciro take off to retrieve the briefcases from the wreckage.

Owen and I exchange a look. Mira locks eyes with Theo. But now's not the moment for a reunion either.

We all turn our focus on Roth. The man we came all this way for.

For different reasons, but with the same purpose.

Yet no one takes the shot.

"What I've built will not die with me," Roth promises.

He places his Lone Star cap back on. Presses his hand to his medals.

Bravado to the end

Delusion.

Owen lifts his gun, but I place a hand on his wrist, lowering his arm.

From the moment Mira and I were born, for our entire lives, I took everything as the firstborn. The microchip, our name, our identity.

It's right for Mira to be the one now.

Everyone else senses it too. Even Alexander stands down.

Mira points her pistol between Roth's eyes. Where he aimed his own kill shot at Father, at Rayla.

But the moment draws out too long.

The weight of killing in cold blood proves too much to bear.

Haven grabs the gun from Mira and pulls the trigger.

And just like that, the man who caused so much turmoil and heartache, pain and division, falls to the ground, dead.

A thousand miles from his home, on the wrong side of his own Big Fence.

No one will ever find his grave.

"It's over," I say.

And now the work of rebuilding begins.

PART IV
THE RETURN

MIRA

I used to spend Tuesdays underground. It was one of Ava's days up, her turn to breathe the outside air, to feel the sun, the rush of seeing and being seen. Her turn at our shared life, while I waited in the basement.

Time moves so much faster when you're truly living.

This Tuesday marks an anniversary. The first year commemorating the Rule of *All*.

The day that power was taken from the governors and put back into the hands of the citizens.

It's been a year since the Loyalists surrendered to the Common and the first peace talks began.

A year since the decisive bullet that saved our country. Changed our future. Rid the world of Governor Roth.

What Owen wanted came true. Our birthday has become a national holiday.

"Mira," Ava whispers, nudging my arm. "We're up."

I pull my wandering mind back to the small auditorium. To the white piano keys in front of me. To Ava at my side on the bench.

Together our hands spring and skip across the keyboard, leading Strake University's choir in my favorite song. Thirty students stack the risers, not a single one in a white uniform or color-ranking sash, every eye on Ava and me.

My sister and I take a deep breath and raise our voices into a harmonizing chorus.

Words our mother wrote and sang.

A tune that made our father smile.

Not the usual lyrics that once bounced off Strake's walls, about power, duty, war, and victory.

This song is about much more important aspirations. Love. Happiness. Hope. A toe-tapping melody that perfectly captures the fleeting euphoria of life at its best.

The choir joins us as we hold the last note, thirty-two voices blending as one.

As soon as I lift my foot from the pedal, and my fingers from the keys, my heart falls.

I close my eyes, trying to hold the transitory high for a few more seconds, but it's gone, and I'm left once again with the raw, heavy feelings that time has not yet healed.

Post-traumatic stress, Ava diagnosed me.

Sometimes I find myself still trapped inside the tunnels. The aqueducts. The basement.

Sometimes I spend entire days roaming the blooming groves of my family's graveyard.

But most days, the good outweighs the bad. With every passing second, I feel stronger. Lighter. More willing to smile at change, and the future that we made.

"Lovely," Choirmaster Dashwood says. "We will open tonight's parade with your song." He swings his head back and forth at the two of us, his grin stretching. "Class dismissed."

Even after almost a year of seeing me walking the university side by side with my twin, many students still can't believe there are two of us. Their heads tilt, their eyes narrow, trying to figure out how exactly they missed what was right in front of them. Naturally, there are those who approach us and lie. *Well,* I *knew all along.* Or my favorite: *I always suspected Ava Goodwin was just too perfect to be one person.*

Some days—usually Tuesdays and Thursdays during the few classes Ava and I share—students and professors gawk or snap photos, shout, *Thank Goodwin you did it!* Other days—usually on Mondays and Wednesdays when I'm alone in my advanced literature classes—students approach like they want to take me down. With words. Threats. Violence.

But a reputation gets you far, I've learned. I have faced and survived the three most dangerous leaders on the continent. A president, a capo, and a governor.

They're all underground now, and I'm alive. Walking and breathing. Feeling the sun.

I'm no longer an easy target.

The muscle and steely glares of Kano and Barend help, of course.

Our bodyguards march toward us from the doorway, Barend with a slight limp, Kano with a bend in his right shoulder. Their injuries left them little choice but an early retirement from the Common Guard.

We won't need their protection forever, I promised them and myself, but we're fortunate to have the former soldiers—*our friends*—as our guards.

As we move out of the auditorium, down the hall, and into the crowded cafeteria, Barend clears his throat, announcing a surprise. "Ciro and I have adopted Ellie. The official documents were sent this morning."

Pawel's little sister, Ellie. One of the thousands of children left orphaned at the hands of the State Guard.

I once made Pawel promise me he'd watch after my sister when I couldn't. I feel lighter now knowing Ciro and Barend will look after his own.

"Amazing news," Ava says, tears welling in her eyes. She often visits the thriving American elm tree Pawel is buried beneath.

Sisterhood, nowadays, is also thriving.

After the announcement of President Moore's illicit dealings and subsequent murder, Ciro's parents and all three of his sisters were released from prison and returned to the States. This past year, two of his siblings have helped Ciro establish permanent Paramount safe houses with their family money. Every climate and political refugee who sought shelter in one of his hotels in Canada has a place to call home. And every US second-born from the Camps is now being raised in grandeur and style.

With a second chance at life. Like me.

I glance at my watch: 12:13 p.m. "Ava, you're going to be late for your cell biology class."

Ava slides her tablet under the scanner of a 3D printer labeled "Kipling's Kangaroo Sticks." Gazing around the dining hall, I wonder what I should choose for my lunch today. Spaghetti? Chicken? Chocolate cake? It still feels novel that I have access to the food printers.

No microchips, no limits, I remind myself.

"You know," Ava says, smiling up at me. "The one thing I do miss about the old days is you doing half my homework."

I laugh, mirroring her grin. My eyes land on the thin scar across her throat. The cut from Valeria. Ava could have bioprinted new skin to help the knife wound heal cleaner, but she refused. *I'm not afraid to show my scars,* she told me.

She pops the jerky into her mouth and curls her lips into a smirk. "Can you tell Theo that Alexander can't come to the party?"

"I'll tell Theo you said hello," I say.

"Fine. The new general and his ego can come if he must. But tell him he *cannot* wear a suit."

"See you soon," we tell each other. Then Ava's off, and I watch her race down the lawn beside Barend, her long red hair bouncing wild in her wake.

"The festivities start at six?" Kano asks, tearing into a slice of pizza before pointing a warning finger toward an advancing freshman.

"Five, if you want to avoid the foot traffic," I say, nodding to the young freshman who waves at me with such eager admiration that my cheeks burn.

Soon, the entire city will be flocking downtown to celebrate a year of rebuilding. In a few hours, concerts, processions, massive balloons shaped like all the Common "heroes" will fill the streets. And I'm grateful that my teammates, now household names, are choosing to be with Ava and me tonight, instead.

I still don't like crowds. Or being in the spotlight.

There are too many eyes on me, even now. The panic starts to rise again, but then I feel a hand slip behind my back, an arm hugging me into the curve of his body, where I fit perfectly, like a puzzle piece.

"Happy birthday, mi amor," Theo whispers in my ear.

I forget about all the eyes and pull Theo into a kiss.

"How was your day?" he says when I finally draw away.

It's a question Ava used to ask me every day, just so we could stay alive. But Theo doesn't know this. He asks just so he can grow closer to me.

"And don't skimp on the details, your retellings are the highlight of my day," he adds, smiling.

Only weeks after we reunited, Theo moved here to Dallas—his birthplace—with his father and mother. He's a sophomore at Strake now, taking eighteen hours of coursework, learning who he is and what he wants to be.

"I'll tell you everything," I say, locking my arm around his, breathing in the moment. Thankful that two souls who never had a place to belong, now belong with each other.

"Ready?" Theo asks me.

"Yes. Let's go home."

AVA

So much of life has changed.

But some things, the small moments, like walking home after a long day of classes at Strake, have stayed the same.

Except now, three days a week, Owen is at my side.

On top of his role on the Cybersecurity Team with Blaise, Owen's earning his degree in criminal justice with the hopes of becoming a computer crime investigator one day. He wants to be a source of good, he says.

Detective Hart. I like the sound of that.

It fits nicely next to Dr. Goodwin.

"Well . . . I got kicked out of class again today," Owen begins, as we stroll our Trinity Heights neighborhood, his hand laced in mine. It's become our routine, something I never thought I'd want again after the repetition of my upbringing. But it's at once familiar and soothing. He talks, recounting entertaining stories from his day, and I listen, a half-hour reprieve from thoughts of my research.

I laugh to hear how Owen, after his esteemed computer forensics professor boldly claimed himself unhackable, hacked the man live in front of the whole class, sending videos recorded by his own security cameras of him dancing around his apartment in his underwear. Just to prove no one is bulletproof.

"Really, he did it to himself . . . He should've learned by now not to challenge me like that," Owen says, his dimples surfacing with his proud smile. "Don't worry, he let me back into class ten minutes later when the sting wore off from being outdone by a former Code Cog."

Sometimes I worry Owen really is too smart for his own good. But that's one of his attractions—he loves to test boundaries, questioning things, always. Like I do.

"This is your stop," I say, turning to a modest prefab eco-friendly home with a rock garden out front. It used to belong to a Loyalist, but now Owen lives here with his parents and Tess, his adopted sister.

Owen's mother's breast cancer is back. It haunts him, knowing how close we were to getting hold of Project Albatross and a possible way to cure his mother's sickness. For curing millions of people's incurable diseases.

But the briefcase was empty. Father's discovery, lost.

We'll never know if Roth really had Albatross, or if it was all just a ruse. He could have hidden the tech, and someone out there in the world could have it right now, could be plotting to finish Roth's plans, or to become the mastermind of some new destruction.

What I've built will not die with me, Roth swore.

Deep down, in that unknowable part of me where I can feel those who have passed on, still with me, guiding me, I know that Father wants me to destroy what he helped to create. But after our return home, after weeks of waking up sweating from nightmares—convinced there was an impending bio attack against Dallas—Mira read these lines to me from our father's favorite poem:

And from my neck so free
The Albatross fell off, and sank
Like lead into the sea.

We have to let go, she told me.

Whatever the truth is, Mira and I will not spend the rest of our lives searching for what Roth may or may not have left behind. Too many people we love sacrificed their lives so we could stop running, take root, and live in peace.

And that's what we intend to do.

I have to let go, and trust that Albatross died with my father, Director Wix, and the governor. *I have to.*

"See you later tonight," Owen says, rubbing his thumb over my knuckles before he lets go. "I'll be there with bells on."

"If you come to my party in a suit, I won't let you in," I say, half-serious. Owen's forgoing the big capital party celebrating the Rule of All, a parade where he would be touted as a national hero, to come to my family's small, far-from-fancy birthday gathering. He could show up to my party wearing a trash bag and I wouldn't mind. But teasing is our way of saying *I love you.*

"Well, we have to ring in your new decade right," Owen insists. "The big two-oh. That calls for a tux."

He kisses me, letting his soft lips linger.

We're interrupted by Duke's sudden arrival. Owen's car pulls into the driveway, the doors fold open, and Tess steps out. She has on a long, UV-protective dress and classic Audrey Hepburn–style sunglasses, her school bag draped over her narrow shoulders.

"How'd the exam go?" Owen asks her, nervous like an older brother.

"Do you remember my nickname?" Tess says, smiling.

The Whiz is a junior at Strake, the youngest student in the school's history. Owen believes she's going to be dean by the time she's our age.

"See you at the party," I tell them both before making my way down the block.

I pause outside my house, four streets down from the Hart's. A three-story sustainable townhome with a rooftop garden and large, open windows that not only let the light in, but show that we have nothing to hide.

Mira and I built our new home with Haven on the site of our childhood residence. Where the latter was sterile, a showpiece full of secrets, this place is full of warmth and openness. And clutter.

The defining feature for me is that this home has no basement. Mira and I both have our own rooms, something I never dreamt possible.

I smell a home-cooked meal as soon as I open the front door. Mira's in the kitchen with Haven, preparing carnitas, Lucía's recipe, sent just for the occasion.

I glance at a collage of photos on the wall. Lucía and Skye together on the motorcycle that took me and Mira from Kipling's west Texas safe house all the way up to our grandmother in Colorado. We shipped the bike's namesake to the woman herself, after she and Skye stayed behind in Mexico City to help the People's Militia maintain control of the Salazar strongholds. Lucía's brother and mother are there too, now that their former home is free of the cartel.

Beside their photograph is Emery—now Senator Jackson of Texas—in her long yellow coat, shaking hands with President Gordon at the White House. She's part of the new crop of senators building the foundation of our country's new government. Slowly, painstakingly, the states are becoming united again.

When I reach the bookcase filled with my grandmother's old journals and our growing collection of stories, I touch the frames of the photographs displayed inside. Photos of our family taken from Rayla's apartment in Denver. The secret photo we found inside my father's Director badge, of our once-illegal family of four, now sits beside new memories we've made with Haven, Owen, and Theo, and all the friends who now make up our world.

"It smells delicious," I say, making my way into the kitchen. "How many have you already had?"

Mira and Haven smile, guiltily.

"Don't worry, we've saved you plenty," Mira assures me.

"It's the best thing I've ever eaten," Haven declares, licking her fingers.

"I think we deserve all the tacos we want today," I say.

I pop a piece of spiced meat into my mouth, and it's like I've never truly tasted real food before. "Holy Whitman, I don't think I'll ever eat printed food again."

We laugh, knowing full well that we all cook about as well as we can dance, which is terribly.

I roll up my sleeves, ready to contribute my part of the meal, a multilayered chocolate cake. I'm determined to make one with my own hands.

It's a family tradition, started by my mother and then perfected by Gwen, our housekeeper and friend.

Except mine will be smothered in vanilla buttercream icing.

New decade, new traditions.

And this one will have twenty candles on top.

Mira and I stand in the greenhouse that Owen and Theo rebuilt for our neighborhood. Our fingers are coated with raw earth, and there's the smell of lightning in the air.

I'm more content than I've ever been.

The birthday girls are late for their own party. But we were missing something. The centerpiece.

"Our first harvest looks beautiful." Mira admires the rows upon rows of bright-yellow black-eyed Susans.

"They look strong," I say, appreciating what we were able to regrow.

The first wildflowers to grow back after a fire. Our mother's favorite.

"Everyone's waiting for us back at the house," Mira says. But her wistful voice doesn't sound rushed.

"I got you something," she says, heading to the corner of the greenhouse. There's no surveillance anymore, just speakers playing gentle music.

She comes back with a bottle of Japanese Nikka whisky.

"Happy birthday, Ava," she says as she holds out the bottle. "Cheers to us."

I smile, take a swig, and smack in satisfaction as the warm liquid burns down my throat to settle in my stomach like a furnace on a cold night.

"Cheers to us, sister," I say. "Happy birthday."

She takes a drink and her eyes water, but she smiles, just as contented as I am. Neither of us makes a move to leave. We just stand there, in the glass-walled greenhouse, listening to the distant thunder rolling in, staring at our garden of yellow flowers.

When the rain strengthens from a pitter-patter on the roof to a full-on downpour, we know we're in trouble.

The first shower of the year and we're caught.

"Nothing for it," I say, taking another shot of whisky.

"You ready?" Mira asks me.

"Ready," I say, grabbing her hand.

We burst from the greenhouse door and out into the storm. Halfway to our house, we stop to dance in the rain.

Two laughing, utterly bedraggled sisters, ready for their party.

Acknowledgments

Thank you to every reader who followed Ava and Mira's story until the end. No characters will ever be more personal to us than these twin rebels, and to share them with you through this trilogy means more to us than any words could capture. To everyone at Skyscape and Amazon Publishing, thank you a million times over. This journey has been a dream. As always, thank you, Mom and Dad, for your never-ending support and love. And lastly, we'd like to thank our two writing mascots, Wyatt and Winston, who have been by our sides the entire seven years it took this story to pour out from our hearts and onto the page.

ABOUT THE AUTHORS

Photo © 2017 Shayan Asgharnia

Ashley Saunders and Leslie Saunders are award-winning filmmakers and the authors of *The Rule of One* and *The Rule of Many*. Hailing from the suburbs of Dallas, Texas, the twin sisters honed their love of storytelling at the University of Texas at Austin. While researching the Rule of One series, they fell in love with America's national parks, traveling Ava and Mira's path. Currently, the sisters can be found with their Boston terriers in sunny Los Angeles, exploring hiking trails and drinking entirely too much yerba maté. Visit them at www.thesaunderssisters.com.